The
OTHER
SIDE of
PERFECT

The OTHER SIDE *of* PERFECT

MARIKO TURK

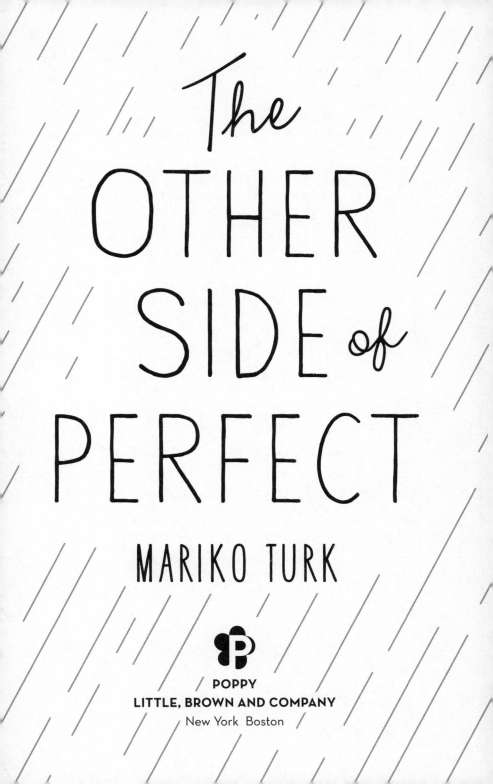

POPPY
LITTLE, BROWN AND COMPANY
New York Boston

Copyright © 2021 by Mariko Turk

Cover art copyright © 2021 by Anne Pomel. Cover design by Jenny Kimura. Cover copyright © 2021 by Hachette Book Group, Inc.

Poppy
Hachette Book Group
1290 Avenue of the Americas, New York, NY 10104
Visit us at LBYR.com

First Edition: May 2021

Poppy is an imprint of Little, Brown and Company. The Poppy name and logo are trademarks of Hachette Book Group, Inc.

The publisher is not responsible for websites (or their content) that are not owned by the publisher.

Library of Congress Cataloging-in-Publication Data
Names: Turk, Mariko, author.
Title: The other side of perfect / Mariko Turk.
Description: First edition. | New York : Little, Brown and Company, 2021. |
Summary: "An emotional story about a former ballerina who is thrust back into 'normal' high school after a life-changing injury, and who comes to terms with life without her passion as well as discrimination in the ballet world." —Provided by publisher.
Identifiers: LCCN 2020029078 | ISBN 9780316703406 (hardcover) |
ISBN 9780316703420 (ebook) | ISBN 9780316703390 (ebook other)
Subjects: CYAC: Ballet dancing—Fiction. | Wounds and injuries—Fiction. |
High schools—Fiction. | Schools—Fiction. | Theater—Fiction. |
Racially mixed people—Fiction.
Classification: LCC PZ7.1.T8745 Ot 2021 | DDC [Fic]—dc23
LC record available at https://lccn.loc.gov/2020029078

ISBNs: 978-0-316-70340-6 (hardcover), 978-0-316-70342-0 (ebook)

Printed in the United States of America

LSC-C

Printing 1, 2021

TO MOM AND DAD

MARCH

PROLOGUE

"WHEN CAN I DANCE?" My voice came out quiet in the small, sterile recovery room. The doctor kept messing with his charts, so I didn't know if he'd heard me. I was about to ask again, but I got distracted by the steel rods rooted into my bones and extending out, attached to a frame outside my leg. Ever since I woke up from surgery, I couldn't stop staring at it. After ten years at the Kira Dobrow Ballet School, I'd seen my share of bodily horrors: weeping toe blisters, a ruptured Achilles tendon, but nothing like this. It was called an external fixator, and it wasn't messing around.

Colleen was staring at it, too—her fingers tapping out the melody of the Kitri variation from *Don Quixote* on the metal post of my hospital bed. I caught her eye, and we had one of our silent conversations.

It's not that bad, right?

Totally not that bad.

I let out a breath and glanced behind Colleen to my parents. Dad's eyes were steadily on the floor so he wouldn't accidentally look at the external fixator and need to sit with his head between his legs again. Mom gave me a smile I knew she meant to be reassuring but was 100 percent not.

"When can I dance?" I repeated loudly. The doctor startled, put down the charts, and sat on the stool next to my bed.

"Let's take it one step at a time," he said, looking at my leg and chuckling. "Pun not intended." When no one reacted, he cleared his throat. "You'll be bed to chair for a couple of weeks until we get you out of that external fixator and into a cast. A few months after that, you can start learning to walk again."

If he wasn't going to answer my question, I'd figure it out myself. I did some mental calculations. The American Ballet Theatre summer intensive in New York was in July. Four months from now. If I was walking in a couple of months, I could dance in four. "That means I can still do the ballet intensive in July," I said. "I can still go."

My parents shifted and the doctor sighed. "Alina," he said carefully. "If it was a clean break, your bones could have healed naturally. You might have been able to dance on pointe in four months. But it wasn't a clean break."

He stopped talking, like that explained everything. When I kept staring at him, he sighed again. "We needed to put in sixteen screws and two plates to keep your bones together. That hardware is meant to stay in there forever. It means your leg won't be as strong or flexible as—"

"So when? If I let it heal and do physical therapy and everything I'm supposed to do, when will it be back to normal?"

"Never," the doctor said simply. "When something breaks like that, you can't put it back together so easily. And when you do, it won't be the same."

That was the epitome of bullshit, but there was no point saying it. "I'll be able to dance in four months," I said coolly. "I'm going to New York." I looked at my parents so they'd know the plan hadn't changed. Dad looked queasy and uncertain. Mom looked like she was holding back tears. Only Colleen was unfazed.

"Definitely," my best friend said, turning to the doctor. "I read this article that said orthopedists can fix anything now, except maybe knees, but she didn't do anything to her knee."

"Yeah," I said, latching on to Colleen's words. "I didn't break my *knee*, just my tibia and fibula."

"Honey…" Mom put a firm hand on my shoulder. "Let's not think about what may or may not happen in the future. All you can do right now is focus on healing. That's the number one thing."

Dad looked at the external fixator again, cursed, and took a seat in the chair at the other end of the room, elbows on his knees. Mom squeezed my shoulder again, like I was supposed to say something back, but I had nothing. Not thinking about the future didn't make any sense to me. The future was everything, and it had only ever looked like ballet.

A wave of drowsiness hit me, the anesthesia making everything hazy. At some point, I registered that my parents were whispering, and it was dark outside the window, and Colleen was gone. I closed my eyes again and felt my body dancing, revolving through the air on the tip of my pointe shoe. Springing across the floor in quick brisés.

As I slipped in and out of sleep, it was hard to tell what was real and what wasn't, what was happening right now and what was a memory.

But one thing was clear. In four months, I'd be on pointe again. In four months, I'd be in New York, dancing.

NOVEMBER

CHAPTER ONE

JEAN-PAUL SARTRE ONCE WROTE: "Hell is other people." I think a more accurate statement would be: "Hell is other people auditioning for Eagle View High School's spring production of *Singin' in the Rain*." Perhaps that's a touch dramatic. But since that dumb doctor turned out to be right about my leg, I had to start junior year as a normal full-time student. And as terrible as the past two months had been, I hadn't, before this moment, been subjected to *this*. To my left, a curly-haired girl belting "Ma may mee moe moo!" To my right, a skinny guy in tight capri sweatpants, belly dancing.

I spotted Margot, my life raft, near the stage of the school auditorium, sipping an iced coffee the size of her head. I wound my way through the packed aisles until I finally reached her side.

"Who *are* these people?" I hissed. She looked at me with an expression I'd never seen on her before. Apologetic? Sheepish? But because it was Margot, it was gone in a second and replaced with a smirk.

"There's no people like show people," she said. Then, sensing what can only be described as my highly disgruntled vibe, she added: "I know it seems weird, but it actually doesn't suck."

I raised my eyebrow at her, still completely surprised she was into this. Margot was so fuck-it-all, and these people were the total opposite. I was pretty sure they fucked nothing. Then again, what did I really know about the essence of Margot? Yeah, we bonded last year in first-period chem. And yeah, she was hilarious, but besides the one time she came over to help me pick out an audition song, I'd never hung out with her outside of school. Lately, I'd been too busy napping and sitting alone in my room eating entire bags of Cool Ranch Doritos to hang out with anyone. But Margot was my life-saver at Eagle View. We had homeroom and ninth-period study hall together, so I began and ended my day with her. Thank God.

On the first day of school this year, I'd told Margot I would be going for the full day now because part-time online schooling only worked for kids who were "pursuing professional careers in the arts," and I...wasn't anymore. I warned her not to say "Everything happens for a reason" or "Maybe it's for the best" or "When life shatters your leg, it opens a window" or any other crap like that. I'd heard enough of it already and didn't believe a word.

But Margot had just looked at me and said: "Nah, I'm glad you broke your leg and have to go to school with us normals. Afternoons without you were kind of boring."

That solidified our friendship, at least on my end. A lifetime of desperately trying to squeeze a word of praise from demanding ballet teachers made me a sucker for people who knew how to throw out a perfectly constructed compliment scrap. If anyone was ever too effusive about me, it turned me right off.

"I mean, you *could* back out now," Margot said, brushing a dribble of coffee from the jean shorts she wore over black tights. The emerald-green stud above her lip caught the light and glistened. With that piercing and her turquoise-dyed bob, she always reminded me of a punky mermaid. "But then you won't get to hear ten thousand overly dramatic renditions of 'On My Own' from *Les Misérables*."

"If you're going to do musical theater references, I'm leaving."

"And I don't know," Margot said, pretending she hadn't heard me. "You might like it."

My hands gripped the straps of my backpack as I looked around at the shabby auditorium. I couldn't help but compare this—the maroon plastic seats, depressingly gray carpet, flimsy black curtains, and cold overhead lights—to the plush jewel-box quality of the Epstein Theatre downtown where the Kira Dobrow Ballet School had its shows. I missed its rich upholstered seats, the golden lighting fixtures around the mezzanine, and the red velvet curtain that Colleen and I used to rub our pinkies over for luck.

Horrifyingly, my eyes started to sting. I coughed and blinked rapidly. "So how does this work?" I asked, my voice coming out crisp and professional.

"Two days of singing auditions, starting today at three. At four thirty, they'll teach us a dance combination. No problem for you. Tomorrow, singing goes until four thirty again, and then we audition with the dance. Callbacks happen Friday for the main parts."

I sighed and plunked my backpack down. Two days of after-school commitments in this genuinely hideous auditorium filled with show people was not ideal. So why was I staying? Maybe it was to avoid my parents' increasingly less subtle suggestions to "do stuff outside the house." Maybe it was because Margot was literally my only friend right now, and abandoning her felt wrong. Maybe it was a reason I hadn't fully thought through yet.

I'd just situated my leg on the edge of the stage for a hamstring stretch, tugging on the hem of my legging to make sure my scars weren't showing, when two white guys shouted "Margot!" and sauntered over.

One of them was tall and rangy, with a mass of artfully messy auburn curls. I recognized him from English—I think his name was Ethan—so he must have been a senior. I was a junior, but I was in senior English because the online schooling got me ahead by a bit. The other guy I didn't recognize. He had swoopy dark hair and a wide, toothy smile that would have looked goofy if his tanned skin hadn't set it off so well. Not that it mattered.

"Margot never lies," Smile Guy said. He looked at Ethan for confirmation. "Right? Margot Kilburn-Correa tells it like it is."

Ethan shook his head. "Nope, Margot is a contrarian. She'll give one answer just because everyone else would say the other one. It's her thing."

Margot smacked Ethan's arm. "It's not my thing."

"See?" Ethan said. Margot smacked him again.

"Fine, I'll ask an outsider." Smile Guy turned to me and I swear there was an actual gleam in his eyes. "Have you ever seen me before?"

"Nope," I said, switching legs.

His mouth did a quick little upturn, like he had won a bet with himself. "Right. So, with fresh eyes and no preconceived notions"— he waved a hand between himself and Ethan—"who's the Fred Astaire and who's the Gene Kelly?"

"I have no idea what you're talking about."

Smile Guy pretended to faint, grabbing on to Ethan for support. And I thought *I* was dramatic.

Ethan held him up and shook his head in disappointment. "Margot, have you brought a musical theater novice into the hallowed halls of the Eagle View auditorium, birthplace of the Happy Crack?" All three of them doubled over at this.

Oh, the joy of inside jokes when you're on the outside.

After an unnecessarily long bout of laughter (the Happy Crack couldn't be *that* funny, whatever it was), Margot finally came to her senses. "Shhh, you're scaring Alina. That's Ethan." She waved her hand at him and he inclined his head, making his curls fall even farther into his eyes. If he remembered me from English, he didn't let on, so neither did I.

"And that's Jude." So Smile Guy had a name.

"Hey, Alina, all kidding aside, we really are very welcoming of newcomers," Jude said, the gleam reappearing. "Are you a freshman?"

Scoff. "Junior," I said flatly, lowering my leg from the stage and taking my phone out of my sweatshirt pocket. He didn't take the hint.

"I thought I knew all the juniors. Why don't I know you?"

I sighed. "I used to only go here in the mornings."

"Why?"

"It was the time of day I was least likely to attack strangers who asked me too many questions."

Margot snorted. Ethan snapped his fingers like he was at a poetry reading. But Jude kept smiling in that irritating way, like he was winning a game I didn't know I was playing. "Ah, yes. Can't be too careful, especially with strangers."

I stared at him. A weirdo in a sea of weirdos.

"All right, dudes," Margot said, shooing them away. "We've got preparing to do. We're not all musical theater gods." The dudes left, and under normal circumstances, I would have roasted Margot for saying the phrase *musical theater gods*. But the auditorium suddenly hushed as two women with clipboards took the stage. The one I recognized was Mrs. Sorenson, the music teacher, whose strawberry-blond hair was slicked back with a mauve headband that matched her sweater set and pumps. According to Margot, she directed the musical every year. Beside her was a tall woman in her fifties with a frizzy pouf of orange-ish hair tied up in a black ribbon. Ms. Langford, apparently. The choreographer. She looked like Mrs. Sorenson's kooky older sister.

Mrs. Sorenson clapped her hands. "Singing starts now," she called out primly. "One at a time, give me your music, stand center stage, and say your name. Ms. Langford will stop you after a few bars. That's all we need to hear right now."

With that, Mrs. Sorenson sat down at the worn piano onstage and Ms. Langford took her seat in the fourth row, clipboard at the ready. Immediately, a gorgeous South Asian girl with black elbow-length waves jaunted up onstage.

"Diya Rao," she said, enunciating crisply. "Singing 'No One Else' from *Natasha, Pierre, and the Great Comet of 1812*."

Margot scoffed. "No one asked what you were singing, Robobitch."

"Friend of yours?" I whispered, glad for the distraction of Margot's commentary.

Margot made a puking face as Mrs. Sorenson started playing in a minor key and Diya sang out in a startlingly clear voice. Her voice vibrated, shimmered. Goose bumps sprang up on my arms. As she went on, the notes became warmer and fuller. The song was about falling in love and she made the words sound like they were flying on top of the melody.

My jaw dropped. It wasn't that I hadn't expected anyone here to be good. I just hadn't expected anyone to be *that* good. I glanced around to see if others were as shocked as I was. But a lot of them looked like Margot did—annoyed. I heard a few scattered mutterings of "Robobitch." So Margot wasn't the only one who called her that.

When Diya finished, she threw a confident smile to the audience and left the stage, taking a seat in the front corner of the room, away from everyone else.

"Robobitch always goes first to intimidate people," Margot said. Sure enough, nobody volunteered until Mrs. Sorenson made Ethan go. His song had an old-fashioned doo-wop rhythm and was about...being a sadistic dentist? Whatever it was, he played it up, strutting across the stage like a weird version of Elvis, his curls flopping every time he cocked his head to dramatically belt out, "I am a deeeeentist!"

It was bizarre, but it relaxed the mood, and things went pretty smoothly from there. People sang, with varying degrees of skill and volume, and then marched back to their seats, getting high fives or ass pats or chest bumps along the way. Everyone was so comfortable here it made me uneasy.

In the middle of the singing time, Jude took the stage. "Jude Jeppson," he announced. I snorted. Somehow that perky name suited him. He didn't have Ethan's swagger or Diya's poise. He was just light and carefree, like he was joking around with friends. Mrs. Sorenson started playing, and Jude began to sing.

Okay, fine. I could see where the musical theater god thing came from. He was *good*. His voice was strong, but tender enough to convey the dreamy happiness of the lyrics, which after a while, just consisted of the name "Maria." I didn't get goose bumps like I had when Diya sang, but maybe that was because the swooning happening all around me was a bit distracting. It seemed no one was completely immune to the charm of a cute guy who could sing a girl's name over and over again in such a romantic way.

On the last "Maria," the "Woos!" and "Ow-ows!" started up, and Jude broke into a grin midnote. Ethan took his phone out and snapped a picture. Maybe Jude would autograph them later for his fans. When he finished, the cheers grew and followed him all the way back to his seat in the second row.

Jude must have sensed my gaze, because he looked over. Whenever I got caught staring, I tried not to look away. So I held his glance and did a golf clap for him. He smiled and tipped an imaginary hat to me.

Our exchange was interrupted by a blond guy in a slouchy beanie walking stiffly down the aisle, clenching and unclenching his hands.

"Holy hell, Harrison Lambert?" Margot said.

"Who's that?"

"He's . . . Harrison Lambert. He's not the musical type. He's the kind of guy who asks what your favorite movie is, and if you say anything other than the most obscure movie ever, he's like, 'Oh yeah, I used to like that movie. In *middle school*.'"

"Ew, he said that?"

"I mean, no. But he would if I ever talked to him."

Margot gave Harrison a hard look as he began a shaky a cappella version of "In the Aeroplane Over the Sea" by Neutral Milk Hotel. Picking an alt-rock song for a high school musical audition seemed weird, but he wasn't bad once he got going. And he finished impressively, looking completely relieved as he walked off the stage.

And he kept on walking, right out of the auditorium. As the door swung shut, the whispers kicked up again, and the guy I'd seen belly dancing earlier let out a loud "Whaaaaaat?" which got some laughs.

"Maybe it was a bet," Margot theorized.

The singing dragged on, and the auditorium got emptier as people left to get snacks or change for the dance audition. Margot went up onstage eventually, singing in a nasal, exaggerated New York accent that simultaneously impressed and confused me.

"So, this might be a good time for you to go," Margot said afterward, checking the time. I looked around, making sure that Jude, Ethan, and Diya had left. I didn't need the best people here watching me suck.

As I walked to the front of the room, I tried to blur out how bizarre it felt to be stepping onto a stage to sing, not dance. I'd asked Margot if there was any way to skip the vocal audition and just do the dancing one—it wasn't like I was going for a lead role—but she said it was mandatory.

"Alina Keeler," I croaked out. Then I sang the first few bars of "Wouldn't It Be Loverly" from *My Fair Lady*. Margot had suggested it because it wasn't too difficult. I was pretty quiet, and Ms. Langford looked bored, but no one covered their ears.

I blew out a breath as I left the stage. Musical theater goddess I was not. But at least I hadn't totally embarrassed myself.

❧

"Let's run through it one more time!" Ms. Langford's raspy voice carried over the noise of the packed stage. It was ten minutes until day one of auditions ended and everyone would go home to practice the combination for tomorrow. It was straightforward—some grapevines, a few hip pops, a Charleston-inspired step, two grands battements (Ms. Langford called them "high kicks!"), and a quick pirouette.

For nondancers it was challenging. Margot was swearing up a storm trying to end the pirouette without stumbling. Diya Rao was doing well, though, and so were Jude and Ethan. Margot had told me that Ethan's older sister taught tap at the Y, and that both boys had been taking lessons with her there for years. Somehow it didn't surprise me.

I hadn't done the combination full-out yet. I'd just been marking it because there wasn't much space to move, and it was already muscle memory. Ms. Langford dismissed us, but then Diya, her hair pulled into a doorknob bun, raised her hand. "Ms. Langford? I have rehearsal for the Shakespeare Festival tomorrow. Can I do the dance audition now?"

Margot rolled her eyes as she fanned the back of her neck. "She does that every year, too. She *loves* saying she's in other stuff. And yeah, like it's *so* impressive that she can do the dance already without practicing it overnight. I'm sure you could, too."

Everyone was clearing the stage as Ms. Langford asked if anyone else wanted to do the dance audition now. Maybe it was because I wanted tomorrow afternoon free to nap. Or maybe my competitive side was kicking in. Or maybe it was a reason I kept trying to ignore: I just wanted to dance on a stage again.

I walked back out and stood beside Diya.

She X-rayed me with her eyes, her gaze lingering on my hair, which I hadn't pulled back like everyone else. It hung, straight as pins, down my back. Her eyes narrowed. "Need a hair tie?"

"I'm good," I said.

Diya raised an eyebrow. Geez. I wasn't trying to be cocky. I just didn't feel like pulling my hair back.

Diya and I took our places at opposite ends of the stage. "We'll do the combination twice so we can get a good look at both of you," Ms. Langford said, pushing Play on the stereo.

And it finally hit me. Sure, it was a stupid little musical theater combination. But for the first time in eight months, I was going to dance. My heart skittered into my throat.

When the music started, something familiar took over. I executed all the steps correctly, but I let the music guide my timing.

As Gene Kelly's voice drew out the lyrics, I slowed down my arm movements, picking up speed only when the horns started again. My Charleston step was light, my battements whooshed against my ears, and I prepped for the pirouette with a delicate pas de bourrée into fourth position. Out of the corner of my eye, I saw Diya do a double pirouette instead of a single. She finished a touch off the music, but I could see Ms. Langford nodding and smiling as we got back into place to do it again.

I felt my mouth curve up. If it was okay to change the choreography, so be it.

The second time, I made my movements even lighter, even airier. I turned the second battement into a développé layout, arching way back as I extended my leg up, toes pointing to the ceiling. At the end, right before the pirouette, my ballet teacher, Kira, popped into my head. White-blond hair, vibrant blue eyes encircled by wrinkles, like rays of the sun. She was watching me, pushing me to be better. So I did a triple pirouette.

Well, I tried to.

My speed was okay, but my right ankle—which had the screws holding it together—couldn't take the pressure. Somehow, I forced my core to balance and keep up my rotation, but I could only do a weak double turn, and I couldn't even finish that with the music.

I didn't see anyone's reaction as I walked offstage, but I heard a few scattered claps. Too many thoughts and feelings were competing for my attention: the quick but steady way my heart beat after a performance, the stomach thrill I got from good old-fashioned competition. Those felt satisfyingly familiar, almost like everything could be okay again. But I couldn't ignore that wobble. The way it knocked me off the music. The way it made me clumsy. The way I'd really, truly never dance on pointe again.

I'd been so stupid to think that dancing in the musical would fill a fraction of the emptiness I'd been clawing around for eight months. Dancing would never be the same. I would never be the same. And nothing could fix it.

I looked for Margot, thinking she would say something sarcastic and snap me out of it. But when I swept my eyes over the rows of seats, I found Jude instead. He was staring at me across the auditorium, his mouth open. It brought back another familiar feeling: the swell of pride when people looked at me like I had just done something beautiful.

I was so homesick for that look. But seeing it now, I only felt hollow. I didn't deserve it anymore. The hollowness filled up with rage.

Jude was still staring at me. His mouth stretched into a smile as he returned the golf clap I'd given him before. But instead of smiling back or tipping an imaginary hat to him, like I really should have done, I flipped him off instead.

CHAPTER TWO

AS SOON AS I SHUT the front door, Mom swept in from the patio and Dad stood up from the piano. "So?" they asked in unison. "How was it?"

They were pretty jazzed about me auditioning for the musical. They'd probably said a little prayer of thanks when they got home from work and didn't find me in my room, buried under the covers and watching ballet videos on my laptop.

"Fine," I said, dropping my backpack roughly onto the foyer floor and then kicking it away from me. And I tried not to, but my eyes swept over the picture frames on the mantel, where my ballet pictures used to be. Still missing.

"Stand down, soldiers." I saluted my parents and headed to the kitchen.

"We'll need more than that, General Grumpy Pants," Dad said, following me.

"General Grumpy Leggings," Mom corrected, pointing at my legs. "That's what those are called. People wear them as pants, but you'll never get me to believe that's what they really are."

I sighed loudly, knowing I'd have to give them something. "It really was fine. My singing wasn't entirely horrible." I opened the fridge, took out a string cheese, and bit into it. "And the dance combination was easy," I said with my mouth full.

I also gave someone the finger for no reason.

I was glad Jude hadn't seemed offended by my spontaneous decision to flip him the bird. Surprised, yes. Confused, definitely. But not mad. I hoped he wouldn't ask me to explain myself.

"You know, we did *Carousel* our senior year at Kalani," Mom said, her smile hopeful.

"*You* guys were in your high school musical?" I asked, the cheese nearly dropping from my mouth. I'd heard more than I ever wanted to about Mom and Dad's high school sweetheart days, but not this.

"Well, no." Dad stroked his coppery beard. "But we had friends in it, I think. And we saw it. And it was really great!"

Yeah, right. Dad was the pianist for a band that played trippy, experimental music. I'd never heard him even mention a show tune. And Mom saw *Carousel* on TCM a couple of years ago and called it "squicky." My parents had resorted to lying to get me out of the house.

"Good for them," I said, popping the rest of the cheese into my mouth and turning toward the stairs.

"Plus..." Mom circled in front of me and put her arm around my shoulders, redirecting me back into the kitchen. "You loved *Singin' in the Rain* when you saw the movie."

"I did?"

"Yes! Don't you remember watching it with Grandma Shiho?"

"Kind of. I was, like, six," I said. It was raining in Honolulu that day, so we couldn't go to the beach like we'd planned. I was bummed, but then Grandma Shiho took me to get ume shave ice from Matsumoto's, and we ate it while watching *Singin' in the Rain*.

I remembered the tart taste of the dessert, and Grandma Shiho laughing a lot—she has my favorite laugh in the world, gravelly yet demure. But I didn't remember anything about the movie.

"Well, I told her about you auditioning, and she's very excited," Mom said. "I watched the movie during my office hours today and it's pretty amusing. It takes place in the 1920s, and there are these two silent movie stars, Don Lockwood and Lina Lamont."

I sighed. Mom's arm was still casually draped around my shoulders. I wasn't going anywhere.

"Don and Lina do all their movies together, but then *talking* movies are invented."

"Uh-oh," Dad broke in with all the subtlety of a cartoon character.

"Uh-oh *indeed*, because Lina Lamont has a terrible voice. It's screechy and has a strange accent and is very annoying. She also has a bad personality."

I rubbed the bridge of my nose. "Okay, okay, what next?" The faster she got through this, the faster I could leave.

"Well, I'm glad you asked, because Don Lockwood meets and falls in love with Kathy Selden. Now Kathy, get this, has acting talent, a pretty voice, *and* a good personality."

"A triple threat," Dad said.

"That's right. So Don's best friend, Cosmo Brown, suggests that Kathy dub over Lina's voice, just for one movie, and then she can move on to her own illustrious career. Of course, things don't go as planned, and there are lots of hijinks and tap dancing, and then everyone lives happily ever after."

"Great," I said flatly.

"I agree, honey." Mom gave me a squeeze and then finally stepped away. "So you'll go back tomorrow for the dance audition?"

23

"No, I did that today, so I'm done for the week." My parents' faces fell, probably picturing another marathon streaming session.

And because I'd already been rude to them *and* flipped off an innocent bystander that afternoon, I added: "Margot was really good."

Just like that, they brightened again. My parents love Margot. She was my savior, as far as they were concerned. When she came over last week to help me pick an audition song, it was the first time I'd had a guest in months. Mom brought us hurricane popcorn and Dad asked if she wanted to stay for dinner and a movie. In my previous life, my parents might have looked twice at Margot's Monroe piercing, eyebrow piercing, and KEEP CALM AND KISS MY ASS T-shirt. But not that day. That day, she was Saint Margot, and she had come to save us all.

Footsteps bounded down the stairs, followed by a slap as Josie skipped the last two and landed on the linoleum. "Last year at lunch," she announced, "Paul Manley kept barking at some girls who walked by his table, and Margot told him he was doing it because he was insecure about his penis."

My sister always took conversations to new and interesting places.

"How do you know? You weren't even there last year," I said. Although I had to admit, that did sound like Margot. And Josie was a freshman now and had her own bustling social life, so she probably knew way more Eagle View gossip than I did.

Josie shrugged. "It's true. And he probably is insecure, because I read that—"

"All right," Mom interrupted. "I'm all for my girls talking about penis insecurity, but not before they set the table."

"Seconded," Dad bellowed, already halfway out the patio door.

Once we'd finished dinner, Josie and I started on the dishes while my parents bundled up to take a walk, talking about the beauty of Pennsylvania Novembers. My parents were both born and raised in Hawaiʻi, so it baffled me how much they appreciated the landscape here. They moved a year before I was born, when Mom got a job as a comparative literature professor at a small liberal arts college nearby. I used to be incredibly grateful for that decision, because otherwise I wouldn't have gone to the Kira Dobrow Ballet School. Now, I dreamt of packing up, moving to Honolulu, blending in with all the other half-white, half-Japanese girls there, and never setting foot in Pennsylvania or Eagle View ever again.

"Plate me." Josie held her hand out for the plate I was over-rinsing. "So if you get in, will you actually do it?"

I thought we'd exhausted musical talk at dinner, but apparently not. "Like I said a gajillion times—maybe."

"Alina." Josie groaned. "You need to get over it."

"Excuse me?"

"Did you really want to spend your whole life measuring your boobs and disinfecting your gross feet and dancing to music written by white men who've been dead for literally a hundred years?"

"Yup," I said without hesitation.

"I'm serious."

"I know." Josie was always so down on ballet. She was a dancer, too, but she did modern at a studio called Variations. She went four times a week, but only in the evenings. Variations didn't have classes during the school day like KDBS and other preprofessional schools.

"I just mean, the whole thing with your leg, maybe it's for the best," she said.

I had to stop myself from flinging the salad tongs at her head. I hated that sentiment. How could losing the ability to do the thing you love be "for the best"? I heard it all the time, though, from teachers and students at Eagle View.

Maybe it's for the best—now you can have a normal high school experience!

Maybe it's for the best, because now you can eat pizza and ice cream every day!

Maybe it's for the best, because everything happens for a reason!

To all these dumb explanations, Josie added: "Now you can try other kinds of dancing for once."

"Like, in the musical?" I asked, raising an eyebrow. "Why do you want me to be in it so bad?"

Josie bit her lip. "Okay. So, you know Laurel Adams and Noah Parker?"

"Nope."

"They're juniors," she said, like that would help.

"Nope."

Josie made an exasperated noise. "Fine, they're in my class at Variations. I'm choreographing something for the student showcase in June, and I want to create it on them. They're really good."

"Okay...," I said, pretending I already knew she was choreographing. She'd always been into that, always developing strange little movements as she stood by the toaster, waiting for it to pop. I just hadn't known she was doing it outside the house now. Then again, I didn't know a lot of things about Josie's life. With my intense ballet schedule, I'd never been the kind of big sister who knew exactly what she was up to and who her friends were and what advice she needed. Not that Josie would ever take my advice.

"The problem is, they both worship Trevor, this senior, and I know he's going to ask them to be in his piece, and they'll say yes to him over me because he's a senior and a guy, and I'm a freshman and a girl."

"So what do you want me to do about it?" I sloshed water around in the salad bowl and dumped it down the drain.

"Noah and Laurel are always in the musical. If they see how good a dancer you are, maybe they'll think prodigies run in the family and take me more seriously."

I shoved the salad bowl into Josie's hands and turned the faucet off, so she could hear me loud and clear. "First, that makes no sense. Second, I was never a prodigy. And third, you're in the advanced class with these people. Don't they already take you seriously?"

Josie put on her *let me educate you* face. God, I hated that face. "Freshmen girls are *never* taken seriously," she said. "If you'd gone to high school full-time when you were a freshman, you'd know that." She bent down, somehow finding space for the salad bowl in the too-crowded dishwasher.

"And I just want an equal shot," she said, straightening up and brushing dark brown bangs out of her eyes. "If Noah and Laurel like Trevor's concept better, fine. But I don't want them to ignore me by default. And I *would* just ask two other people in my class, but they're the best and I want them. My piece is going to be this super-intense duet about oppositions and contrasts in the world, and how those things can clash but also merge to create strange harmonies—that's what I'm calling it. *Strange Harmonies.*"

My heartbeat kicked up as I watched her describe the piece, because I recognized something in her face. A mix of inspiration, ambition, and hunger. The same expression I'd seen reflected back to me thousands of times in the mirrors at KDBS.

Josie turned to the sink and scooped up the silverware. "So

will you do it? Be in the musical and impress everyone with your dancing and get Laurel and Noah to at least consider being in my piece?"

And then it was happening. Josie standing there all happy and unbroken and able to do what she loved set off the *tick, tick, tick* inside me—the jealousy bomb that was about to explode and make me hate her and everyone and myself.

"I don't know, Josie. And your shitty dance won't be the deciding factor." I whipped around and walked upstairs. As I crossed the hallway to my room, I heard Josie shut the dishwasher, no doubt unfazed by my dramatic exit. It wasn't a rare occurrence these days.

I shut my door and sat at the edge of my bed, staring at my peach walls with their light rectangular patches, the ghosts of pictures that used to hang there. Colleen and me in *The Nutcracker*. Colleen and me in *Coppélia*. Colleen and me in *A Midsummer Night's Dream*.

Over the summer, I'd stuffed them all in a shoe box at the back of my closet. When Mom and Dad saw what I'd done, they'd shared the tense, worried look I'd grown used to. I expected some kind of talk to come from it, but the next morning when I went downstairs, all my ballet pictures were gone. From the mantel, from the fridge, from everywhere. In their place were school portraits and candids from my birthdays and Christmas. No one said a word about it.

It was like I'd never done ballet. Like it had all just been a dream.

I jumped when my phone buzzed and Colleen's name flashed across the screen.

Kira made us do THREE adagios today. My theory: She hit the vodka hard last night and slow music was better for her hangover. No one believes me.

I took a breath and slowly let it out. Colleen and I kept hanging out for a while after my injury. But when she came over last July after finishing the Boston Ballet summer intensive, all lovely and whole and strong, it was just...too much. I couldn't look at her and not see ballet. Not be consumed by jealousy. After that, I texted her to say I couldn't talk to her for a while.

She wrote back that she understood but asked if she could still talk to me.

You don't have to text back, she wrote, **and we don't have to see each other for now. Text no if you don't want that. Don't text anything if it's ok.**

I hadn't responded, so I got messages from Colleen a couple of times a week. She'd text about random stuff—her pit bull, Ferdinand; Kira, of course; and Juliet and Spencer, the girls in our level who always got the best roles.

I read Colleen's text again, hearing her bright, bubbly voice in my head. Of course no one believed her hangover theory. Colleen had floated a lot of unbelievable theories over the years: that Kira used to dance burlesque. That the rehearsal pianist, Darcio, was an exiled Belgian prince. That Khloé Kardashian was a secret genius. I knew Colleen didn't 100 percent believe in her own theories. She just liked the idea of them being true.

I put my phone on my nightstand, trying to ignore the tightness in my stomach. I was so glad Colleen hadn't disappeared entirely, like my pictures had. Still, every time I didn't reply, I felt this horrible gut punch. Because Colleen was my best friend, and I hadn't talked to her in four months. Which probably meant she wasn't my best friend anymore.

I fell back onto my soft pink comforter and tried to zone out.

At some point, a crack of thunder startled my eyes open. Downstairs, I heard Josie and my parents laugh as they covered the patio furniture and hurried back inside. My right leg, where the metal was, throbbed with an ache that took over my whole body. It happened every time it rained. I curled into the fetal position, reliving the horrible split second that had changed everything.

I'd been practicing fouettés after class at KDBS. My arms had been hyperextending when I pliéd, and I didn't want to leave until I'd corrected it. Maybe I hadn't put enough rosin on my shoes. Maybe I was exhausted from class and should have taken a break. All I know was that one second, I was whipping through the air, and the next, I wasn't. A sickening crack echoed around the walls of the studio. My bones were in pieces. And nothing would ever be the same.

And now, I felt out of place in my peachy-pink room where I used to have sleepovers with Colleen, staying up all night fantasizing about being professional ballet dancers in New York. We'd be company members in the American Ballet Theatre. Roommates. Regulars at fancy sushi restaurants and romantic cafés. We'd dance our favorite role: Giselle.

I pulled the comforter over my head and dragged my laptop inside. Harsh light filled my sad little blanket fort as Marianela Núñez danced on-screen, the second-act score of *Giselle* radiating weakly from my laptop's speakers.

In the ballet, Giselle dies of a broken heart because the man she loves betrays her, and then she turns into one of the Wilis—ghosts of jilted girls, doomed to haunt the forest forever, killing men who wander in at night.

I wasn't dead. And nobody had jilted me. But some*thing* had. I still loved ballet, but it didn't love me back. All I could do was linger on, like a sad, rejected ghost, hurting people who didn't deserve it.

CHAPTER THREE

I FELT A LIGHT SLAP on my arm and turned to face Margot. Thank God we both had last names starting with *K*. It meant I had a distraction in the bleak place known as homeroom.

"I'll text—" Margot started, but was overpowered by a huge yawn. I yawned, too, and not just because Margot did. Between late-night *Giselle* viewings and the slurry of memories that kept me awake (highlights included the God-awful sound of my bones breaking, the searing pain I felt after I got to the hospital, and the doctor pointing at my X-ray and saying, "You shattered it good") I never got enough sleep.

"Jesus, I'm tired," Margot said, tapping her pencil on a half-finished geometry work sheet.

"Wild night?" I asked, rubbing my eyes.

"If watching *Little Shop of Horrors* with Ethan is wild, then yes."

I shook my head. Ethan went over to Margot's house for a movie night every Thursday, and they only watched musicals. "Don't you guys ever get sick of musicals?"

"How dare you."

I rolled my eyes. *I* was sick of musicals after a single day of auditioning for one. The first run-through of my dance audition had actually felt kind of good, letting my body move to music again. But the second had been certifiably horrible, and afterward I completely freaked out.

"Really, though. Why do you like them?" I asked. "They're so..." I tried to think of a description that was true but wasn't super rude.

"Cheesy? Embarrassing?" Margot said.

"Exactly. And you're neither of those things."

"How do you know? My outside may be sarcasm, but inside I'm cheese."

I smirked. "Can that be your yearbook quote?"

"'Chaos is what killed the dinosaurs, darling,'" Margot said, spinning her pencil around her middle finger.

"What?"

"That's my yearbook quote. It's from *Heathers*."

"Is that a musical?"

Margot squinted one eye at me, trying to figure out if I was kidding. "It was a movie and then it got turned into a musical. And to answer your judgy question, I like musicals because they're loud and weird. And I'm loud and weird. Plus, the people who do the musical here don't care if they're cool or popular or whatever. It's refreshing."

I nodded. I guess that made sense. As far as I could tell, everyone else at Eagle View cared a lot about being "cool." Over two thousand kids went here, so you'd expect some variety. But mostly, people traveled in big, samey packs, talking about things that didn't matter while looking generally unimpressed with the world.

"Were ballet people like that?" Margot asked. "Did they care about being cool or were they too focused on their dancing?"

I stiffened. I didn't want to talk about ballet. I knew that was what friends were supposed to do—talk about the hard stuff—but this friendship was new and fun and as free from awfulness as anything could be right now. I didn't want to weigh it down. And Margot couldn't really understand what I was feeling, anyway.

"Wait, so, what were you going to say earlier? You said you were going to text me," I said, deflecting.

"Oh. Yeah. I was saying I'll text you when I see the callback list." Margot had music appreciation in the choir room first period, where Mrs. Sorenson would post the list.

"Sure, but I'm not going to be on it if they only do callbacks for the main parts. You heard me sing, right? Not musical theater god material."

"Never know," Margot said. "And speaking of musical theater gods, did you give Jude the finger?"

"No comment."

"You *did*?" She sat up straight, looking equal parts delighted and confused. "Why? I mean, I totally support it, but what did *Jude* do? He's like the textbook definition of a sweetheart."

I shot her a knowing look. "A sweetheart? The kind who could break your no-dating-someone-at-the-same-school rule?"

"Hard no. He's too pure. But back to why you gave him the finger." She made impatient circles with her hand.

"Ugh, fine. He didn't do anything. I was in a bad mood and he was just there. All smiley and nice and...*there*."

Margot tilted her head at me, confused. "Yeah, what a jerk."

"No, it's just, when people are too nice or too complimentary or whatever, it freaks me out. It's like, what are they after?" I skipped the part about me almost having a panic attack after flubbing that stupid pirouette.

Margot took it in for a second. "So just to be clear, you *don't* like

33

it when guys are nice to you? You're not one of those girls who like assholes, are you?"

A few guys sitting in the next row snickered loudly. Margot stared at them and started slow clapping. "Wow, you just won the Oldest People to Still Laugh at the Word *Asshole* award. Congrats, you should be *so* proud."

Embarrassed, the guys quickly moved seats. I smiled and shook my head at Margot. "What?" she said innocently. I'd gotten used to Margot's Margot-ness over the last few months. She never let things go, which could have been exhausting to be around, but she made it entertaining.

"You didn't answer my question," she said.

"No. Hate assholes," I said, remembering we were still talking about why I gave Jude the finger. "I was just having a bad day. Hopefully he's not mad."

"Nah." Margot shrugged. "I don't think Jude gets mad."

Right. Jude Jeppson, with the angelic voice and swooning fan club, probably lived in a happy little bubble.

The bell rang. Margot stuffed her work sheet into her backpack and stood up the way she always did, taking her damn time. The only indication that she was excited to see the callback list was the slight rise of her voice when she said: "Watch your phone."

"Good luck, Lina," I said. Even though Margot had never told me she wanted the Lina Lamont role, I'd figured it out after Mom said the thing about Lina having a weird voice. That explained why Margot had used that accent at auditions.

Margot looked surprised for a second. Then she smiled. "Thanks."

I turned and started the trek to first-period English. Eagle View was constructing a new, massive building that would eventually hold the entire student body, but until it was finished, the old school and the completed wing of the new school were connected by a long tunnel. I didn't mind the lengthy walks between classes. It was a welcome break from sitting still all day and listening to teachers lecture while the girls behind me whispered about how bored they were or how difficult it was to find a "classy" silver dress online. Before, these kinds of conversations didn't bother me. They hardly even registered. Because every day at 11 AM sharp, I'd leave for the sunlit KDBS studio, where everyone was razor-focused and driven and the opposite of bored.

Now there was no leaving. I was stuck listening to vapid conversations and worse, the spectacularly dumb comments of certain boys. Since I hadn't spent much time at school freshman and sophomore year, a few of the guys saw me as fresh meat.

I turned into English and saw Exhibit A: Tweedle Dumb and Tweedle Douchebag. Their real names were Jake Lux and Paul Manley, of the purportedly small penis. They sat in the back corner, made jokes about Ms. Belson's clothes, and never read the assigned books.

Paul put his hands together and bowed his head to me. "All hail the Ice Princess of the East."

Well. That was a new one. I rolled my eyes as I walked to my seat. I'd made the innocent mistake of sitting in front of Paul and Jake on the first day of school, and then Ms. Belson passed around a seating chart and I was stuck there forever. And because I never laughed at their dumb jokes, I was deemed an "ice princess." Today, I guess they got tired of being regular jerks and wanted to try being racist jerks for a while.

As I was about to sit down, Paul bowed to me again, then winked. I gave him the death stare and sat down.

I didn't have Margot's slash-and-burn philosophy when it came to bullshit. My philosophy was deflect and ignore. In the end, there

35

would always be bullshit, so why spend all your energy slashing and burning something that would never actually change?

When I opened my bag, something felt different in the room. Usually no one else in class paid attention to what Paul or Jake said to me, or at least they all pretended not to. And Ms. Belson was on some advising committee that met in the old building, so she was never in the room until the minute class started.

But I had the feeling someone was watching me. I looked toward the front corner of the room, by the windows, where a pair of blue eyes surrounded by messy curls blinked back at me. Ethan. The sadistic dentist from auditions. He passed a balled-up piece of paper to the person next to him, and I watched as it zigzagged its way back to me.

I tensed as my hand grasped the paper, waiting to hear if Paul or Jake would comment, but they were absorbed in some conversation about a girl on the soccer team. I unfolded the note.

> It was my moral duty to tell you not to sit near the Neanderthal twins on the first day of school. I failed. Please accept this crumpled piece of paper as my apology. Also please don't give me the finger. That would be rude. And confusing. And kind of hilarious.

I looked up at Ethan, who was considering me with a curious expression. Embarrassment crept up my spine as I imagined Jude telling him about how I gave him the finger for no reason.

Don't worry about it, and no guarantees, I scribbled, and sent the note on its way. When Ethan read it, his mouth quirked up. Then he gave me a small, respectful nod.

I nodded back, and actually felt myself smile.

Wow. Having an interaction in English that didn't make me want to gouge my eyes out with a pen was new and different. It was kind of sad to admit how much better it made me feel.

My phone lit up with a text from Margot, and since Ms. Belson wasn't in the room yet, I opened it.

"Who ya texting?" Paul leaned over my shoulder.

"My friend Personal Space," I said, shifting forward and lowering my phone into my lap.

"It's a cold one today," Jake whispered. "Get out the blankets."

Margot had sent two photos. The first was of her name under callbacks for Lina Lamont. I knew it! The second was of my name under callbacks for something called the Vamp.

A moment later another text arrived from Margot: **Dude, congrats! Check out Cyd Charisse, the original Vamp!** Underneath was a link to a YouTube video. The thumbnail showed a glamorous woman in bright green, her dark hair in a sleek bob, her long leg extended above her head.

My brain was beyond scattered—I hadn't been sure I'd actually get into the musical, or if I even *wanted* to after the disaster at auditions. And now I had a callback?

I didn't have to go. I could head home and nap. I kept telling myself that as I stared at Cyd Charisse's extension, the curve of her high-arched foot.

When Ms. Belson came in, I put my phone away and mentally prepared myself for her forty-five-minute lecture on existentialism, whatever witty remarks Paul and Jake were sure to have about her magenta sequined sweater, and the prospect of another day of staying after school. I was exhausted just thinking about it.

CHAPTER FOUR

ACCORDING TO WIKIPEDIA, Cyd Charisse's real name was Tula Ellice Finklea (kudos to her for changing it), and she had apparently studied classical ballet before going into movie musicals. Margot and I huddled over her phone in the auditorium during callbacks, watching Cyd Charisse dance with Gene Kelly in a small segment of "Broadway Melody," which Margot said was the biggest, longest dance number in *Singin' in the Rain*. I could see the ballet training in her turnout and the way she held her head. Still, the dance was far from balletic.

Gene Kelly was in a yellow vest and dorky glasses, and Cyd Charisse, the Vamp, was dance-seducing him. She slithered around on her long legs in a way that was aggressive but aloof, raunchy but dainty. I couldn't figure out how she was able to create that effect.

"So, what else does she do? Does she sing?" I asked, my eyes still glued to the screen.

"Nope," Margot said. "She doesn't sing or have any lines. She just dances in this."

With all my years of classical training, I'd never danced like that.

Margot clicked her phone off and fanned herself with her callback script. She'd already finished her Lina Lamont scenes but was sticking around for support. She scanned the stage, assessing the three guys who had been called back for Don Lockwood: Jude, Ethan, and, to everyone's surprise, Harrison. They'd already sung but were staying to partner the three girls called back for the Vamp.

"Bang, Marry, Kill with those three," Margot said, pointing to the Don Lockwoods. "Go."

"Nothing with any of them."

"Oh, come on, one of those guys is going to be your dance partner. You have to seduce them *and* do ballet with them, which means—"

"What?" I interrupted. "Ballet?"

Margot wrinkled her eyebrows. "Oh, I thought you knew. There's the sexy Vamp part first, and then later in the song she comes out in white and she and Don do a ballet duet."

I practically stopped breathing. "It probably won't be what you're used to," Margot said carefully. "Last year in *42nd Street* we did a ballet number, but it was really more like swaying while holding flowers. Ms. Langford is more tap and jazz. She doesn't have much ballet experience, so the ballet duet will probably be more like a 'ballet duet.'" Margot did exaggerated air quotes. "Sorry." She said that word quietly, like she really was sorry.

"It's fine," I said, and my voice actually sounded half convincing. But then I thought of something horrible. What if we had to do ballet at the callback? A wild panic filled me and I gripped the edge of my hard plastic seat. I calmed down by reminding myself that if we did, it would just be flower swaying, like Margot said. Ballet in air quotes. Not the real thing. My pulse slowed down, back to normal.

"So hey," Margot said, her voice surprisingly gentle. "What are you doing tonight? There's a new record store opening in Harrisburg that looks cool. Want to go?"

"Oh, um, sorry. I'm kind of tired. I think I'm just going to go home and sleep." I already wished I were in bed, under the covers, watching *Giselle*.

"Okay," Margot said. "Then you should come to me and Ethan's movie night next week. We don't even have to watch a musical. And you can pick the snacks." She smiled at me expectantly.

"Um, maybe." It wasn't that I didn't want to hang out with Margot. I just needed her to stay in the school zone. If she crept too much into my real world, she'd see how pathetic it was. How pathetic *I* was. She'd pity me. Or worse, she'd say "Get over it," which I wouldn't be able to stand.

I looked around for Ms. Langford, wondering when the Vamp callback would start so I could do it and go home already. When I turned back to Margot, she was tracing her fingernail over a lengthy run in her black tights, a frown pulling at her mouth.

When she saw me looking, she straightened up. "I still can't believe Harrison's here," she said. I swiveled to see Harrison sitting on his own. He kept nervously pulling off his beanie, smoothing out his hair, and putting it back on.

"Vamp girls and Don Lockwoods, line up!" Ms. Langford finally called.

"Go get 'em, champ," Margot said as I stood and joined the other two girls called back for the Vamp role—Laurel Adams and Diya Rao—onstage. Diya X-rayed me with her eyes again. What was her deal? She'd also been called back for Kathy Selden, a role with actual lines, so she probably had no interest in being the Vamp.

Diya and Laurel were both wearing leotards and dance shorts, their bare legs on display. I felt out of place in my jeans and gray Henley, but there was no way I'd change. I wasn't showing anyone my scars.

Ms. Langford matched up the partners according to height. That put the tall Diya with Ethan (which seemed to piss them both off), the petite Laurel with Harrison, and me in the middle with Jude.

"Hey, Alina," Jude called, walking over with his toothy, carefree smile, like I hadn't flipped him off the other day. Which...all right. If he was going to give me a pass, I wasn't going to bring it up.

"Partners, stand facing each other, two feet apart," Ms. Langford directed. "Look into each other's eyes. Connect."

Extended eye contact was never not awkward, but I was used to it from partnering class. I liked being clinical about it. Eye color. Eyelash situation. That sort of thing. Jude had full, dark eyelashes that gave the impression of eyeliner. His eyes were a rich hazel. Little creases were forming in the outer corners from the slow smile spreading on his lips.

Somehow, we were doing the best out of everyone at this part.

Ethan and Diya were standing way more than two feet apart, and it sounded like they were trying to sigh and scoff each other into oblivion. Laurel kept breaking into giggles while Harrison kept saying "What?" I broke eye contact for a moment to glance at Laurel, remembering Josie's bonkers plan for me to dazzle her and Noah with my classical dance training so they'd consider being in her piece for the student showcase.

Even if that plan made any sense, I learned that I wasn't going to be doing any impressive classical moves at the callback. The routine Ms. Langford taught us was shockingly simple. All I had to do was slide Jude's prop glasses off, circle around him, twirl the glasses while doing a high-kneed sexy walk, blow on the lenses, and then rub them kind of scandalously on my thigh. Ms. Langford said she was looking for style rather than technique at this point.

"Cyd Charisse contained wonderful oppositions," Ms. Langford said, her orange curls bouncing as she gestured with her hands. "She was sensual but refined. Serene but explosive. Fred Astaire once called her 'beautiful dynamite.' That's what I'm looking for today."

As we ran through the combination, Ms. Langford shouted things like "Smolder!" and "Beautiful dynamite!" But it was hard to make adjustments to my dancing when I didn't know what part of my body to adjust. In class, Kira used to yell specifics: "Shoulders down!" "Point your feet!" "Turn out from the hips!" Plus, it was hard to "smolder" after spending the whole day at Eagle View, sitting in uncomfortable chairs, getting a permanent crease in my forehead from trigonometry, and eating something called chicken shoestrings for lunch. Double plus, I kept almost poking Jude's eye out with the stupid glasses.

"This isn't a common ballet move, I assume?" he asked, rubbing his eye.

"How do you know I do...did ballet?" I asked while craning my neck around, trying to see how Diya and Laurel were doing with the glasses thing. Laurel had it down, but Diya took them off Ethan's face too roughly, and the tip went up his nose. I wasn't entirely sure she hadn't done it on purpose.

"Oh, I can tell," Jude said. "The way you dance, the way you move, the way you walk with your feet turned out like a duck." My gaze snapped back to his. He was smiling. "My cousin does ballet. I learned the signs."

I glanced down at my feet. Turned out as always. Then I looked back at him with narrowed eyes.

"Uh-oh, you going to give me the finger again?"

"Not yet."

Jude studied me with a squinty expression. "Just out of curiosity—"

I waved my hand in front of his face. "Shh, I need to become beautiful dynamite."

❧

Once callbacks ended, I walked out to the already-darkening parking lot, trailing behind Margot, Ethan, and Jude as they chattered incessantly. When my phone dinged with a text from Colleen, I slowed down even more.

Two new girls joined today. Jodys, obvs. Seem nice.

I sighed even though I wasn't surprised. Jody was the name of the main character in *Center Stage*, a ballet movie Colleen and I had seen a million times. We used Jody to describe a particular kind of girl— the blond, blue-eyed beauties who, despite how excellent or mediocre their technique was, always threatened to secure Kira's favor based on some "it" factor they all seemed to possess.

On the whole, KDBS was full of Jodys, which meant Colleen and I always had to work extra hard to get noticed. We never talked about how outnumbered we were, but we definitely were. There were a few other East Asian girls in the lower levels of the school, and a couple had cycled in and out of our class over the years. Colleen had always been the only Black girl at KDBS, though.

It took me a second to notice that the chatter had stopped and an odd silence filled the air. I looked up from my phone. Margot, Ethan, and Jude stood several paces away, staring at me. "Sorry, what?" I said.

"Want anything?" Margot jabbed her thumb at the two lit-up vending machines by the side of the school.

"I'm good." I dropped my phone into my jacket pocket. The gut-punch feeling I always got when I ignored a text from Colleen now combined with embarrassment for being so oblivious to where I was. I wasn't in my room, free to zone out, yet.

Margot and Jude walked over to the machines while Ethan and I stayed put. I was about to head off to my car when Ethan popped the hood of his sweatshirt over his head and turned to me. "So I take it my apology note is accepted?"

Oh, right. English. Paul and Jake. "Sure," I said, smirking. "Neanderthal twins. That's good."

"Thanks. And hey, since you're new, I'll tell them off for you."

"What?" My eyes widened as I looked up at him. He couldn't be serious. He looked serious. "Please don't."

"It's long overdue. In fifth grade, I wore a pink flamingo costume to the Halloween parade, and Paul and Jake said I was gay and anyone I touched would turn gay. I mean, I *was* gay, and it was a phenomenal costume, so I don't entirely blame them for thinking it had powers, but still. It would be cathartic."

"But..." I paused, confused about why he thought it was a good idea. "I doubt it will change anything." It was like KDBS being full of Jodys. It was the way things were, and I'd rather focus my energy on the stuff I could actually control.

"Are you sure?" Ethan eyed me doubtfully. "I may not be as gifted as Margot in the art of intimidation, but I can be devastating when I want to be. *Devastating.*" He made his eyes go all big and intense, like they'd been during his sadistic dentist audition song.

Jude and Margot joined us again, crinkling plastic snack bags. "What's devastating?" Margot asked around a mouthful of chips.

I looked hard at Ethan, shaking my head a little. I didn't need anyone else knowing about Paul and Jake's douche act in English.

"Dancing with Robobitch," Ethan said smoothly. "I'm still recovering."

Margot snorted and I nodded to Ethan, glad we were on the same page. The group split up after that. Jude's car was near mine, so we walked together through the parking lot.

"So...are you nervous about getting the part?" I asked to fill the silence. Just a few more seconds and I'd be on my way home after this way-too-long day.

"Nah." Jude shrugged one shoulder. "If I get it, awesome. But if I don't, it's not the end of the world. Life goes on. Et cetera, et cetera."

That wasn't what I expected, and it annoyed me for some reason. "How mellow of you," I muttered.

"Wow." Jude looked at me. "You didn't like my answer at all."

"No, I'm just surprised. From what I've seen of you, I thought you'd care more. About getting the best role."

"Ah, from what you've *seen* of me. So you have good observational skills?" There was that gleam in his eye again, accompanied by a knowing smile.

Something about those two things made a whole lot of words come out of my mouth. "Yes, actually. I do. I observed that you're the best guy singer here. And I also *observed* that you dance with a kind of loose, aristocratic elegance. More like Fred Astaire than Gene Kelly. And yes, I do know who they are. I just didn't say anything at auditions because I didn't feel like it. So I assumed that you would want, like really *want*, the part that gives you a chance to do what you're good at."

Jude blinked at me, his expression shifting from confused to really, really pleased. Proving I had good observational skills somehow turned into me complimenting him a million times.

"Wow, thanks," he said. I glanced at him, taking in his eyeliner lashes, his coffee-brown hair that fell to the side in a gentle swoop, the pink flush spreading across his cheeks—all of which I hated to admit was kind of adorable.

I looked away. "Don't let it go to your head," I said sharply. "Arrogance kills elegance. It, like, murders it in cold blood."

"Good to know." The corner of Jude's mouth lifted as he reached an old white SUV and pulled out his keys. "And don't worry, I won't let it go to my head."

"I'll be able to tell if you do. Observational skills, remember?" I said, tapping a finger on my temple as I walked to my car, a few spaces down from his.

"Nothing gets past you." He gave me a small wave.

Driving home, I felt...surprisingly okay. Yeah, I was tired, and the idea of Colleen contending with two new Jodys without me stung a little, and I still didn't know how I felt about the whole Vamp thing. But suddenly, I wondered what it would be like if Jude and I got the parts and we got to dance together. If I could make myself stay after school for rehearsals instead of retreating to my room. And if the musical didn't keep reminding me that what I really wanted—everything I'd worked for—was impossible now.

All of a sudden, I felt less okay. I slammed the brakes a little too hard at a red light, and an ache radiated up my leg. I closed my eyes and took a deep breath, something my physical therapist, Birdie, used to tell me to do whenever I felt like curling up into a ball and disappearing. Or crying. Or screaming obscenities. Deep breaths were pretty much Birdie's go-to solution for any publicly inconvenient emotion, and I was kind of shocked to realize how decently they worked in a pinch.

Deep breaths didn't cure you of the desire to disappear or cry or scream. But they dulled it enough so you could go about your day looking and acting like a relatively normal person. I called them Nature's Advil.

Once in physical therapy, I'd asked Birdie if she ever used the deep breathing trick on herself. "Like when people touch your stomach without asking," I'd said. Birdie was six months pregnant and hated that.

"Deep breaths don't work for that," she'd said, putting a bandage on my hand where I'd scraped it falling down the physiotherapy stairs and then had a swearing, crying meltdown.

"I calmly tell those people to unhand me or die," Birdie went on. "Deep breaths only work if the rage is coming from inside the house." She tapped me on the chest.

Birdie was always saying weird stuff like that. She was going to confuse the hell out of her baby when it was old enough to have problems. Still, I didn't know how I would have gotten through the summer without her. I couldn't break down in front of my parents because I knew it killed them, and Josie didn't remotely understand, and Colleen tried, she really did, but watching her go off to class or rehearsal just made me feel worse. And then, of course, in July I stopped talking to her altogether.

I was discharged from physical therapy in July, too, since I could walk fine. I hadn't seen Birdie since.

The deep breaths had done the trick, dulling the rage to a quiet rumble.

At another red light, I checked my rearview mirror. Jude was behind me in the old white SUV, bopping away to a song I couldn't hear. I still didn't understand how he could be so casual about something he invested so much of his time in. I wondered if he worried about anything, ever.

As I made my way home, Jude followed along behind me. I figured he lived in one of the gazillion developments on this side of town, until I made the right turn into my neighborhood and he was still in my rearview mirror.

As I pulled into my driveway, his SUV passed by, turning around at the stop sign and circling back, coming to a rest at the house directly across from mine.

I slowly got out of my car.

"Howdy, neighbor," Jude yelled, the knowing smile at full wattage now.

CHAPTER FIVE

SNIPPETS OF OUR CONVERSATIONS fired rapidly in my head: Jude asking if I'd ever seen him before, me calling him a stranger, his praise of my observational skills—sarcastic praise, I now realized. Damn.

"How long have you lived there?" I asked warily.

Jude walked across the street to me. "Only three years."

I pinched the bridge of my nose. I'd lived here all my life. How had I not recognized him? I looked around at all the other houses surrounding me, realizing I probably couldn't pick anyone living in them out of a lineup.

Of course Mom chose that moment to pull up in the minivan, waving theatrically at Jude from the window. Josie hopped out with an armful of library books. "Jude!" she called. "How's it going?"

"Not bad. How's Mrs. Palladino's class?"

Josie held up her library books. "You were right, she's a fiend." My mouth hung open as I looked between them.

Mom got out, talking on her cell. *Hi, Jude,* she mouthed before turning up the walkway. And she tried to hide it, but her eyes lit up when she saw Jude and me standing together. It was the same look she had when Margot came over that one time. *Oh boy*, she probably thought. *My daughter has two whole friends now!*

"You'll make it," Jude said to Josie as she followed Mom inside. "Oh," he called after them. "Tell Arthur I have that book he wanted to borrow."

Arthur. My dad. Jude was loaning books to my dad.

The door shut and we were alone again. Jude had the good sense not to say anything, but his smile sure was loud.

"*Fine*," I said. "You got me. My observational skills are shit."

"Not shit, necessarily. You just never observed in this direction." He pointed to his house. "Or these directions." He pointed to both sides, like a flight attendant. He wasn't wrong. Until eight months ago, my whole world was ballet.

"I was...busy."

"Oh, I know. It's not an insult. Just an *observation*."

I snorted. Then I surprised myself. "Want to go for a walk?"

Jude's eyebrows shot up. Guess I'd surprised him, too. "Okay."

I felt a little bad about being so oblivious to him before. Also, if Mom and Dad saw me doing something social after I'd done an extracurricular activity, I'd probably get away with staying home for the rest of the weekend.

I held up a (pointer) finger, asking him to wait. Then I jogged to my front door, opened it, and called in: "I'm going on a walk with Jude. Please note that I've spent three nonschool hours out of the house today. Adjust your nagging accordingly."

"Will do, sweetie," Dad said, giving me a thumbs-up from behind the piano. Mom, standing suspiciously close to the front windows, saluted.

Jude was going to see a movie at 6:15, so we had about half an hour to walk. As we wandered up the sidewalk, I pulled my red fleece jacket tighter around me. With the sun already down, fall nights like these got pretty cold. Not hat weather yet, but close. "So how did you meet my whole family?" I asked.

"My mom throws a neighborhood Fourth of July barbecue every year."

"Ah." I was hardly ever home in July. It was the prime month for summer ballet intensives—the rigorous, audition-only ballet programs that opened doors later on. Now that I thought about it, I could vaguely remember my parents saying stuff like "We've got that barbecue at the Jeppsons' tonight" when we talked on the phone while I was away. I'd just never asked who the Jeppsons were.

"They're pretty great. The burgers are amazing, and Mrs. Garber always gets drunk and imitates Elvis." When I didn't react, Jude said, "That would be funny if you knew who Mrs. Garber was. Trust me."

He put his hands in the pockets of his brown bomber jacket. There were patches going down the left sleeve: a slice of pizza, the bat signal, a rainbow ally flag, and a pair of red lips surrounded by the words *Rocky Horror Picture Show*. The patches should have made the jacket look cartoonish, but somehow, with his side-swooped hair, it looked kind of retro and cool.

I cleared my throat and looked away. "So can I ask you something? How were you so sure I wouldn't recognize you? When you asked me at auditions if I'd ever seen you before, you seemed pretty sure I'd say no."

Jude smiled and glanced up at the dark sky, like he was remembering something funny. "Okay. So once, a couple years ago, my aunt Liddy was visiting, and she was helping me wash my mom's car. You were sitting on your porch with your headphones on. Aunt Liddy bet me ten bucks that you'd smile at me in two minutes or less.

I said I'd bet her twenty bucks you'd never look over. Not even once. I knew I'd win, and I did."

"But *how* did you know?"

"Just, you always looked like you were somewhere else. Especially when you had your headphones on. That day when we washed the car, we'd look over and you'd be sitting there, doing these little moves, like..." Jude demonstrated by tilting his head slightly and turning his hand in delicate circles.

I nodded. The memory of it made my throat seize up. I used to listen to the music of whatever role or variation I was working on over and over again. As I listened, I'd do the dance in my head, and my body would follow with little ghosts of the movements. It helped me make the music part of my body. When I was sitting on the porch, I wasn't really there. I was dancing, even when I wasn't.

"I—" Jude hesitated. "I heard about your leg. Your mom told my mom about it. It must have been hard not to dance for so long. Especially for someone as good as you are."

"As I *was*," I corrected. Then reminded myself to save the melodrama for later, when I was alone in my room.

Jude looked confused. "But you still are. You were great at auditions. And I'm not just saying that because you called me elegant."

"I said you *danced* elegantly."

"Right. And so do you."

"I mean, yeah, I can still dance. But I can't..." I tried to find words to describe what it felt like to dance before. Lifting up onto pointe, becoming light in an instant. Skimming along the floor in quick bourrées. Exploding through the air in a grand jeté. Becoming something other than myself. A fairy or a spirit or an enchanted bird—things that didn't exist in real life but did when I danced them.

I couldn't say any of that, though. Not now. So I went with

the practical problem. "I can't dance in pointe shoes anymore. And without pointe, you can't do ballet. Not seriously, anyway. And I don't want to do it if it's not serious."

"But..." Jude tilted his head. "Even if you can't do it seriously, like as a career, couldn't you just—"

"No." I couldn't "just" do ballet casually, or for fun, or in any other way besides a career. Without the strength and ability I once had, ballet would be a sad echo of what it was before. It would hurt too much to do it like that.

I forced a smile. "I don't expect you, Mr. Life Goes On Et Cetera Et Cetera, to understand what doing something seriously means."

"First of all, awesome nickname," he said wryly.

"Thank you."

"Second of all, I do things seriously. Just because I'm not freaking out about getting the Don Lockwood part doesn't mean I'm not serious about it. I just like doing a lot of things, and the musical happens to be one of them."

"A lot of things," I repeated. "Like, sports?" I remembered Margot saying something about Jude missing last year's musical because of soccer.

"Nah. I did lacrosse and soccer for a long time, but I quit this year. They took up too much time."

"Oh. So what other things do you like doing, then?"

"Hmm, let's see. Playing video games, playing Whiffle ball, watching horror movies, doing Taylor Swift karaoke, drinking green tea in the bath, reading, especially mysteries, hanging out with friends, knitting—oh, and working at Fly Zone. It's an indoor trampoline park," he explained, seeing my bewildered face.

Okay, Fly Zone wasn't what I was confused about. That one actually made a lot of sense. But I couldn't wrangle all the others into a portrait of a single person. I mean, the mysteries and the video games and the Whiffle ball, sure. And he was a musical theater god, so maybe that explained the Taylor Swift karaoke. But green tea in the bath? Knitting? I'd never heard a guy my age admit to liking such things, even the boys in ballet, who were used to defying stereotypes. Which reminded me...

"Don't forget tap dancing at the Y. Margot told me."

"Oh, yeah, tap." He snapped his fingers. "I knew I was forgetting something. But yeah, basically I like doing the things I like doing." He turned to me with a proud smile. "I guess I'm serious about enjoying life."

"Oof." The noise escaped me before I could stop it.

"What, too cheesy?"

Yes. "No, sorry. I'm just not really enjoying anything these days, so..." I trailed off and mentally slapped myself in the face. Way to go, Alina. Invite a near stranger on a walk in the cold and then hit him with a self-pitying downer like that.

"Oh." Jude took a breath like he was going to say something else, but didn't.

"Don't listen to me, I'm just tired," I said. We walked by a few more houses as the wind picked up speed. The streetlamps gave a soft glow, casting the neighborhood in a goldish hue. Jude kicked a rock. It scuttled down the sidewalk and disappeared, with a brittle whoosh, into a raked pile of leaves.

"So I'm aware we've literally only known each other for five days," he said. "But since we *are* neighbors, I could give you some neighborly advice."

"Uh, okay..."

"I'm no expert or anything. But I think when you have a reason to be sad, you should do two things. Want to hear them?"

He sounded like a motivational speaker. But whatever, I'd humor him. "Sure."

"The first thing is hard. It's making peace with why you're sad. Like, not wallowing in the pain but not trying to erase it, either."

I thought about the empty walls of my room. The freak-out at auditions. The flipping of the bird. The jealousy bomb exploding. I felt no peace at all. I was spectacularly failing at the first thing.

"The second, more fun thing, is finding something that makes you happy and doing the hell out of it. Especially if it's something you couldn't do before."

"What do you mean, something you couldn't do before?"

"Like something you never had time for, or didn't do because you felt like you couldn't..." He paused, his mouth still open, like he was trying to figure out how to phrase what was in his head. Instead he shrugged and said, "Or whatever."

"Did you get this from one of those self-help books they sell at the grocery store?"

He laughed. "Sadly, no. I stole it from my mom. It's what we did after my dad left."

"Oh...I'm sorry." How awful. Of his dad. Of me. I didn't know why I assumed he'd gotten all this stuff from a dumb book instead of his actual life. We took a few more steps in silence. "I didn't mean to be so jokey," I said.

"Hey, you can be jokey all you want. If it makes you happy," he added with a wink. I must still have looked uncomfortable, because he added: "It's okay, really. It happened two years ago now." He dug a pair of thick green gloves out of his jacket pocket and slipped them on.

"It was awful at first. And it's still hard sometimes, but I think my mom had the right idea. Like for example, one of the things she never really got to do was grill. That was always my dad's job. He grilled the fancy burgers and she was on salad duty. When he left, she bought a Magellan Deluxe gourmet grill and started throwing Fourth of July barbecues. And because of that, we get to hear Mrs. Garber drunk-singing 'Love Me Tender' every year, which, again, you just have to trust me, is hilarious."

I smiled. I wanted to ask more questions, like if he ever saw his dad now or not. But I didn't know him well enough for that.

We made it back to the middle of the street between our houses. I checked my phone: 6:14. He should have left for the movie a while ago. Plus, it was getting really cold out here. But I didn't want to end on such a heavy subject, so I searched my brain for something else to say.

"Did you knit those?" I pointed to the green gloves.

"Yup. My first attempt at gloves, so they turned out a little wonky." From the golden light of the streetlamps, I could see they were lumpy in places, and one of the fingers was misshapen. Still, they looked warm.

I shrugged. "They're not bad."

Now 6:15. But Jude didn't seem like he was in any hurry to leave. Surprisingly, I wasn't, either. Then I remembered something he'd said to me back at auditions. "Hey, wait, if you knew who I was this whole time, how come you asked me if I was a freshman?"

Jude laughed. "Okay, that was a cheap shot. But come on, I'd known who you were for years and you'd just confirmed you had no idea who I was. I blame my fragile ego."

That made me think about Jake and Paul. I'd violated their truly fragile egos by not laughing at their stupid jokes, and it had led to a pretty awful sort of retribution. Jude—who'd walked with me on this particularly cold fall evening because I asked him to, who'd tried to make me feel better after I said a rude thing—was altogether different.

"I think your ego is just fine."

"You do?" He leaned a little closer, like we were sharing secrets.

I had a flashback to all the girls swooning when he sang "Maria" at auditions. "Yeah," I said dryly.

During the lull that followed, I checked my phone again: 6:17. He obviously wasn't the type to care that he was late to movies, which made sense. I pictured him waltzing into the movie theater, asking everyone what he missed, and they'd all be glad to tell him, because he was Jude Jeppson, singer of songs, jumper on trampolines, enjoyer of life.

But I stopped myself from falling back into that easy picture of him, the one I'd drawn up over the last few days. It wasn't that I thought his whole peppy vibe was fake now that I knew about his dad leaving. I just knew that he'd worked for it. That somehow he'd trudged through the weight of sadness and come out on the other side.

"So," he finally said. "Would a horror movie about a zombie clown make you happy? Because that's what I'm going to see."

"That shouldn't make anyone happy."

He smiled. And I realized that, even though I'd only known of Jude Jeppson's existence for five days, I could honestly say he had one of the best smiles I'd ever seen. I gave a quick wave and started walking toward my house, but I was still picturing his grin. It was happy and goofy and sweet and sincere. So sincere it drew me in and made me want to back away at the same time.

"Have a good weekend, Alina," he called after me.

"You too." I turned and watched Jude walk to the SUV, his steps light and elegant, as always.

CHAPTER SIX

MY PARENTS LEFT ME ALONE over the weekend, just like I'd planned. But Monday morning, as I tried to eat breakfast in peace, Mom started badgering me to "invite your musical friends Margot and Jude over to hang!"

I pretended I'd left something in my room and headed to the stairs. Josie blocked me halfway up.

"Will you pick me up from dance later? Dad's playing at a jazz night thing and Mom has some talk she has to go to. I *really* don't want to get a ride with Fiona's mom. She keeps trying to sell me crystals."

"So buy one to shut her up."

Josie scoffed. "That's what she *wants* me to do. I can't give in!" she yelled after me as I went back down the stairs. There was no way I was picking her up. That was a slippery slope, and I wasn't about to chauffeur her to and from dance all the time. *Hell* no. If she wanted to dance, she could find her own damn ride.

Margot texted then, asking me to meet her at school early. She even bribed me with a caramel apple latte, my favorite of all the fall-themed hot drinks. I grabbed my jacket and backpack and left.

Hot caffeine was all I could think about as I walked from the parking lot to school, the chilly morning air sweeping through my still-damp hair, making me shiver.

"So why are we here fifteen minutes before we need to be?" I asked Margot after she handed over the latte. I knew it would burn my tongue if I drank it now, but I took a sip anyway.

"Cast list is going up," she said, leading me to the choir room, which was at the opposite end of the building. When we got there, a small crowd had already formed outside the double doors.

Ethan elbowed his way through to us, running a hand through his messy hair. "Happy Casting Day," he said sleepily, fist-bumping Margot and clinking his bottle of chocolate milk against my latte.

"Okay, party people, listen up!" Davis, the senior guy I'd seen belly dancing at auditions, was lifted onto two other guys' shoulders and clapped his hands above his head until everyone stopped talking. "Pre–cast party, my house tonight at seven. Don't bring losers. Car-pool to save the environment. That's it." Davis was lowered back down to the floor as everyone cheered.

It was so loud and so early. Both of these factors contributed to my desire to tuck my head into my hoodie and curl up in a ball on the hallway floor.

"The pre–cast party is special. *So* different from the cast party after closing night," Ethan said.

"How so?" I asked, stifling a yawn.

"At the regular cast party, after closing night, everyone has seen each other at their best and their absolute worst. Romances have begun and ended. Feuds have blazed and burned out. It's fun, but it's *fraught*." He looked at Margot for confirmation.

"That's pretty dramatic, but kinda true," she said.

"The pre–cast party is less weighed down," Ethan went on. "It's all about beginnings and possibilities. Sweet, sweet possibilities." He smiled cheerfully at Davis, who flipped his dreadlocks behind his shoulder and winked.

"The pre-cast party also happens on a weeknight, so it ends at nine thirty," Margot added.

Ethan sighed. "There is also that."

Margot glanced around. "Isn't Jude coming?"

"I don't think so," I said at the same time Ethan said, "He's on his way." They both stared at me.

"Oh, I saw his car in the driveway when I left, so I didn't think he was coming."

"Look at you, finally realizing Jude's your neighbor." Ethan grinned and Margot laughed.

My stomach did a weird fluttering thing. Ethan knew we were neighbors, which meant Jude had told him, which meant...Jude was talking about me with his best friend? I didn't know how I felt about that.

Margot and Ethan were staring at me again, waiting for my response. "Yeah, it only took me three ye—" I started, but was interrupted by Jude jumping in front of me.

"Do pre-cast parties make you happy?" he asked, doing a dorky dance that involved a lot of elbows. Margot and Ethan looked back and forth between us, eyebrows raised.

My cheeks went hot, which was dumb. I needed to get it together. "I've never been to one, but I hear they end at nine thirty. So maybe."

Ethan shook his head and turned to Jude. "I sold it better than that, I swear."

"I'm sure you did, Gene." Jude lightly punched Ethan's shoulder.

"Thanks for believing in me, Fred." Ethan punched Jude back.

Margot rolled her eyes. "What's this now?"

"Alina settled our Gene Kelly/Fred Astaire debate," Jude said. "He's Gene." He pointed to Ethan.

"He's Fred." Ethan pointed to Jude.

"Yeaaah, that's not going to get annoying," Margot said. "This is why you never answer their questions, Alina. It just leads to this."

"Noted," I said, watching Ethan and Jude's Gene and Fred routine escalate. Soon they challenged each other to a duel and started fake sword fighting in the hallway. I took a long drag of caramel apple latte. It was way too early for this.

Excited whispers built up around us, distracting me from Jude and Ethan's musical theater god shenanigans. Mrs. Sorenson's pumps clicked sharply on the floor as she walked up, sheets of paper in hand. "I won't make you wait any longer," she said, and tacked the papers onto the bulletin board.

Everyone rushed forward. I stepped back. A moment later, Margot burst out of the crowd and shoved her phone in my face. She'd taken a picture of the top part of the list.

Don Lockwood . . . . *Jude Jeppson*
Kathy Selden . . . . *Diya Rao*
Cosmo Brown . . . . *Ethan Anderson*
Lina Lamont . . . . *Margot Kilburn-Correa*
R. F. Simpson . . . . *Will Braddock*
Production Tenor . . . . . . *Harrison Lambert*

"Wow—" I started.

"Wait for it," Margot said, pulling up another photo. This one was of the chorus list. My name was on it. And beside my name, it said: *The Vamp*.

Before I could react, Margot whacked me hard in the bicep. "Congrats, dude."

"Ow!"

"Sorry, I'm not really a hugging person, but I had to do *something*."

I glared at her, but I wasn't actually mad. Margot's smile was bigger than I'd ever seen it.

"Congrats to you, too," I said, returning her bicep smack. Over her shoulder, I saw Jude and Ethan doing an elaborately choreographed handshake full of jumps and spins. A bunch of people surrounded them, cheering.

Diya Rao skirted the group, rolling her eyes. When she got to the cast list, she gave a small nod, like all was right with the world. Then she disappeared around the corner. After a few seconds, Ethan spotted Margot and me off to the side. He ran in our direction, tugging Jude over with him.

I thought a forced group hug was inevitable, but just before they got to us, they both slid onto their knees, brandishing jazz hands. "Za-zow!" they shouted in unison.

I waited for Margot to groan, but she threw her arms in the air and yelled "Za-zow!" back. Then they all broke into hysterical laughter. Oh, God. It was another Happy Crack situation.

"It's something Ms. Langford says when she's choreographing," Margot explained when she caught her breath. "You'll see."

A jittery feeling spread through my body, making my heart beat at a loud, insistent speed. I was actually in the musical. I even had a part, a dancing part. I thought about Cyd Charisse's intriguing style and the little routine Ms. Langford had us do at callbacks, which I'd done okay with. It wasn't at all like ballet, so it would be fine. Still, it was all happening too fast for me to sort out what was making me so nervous.

I calmed down enough to register that Ethan and Jude were standing up again and talking to Margot about the pre–cast party. "Should we all go together?" Margot asked.

Ethan nodded. "Of course."

"I can pick everyone up at seven," Jude said. They all looked at me.

Everyone? When did I become a part of everyone? "I'll just drive myself," I said.

"Oh, okay." Margot looked disappointed, but there was no way I was going to be stuck at this party until nine thirty.

❧

Ten minutes after I got to Davis's house that night, I cursed my decision to drive separately without checking to see if Margot, Ethan, and Jude were here yet. A raucous dance party had erupted in the living room, so I inched my way to the kitchen, where I planned to stay for the next fifteen minutes. After that, I'd leave whether Margot was here or not.

Davis's kitchen was spacious and quiet. A large island with stools around it sat in the middle, laden with chips and store-bought cookies. I was picking at the chips when someone cleared their throat behind me and I whirled around.

A blond guy in a beanie was leaning up against the refrigerator in the corner. Harrison. "Sorry. Didn't mean to startle you," he said. His voice was low and raspy, like someone in a whiskey commercial.

"It's fine," I said, pointing a chip at him. "Harrison, right?"

"Yeah." He did an awkward half wave. "And you're . . ."

"Alina."

"Cool." Harrison nodded. "Cool."

I ate another chip and wondered if Harrison wished I'd get out of his lurking space. I definitely wished he'd get out of mine. He was here first, but whatever.

"So . . . ," he started, drumming his fingers against the refrigerator door, searching for something to say. He didn't find it.

"What part did you get?" I asked.

"Production Tenor."

"What's that?"

Harrison shrugged. "I have no idea. I haven't seen the movie."

I remembered Margot saying Harrison was the kind of pretentious guy who only liked obscure, artsy films. There were an awkward few beats of silence, and then someone in the living room screamed so loudly I dropped the chip I was holding. The scream shifted into a witchy cackle and the room erupted into laughter.

"Jesus," I muttered, trying to slow my heart rate down.

"Yeah," Harrison said, pulling off his beanie, smoothing his hair back, and putting the beanie on again. "I needed a breather for a minute. Or twenty."

I snorted. Harrison was as uncomfortable here as I was. "I get it. I've only been here for ten minutes and I'm already exhausted."

"*Right?*" Harrison said, pushing off from the fridge. "Everyone's quoting lines from stuff I've never heard of. It's a whole different planet out there, man."

"A very weird planet."

Not that I didn't like weirdness. Ballet dancers were ultraweird. I thought about a typical preclass scene at KDBS: Juliet scraping the sole of her pointe shoes with a knife. Spencer picking up marbles with her toes. Colleen talking to her foot calluses ("Well, hello, Maria. You're looking extra pretty this morning.")

But that was my kind of weird. Out there . . . wasn't.

"I say we stay here as long as we want," I said, planting myself on a stool.

Harrison smiled. "Agreed." He settled into a stool on the opposite side of the island and popped open a cookie container.

"Can I ask why you auditioned?" I said after a minute. "People seemed surprised."

"I was, too, if I'm honest." Harrison finished a cookie and grabbed another one, gesticulating with it as he talked. "I always thought musicals were so commercial. Soulless entertainment instead of real art."

A chunk of cookie broke off and sailed across the kitchen when he said the word *art*. Somehow, it made his comment seem less pretentious. I smiled. Harrison did, too. He sheepishly scooped up the cookie chunk with a paper towel and threw it in the garbage.

"Why are you in it, then?" I asked as he sat back down.

"I, uh, I saw *42nd Street* when they did it last year. My girlfriend at the time wanted to go, and I kind of..." He paused, staring out the small window over the sink. Then his eyes shot back to mine, like he'd just remembered I was there. "I don't know, I just liked it," he said quickly, stuffing the remainder of the cookie in his mouth.

Sharp heels sounded above the music, and Diya Rao walked into the kitchen. She was wearing a black sweaterdress, gray tights, and black boots, her voluminous waves shining under the light. She stopped short when she saw me and Harrison, but just for a second. Then she walked over to the fridge, picked out a LaCroix, and cracked it open. She took a sip before perching on the stool next to mine.

"So why don't you go to ballet school anymore? Is your leg that bad?"

Wow. Blunt. Maybe I was beginning to understand the Robo-bitch nickname. "Yup," I said. Diya looked at me, expecting more.

But I felt no need to elaborate. So she sipped her LaCroix in silence, still eyeing me and blatantly ignoring Harrison.

"Well, uh, guess I'll get back," Harrison said, standing up. I wanted to mouth *Sorry* to him. I felt like I was betraying the kitchen lurker's code or something. But it was Diya's fault, not mine. I watched Harrison take a deep breath and disappear into the noise of the living room. I ate a few more chips in silence.

"You got into that school in New York," Diya said. "I saw it in the paper."

I froze, surprised she'd read it. It was a small article that ran last March about kids going to various specialized camps.

> *16-year-old Alina Keeler will go to New York City for American Ballet Theatre's summer intensive. Summer intensives are rigorous programs designed to improve a dancer's technique, strength, and flexibility. They also serve as an extended audition. If Alina does well at the five-week intensive, she could be invited to stay at the school year-round. If she distinguishes herself at the school, she could be one of the elite few who joins the American Ballet Theatre, one of the most prestigious ballet companies in the world.*

I'd read those lines over and over, never quite able to believe them. ABT was my dream company, and I'd gotten into their summer intensive. *Me.* I was so used to being a runner-up to Juliet and Spencer I hadn't thought I had a real chance. At the time, it made me wonder if ABT saw something in me that Kira didn't. Maybe my dream could really come true—dancing in New York, playing Giselle at the Metropolitan Opera House. It was a sparkling, ecstatic little idea that I almost started to believe. But a couple of weeks after the article ran, I broke my leg.

I knew I should have responded to Diya, but the weight of my hopes froze my tongue. Finally, after what felt like a very long silence, she said, "I bet you wish you were there, instead of here."

I looked at her. She was being blunt again, but it didn't sound bitchy. Actually, after so many "maybe it's for the bests," it just sounded *true*. "Here" didn't just mean the party. It meant the whole thing—high school and the musical and normal, teenage life. And "there" was my dream—ballet. Being in a company. Devoting my life to dance.

Diya's eyes, which had been considering me closely, shifted to the living room. I turned and saw Margot, Jude, and Ethan walking in the front door. *Finally.* My body relaxed, and Diya noticed. "They're your friends," she said. I couldn't tell if that was a statement or a question.

"Um, yeah?"

"What do you think of them?"

I shrugged, confused. "I don't know them that well, but they've been really nice to me."

Diya sighed. "Well, of course they're nice to you now. But you were...you were an amazing dancer." She looked me right in the eye again, her expression hardening. "They didn't like you so much then."

She held my gaze a moment longer. Then she finished her La-Croix, popped it into the recycling bin, and brushed past Margot, who stood in the kitchen doorway.

CHAPTER SEVEN

"WHAT WAS *THAT* ABOUT?" Margot asked. Jude and Ethan had been pulled into the living room to dance by some senior girls, so it was only me and Margot in the kitchen.

What did Diya mean that they didn't like me when I was still doing ballet? I hardly knew Margot then and didn't know Jude and Ethan at all.

Margot cleared her throat loudly.

"Oh, she was just asking me what I thought about you guys. You and Ethan and Jude. I have no idea why."

"Pfft, I know why," Margot said, coming around to the other side of the island and grabbing a cookie. "Diya and Jude dated their sophomore year."

"Really?" I couldn't picture it. They seemed like polar opposites.

"Yeah. For, like, two seconds. They were a musi-couple. Those happen every year, and hardly ever last after closing night. But Jude and Diya didn't even last through winter break. I forget exactly what happened, but she probably got too full of herself. Anyway, Jude's a sweetheart, and everyone in the musical loved him, so they weren't kind to her when it all went down."

Something occurred to me then. "Is that when the Robobitch nickname started?"

Margot glanced over my shoulder at the dancing. "Probably. Jude didn't start it. But it fits her, so it stuck. Anyway, I bet she saw you dancing with Jude at callbacks and got jealous."

"Maybe," I said. But Diya's words didn't sound like they were about Jude at all. Anyway, why did I want to defend Diya? I hardly knew her. And she'd just thrown some cryptic shade at the only three people I talked to at school.

The music in the living room changed and got louder, so I couldn't think anymore. Gasps and shrieks rippled through the crowd. Margot shot me a devious look, grabbed my elbow, and pulled me into the chaos of the living room.

A reedy male voice was speaking over a swift beat, and everyone was gathering into two parallel lines facing each other.

"What's happening?" I yelled to Margot. I'd never heard of the musical kids being into hazing, but who knew?

"The Time Warp," Margot said. "It's tradition. Just go with it and don't ask questions."

The beat got faster and the man's voice started scream-singing. That was apparently the cue for everyone in the two lines to start dancing. Well, not dancing so much as collectively freaking out.

There was head-banging, the Charleston, the twist, good body rolls, bad body rolls, something that looked like voguing, something that looked like electrocution, break dancing, and a bunch of other things I couldn't name. Ethan was flossing, and Jude was trying to, but his arms and hips wouldn't quite coordinate, so he looked like a demented wind-up doll.

Across the room, I made eye contact with Harrison, who mirrored me with an utterly terrified expression on his face.

Despite my fear, a laugh bubbled up from my chest. It escaped as a high-pitched giggle before I clamped my hand over my mouth. I didn't know where it came from, but between Harrison's face, all these random people convulsing to the beat of this bizarre song, Jude flossing, the swoop of his hair bouncing with every jerky move...

Another speaking voice came over the song, instructing everyone to jump to the left and step to the right and then thrust their pelvises out repeatedly. I was still coming to terms with all the pelvic thrusting when suddenly, someone pushed Ethan and Davis into the middle of the two lines. Everyone hooted and clapped as Ethan twirled Davis around a few times and dipped him. After eight counts, Ethan pulled Jude in to take his place in the middle.

And Davis, with a wicked smile on his face, pulled Harrison in.

Jude immediately started doing the running man while Harrison looked completely paralyzed. I felt for him, I really did. I almost shut my eyes so I wouldn't have to witness the humiliation. But then, with no warning, Harrison just...started doing the running man, too.

The crowd went wild. Margot howled beside me. Harrison's smile went from self-conscious to genuine. When Jude and Harrison finished their eight counts, they turned to choose the next pair of victims.

I stupidly made eye contact with Jude as he scanned the line, and he headed straight for me. *Hell* no. I ducked behind Margot. She blew a raspberry in my direction but blithely joined another girl in the middle. I watched as Margot bent her knees, tipped her head to the ceiling, and shook her shoulders back and forth. She had her signature *I don't give a shit what you think* look on her face, but it wasn't defensive now—it was just there, plain and simple. And everyone was cheering her for it.

I understood why Margot liked being in the musical so much. She could dance goofily to the Time Warp. She could sing. She could pelvic thrust. Just like Jude and Ethan, she was in her element here. As I watched everyone dancing around me, I realized why they all loved being in the show. It let them be whoever they wanted to be.

All of a sudden, my eyes stung and my nails dug into my palms. I sucked in a few deep breaths.

But the jealousy bomb exploded anyway.

I'd never be who I wanted to be. And it wasn't fair. They hadn't even sacrificed what I'd sacrificed. They hadn't spent their whole lives practicing until everything ached, and stretching until their muscles were numb, and watching Kira pass them over for—

"It's from *Rocky Horror!*" Margot yelled, shaking my shoulder and snapping me back to the present. The Time Warp had ended.

"We do it at the closing-night cast party in the spring, too," she said. "Now you'll be ready."

My mind raced ahead to March, when we'd perform *Singin' in the Rain.* In February and March, KDBS always performed a big story ballet. They were doing *Giselle* this year—my favorite, the one with the jilted girls becoming Wilis. So while Colleen and Juliet and Spencer would be there, bringing those beautiful spirits to life, I'd be here. At another cast party, faking my way through the Time Warp, still wishing I was somewhere else.

I couldn't catch my breath. I couldn't be here. I couldn't do the musical.

Ethan shouted something to Margot, and while her head was turned, I quietly backed away. Then I dug my jacket out of the pile and sprinted to my car.

On the way home, I gripped the wheel, trying to make my mind go blank. My phone buzzed as I pulled into our empty driveway. Margot: **Where are you?**

Sorry, went home. Had a headache, I typed back.

Are you ok?

I dragged myself out of the car without answering. At least my parents weren't back from Dad's gig yet, so they couldn't grill me about the party.

When I walked inside, Josie was spread out all over the kitchen floor, gluing paper amoebas onto a glittery trifold poster board. She paused, looking up at the microwave clock. "Couldn't make it to nine thirty, huh?"

"Shut up." I wished I could bypass her entirely and go straight to my room, but my throat was super dry and I needed water.

"Careful!" she whined as I stepped over all the paint tubes, glitter jars, and paper cut-outs. I grabbed a plastic cup and held it under the faucet. My hand was shaking, so water sloshed over the sides. When I turned to go upstairs, the cup slipped out of my hands and clattered to the floor.

"Oh my God, what's *wrong* with you?" Josie screeched, snatching up the poster board, its corner dripping with water. She gasped when she saw that a few of her amoebas were now swimming in a puddle on the floor.

"It was an accident," I said, grabbing a dish towel. "Calm down."

"This is due tomorrow!"

"You'll be fine. You have like a million amoebas on that thing already."

"They're *parameciums*," she snapped, grabbing the dish towel from me and dabbing furiously at the wet corner.

I rolled my eyes, found another towel, and started mopping up. Josie wouldn't look at me, her mouth scrunched into a defiant pout. I sighed. "I really didn't mean—"

"Yeah, right," she said. "You do and say whatever you want and we all just have to take it 'cause you're *sad* about *ballet*."

71

I froze, my mouth hanging open. "Go to hell, Josie." I knew she had never understood what I felt about ballet, but I was so sick of her treating this whole thing like it was no big deal. She hadn't lost anything in her entire life. Not one thing. Not even her stupid amoeba poster. I got the sudden urge to rip it to shreds and throw it down the garbage disposal.

As Josie kept fanning her hand over the wet corner, I saw her grudgingly realize I was right. The dumb thing looked completely fine.

"I'm just saying," she muttered.

"What?" I snapped. "What are you just saying?"

Josie picked up a tube of green puff paint and started decorating the top of the board. "That maybe ballet and Kira weren't so great to begin with, and maybe you should be glad you're not dancing for her anymore."

"Your opinions about Kira and ballet are so irrelevant to me it's not even funny."

Josie was silent for a second. Then, with irritating casualness, she said, "What would you be doing right now if you hadn't broken your leg?"

I narrowed my eyes. It was November. I'd be at *Nutcracker* rehearsal. Every year since I was seven, I'd been in KDBS's performance of *The Nutcracker*. It was more a part of fall and Christmas to me than cold weather and twinkly lights and snow. And I'd been doing my best not to think about it, but of course Josie brought it up.

"You know what I'd be doing," I said tightly.

"And what role—what *amazing* role—would you be rehearsing?"

My face heated up. "Why does that matter?"

Chinese Tea. I was always cast in the Chinese Tea role. After Marie and the prince arrive in the Land of Sweets, everyone comes to welcome them—Spanish Hot Chocolate, Chinese Tea, Arabian Coffee, and so on. Each performs a short divertissement, a brief dance showing their skills. In most versions, there are three people who do the Chinese Tea dance. But when I was thirteen, Kira made it a solo. My solo. The movements were similar to what was in most other versions—lots of delicate jumps, tiny shuffling steps across the stage, and bowing in time to the swift music.

It was never my favorite, but I always tried not to think about that. Because the rest of the show was so magical—the growing Christmas tree and dancing dolls and the little bed that floated across the stage as Marie dreamed.

"I never knew what was worse," Josie went on, capping the green puff paint and reaching for the blue. "The racist choreography or the fact that Kira made you dance it every year because you're Asian. And don't even get me started on Arabian Coffee."

"Stop," I said, anger bubbling up. I hated what Josie was doing right now. Finding the tear in a beautiful bolt of silk. The scratch on a diamond.

"Why do you always have to go looking for bad things in ballet?"

"Um, I'm not *looking* for them, they're just there. And if you opened your eyes, you'd see them, too."

An incoherent noise escaped from my throat. Josie was wrong. Ballet made me feel invincible, like a sorceress. Ballet was everything. "Do you know what it felt like when I did petit allegro?" I asked, my voice sharp. "Like I was literally flying across the floor. And when I turned with perfect balance, it felt like the room was spinning around me while I stayed still..." I trailed off, not sure why I was saying all this to her. She would never understand, so I went with something more concrete. "And Kira let me do Sugar Plum last year, remember?" I said triumphantly.

Because of high ticket sales, KDBS had scheduled an extra performance of *The Nutcracker,* and Kira let the understudies dance the main roles. I did Sugar Plum and Colleen did Dew Drop. We had skimmed our pinkies over the red velvet curtain an extra time that night, thanking whatever ballet gods were responsible for that miraculous turn of events.

I looked at Josie expectantly, but she just scoffed. "Yeah, once. That show ran for two weeks, and the whole rest of the time you had to do Chinese Tea." She scrunched up her nose like she was smelling something foul.

"God, it was just one stupid dance! Why do you even care?"

"Why *don't* you care?" Josie said.

I dropped the towel on the floor and went upstairs without another word. I collapsed onto my bed, pulling up *Giselle* on my laptop. I tried to lose myself in the soaring violins. But as Giselle whirled across the stage in her piqué manège, my brain kept thinking about last season's *Nutcracker* auditions.

Colleen and I knew we had danced well. Colleen's jumps were light as air, her upper body moving with such willowy grace it looked like she was dancing on top of a breeze. When I did my bourrées, the younger girls watched my every move, drawn into my performance. We danced better than Juliet. Better than Spencer. And we'd been their understudies for Sugar Plum and Dew Drop the year before. I was certain it was our turn now.

And yet when I walked up to the cast list, there was my name next to *Chinese Tea* again, and Colleen's next to *Arabian Coffee.* We were understudies again, too.

When I looked at Colleen, her careful, placid expression—the one we'd all mastered over the years to hide outrage or pain—was gone. We were both confused. Angry. Something wasn't right.

On shaky legs, we approached Kira.

"Yes?" she asked, her blue eyes piercing us as she wrapped an eggplant-colored scarf around her shoulders. I opened my mouth but couldn't find my voice.

"What did we do wrong?" Colleen asked, her fingers tapping a nervous rhythm on her thighs.

"What do you mean? You both got cast in excellent parts."

"I mean—we thought..." Colleen paused.

"You thought you'd get Sugar Plum and Dew Drop." Kira looked back and forth between us. "You thought that because you were understudies last year, you'd get the parts this year. That's not how it works in the professional world, and it's not how it works here. The purpose of being an understudy is to learn, to improve. You've done that. Now you bring that experience to the roles you do have."

I knew that was how it worked, and it made sense to me. Still, a question wouldn't leave my mind. "But why are *we* always cast in these roles?" I asked, my voice shaking.

Kira blinked at me, astonished. "What are you implying?"

"I—" I wasn't exactly sure, so nothing came out.

"My casting decisions have never been anything but fair," Kira said in a clipped voice. She gestured to me. "You need to work on your entrechats, and Chinese Tea helps you do that." She turned to Colleen. "Arabian Coffee lets you work on softening your arms, keeping them graceful instead of athletic. My job is to train you to enter the most competitive programs and companies in the world. *That's* why you have these roles. How dare you imply anything different."

My heart beat in my ears as I started to sweat from shame and embarrassment. I hadn't meant to accuse her of anything. It had just *felt* so unfair. But Kira was right—she was training us to be professional ballet dancers. She'd done so much for us. Taught every class since I was seven, never missing a day. She'd even driven me home after class once when Dad's car got a flat. During the ride, she'd told me stories about performing *Firebird* when she was eighteen, and how she was so nervous she fell flat on her face during her big entrance.

"I'm sorry," I said, hardly above a whisper, tears clouding my eyes.

Kira nodded perfunctorily and slipped into her coat. "Don't get emotional, dear. Remember, ballerinas do what they're told and they make it beautiful. You two want to be ballerinas, yes?" I nodded quickly and blinked away the tears, ashamed of them on top of everything else. Of course I wanted to be a ballerina. I needed to be. "Yes," Colleen said beside me.

"Then you accept the role you're given." Kira lifted her chin as she buttoned her coat. "*The Nutcracker* is a grand ballet tradition. You get to be part of it, in roles the audience adores you in. You should be grateful." I stood up straighter, mirroring her posture. She was right. I was part of a ballet tradition. I made two resolutions right then: I would make Chinese Tea beautiful and I would never question my role again.

I hadn't thought about that day much since. It was like Colleen and I made a silent agreement to never bring it up. And then the miracle happened and Kira let us dance the leads, and it felt like proof that she really did believe in us, proof that the whole awful conversation on casting day was gone, erased.

But now I couldn't stop thinking about Kira's words on casting day. Uncomfortable questions wormed their way into my brain, and I pressed Pause on *Giselle*.

Had Colleen and I not gotten the lead roles because she needed to work on softening and I needed to work on entrechats? Or was it part of the grand tradition for us to be Chinese Tea and Arabian Coffee, and for Spencer and Juliet—and the rest of the Jodys—to be Sugar Plum and Dew Drop?

There was another thing, too. Colleen was Arabian Coffee again this year—she'd texted me about it back in October. Colleen was one of the most willowy dancers I'd ever seen. How could she *still* need to work on softening her arms?

Before all the questions could settle in, my phone buzzed. Colleen.

ABT summer intensive audition: Jan. 18 in Philly. The parents said I could go.

I stopped breathing. The questions faded into the background and all I could focus on was three letters. ABT. American Ballet Theatre. Her dream company. My dream company. My eyes glazed over as more messages came in.

Dad said put it on Google Calendar so I remember. I said it's one date I think I'm good. He literally lectured me about the importance of calendar apps for half an hour. What is life.

Miss you, Ali-oop.

If Colleen did well at the ABT audition in two months, she would get into the summer intensive. If she did well there, maybe they'd invite her to stay at the school year-round. Maybe she'd get into the company in a couple of years.

I read the texts again, hearing Colleen's voice in my head, but it sounded far away. Like she was already in New York. Already there, forgetting about me.

I pressed Play on *Giselle* and turned up the volume, letting the violins drown everything out.

CHAPTER EIGHT

TUESDAY AFTER SCHOOL was the first rehearsal for *Singin' in the Rain*. It had taken me even longer than usual to fall asleep the night before, so I was dragging by the time ninth period rolled around. As I turned into study hall, I mentally practiced my "Sorry, Margot, but I'm quitting the musical" speech. It was a ridiculous idea in the first place. And I'd already had more major freak-outs since I auditioned than I'd had in the past couple of months combined. Clearly I wasn't ready to be anywhere else but in my room, under the covers.

I fidgeted with my sweater sleeves as I took my normal seat in the back row. I didn't know why I was so nervous about telling her. Yeah, she'd pushed the idea of the musical and helped me pick an audition song, but she had Ethan, Jude, and everyone else in the cast who'd cheered for her at the party. The musical was her happy place. I'd just bring it down.

A few seconds later, Margot strode in and heaved her stuff onto the desk beside mine—a bloodred water bottle and an army-green backpack with the words *If you can read this back the F up* scrawled across it in Sharpie. It all clashed horribly with her drapey burnt-orange sweater and turquoise hair, but somehow she always made her ensembles look like a mood.

"You're alive," she said. Since I'd overslept and missed home-room, it was the first time I'd seen her since bailing on the party.

"Yeah, I'm feeling better now."

"Good," she said as she sat down, giving me the side-eye.

I took a breath. "So—"

"You didn't miss much," Margot said at the same time. "Although I did kind of miss *you* in the middle of all those strangers."

"Strangers? They all love you."

She pointed at herself. "Love? Me?"

"They were cheering for you during that *Rocky Horror* thing!"

Margot glanced at the teacher's desk before responding. Mr. Dale always let us talk during study hall, but he had a weird way of jump-ing into the conversations and pretending to relate. Now he seemed pretty invested in Teddy Hansen's monologue to Pauline Caffrey about Hitchcock films, so Margot went on.

"Okay, there's a difference between cheering for someone and loving them. They respect me, I guess. But I'm not *friend*-friends with many of them."

"Why not?" Margot had been in the musical every year since she was a freshman, and she'd seemed in her element last night. But now that I thought about it, at auditions and callbacks and the party, she'd only talked to me, Ethan, and Jude.

"So . . ." Margot fiddled with the ends of her bob. "I used to hang out with a different crowd."

"Which one? Wait, was it the Hitchcock crowd?" Teddy was still yammering on to poor Pauline. It was hard to ignore.

Margot snorted. "I like that you don't know anything. I mean, that you don't know anything about anyone who goes here. But I guess it had to come out sometime. I used to be friends with Izzy Kramer."

I actually did know of Izzy Kramer. It was hard not to, considering her face was plastered all over the school's trophy cases, as a homecoming court "princess" and captain of the state champion volleyball team.

Last week on my way to trig, I was behind Izzy and the pack of girls she always hung out with. She turned to one of them and said, "Olivia, you smell like Snausages. Move over." Just like that. The other girls cackled. I couldn't picture Margot among them. Margot knew how to hurl a good insult at a jerk, but she wasn't mean to innocent people like that.

"We had nothing in common," Margot said. "We just lived in the same neighborhood growing up. Anyway, Izzy and the others were super cliquish and judgmental and mean, and I got sick of it. I'd known Ethan since I was a kid, and I liked him so much more. So when I was a freshman, he convinced me to try out for the musical. And soon I was excommunicated from Cool Girl Island."

"You were excommunicated because you were in the musical?"

"Well, no. There was an incident." I gestured for her to keep going and she heaved a big sigh. "Last year at the Galleria ice rink, Izzy's stupid boyfriend R.J. was supposed to do this big, elaborate proposal to ask her to Winter Formal. Izzy spilled strawberry Frappuccino on her sweater and told me to go to her house to get her a clean one. She was already mad at me for some dumb thing or another, so when I said no, she called me a skank, I called her human garbage, and it was a whole big thing."

"Geez." That did sound like a whole big thing.

"I haven't talked to her since."

"Are you okay with that?" I asked.

"Of course I am." Margot leaned back in her chair. "Because *I'm* only mean to people who deserve it. Like..." She checked to make sure Mr. Dale had turned his attention to another conversation on the other side of the room. Then she kicked Teddy's chair with her foot. "Dude. Stop. Pauline wants to read her book, not listen to your film interpretations."

It was true. Pauline had her finger on the place in her book where she'd stopped reading, and kept lowering her eyes to it until politeness won out and she'd look up at Teddy again, smiling mechanically and nodding.

Teddy gave Margot a withering stare. "No one cares what you think, *Margot*." Still, he slouched down in his desk and left Pauline to read in peace.

Once I was done silently laughing, Margot's face turned thoughtful. "Ethan thinks I should be nicer, even to idiots. He says it's not always my job to butt in. He says it makes other people, like the ones in the musical, scared to open up to me."

I remembered Josie telling me the "Margot made Paul Manley insecure about his penis" anecdote, and Josie hadn't even been at Eagle View when it happened. Stories of Margot's badassery spread far and wide, but they probably did scare people a little, too. Even just now, Pauline had given Margot a quick smile to say thanks, but she'd lowered her eyes just as fast, like she didn't want to be too associated with her.

"Well, you don't scare me," I said.

Margot smiled and looked down at her hands. "I know. That's why I'm glad we're friends. Ethan and Jude are great, but they have their whole senior crowd. Plus, I haven't had a *girl* friend since the whole Izzy disaster, and that's been kind of rough." She looked up at me. "I've been meaning to say this, but thanks for doing the musical with me. It means a lot."

I blinked at her. If anyone was eavesdropping on our conversation, they would have undeniable proof that underneath Margot Kilburn-Correa's badass image, there was another layer. One that could feel lonely and unsure. One that needed things from people occasionally.

Like for me to be in the musical with her.

Damn.

～

The whole cast—from the senior veterans to the couple of tiny freshmen who made the cut—settled into the maroon auditorium seats with fresh packets of sheet music. "Today we're going to sing all the music in the show," Mrs. Sorenson announced. "We need to immerse ourselves in the world of *Singin' in the Rain*."

Wonderful.

At least Margot had chosen a seat in the back corner, out of Mrs. Sorenson's direct line of sight and close to a door, in case I needed to take a stealth break.

Jude and Ethan began with an old-fashioned vaudeville number called "Fit as a Fiddle." Despite the supreme cheesiness of the song, and the even cheesier T-shirt Jude was wearing (it said KNIT HAPPENS above a ball of yarn), he looked weirdly good singing it.

When they finished, the room broke into applause and wolf whistles. Jude and Ethan did a few flourishing bows until Mrs. Sorenson shooed Ethan away so she could move on to Jude's solo, "You Stepped Out of a Dream." When Jude started to sing, his expression shifted. His eyes had this focused look, his cheeks were flushed from performing, and his lips...

"Bet you don't want to give him the finger now," Margot whispered.

"What? I—why would you say that?" I whispered back.

Margot squinted at me. Then she waved in Jude's direction.

"Because look at him." I did, taking in his earnest expression, his knitting humor shirt. "It would be like flipping off a baby otter," Margot said, snickering at her own joke.

"Oh. I just thought you meant—never mind."

"What?"

"*Nothing.* Never mind."

Margot raised her eyebrows. "Oookaaay."

For the rest of Jude's solo and the next few songs, I studied the sheet music like it contained the secrets of the universe. I didn't want to look up and start noticing Jude's lips again.

"This should be interesting," Margot said. Harrison was walking to the piano for his solo, "Beautiful Girl." His face was red already.

Mrs. Sorenson played the opening chords and Harrison warbled out the first few lines of a song that crossed the line from cheesy into straight-up cringey. He looked like he was in pain. I would be, too, if I had to sing such an embarrassing love song in public.

If Ethan or Jude were singing it, they would have played it up for the crowd. Probably thrown in a few winks and finger-guns. Even though Harrison had running-manned it up at the cast party, he obviously didn't feel completely comfortable here.

But then Ethan started snapping to the beat of the song. As he snapped, he snaked his head from side to side. Other people followed Ethan's lead, snapping and swaying along. The energy in the room relaxed and Harrison must have felt it, because he finally cracked a smile. The final verses weren't quite as painful, and there was a healthy smattering of applause as Harrison went back to his seat, still blushing but smiling.

I thought back to English, when Ethan had passed me that note. He was good at making people feel like they were less alone, at least for a moment.

After Harrison sat down and Diya went up to do her solo, the mood in the auditorium shifted immediately. As her crystalline voice poured out, everyone slouched, whispered, or looked at their phones.

Geez. She must have done something terrible to Jude. I looked at him to see if I could gauge anything, but I could only see the back of his head. When Diya hit the last, gorgeous note, my eyes automatically swiveled back to her.

"Robobitch," a guy pretend-coughed a couple of seats away, and everyone around us tittered. I glanced at the guy. I didn't recognize him, but he was sitting beside Laurel, whose shoulders were shaking with laughter. Amazingly, though, Diya was still holding the note, completely unfazed.

She finished with a flourish and smiled at Mrs. Sorenson, who nodded proudly at her. "Five-minute break," Mrs. Sorenson announced. Diya strode out of the auditorium with a contented smile.

"Who's that guy?" I gestured to the one who'd pretend-coughed as everyone emptied out of the aisles to get snacks.

"Noah Parker," Margot said. Ah, so that was the other person Josie wanted in her dance.

"Is he friends with Jude?"

"Mmm, I don't think they know each other that well. Why?"

"I just thought...I mean, you said..." I wanted to say it seemed odd that people who didn't really know Jude were still mad at his ex-girlfriend from two years ago, but I didn't know how to phrase it without sounding weird. Or accusatory. Or like I was too interested in Jude's dating history. So I dropped it.

My mind wandered for the rest of the break. And during the next songs, drowsiness weighed my eyes down. Staying after school was really cutting into my napping time.

I was barely keeping my eyes open when Jude went up to do "Singin' in the Rain." As he sang in his clear voice and swayed along to the rhythm, I found myself swaying with him. My eyelids dropped down all the way and I drifted off...and I was in Jude's arms, dancing instead of walking down the streets of our neighborhood.

As Jude sang about the rain and being happy again, he twirled me under his arm and leaned in close, his lips almost brushing mine.

I opened my eyes with a start and was back in the auditorium. "Morning." Margot smiled.

"Ugh." I rubbed my eyes and straightened up, hoping my face hadn't given anything away about my sappy dream. Not that it meant anything. I stretched my eyes wide, ordering myself to stay awake.

By the time we reached the finale, I was more than ready to go home. I'd been avoiding thinking about Colleen and ABT all day, but it was nudging more insistently around the edges of my brain, making me feel both jealous and like the worst person in the world for not answering, not wishing her luck, because I knew what a huge deal it was.

Mrs. Sorenson ended rehearsal by giving us a motivational talk about how we needed to work hard over the next four months to produce a "fantabulous" show.

Oh boy. Four months of fantabulous.

As everyone gathered their things, I looked at the schedule for the next two weeks, taped onto the auditorium door. I had rehearsals after school on Wednesdays and Fridays. On those days, the girls in the chorus along with Harrison would learn the choreography for "Beautiful Girl."

There was nothing about the Vamp dance yet. I started wondering again about what it would be like to dance with Jude. What it would feel like if he lifted me, his hands gripping my waist.

"Nothing like a first rehearsal," Jude said behind me. I jumped, and the ridiculous notion that he could tell what I'd been thinking flashed through my head. He could *not*, I rationally told myself.

Jude scanned the schedule and put his rehearsal times (nearly every day) into his phone. "Oh, hey," he said, tucking the phone into his back pocket. "Would you mind giving me a ride home? My mom needed the car today, so she dropped me off."

"Sure," I said, pulling myself together. "Where do you live again?"

"Ha, ha."

We turned out of the auditorium and went through the lobby and past the freshman lockers lining the hallway. A lot of clubs had just let out, so we swerved around clusters of chattering overachievers, including Josie and a few friends. I felt her watching me as I shoved by, but I didn't look up. I was still mad at her for what she'd said last night.

Jude slowed down and looked back. "Are we waiting for your sister?"

"She takes the activity bus," I mumbled.

He tilted his head in confusion. "Her friend Fiona has to ride the bus, so she does, too. It's a solidarity thing," I explained. I didn't want him to think I was a complete monster.

"Wow. Riding the activity bus when you don't have to," Jude said, impressed. "She should win some kind of friendship award for that."

"Mmm," I said, still stewing. If Josie was such a great friend, why was she being such a shitface to me lately? I mean, we'd never been the super-close-best-friend type of sisters. Since we started going to different dance schools years ago, it was like our lives had steadily drifted apart, each of us pursuing our own interests. But things had gotten undeniably worse after my injury. I knew I hadn't been the most pleasant person to be around, but she was impossible sometimes.

I sped up, needing to be out of here. We were almost at the doors to the parking lot, but then Jude spun around. "Josie Keeler!" he yelled through cupped hands. "I salute you for your epic display of bus loyalty!"

Josie and her friends broke into giggles, shooting Jude glances and whispering among themselves.

"*Hey*, there's a seat left on the activity bus if you want to join them," I snapped, pushing open the door.

"Coming," he said with an infuriating grin.

CHAPTER NINE

A COLD DRIZZLE HIT US on the way to the car. I picked up the pace, trying to ignore the slight limp in my gait. My leg got so much stiffer on cold, damp days. It made me even grumpier than I already was.

As soon as we pulled out of the parking lot, Jude fiddled with the buttons until he found the Broadway channel on satellite radio.

"Oh my *God*," I said, glancing at him in disbelief. "We just spent two hours singing musical music. Aren't you sick of it?"

"It's musical season, Alina. You gotta lean into it." A new song started and Jude sang along to the bouncy rhythm. He looked at me. "You do know what this song is, right?"

"No."

"It's *Cabaret*! It's Liza!" He threw his hands in the air.

"You're going to have a frustrating ride home if you expect me to know any of these songs," I said as I looked over my shoulder to switch lanes.

"Huh. Interesting." He squinted at me. "Veeeery interesting."

I rolled my eyes when he didn't elaborate. "What?"

"You shamed me for not caring enough about getting the lead

in the musical, and yet you seem completely indifferent—almost hostile—to musicals."

I shrugged. "Because the musical is your thing. You should care about your role in it. The musical is not my thing. And yeah, I know I'm in it, but still, it's just not."

"Hmm." Jude kept squinting. "I guess it is my thing. I have a lot of things, though."

"I remember." Trampolines and baths and mysteries and green tea and knitting. "Is anything *not* your thing?"

Jude looked out the rain-streaked window. "Goat milking."

I smiled even though I tried not to. "Oh?"

"Yeah, I went to the farm show when I was eight and milked a goat. They gave me a ribbon for it and everything. But even though the ribbon was cool, I knew that goat milking was not my thing."

"God. So picky."

He laughed. "But hey, back to the musical for a sec. Did you at least like any of the songs we did today?"

Jude's singing drifted into my head, along with the cheesy dream of dancing with him, twirling under his arm... The cheesy dream that didn't mean anything, I reminded myself.

"Not really," I said. We were quiet for a bit after that. Every time a new song came on, Jude would point to the radio and raise his eyebrows, silently asking if I knew it. I would shake my head and he would sigh dramatically.

"Why are you going this way?" he asked when I turned into a small neighborhood instead of continuing on the main road.

"It's a shortcut."

"No way."

"This way is two minutes faster than staying straight, sometimes three."

"Wooow," he said slowly. "You don't know Broadway, Alina Keeler. But you do know *the road.*" He made his voice gravelly when he said "the road," like we were in a noir film.

I breathed out a laugh, but it was kind of true. When I finally turned sixteen and a half last March and traded my permit for a license, my parents were so relieved they didn't have to ride with me to ballet every day that they let me use the Honda whenever I needed. I was allowed to pick Colleen up, too, which was perfect. She lived about fifteen minutes away, and we weren't in the same school district, so carpooling meant we got to spend more time together during the week, outside of class and rehearsal. The first time I came to get her, her father did a whole bit about examining my license—bringing out a magnifying glass while we rolled our eyes at the dadness of it all. But between Colleen's ballet schedule and all the activities her parents had to drive her two younger brothers to, I knew they were more than happy to let Colleen ride with me.

It didn't last long. Only ten days. When I broke my leg and lost ballet, I lost driving, too, though I hardly noticed at the time. It felt strange driving again—with a leg that stiffened and ached when I held the brake for too long—especially on cold, damp days like this. But it felt good to drive, too. It was something I could actually do again, something I could control.

As I turned into our neighborhood, a familiar wailing melody blared out of the speakers, breaking me out of my trance. "Oh, I know this one," I said, searching my brain. "Is it... 'Memory'? From *Cats*?"

I waited for Jude to praise me, but he buried his face in his hands. "Do *not* tell me the only song you knew this entire ride was 'Memory' from *Cats*."

"What?" I pulled up to my house and put the car in park. "Is that worse than not knowing any?"

"Kind of." Jude clicked his seat belt off but stayed where he was. "Have you ever been down a YouTube rabbit hole?"

"You mean, like, watching one video, and then another and another and another until you lose all sense of time? Of course."

"Well. Since we're neighbors *and* dance partners now, I feel it's my duty to take you down a very special kind of rabbit hole."

I snorted. "That sounds bad."

"Mind out of the gutter, Keeler." He opened the passenger door. When I just stared at him, he gave a grandiose wave of his arm. "Come on, I think you'll like this very special kind of rabbit hole."

"Ew. Okay, just... never say that again." I turned off the ignition and followed him across the street to his front door, ducking my head against the drizzle. As Jude got out his keys, I texted Mom and Dad to tell them I'd be at Jude's for a while. Dad sent me ten thumbs-up emojis. Mom said, **Great!! I saw an ad for midnight bowling at Sparkle Lanes this weekend. You guys should go!**

I hated bowling. And my curfew was before midnight. And the Sparkle Lanes snack bar gave a few kids food poisoning last year. Mom was truly desperate for me to have a social life.

Inside, Jude's house reminded me a little of ours. A bit messy, but the mess was interesting. Succulents in mismatched pots crowded every windowsill, colorful knit throws were draped over the couch and armchairs, and pretty much every surface was covered with paperbacks.

In the kitchen, the refrigerator was full of photos. I looked at one of a very sleepy Jude, eyes half closed, hair sticking up in different directions. Beside it was one of a woman, his mom I guessed, looking like she'd just tasted something terrible. All the photos were like that—super-unflattering shots of either Jude or his mom.

"A joke that escalated," Jude said when he saw me looking. "You put *one* funny picture of your mom at Aunt Liddy's wedding on the refrigerator, and a year later, you have this. But neither of us wants to back down yet."

"Understandable. Tell her if she needs help, I'm available to shoot during rehearsals."

"She would so take you up on that offer," Jude said, pouring us two glasses of water. We headed back to the living room, and I sat down beside him on the brown leather couch as he picked his laptop up off the coffee table. "Okay. Any good Broadway rabbit hole begins with a ballad." He typed something into the search bar and scrolled a bit. I wrapped my arms around myself, still cold even though I'd kept my fleece jacket on. Without taking his eyes off the screen, Jude dragged a burgundy throw off the arm of the couch and dropped it onto my lap.

"Thanks." I ran my fingertips over the simple but neat pattern. "Did you knit this?"

"Of course not," Jude said. "I crocheted it." I stifled a laugh and wrapped it around myself, feeling instantly warmed to the core.

"Ah, here we go." Jude propped the laptop on a stack of books on the coffee table.

We watched Jennifer Holliday sing "And I Am Telling You I'm Not Going" from *Dreamgirls* at the 1982 Tony Awards. The power and desperation of her voice, coming through even in the old, grainy video, was extraordinary, I had to admit. After that we checked out the options on the sidebar and watched "Defying Gravity" from *Wicked*—a little over-the-top, but catchy. That led us to "Maybe This Time" from *Cabaret*, and then to "Not Getting Married Today" from *Company*.

"Not Getting Married Today" was a dizzying song where a woman sings faster and faster about how she doesn't want to go through with her wedding. The lyrics were inventive and intricate, and they weaved in and out of the accompanying music like they had a life of their own.

"Who wrote that?" I asked when the song ended.

"Stephen Sondheim. I can't believe I just witnessed your first Stephen Sondheim. I'm honored." I requested more Sondheim, so Jude clicked on "Finishing the Hat," a song from a musical called *Sunday in the Park with George.*

Jude told me the musical was about the famous painter Georges Seurat. In the video, George sat in front of a painted backdrop of a park, a sketchbook on his lap. He sang about a woman who left him because he was too involved in his art, but then he started singing about his need to paint the hat he was working on exactly right. The song went on like that, back and forth, and by the end, he seemed to forget about the woman because he had painted the hat perfectly.

"Whoa." I sat back on the couch, realizing I had inched closer to the screen. "That song is so..." I paused, searching for the right word.

"Tragic?" Jude said. "I know."

My mouth fell open. "I was going to say inspiring."

"*Inspiring?* He basically says he can never be with the woman he loves because he's always obsessing over his work."

"Obsessing over his *art*," I corrected. Jude looked at me like he didn't understand the difference. "It's not just some job," I said. "His painting is part of him. I think it's inspiring that he knows he'll always be creating art, no matter who is or isn't in his life."

"But..." Jude shifted on the couch so he was facing me. "Doesn't that also mean he's kind of...detached from other people because of his art? And is that really a good way to live?"

"Why wouldn't it be?" I said, my voice loud. I couldn't believe I was getting so amped over a Broadway song.

"Because he's separating himself from the world," Jude said.

I shook my head. "He's separating himself from the world so he can see it more clearly, so he can capture it on a canvas. It's like, he paints"—I drew my hand out from under the blanket and pointed to George, frozen on the computer screen—"so he can bring beauty out of all the ugliness in the world. And then when people see his paintings, they get to see that beauty. They get to focus on it, and not worry about the ugliness for a while."

"And that's good, but..." Jude ran a hand through his hair, thinking. "Is it worth giving up real things, like relationships? I mean, what's more important, people or art?"

"Well, people and relationships are obviously important. But art is real, too. Art can make you feel alive and understood and like anything is possible. Which people can't always do."

My mind flew to Jake and Paul. To the doctor who'd made a stupid pun when I asked him when I'd be able to dance again. "Sometimes people can make you feel the opposite," I said.

We were both talking loudly, our cheeks a little flushed. I wasn't used to debating. You were never supposed to debate in ballet class. The main rule was to listen to your teacher and obey. But it was kind of fun to disagree. And judging from the smile that was slowly spreading across Jude's face, I think he might have agreed with me on that, at least.

"I think we had our first philosophical argument," he said.

"An important step in any neighbor slash dance partner relationship," I added.

Jude tilted his head, like he was considering me from a new angle. "It makes sense, though, that you would interpret the song that way. You're an artist. You're George."

But I wasn't, I only now remembered. Somehow when I was

94

listening to that song, I'd been swept up in the feelings I always got when I saw or heard a beautiful work of art—a pas de deux or a variation or a symphony. I felt full and exhilarated and like the world was teeming with all the best things: joy and love and the kind of beauty you can eat and keep inside you.

I'd forgotten that *I* couldn't create those things anymore. That I'd never finish my hat. I took a deep breath, reminding myself this wasn't the place to sink down completely.

I picked up my backpack. "I should probably go. Thanks for—"

"Sorry. I didn't mean to bring up..." Jude trailed off, watching me closely.

"It's fine." I stood, leaving the burgundy blanket in a heap on the couch.

Jude followed me to the door. "You're still an artist. You know that, right? You're still a dancer. A really good one."

"Bullshit." I spat it out before I could stop myself. It hung, bitter and ugly, in the air between us. The dancing he'd seen me do was miles away from how I danced before. I wanted to yell that at him, but what was the point? Anyone who thought it was that simple, that dancing in the musical was the same as dancing ballet, would never understand.

I reached into my bag and dug my keys out before remembering my car was already at my house. I tried to put them back, but they dropped to the floor with a clang.

"I got it," Jude said softly. He knelt in front of me and looped the key ring around his finger. I waited for him to stand up, but he didn't. "I know some people say nice things just to say them," he said, eyes hovering around my ankles. "But I don't. I really meant that."

His voice sounded honest and a little bit hurt.

But fuck that. He didn't get to believe in nice things when I couldn't. Anger roiled inside me, threatening to explode. He *meant*

95

it when he said I was still a dancer? And what exactly did he know? Absolutely nothing.

Jude didn't know that last July—a week before the ABT summer intensive—I got out a pair of pointe shoes when no one was home. The pink satin was smooth under my fingers. The shank bent with just a bit of pressure. The box was still firm. They were perfect. Broken in but not dead yet.

As I slipped my feet under the elastic and wrapped the ribbons around my ankles, a feeling of power zipped through me. I'd cleaned the rods sticking out of my bones every day so they didn't get infected. I'd injected myself with blood thinner so I didn't get clots. I'd done all Birdie's exercises. I'd done everything I was supposed to, all so I could dance on pointe again.

I went to the basement and dragged my plywood practice board away from the wall, lowering it carefully to the floor. I stepped onto pointe with my left leg, wobbling from rustiness but getting a good balance after a few tries. I inhaled and transferred my weight gently to my right leg.

The pain was unnatural. Like a sharp metal claw scraping against my bones. I fell to the floor in shock, landing hard on my left knee.

I tried again. Another burst of metallic pain. Another fall. Again. And again. And again. Until my knees were red and raw and my face dripped with sweat and snot and tears. It wasn't the pain that made me cry. It was the doctor's words all those months ago in the hospital. The ones that seemed so impossible.

When something breaks like that, you can't put it back together so easily. And when you do, it won't be the same.

That was when I knew, for absolute certain, that the bizarre, beautiful magic of ballet was gone forever.

It took me a second to register that Jude was still kneeling in front of me, staring at my ankle. "Does it still hurt?" he asked, barely above a whisper.

Yes. It hurt all over, it hurt everywhere. I opened my mouth to yell that at him, but before I could take a breath, the anger seeped out of me, and I got a new urge. To tell him about that night in the basement. But the words wouldn't come. Instead, I bent forward, grasped the cuff of my jeans, and rolled it up, revealing my scars.

The one on the outside of my leg was king. Eight inches long, framed by little dots where the staples had held my skin together. The one in front was tiny in comparison, just four inches of raised, jagged skin. The last two were indentations in my shin, where the metal rods of the external fixator had been rooted into my bones.

Jude's eyes grew as he took it all in. Then they turned gentle, like they usually were, and he finally looked back up at me.

I felt my cheeks warm. No one besides my family and Birdie and the doctors had seen my scars. And I'd shown Jude. *Jude.*

I leaned forward to cover them up again, but his hands were already on my jeans. He unrolled the cuff back down to my ankle slowly, carefully. His fingertips only brushed my calf once. When they did, a shiver traveled up my body.

Finally, he stood up. "It aches a lot," I said quickly. Because maybe if I answered his question like a normal person, he'd forget I'd shown him my scars. "And it's stiff, especially in the cold. It's hard to loosen it up sometimes. There's um, metal in it. Stainless steel." Oh my God. Why had I done that? Shown him?

"Like Wolverine," he said.

"I—what?"

"You don't know Wolverine?" Jude smiled faintly. I could see all the different shades of brown in his eyes. We were standing so close.

As soon as I thought it, he took a small step back. He fiddled with the zipper on his hoodie. "We'll go down another YouTube rabbit hole, superheroes next time," he said.

My stomach did a confusing flip at the words "next time."

"And hey." He opened the door for me. "That must have been so...painful, all that stuff." He nodded to my leg. "And I swear I won't say anything more about it after this, but scars and steel don't decide if you're a dancer or not."

I bit back the curses this time. He'd been honest with me, so I'd be honest with him. "They do, though. In my case, they do." I slung my bag over my shoulder and left.

CHAPTER TEN

WHEN I WALKED INTO the auditorium for rehearsal the next day, I cast my eyes around for Jude, unsure if I wanted to see him or not.

He wasn't there. My shoulders relaxed, and I decided I was going to avoid him for a while. I clearly couldn't be trusted to not do ridiculous things around him. And considering I'd flipped him off and showed him my scarred-up leg within the span of a week, I was sure he'd enjoy the break from me as well.

I looked for Margot then, but of course she wouldn't be here, either. Today we were learning the dance portion of "Beautiful Girl," where the girls in the chorus waltzed around as showgirls while Harrison objectified us in song. I hadn't really thought about how since Margot had a lead role, she wouldn't be in chorus rehearsals with me. Damn.

"Semicircle around Harrison! Go!" Ms. Langford shouted in her deep voice as a blur of girls in colorful dancewear surrounded Harrison, who stood rigidly in the middle.

"First eight counts!" Ms. Langford called, and proceeded to go through the first eight without too much downtime, which I liked. It was a simple combination, but there was a flow to it, so that each movement carried into the next.

"One, two, three, four, and pose!" Ms. Langford yelled after we'd run through the whole thing with music for the first time. Groans echoed through the auditorium because most people didn't have the steps down yet.

"You'll get it," Ms. Langford said, running her hands through her orange curls, frizzing them out even more. "Girls, take a short break. We'll run through it one more time in five. Harrison, stick around so we can go over that footwork."

As most of the chorus stampeded off the stage, I stayed put, stepping into a calf stretch. Of course I was staring at the auditorium doors when Jude walked in, followed by Ethan, Diya, and Celia Breed, a bouncy-haired blond senior. Diya immediately broke from the group, setting her things down in the front corner of the auditorium while the rest of them stayed in the back, joking around. I looked away before Jude saw me, my heart pumping fast.

"Hey." Someone tapped my elbow and I jumped. It was a sophomore girl with pale, freckled skin and dark hair swept into a high ponytail. She was wearing the brightest shade of pink lipstick I'd ever seen. Beside her was a tiny blond girl in a cat-ear hoodie. "Whoa, sorry," Lipstick Girl said, backing up a step. "We were just wondering if you could show us how to do that lean steppy thingy?"

"The tombé pas de bourrée?"

"Uh, yeah." She smiled. "That."

I showed them how to do it slowly, breaking down each part. The lunge, the three-stepped pas de bourrée with flowing arms, and the ending pose—our upstage arm stretched up into fifth position as we looked out into the audience. They kept laughing about their arms. "I feel like I'm flapping!" Cat-Ear Girl said.

"Try relaxing them first," I said, taking her forearm and gently tugging it up and down, like Kira used to do. "And then keep your elbow in line with your wrist. There should be less flappage that way." She laughed, and I demonstrated the steps for them again.

Lipstick Girl sighed. "Seriously, how does it look so pretty when you do it and when I do it, it's like, ca-caw! Ca-*caw!*" She flapped her arms like the most ungraceful bird in the world as she "ca-cawed" so loudly several people looked over.

Including Jude. I dropped my eyes again.

"Shhh," Cat-Ear Girl said. "This is why Harrison doesn't want you to meet his friends." We all looked over at Harrison, whose forehead was wrinkled in concentration as he watched Ms. Langford demonstrate the steps for the hundredth time.

"Are you and Harrison dating?" I asked Lipstick Girl. I didn't know if sophomores dating seniors was a common thing, but it would easily explain why he was in the musical.

"Only in our imaginations," Cat-Ear Girl said.

"Okaay," I said slowly.

"I'm Laney," Lipstick Girl cut in, giving her friend a warning look. "That's Ada."

"Alina," I said.

"Cool." Laney stretched her arms above her head. "Now we don't have to call you Ballerina Girl anymore."

I stiffened. I was always surprised when someone at Eagle View knew about my ballet past. I assumed they were all as oblivious to me as I was to them.

"You *do* ballet, right?" Laney asked, brow furrowed. "I just figured you did because you're a great dancer and your posture is absurd. In a good way," she added quickly.

A sharp clap saved me from having to answer. "From the top!" Ms. Langford called, and everyone rushed to their positions around Harrison. As the music started and I swayed from side to side, I noticed Laney and Ada watching me, carefully adjusting their arms to match mine.

I looked away, out into the auditorium, where Jude was. My breath caught when I saw he was watching me, too. His expression was hard to read from up here, but his eyebrows were wrinkled, and his head was slightly tilted, like he was looking for something.

Scars and steel don't decide if you're a dancer or not.

Self-conscious sweat broke out on my forehead. I concentrated on swaying my arms, grapevining to stage left, and lining up behind the other girls as Harrison took our hands one by one and twirled us to his other side. I did the tombé pas de bourrée into the ending pose, raising my arm into fifth.

I glanced out into the auditorium again, and Jude was gone. My stomach dropped, but I didn't know why. I wanted to avoid him, right?

☙

When I walked into rehearsal on Friday, a shrill "Ca-caw!" echoed off the stage. Ada and Laney were laughing and waving for me to come up. "We're going to stand behind you today," Ada said when I wandered over. "We have a theory that if we're close to you, we'll pick up your dancing skills through osmosis or something."

"Seems logical," I said dryly.

They laughed liked I'd just made a brilliant joke. "You guys need to lighten up," I said, which made them laugh again. They were clearly an easy audience, but I smiled anyway.

During rehearsal, the little weirdos stuck to their plan, standing right behind me as we practiced "Beautiful Girl" a bazillion times. During the downtime, I heard snippets of their conversation, though I couldn't understand any of it. It was filled with unfamiliar names and abbreviations and inside jokes. It reminded me, with a spasm of loneliness, of how Colleen and I used to talk.

"Alina." Ms. Langford came up to me after she dismissed the chorus for the day, Harrison standing sheepishly at her elbow. "I need to work on 'Make 'Em Laugh.'" She gestured to Ethan, who was climbing onto the stage. "Would you mind going over 'Beautiful Girl' with Harrison before you leave?"

"Oh. Sure."

"You're a doll," Ms. Langford said, slapping me on the back and handing me an ancient CD player. As Harrison and I headed to the back of the auditorium, Laney stared after us with a wide-eyed expression.

"I'm sorry you have to do this," Harrison said as I set the CD player on the rough gray carpet and plugged it in.

"It's fine." Harrison's choreography was mostly rhythmic walking, a few box steps, and some spins. It wouldn't take long to go over it with him. "So. Let's see what you remember." I pressed Play.

Harrison did the whole thing without stopping, which was good. What was *less* good was that every step had a lurching, unnatural quality, like he was a drunk marionette.

"Huh," I said when he finished. It was truly the only word that came to mind.

"Yeah." Harrison sighed deeply, pulling off his beanie, running a hand through his hair, and putting it back on. I'd seen him do that before, when he was sitting alone at callbacks and in the kitchen at the pre–cast party.

"Okay," I said, realizing the problem. "You feel really awkward doing the dance, and that's making you look really awkward doing the dance."

"Right," he said slowly. "So how do I, like, fix that?"

I thought about what I used to do to make a variation flow naturally. "I think you have to really listen to the song. Maybe not the lyrics," I said quickly, because the lyrics were truly terrible. "But the melody and the rhythm. The more you know the song, the more you can feel the music in your body, and that's what'll turn you into that cheesy, overconfident creep who loves singing about beautiful girls."

Harrison grimaced. "That's your suggestion? Listen to the song and become the cheesy, overconfident creep?"

"Afraid so."

Harrison closed his eyes and took a swift, bracing breath as I cued up the music. Then he plastered a bizarre smile onto his face and launched into the combination with the same drunk marionette quality as before.

"I'd...lose the smile," I said.

Harrison rubbed his face. "How am I so bad at this?" His eyes drifted behind me to the stage, where Ethan was doing a smooth series of barrel turns.

"He takes lessons," I said encouragingly. "You can't expect to be as good as someone who takes lessons."

Harrison did the beanie thing again, looking at the floor. "Right."

I considered him. He looked miserable. If he was hating rehearsal this much, maybe he should quit. He could walk out of here right now and forget it ever happened.

"Don't take this the wrong way, but are you one hundred percent certain you want to be in the musical?"

He sighed. "I don't know. I wanted to try. I knew I might not like it, I knew I'd probably be bad at it, but I just had to...try."

"Why?"

"There might be some...personal reasons," he mumbled, his face going pink.

Personal reasons? I sucked in a breath. Oh my God—Harrison joined the musical because he liked someone in the cast? My chest squeezed, because Colleen would be all over this. She was a romantic—in love with people falling for each other and doing embarrassing things because of it.

Awwwww! I could practically hear her squealing. *You* have *to help him!*

Suddenly, I really wanted to. His dumb romantic plan was going to work, damn it.

I grabbed the CD player, gestured for Harrison to follow me, and went out the back door into the lobby. "Okay, look," I said, finding an electrical outlet. "The fact that it's hard for you to act like an overconfident creep is a good thing in general. It'll take practice, that's all."

Harrison raised an eyebrow. "Really?"

"Yup. Now, watch my arms." I pressed Play before I could think better of it. As the jaunty drumbeat and swirly strings kicked in, I made my body go loose-limbed. Then I did the dance, infusing each step with a cocky sureness. When I finished, Harrison's eyes were wide.

"How did you do that?"

"You just have to do what the song tells you. And do it confidently. And relax your shoulders. Try it again."

It looked marginally better this time. Still stiff, but definitely less painful to watch. Laney and Ada came out of the auditorium just as Harrison got to the part where he was supposed to start twirling the line of girls, and I had an idea. Laney was probably too young to be his costar crush, but maybe it would help him get into character if he danced with an admirer for a bit.

"Hey, Laney. Do you mind partnering Harrison for the spin part?" I asked.

Laney dropped her backpack with a thud and came over, nervously giggling. "Yeah, I guess I can do that." Ada sat on the floor, breaking out a pack of Skittles like she was at a movie theater.

I had Harrison and Laney go through the combination a few times. My plan was kind of working. Laney's bubbliness was loosening Harrison up, making him take himself less seriously and lean into the movements.

Soon, I felt like Harrison was ready to practice on his own. "Thanks," he said, shrugging on his plaid jacket and smiling at us as he turned to leave. "You guys saved my dignity."

Laney stared after him with a dreamy expression. "Thanks," she echoed when he was gone.

"I expect to be invited to the wedding." I picked up my jacket from where I'd draped it over my backpack.

"We're keeping it small, but that can be arranged," Laney said.

"Um..." I wasn't sure how to respond to that.

Ada snorted. "I'm just going to tell her. We play this game called Love Realism. We pick someone in the cast who we have a crush on, and we go through how our lives together would pan out from now until death. Laney picked Harrison."

"Ah." I smiled. "What's happened so far?"

"*Well*," Laney said, "we both went to Penn State. He spent a lot of time with his frat brothers, which was whatever. But now we've graduated, and I want to get married, but he wants to wait until we're more financially secure. So it's a little tense."

I laughed. "Who's yours?" I asked Ada.

"Laurel Adams. I have a long-distance boyfriend, so I wasn't sure if I was going to play this year, but it's not like I'm actually pursuing her. Right now we're backpacking through Eastern Europe together. Want to play? Have anyone in mind?"

Jude's face floated into my brain. His hazel eyes. His smile. "No," I said quickly. "Nope."

※

For the whole drive home, "Beautiful Girl" was stuck in my head. Which was okay, because it distracted me from thinking about Jude's face again.

When I walked in the front door, the warm, delicious smell of shoyu chicken enveloped me. It was my favorite food in the world. "Hey, sweetie," Dad called from the kitchen as I shut the door.

"Hey." I dropped my backpack on the foyer floor and walked over to the stairs, leaning my hand against the banister as I looked into the kitchen, breathing in the magical mixture of shoyu, ginger, garlic, and brown sugar.

Mom waved at me from the counter, where she was shaping rice balls. "Did you have fun at rehearsal?" she asked.

I thought about it for a second. I'd expected rehearsals without Margot to be painful, but they hadn't been that bad. Laney and Ada were kind of entertaining. And helping Harrison had felt kind of good.

"I didn't . . . *not* have fun."

Dad paused as he lifted a stack of plates from the cupboard. "Well, I'm not not glad to hear it."

"I am also un-unhappy about it," Mom chimed in.

I rolled my eyes as my parents laughed way too hard at their dumb joke. "Bye," I said, going upstairs.

"Dinner in ten!" Mom called after me.

In my room, I fell back onto my comforter and stared at my blank peach walls. I closed my eyes, but even though I'd had a full day of school and rehearsal, I felt wide awake. I opened my laptop and typed *Giselle* into the YouTube search bar.

Then I erased it and typed *Beautiful Girl Singin' in the Rain*. A clip from the movie came up. I watched it, glad that Ms. Langford had put a lot more choreography into her version. I played it again and found myself standing up, doing the routine, my bare feet brushing over the soft carpet. After I stepped into the ending pose with my arm raised, I felt my body arching back into a slow cambré.

It wasn't in the choreography, but it fit the delicate dip in the music. I straightened up, feeling a slight pull in my back muscles. I hadn't stretched them properly in forever.

I got on my hands and knees and slowly arched my back up, then down, then up again, stretching the sore spot. I breathed in deeply as I held each position, feeling my muscles warm, loosen, expand. I stretched my obliques, then my shoulders, then my hamstrings. Finally, I stood up, dabbing at a light sheen of sweat on my forehead. I glanced at my bed, but I still didn't feel like crawling into it.

I wandered over to my window and peeled back the curtain. Across the street, an upstairs light was on in Jude's house. I wondered if it was his room. I stared at the lit-up window until a text from Colleen came in.

Did I just spend two hours making Ferdinand gifs? Yes. Do I regret it? No.

Underneath was a gif of Ferdinand sashaying down the sidewalk to the beat of "Stayin' Alive." A wave of missing Colleen swept through me. I wanted to see all the Ferdinand gifs, and laugh at them until my eyes watered, and make a few of my own while lying next to her on the constellation rug in her room.

If I could text back, I'd compliment Ferdinand's swagger. I'd say I was sorry for disappearing. I'd tell her about Jude.

Did I show Jude my scars? Yes. Do I regret it...

I thought back to that moment, that suddenly overwhelming urge to give some of my hurt away. How Jude's eyes were kind and sad when he looked at me, like he understood, even though he couldn't.

I looked again at the lit-up window across the street. Showing Jude my scars was embarrassing, and I was definitely going to avoid him for a while, but I couldn't bring myself to say I regretted it. Not even in a fake text message to Colleen.

I had no idea what that meant.

DECEMBER

CHAPTER ELEVEN

FOR THE NEXT COUPLE OF WEEKS, I stretched every night and slept surprisingly well. And when I woke up in the mornings feeling less like a zombie, I also felt less like I wanted to kill everyone. Which was a nice side effect.

I still needed my weekend sleep-in time, though. Which was why, when I woke up to a constant buzzing noise at 7:30 on a Saturday morning, a bit of the old murderous rage crept back in. I snatched in the general direction of my phone, knocking it off the nightstand. I pawed the carpet until I found it.

Margot.

abuela visiting. taking me shopping for Winter Formal dress. couldn't say no. help??

whayrt? My fingers weren't very coordinated this early in the morning.

can you distract her? meet at capital mall Macy's now please? please now?

I closed my eyes again, not wanting to move, let alone go to the mall. It was a week into December and, as Margot put it yesterday, "cold as frostbitten balls outside." My phone rang. I pressed the answer button to shut it up. *"What?"*

"PLEASE??" Margot yelled.

I yanked the phone a few inches away from my ear. "Is Macy's even open now?" I croaked out.

"They have special hours for the holidays. Come *on*," Margot said insistently. Then she started singing "Jingle Bells" with her own made-up lyrics. "Come to Macy's. Come to Macy's. Save me from Abuela!"

I made a sound between a groan and a laugh. *"Fine.* Hanging up now." I rolled out of bed and put on my fleece-lined leggings, boots, and the chunky mustard-yellow sweater that was my grandma Shiho's in the sixties, when she lived in New York. After she moved to Hawaiʻi with Grandpa Kenny, she packed all her sweaters into boxes, figuring her future kids or grandkids might like them one day. And she was right—as soon as it dropped below forty degrees, Josie and I always broke out the Grandma sweaters.

When I went downstairs, Mom froze on the couch, her pen poised above the essay she was grading. "Am I dreaming? Or are you actually up before noon?"

"I'm meeting Margot at the mall. Can I take the car?"

Mom smiled. "Ooo, what are you going to get?"

If I told her Margot was looking for a Winter Formal dress, she'd think I was looking for one, too, and get way too excited. "Nothing. Margot's abuela wanted to take her shopping, and I'm meeting them there."

Mom smiled even wider, probably imagining Margot and me trying on a bunch of wacky outfits while dancing to a pop song, like in a movie montage.

"So can I take the car?"

"Sure," Mom said, turning back to the essay. "But you'll have to pick Josie up from dance at eleven thirty."

I paused as I reached into Mom's purse for the keys. "Can Dad do it?"

Mom shook her head. "He's playing at a wedding today."

I sighed. "Fine." I shrugged on my down puffer coat, pulled my knit cap over my head, and opened the front door. A burst of icy air slapped me in the face and I cursed Margot all the way to the car.

Twenty minutes later, clutching a caramel apple latte, I stepped into the Macy's juniors' section, yawning. It was depressing to think that soon I'd have to get up this early every Saturday for extra rehearsals, which would start after winter break.

As I looked for Margot, "Waltz of the Snowflakes" came on over the speakers. Ugh. Besides the Christmas trees and twinkly lights everywhere, the fact that you couldn't go to any moderately upscale place in December without hearing *Nutcracker* music was not helping my withdrawal.

"Alina, thank *God*." Margot barreled out of the dressing room. Her sweatshirt was crooked, and her usually sleek turquoise bob was staticky and disheveled. "I told her I wasn't going to Winter Formal. The theme is 'Neon,' for God's sake. That's not even a theme, it's a gas!"

My eyes widened. I'd never seen Margot so frazzled.

A tall, elegant woman walked out of the dressing room, several gowns with varying degrees of pouf and sparkle draped over her arm. She wore a wide-leg jumpsuit in taupe, belted at the waist, and her hair was pulled back into a low bun. I would have mistaken her for a runway model if she hadn't been in her seventies.

"Abuela," Margot said, "this is Alina. She's looking for a dress, too." *Sorry*, she mouthed, but I didn't mind. I figured this was what

Margot had had in mind when she said "distract her." And it didn't mean I was going to Winter Formal. It meant I'd help placate Margot's abuela for a while by trying on some dresses.

"Isabel Correa," the woman said as she shook my hand. "I'm very pleased to meet you." She did look very pleased. And a little surprised. "Margot, it's wonderful you have a friend to try on dresses with. That's a very important thing in life."

"Oh, geez," Margot said under her breath, but only when Isabel had safely turned away.

Isabel started hanging the rejected dresses on the rack outside the fitting room. "Sometimes the friends we choose when we're children disappoint us," she said. "I always find it admirable when young people who outgrow their old friends find"—she glanced at me, taking in my vintage sweater and seeming to approve—"better ones."

"Okay, can we get on with this, please?" Margot said, inching away, clearly ready to end the conversation.

Isabel barely hid her smile. "Okay. I'll let you two look. Pick some things out together, and I won't give my opinion until the dressing room."

Margot grabbed my elbow and darted away. "Sorry about that," she said as we snaked through racks of dresses to the far end of the department. "I kind of vented to her a lot when the whole Izzy thing blew up, so she's been treating me like a pity project ever since, making sure I go to stupid school things so I don't 'miss out.'" Margot scoffed. "Like I'd miss out on anything by not going to Winter Formal. God, what even *is* this?" She picked up a dress that had the color and texture of pulpy orange juice.

I couldn't hold back my laughter anymore.

"Alina!" Margot yelled. "She made me try on so much taffeta! I'm *traumatized*!"

116

I was full-on laughing now, and so was Margot. Once we recovered, Margot wandered to another rack. "Okay, let's just get this over with. We'll pick out some dresses that don't make us look ridiculous. Those yearbook photographers will be everywhere, and—"

"Wait, you're really going? You're not just trying on dresses for your abuela?"

"No, we are really going. Abuela will be here until after Christmas." Winter Formal was on December twentieth, the last day of school before winter break, and it hadn't been remotely on my radar. Margot flashed her teeth at me. "Come on, we can literally walk in, take one picture for Abuela, then walk out and go to Waffle Country."

I smiled inadvertently when she said "Waffle Country." It was this retro place with checkerboard floors, powder-blue booths, and sparkly red tabletops. A total eyesore, but their waffles were life-changing.

I eyed the rack and lifted up a magenta ball gown with a heart-shaped cutout in the back. I held it up to Margot's chin. "I'll go if you wear this."

"Honestly," Margot said, taking the dress and eyeing it warily, "I've tried on worse."

As we pawed through racks of dresses, I learned that Isabel ran an art gallery in New York that showcased Mexican-American artists, and that her visits to Pennsylvania were often unannounced. "I swear, she just decides to get on the train sometimes. She's my favorite person in the world, but whenever she gets an idea in her head, there's no stopping her. Today's idea was: get Margot a Winter Formal dress. I knew something like this was going to happen when I didn't let her buy me a quinceañera dress last year," Margot muttered. "Damn last year me!"

"You had a quinceañera?" I asked, curious. I didn't know much about them. But I'd read a magazine article once about Latinx girls

117

celebrating their quinceañera, and in the picture, they were all wearing big, beautiful ball gowns and tiaras. I couldn't imagine Margot all dressed up like that.

"A small one, yeah," she said, swiping through a rack of dresses at lightning speed. "I didn't want a special dress for it, obviously, but Abuela did buy me this kickass pair of four-inch heels. They made the waltzing a little harder, but we all have to make sacrifices."

I smiled. "Waltzing?" Again, I couldn't picture it.

Margot looked a bit sheepish, but then kind of proud. "Yup. I wasn't going to have one, but then Abuela told me about hers back in the day, and what it meant to her, and then I wanted one." She plucked a black cocktail dress off the rack and tossed it over her arm. A thoughtful look passed over her face. "Sometimes I feel like because I'm only half Mexican and my abuela was born and raised in the US, I don't have that much of a connection to Mexican culture. And I want to feel more connected."

I thought about that. "I know what you mean."

"Yeah?"

"My grandparents on my mom's side were both born in the US. I don't speak Japanese, and I've never even been to Japan. I really want to go someday, but yeah, there are lots of times when I feel like I'm not that connected to Japanese culture." Margot nodded. I rubbed the soft fabric of a burgundy dress between my fingers. "Once when we were visiting Hawai'i, my grandma Shiho had a bunch of women over to play bridge, and a couple of them kept commenting on how 'Americanized' me and Josie were."

Margot smirked. "Aren't old ladies the best? No filters. What did your grandma say?"

"She was just like, 'Well, yeah, they're American. They're Japanese-American.'"

"Nice."

I smiled. It hadn't bothered me at the time, what those old ladies had said. But I also remembered feeling that my grandma was right. We were Japanese-American. And being Japanese-American could mean all kinds of things. I liked that it was so open—so full of ways to think and act and be, not bound to some strict set of rules.

Suddenly, I really missed Grandma Shiho, her cluttered house in Honolulu, the plumeria tree in her yard, her scruffy cat, Gyotaku. "I wish my grandma could get on a train to visit," I said.

"Yeah, but going to Hawai'i to see her has to be amazing," Margot said. "Take me with you next time, okay? We can hang out on the beach all day and then find weird shit to do downtown at night."

I laughed, picturing vacationing in Hawai'i with Margot and Colleen. Colleen would develop a million crushes a day and Margot would find entertaining ways to shoot them all down and I'd probably never stop laughing. The fantasy was so amazing I momentarily forgot it had been five months since I'd talked to Colleen.

I put the fantasy out of my mind.

When Margot and I each had three nonterrible dress options, we headed back to the fitting rooms, where Isabel was waiting. Margot locked eyes with me before we went into our separate stalls. "You have to come out, okay?" she said.

Both of our first picks—the little black dress for Margot and a navy one-shouldered dress for me—received a firm no from Isabel. She said they were too conventional for such "fascinating young women."

But Margot's second pick, a glistening metallic gray dress with a halter neckline, a floor-length skirt, and pockets, got Isabel's approval. "Finally! Thank you, Jesus!" Margot fell to her knees and threw her hands up until Isabel told her to compose herself. Mine got another no.

Margot turned to me and said, "I'm pullin' for you, champ."

I returned to the dressing room and put on my third and final option. It was a soft, rosy pink, with a simple scoop neck and a black velvet ribbon that crisscrossed in the front and tied in a bow at the back. The skirt was soft tulle and a little bit poufy, falling just below my knees, leaving my scars uncovered, which obviously ruled it out. But there was something else.

I frowned at my reflection. With the color and the skirt, this dress was way too ballet-esque. Still, I had to show it to Margot and Isabel. I'd promised. I quickly pulled my leggings back on underneath the skirt, making sure they were fully covering my scars, and came out of the dressing room. Isabel's face lit up, and Margot said, "Niiiice."

"Lovely," Isabel cooed. "You move so gracefully in it."

"Of course she does," Margot said. "She's a ballerina." Isabel lifted her eyebrows, looking at me expectantly.

"I used to do ballet, but I don't anymore."

"I love the ballet," Isabel said. "I go whenever I can. I met a dancer from American Ballet Theatre at a dinner once. She told me that ballet isn't something you *do*. It's something you are. I've never done ballet, but that sounds right to me."

I smiled a little. Part of me wanted the conversation to end. But another part, the stubborn part that had picked out this dress, wanted to grasp on to the notion that ballet was in me somehow, forever, even though I couldn't do it anymore.

Scars and steel don't decide if you're a dancer or not.

But if scars and steel meant you couldn't do pointe or hold yourself up in a relevé or do a steady pirouette, then that was exactly what they did.

"I actually have a dress from my cousin's wedding a couple of years ago," I said, backing into the dressing room. "I'll just wear that." I didn't know why I hadn't already thought of it. The dress had a lacy lavender bodice and a long, flowy skirt. It would make a perfectly fine pretending-to-go-to-Winter-Formal dress.

Isabel's eyebrows rose in surprise.

"Are you sure?" Margot said, examining the velvet ribbon. "This one looks amazing on you."

"Yeah. The other dress fits me better." I shut the dressing room door and shed the dress as quickly as I'd put it on, wondering why I'd let myself pick it out in the first place.

∼⤳∽

I was still thinking about the dumb dress as I sat outside the redbrick Variations building, waiting for Josie's class to end. Through a large ground-floor window, I glimpsed bodies dashing through the air to a strong drumbeat.

I couldn't help noticing how different it was from KDBS. Not just the movements but the dancers themselves. The class was still mostly white, because our town was mostly white. But there were more students of color in this class than in any at KDBS. And the teacher was Asian-American. Somewhere in the back of my mind, I remembered Josie mentioning that. All of a sudden, what Josie had said about Kira that night I spilled water on her science project popped into my head. *Maybe you should be glad you're not dancing for her anymore.*

I turned up the heat and shook the thought away.

I spotted Josie in the back of the room as a small group did the combination in front. She was whispering with a boy instead of practicing. When it was her group's turn to go, she hesitated a bit on the last few steps, probably because she couldn't remember them. A mistake that could have easily been fixed if she'd bothered to go over the combination. She clearly didn't take class seriously. And yet she got to be there, dancing, while I sat out here, waiting to drive her home.

The jealousy bomb stirred in my stomach. I closed my eyes and breathed as the unfairness washed over me, remembering the time I'd unloaded to Birdie about Josie's lack of dedication.

"She just . . . she doesn't even care!"

"Why do you say that?" Birdie asked, rubbing my scars in firm, circular motions to break up the scar tissue.

"She missed class today because she was tired from a stupid sleepover. It's like it doesn't even matter to her."

Birdie shrugged. "There are different ways to care."

"Whatever."

"Nuh-uh, you don't get to be mad at me, I'm mad at you."

Earlier during our session, I'd made the mistake of looking at one of those websites that compared fetuses to fruits and told her that her baby was the size of a butternut squash. "Fine," Birdie said after a few moments of silence. "We can be mad at each other."

Even then, I knew that Josie's dancing had nothing to do with my injury. Still, I couldn't get past the injustice. I guess I still hadn't let it go.

Class finally ended and Josie came out, wrapped in her white parka. Someone called her name and she paused in the middle of the parking lot. The boy she'd been talking to in class jogged over. They laughed at something, their breaths turning into wispy clouds. Every time I thought the conversation was ending, one of them made an oversized gesture and kept going.

I jammed my hand onto the horn, feeling a deep satisfaction when Josie and the boy jumped like startled squirrels. Josie squinted into the windshield before saying something to the boy and then trudging over to the car.

"That was so unnecessary," she said, clicking on her seat belt. I shrugged and pulled out of the parking lot. "Why are *you* picking me up, anyway?"

"I was already out."

"Before noon?" She put her hand to her chest in mock surprise. I didn't dignify that with a response, and we settled into the tense silence that had become our norm. We hadn't said much to each other since our fight about ballet. So it surprised me when I stopped at a red light and Josie asked, "Did you see me do the combination?"

"Yeah," I said slowly.

"And?" Josie looked at me. "What did you think?"

That confused me even more. We never asked each other for critiques. "I don't know."

"Scale of one to ten," Josie said.

"Five."

Josie scoffed and looked out the window. I knew that would shut her up. I enjoyed a full minute of silence before she asked, all huffily, "What should I do differently, then?"

"Oh my God, I don't know, Josie. You have a dance teacher. Ask her."

Josie narrowed her eyes. "You're in an even worse mood than usual. Is it because you haven't seen *Jude* in a while?"

"Excuse me?" My fingers squeezed the wheel. I'd gotten so good at avoiding Jude that his name affected me like an electric shock.

Josie smiled haughtily. "I ran into him at lunch and he asked how you were doing because he hadn't seen you in a while."

"What did you say?" I asked casually.

"Not important. So is that why you're so grumpy?"

"No." I switched on the radio and turned it up, my go-to move when Josie was being annoying, and spent the rest of the drive ignoring her.

CHAPTER TWELVE

"THAT'S THE SADDEST IDEA EVER. You can't get dressed up for Winter Formal and then eat waffles instead," Ethan said. We'd started meeting by the senior lockers and walking to English through the tunnel together.

"You say that like they're any old waffles. We're talking Waffle Country waffles. It's different."

Ethan held out his hand. "I'm not questioning the superiority of Waffle Country waffles. I'm not a monster. I'm just saying, sometimes Margot decides she doesn't like something just because other people here *do* like it. She doesn't give this school enough credit."

"Or maybe you give it too much credit?" Ethan had a confusing amount of school spirit. His Instagram was famous because he documented all Eagle View's happenings. Football games, band concerts, Quiz Bowls, charity car washes, dances, and everything else, all in his signature warm, saturated colors that turned every mundane moment into a work of art. When he posted something new, it got hundreds of likes within the hour. The local paper had already used a few of his pictures for their website.

"Look, I'm not an idiot," Ethan said. "I know a lot of people here only talk to me because I make them look amazing on Instagram, and they're afraid that if they don't talk to me, I'll make them look bad on Instagram. But I don't care. Interesting things happen here. I like taking pictures of them."

"What interesting things?" I asked, highly skeptical.

"Lots of stuff. Victories, defeats, the soul-crushing awkwardness of a first slow dance, declarations of love. Well, no love declarations yet. But maybe one day."

"Love declarations?"

"Like if someone professed their feelings to someone else in a super-public way. It would be an amazing shot. The emotion! The stakes! But no one here has the balls."

We slowed down as a guy and a girl walking a few feet in front of us stopped short, causing a hallway traffic jam. "I thought you said you blocked her number, *Devon*," the girl said.

"I did, dude, it must be some problem with my phone."

"Don't call me dude, you know I hate it when you call me dude!"

I looked at Ethan as we skirted the couple. "Wow. *So* interesting. I'll wait if you want to take a picture."

"Stop deflecting," Ethan said. "Come on, you and Margot have to come to Winter Formal. The theme is 'Neon.' The best worst theme in the history of formals. And it's just one night. What's the problem?"

The problem was, I didn't want a repeat of the pre–cast party. Running away and practically hyperventilating in the car. "I don't know. I just...I think waffles would be better. Anyway, are you going with anyone? Davis?" I knew that Ethan and Davis had hung out a few times since the pre–cast party.

"No, Deflector." Ethan sighed. "Davis is great, but we both realized there's nothing extra there. We talked about still going together—two openly gay seniors, walking into the gym, making a statement. But it's our last Winter Formal and we both want to go with our friends. He's got Pauline and Brad and that whole group, and I've got Jude and Celia and the other musical people, including you and Margot, if you stop being too cool for school. Plus, of all the dances, Winter Formal has the most baggage. It'll be good to be all together."

"Baggage for who?" I asked. I knew Margot had had the blow-out with Izzy at the ice rink, but that was before Winter Formal.

"Mmm, what?" Ethan looked at me a little too innocently. I could have let it go gracefully, but screw that.

"Whose baggage? Yours?" Ethan's face didn't change, so I assumed not. "Jude's?"

"Alina, I'm trying to subvert the 'gay boys are gossips' stereotype. You're not making that easy."

"Oh, come on, it's not gossip, it's...information. Information that you're giving to a mutual friend, which will help her be more sensitive if she ever talks about Winter Formal with Jude."

Ethan stepped in front of me and started walking backward so he could look me straight in the eye. "Alina Keeler. Why would you be talking about Winter Formal with Jude?"

"I won't be," I said so loudly a few people looked over. "I just meant, in case it comes up. When Jude's around."

Ethan kept staring at me, still walking backward. A few seconds later he returned to my side, but he still didn't say anything. We got out of the tunnel and climbed the stairs to the second floor. "Maybe you should know," he finally said. "A cautionary tale."

"What?"

"Never mind. Now I've built it up. It's not juicy or anything. Sophomore year, when Jude and Diya were a thing, Diya got a finalist spot in some musical theater song contest in Pittsburgh."

"I didn't know they had those." I wondered if it was like ballet competitions, where you performed a variation in front of judges for the chance to win a shot at a prestigious school or summer intensive. "Do they give scholarships?" I asked.

"*I* don't know, that's not the point. The point is, the contest was on the night of Winter Formal, so she ditched Jude."

"Oh."

"Yeah. The freaking night of the dance, she just calls him and says she's not going. You should have seen it. Jude in his suit, holding a corsage box...I know it sounds like a scene from a bad teen rom-com, but the pain was *real*."

The "Finishing the Hat" debate came back into my head, how Jude thought it was tragic to choose art over relationships. Then I thought of something else—Jude had said his dad left two years ago. Winter Formal his sophomore year was probably not too long after it happened, which I was sure made the whole thing even more heartbreaking.

Poor Jude.

I'd never really dated anyone before—I'd had an undefined thing with a boy at a summer intensive in Philadelphia once, but nothing official. Still, what if *I* was in Diya's situation? If I got a last-minute chance to audition for the ABT summer intensive and it meant ditching someone I cared about, what would I do?

Something inside me knew the answer. Ballet. I would have chosen ballet. And I would have wanted the person I was dating to understand, even if they were angry, even if they were sad, even if they had to break up with me. I would have wanted them to respect why I chose what I chose.

"Anyway, I've hardly spoken to Robobitch since," Ethan said.

"Seems like no one else in the musical has, either." I was careful to keep my voice casual, so it wouldn't seem like I was criticizing.

Ethan shrugged. "She brought it on herself."

Ugh. There was that weird defensive twinge again. I could understand why Jude would be angry with her for ditching him—they wanted different things. But why did the rest of the theater crew give a damn?

And was *Ethan* the one who started the Robobitch nickname? I mean, in the glossary of nicknames I'd heard at this school, Robobitch wasn't the worst. It was still mean, though. It still implied that Diya was a cold, emotionless, robot bitch because she'd chosen musical theater over her boyfriend. Her future over Winter Formal. Art over Jude.

The question was on the tip of my tongue, but I swallowed it. Ethan was my friend. He was amazing and funny and made me feel less alone while surrounded by Paul and Jake. I wasn't going to look for a reason to tarnish that. As we made our way farther down the hallway toward class, my mind landed on something else.

"Wait, why was that a cautionary tale?"

Ethan hesitated but then plunged in. "It was to let you know about Jude's most recent history in that department. Like, in case you were fooled by his peppy exterior, and thought he was just a carefree guy who sings and dances and flirts but never takes it seriously and never gets hurt." He gave me a pointed look.

Was that what Ethan thought *I* thought of Jude? And why did I even need this cautionary tale? Jude and I hadn't talked to each other in weeks. I looked up at Ethan, but he was staring straight ahead with an annoyingly neutral expression on his face.

Well. Ethan was a lousy gossip. I was more confused about Jude than ever.

We were still a few minutes early when we got to the classroom, so we lingered in the hallway. "So what's it going to be?" Ethan asked. "Winter Formal or waffles?"

"Waffles," I said.

Ethan leaned the side of his head against the wall and closed his eyes. "Tragic. It's so tragic it's killing me. I'm dead."

I snorted. Over Ethan's shoulder, I spotted Harrison walking down the hall. When he saw us, he stopped, then frantically glanced between Ethan's back and the floor before heading our way. He took off his beanie, smoothed out his hair, put it back on, and...oh my God.

It was Ethan. Harrison had joined the musical for *Ethan*. I knew that to an outsider it would seem like pretty weak evidence, but I'd spent years listening to Colleen explain how a walk or a gesture or a hair flip proved that so-and-so had a crush on so-and-so, and she was almost always right. I was weirdly certain about this.

I looked at Ethan, who was still pretending to be dead. I jabbed him in the stomach, and he opened his eyes just as Harrison came up. "Hey, guys," Harrison said. "How's it going?"

"Not bad." Ethan smiled. "Just minimizing the time we have to spend in English." He gestured to the classroom.

Harrison laughed a bit too loudly. "Right, right, I hear that." There was a pause, and I tried not to look between them too much. Ethan seemed like he always did—friendly, jokey, laid-back. I didn't know if that was a good or a bad sign. "Um, anyway..." Harrison stepped back. "Gotta get to calc. See you later."

I watched Harrison walk off, and Ethan turned back to me. "Did you do the reading for today?"

"What do you think of Harrison, he's cool, right?" I said.

"Um." Ethan raised an eyebrow. "Right..."

"I heard he likes someone in the musical."

"You *heard*? You're too cool for Winter Formal, but now you're all plugged in to the Eagle View gossip?"

"Again, not gossip. Information."

Ethan brushed his hair out of his eyes and gave me a stern glare. "Well, *I* haven't heard that. Or anything else about Harrison's sexuality. So whatever you're trying to do...don't."

I sighed. "Fine." Ethan had kept quiet about the whole Paul and Jake situation when I asked him to, so I wouldn't meddle in his business. "Just keep your eyes open," I said quickly.

"Excuse me, I don't take advice from people who choose waffles over neon-themed dances." I rolled my eyes as a passing teacher shooed us into the classroom. Ethan squeezed my shoulder before going to his seat in the front corner, his small way of bolstering me so I could make it through forty-five minutes in the company of morons.

Paul put his palms together and bowed to me. "Ice Princess, you going to Winter Formal?" he asked as I sat down. "You could make it all frigid in there. Really add to the décor." He and Jake shivered dramatically.

"Mm-hmm," I said without turning around. My phone flashed in my bag.

Ethan had texted a series of emojis. Two boys, an equals sign, and a pile of poop. I snorted. Another message popped up. **Are you sure I can't tell them off for you? I'd make it good.**

Still very sure, I wrote back quickly.

Okaaaaay.

I felt Paul craning over my shoulder, so I lowered my phone to my lap and texted back a heart.

CHAPTER THIRTEEN

"HMM-HMM-HMM-HMM-HM-HM . . ." Josie was humming "Waltz of the Snowflakes" in the car on the way to school. Her bus friend Fiona was sick, so I had to take her. "La, la, la, la-la-la, la..." She was full-out singing it now. It was the blessed last day before winter break, so I should have been happy. Instead, I wanted to murder Josie.

"*Stop*," I said sharply.

"Sorry, geez." She held her gloved fingers up to the heating vent. "You know, you don't own that song. I'm dancing to it, too."

"Kind of," I mumbled. Variations was doing its own version of *The Nutcracker* this year, which apparently mixed Tchaikovsky's score with "noise music," whatever that was. I was *not* looking forward to going but knew I'd have to.

"What do you mean kind of?"

"I'm not talking about this now," I said, switching on the radio, where "Waltz of the Snowflakes" promptly boomed through the speakers.

Josie cracked up as I turned it off. She was still laughing two traffic lights later.

"I will throw you out of this car, run you over, and go to school like nothing happened!" I yelled.

The rest of the ride was silent.

When I pulled into the parking lot, Josie didn't even wait for me to turn off the car before getting out and slamming the door. Guilt nagged at me as I walked into school and headed to the choir room to check the rehearsal schedule. It wasn't like me snapping at Josie was a new occurrence. Though I guess I'd never threatened to run her over with a car before. But whatever. She shouldn't have been singing that song when she knew it would make me homicidal.

I scanned the schedule, stopping abruptly at January sixth. The first Monday after we came back from break. Only my name and Jude's were printed there. Our first rehearsal for the Vamp dance. I took a breath. The last time I was alone with Jude, it had ended badly, but it didn't have to this time. A month had passed since I'd shown him my scars. Enough time to forget about it. At rehearsal, I'd be calm, composed, and completely professional.

When I walked into homeroom, Margot fluttered her eyelashes. "Pick me up at seven?" she said.

"For..." I pretended to be confused.

"Don't make me say it."

"I really don't know what you're talking about." I smiled dumbly as I took my seat.

"Winter Formal, okay? *Winter Formal.*"

I laughed. I'd told Margot I would go along with her plan: go to Winter Formal, get photo evidence for her abuela that we attended, and immediately leave for the warm, syrupy haven of Waffle Country.

It was a good plan. It made Margot happy. And it made my parents positively ecstatic, which was useful. They had chilled out about the social stuff since the musical, but who knew how long that would last. I figured if I went to Winter Formal, maybe they'd think I really had made progress. Then I could skip Spring Fling and prom and every other school dance in existence.

"I'll be there," I said.

"Thanks." Margot looked genuinely relieved I wasn't bailing on her. I wondered what she would've done if I had. Probably just gone with Ethan and the other musical people. Like Jude. Was he going? Jude liking school dances wouldn't surprise me at all. Maybe he wasn't going because of the Diya baggage. Or maybe he was going with a date.

My brain traveled back and forth between those two scenarios so much that by the time school ended, I was thoroughly annoyed with myself.

I was waiting in the parking lot for Josie when I got a text from her saying she was getting a ride with a girl from her dance class, who was "stable" and didn't "yell for no reason." Guess she hadn't forgotten about this morning. I sighed, the guilt coming back full-force.

When I got home, Josie was splayed on the couch, watching a Willa Hoang makeup tutorial. She'd been watching Willa for years and used to ask if she could try the different looks on me. I always said no, so she hadn't asked in a long time.

As I took off my coat, Josie gave me a withering stare before flicking her eyes back to the screen.

"Look, Josie, I—" I stalled, distracted by her bare foot slung over the back cushions of the couch. She was pointing and flexing it unconsciously, her high arch curving like a hook. She had the kind of feet ballet dancers would kill for. Like mine.

"I..." I stopped again. I couldn't apologize. What did she have to be angry about? So I'd snapped at her—so what? She could still dance. She'd be just fine. "I'm...I'm not going to stay for long, but

I'm going to Winter Formal, so maybe you could do my makeup."
There. Not an apology, but something.

Josie's eyes shot to mine suspiciously. "Can I do this one?" She
turned her laptop around. *Shimmering Winter Goddess Look!* it said
above Willa, with loose curls, silvery eyeshadow, blush-pink lips,
and rhinestones over her eyebrows.

"Fine. But without the rhinestones."

"Obviously without the rhinestones," Josie muttered, brushing
past me as she went upstairs.

Josie kept one eye on the tutorial as she held a curling iron centime-
ters away from my neck. I watched her closely in the oval mirror of
her tiny purple vanity. She'd gotten it years ago, and I hadn't realized
how much she'd outgrown it until now, as I balanced one butt cheek
on the stool.

I breathed in sharply as she twisted up a lock of hair, the iron
coming dangerously close to my ear. "If you burn me, I'll burn you
back," I said.

"I'm not going to burn you." Josie rolled her eyes. "Though
maybe I should."

"I shouldn't have yelled at you, okay?" I said, hoping she'd forget
about it.

"It's not even that, it's...never mind." Josie slowly unwound my
hair from the iron and tested the curl with her fingers.

"Say what you want to say, Josie."

"I don't want to get into a big *thing* right before the dance."

Josie was going to Winter Formal with a gazillion friends who
were coming over to take pictures with her later. I looked at her
reflection in the mirror. She was wearing a black halter dress with a

sparkly silver belt. With her hair in loose waves over her left shoulder, her bangs slicked to the side, she looked so grown-up.

"I won't make it a big thing," I said quietly.

"Fine. I was going to say, it's not what you yelled at me in the car that made me mad. It's the fact that you don't yell that stuff at the people who really deserve it. Like..." She hesitated. "Like Paul Manley."

My eyes widened. "What do you know about Paul Manley?"

"I know he says racist, sexist things to you and you just ignore him. *That's* the kind of person you should explode at. Not innocent people who hum."

I was about to argue, but instead my mind went to how I'd flipped Jude off after the dance audition. He had been innocent, too. He hadn't wronged me. Neither had Josie. They simply happened to be there when all the wrongness I felt inside refused to be held in any longer.

I'd never explode at Paul, though. It wasn't worth it, and it wouldn't change anything. "Whatever. I don't care about what he says."

Josie shrugged, winding up another lock of my hair. "Maybe you should. I mean, you held your tongue about this stuff when you were in ballet, but—"

"Josie," I warned.

"What?" she said, exasperated. "Why can't you talk about it? Did Kira brainwash you or something? She's not here right now. She can't get you."

I inhaled slowly, ignoring Josie's patronizing tone. "Kira's casting decisions might have sometimes felt...unfair," I said, testing the words I'd never said out loud. "But she had her reasons." I thought again of the *Nutcracker* casting day and the deep-down feeling that something wasn't right. It was easy to squash it after Kira's explanation, and especially after she let us dance the leads. Now it was harder to ignore, but weirdly, some part of me still wanted to trust her.

135

"Fine. Let's say she cast you as Chinese Tea every year because of your skill, not race. What about the choreography?"

Well, that was an easy one. "The choreography's not Kira's fault. It's been that way forever."

"Why can't she change it?"

"Because..." I paused when the words didn't automatically come to me. Heat rose to my face as I scrounged around for an answer. "Because of tradition! Ballet companies around the world have been doing it that way for decades."

Josie put down the curling iron and swiped highlighter onto my cheeks. "Yuna always says that just because something's been a certain way forever doesn't mean it shouldn't change."

"Who's Yuna?" I asked absentmindedly.

Josie rolled her eyes. "My dance teacher."

"Oh." I was sure Josie had mentioned her before. I just hadn't remembered.

"Anyway," Josie said crisply. "She's right. That dance is all kinds of awful. I mean, come on, those dumb little steps, the *bowing*..." She shuddered.

"I mean, it's...outdated," I admitted. It was choreographed in the 1800s, so of course it is. I was about to argue that Chinese Tea was one little dance in the middle of a whole ballet, that it didn't even matter that much, but I froze as an image of Paul bowing to me in English popped into my head.

That was different, though. I mean, I guess it *looked* similar to what I'd do in the Chinese Tea dance—palms together, bobbing my head up and down. But when Paul did it, it was to be "funny" at my expense. The audience never laughed when I did the Chinese Tea dance. Though sometimes, after a performance, I'd see kids running around, doing the bobbing head thing and laughing...

But Paul was doing it to be an ass. I was doing it because it was my role in *The Nutcracker*, a beautiful ballet with choreography that went back over a hundred years, which again, Kira couldn't drastically change...right?

My brain felt tired all of a sudden.

"Well, whatever," I mumbled, hoping that would end the conversation.

I avoided meeting Josie's eyes in the mirror, glancing around her room to distract myself instead. I paused when I saw an old picture of Josie and me on the ribbon bulletin board above her desk. In it, I was seven and she was five, and we were wearing the navy-blue sailor costumes from the one and only duet we ever did together—at the community center dance school's summer recital. It was a jazz piece to "Beyond the Sea," and we practiced it in the living room religiously for months. Mom warned me that Josie was younger and wouldn't have the attention span to practice as much as me. But every time I cued up the music, she was right there at my elbow. She never complained, no matter how many times we ran it. God, it was probably the most time we ever spent together, practicing that summer.

After that recital, Josie wanted more freedom and I wanted more structure, so my parents enrolled Josie at Variations and me at KDBS. We couldn't practice together anymore because we were doing such different things, but we'd sometimes show each other the new steps we were trying to nail. A switch leap. A tour jeté. But as I got more serious about ballet, Josie's dancing seemed less relevant to me, less important. Now I couldn't remember the last time Josie or I had even talked about dance without one of us tuning out or getting mad.

Josie followed my gaze to the picture. "Those costumes were butt-ugly. But the dance wasn't bad."

"I was just thinking about how much we practiced it."

"A lot."

"Mom was surprised you were able to spend so much time on it, since you were only five."

Josie shrugged. "I cared about it."

Her eyes met mine in the mirror before she turned and pulled out a container of half-used perfumes from her closet. Glass bottles clinked as she dug around, sniffing a few options.

"Listen," she said, bunching up her nose and dropping a sparkling purple bottle back into the container with a thunk. "I know you kept quiet about all the bullshit before because you were going for the big picture. A professional ballet company. I wouldn't have been able to stand it, but I get it. Sort of. Actually not at all, but whatever. The point is, you're not doing ballet anymore. So why are you still being quiet about that stuff?"

Normally, everything about that smug little speech would have made me snap. But for the first time, I felt Josie's questions seeping into my brain and stubbornly taking root there. Maybe ballet had taught me to be quiet. To keep my anger and hurt inside. Maybe my outbursts meant that strategy wasn't working for me anymore. But if I wasn't the quiet, dedicated ballet girl, keeping her head down and moving forward even if things were unfair, then who was I? And if ballet was so unfair, why did I miss it so much?

Josie sprayed a vanilla fragrance on the back of my neck and plumped my waves with her fingers. "Voilà," she said.

I stared at my reflection. I looked amazing. Every curl, every sweep of silvery shadow and blend of pink on my cheeks and lips, was perfect. Josie had put a lot of work into this, even though she was mad at me for threatening to murder her this morning.

Josie shoved the perfume container back into her closet and unplugged the curling iron. My eyes caught again on the picture of us from years ago, and a surprising thought occurred to me. Maybe Josie didn't keep bringing up all this stuff about ballet to be a jerk.

Maybe she did it because she cared.

~

On my way to pick up Margot, I couldn't stop thinking about *The Nutcracker*. Kira. Chinese Tea. The choreography. Paul and Jake. It was all a big mess in my head.

When I stopped at a red light, I caved. I brought up *The Nutcracker* score on my phone, scrolled to the Grand Pas de Deux, and hit Play.

As soon as I heard the familiar harps floating peacefully up and down the scale, everything started to feel okay again. And even though I was in traffic, inching past strip malls and car dealerships, I was really somewhere else: December last year, in the Epstein Theatre, performing the role of the Sugar Plum Fairy for the first time.

Onstage, I touched the stiffness of the pink tutu extending a foot and a half away from my body. Felt the weight of the glistening silver crown, secured onto my head with bobby pins. Danced the movements that had become so familiar to me and yet never lost their specialness.

The Sugar Plum Fairy was a beautiful puzzle. She was a fairy, obviously, so she was delicate and whimsical and dainty. But she was also a powerful, benevolent ruler. It took me ages to figure out how to dance like that. Took thousands of little adjustments to my arms and legs and fingers and feet as I stood behind Juliet and Spencer, practicing as their understudy. Once I finally got the perfect balance of delicacy and power into each arabesque and piqué, I polished them until it all felt natural, like I had always moved that way.

When I got to do it for an audience, I soared over the stage, the bell-like notes of the celesta emanating from my body and whirling around the theater, filling it with warmth and light and loveliness.

Back in the car, the orchestra came to its final dramatic note. I took a breath in the silence that followed, recalling that my favorite part of the whole night had come after the dancing.

In ballet, a curtsy is also known as a reverence. It's not a simple bow to say "Thanks for clapping." It's a gesture of love and respect to your classmates, teachers, the music, the orchestra, the audience, and most of all, to ballet itself. It's the embodiment of gratitude for being able to do what you just did.

Onstage that night—to the rhythm of my wild heartbeat and the applause of family, friends, strangers, ballet lovers, and people who had just seen ballet for the first time—I extended my right arm, and then my left. Then I knelt into a deep curtsy, slowly lowering my head.

I'd cried a lot of tears and held back even more before I got the chance to dance this role. But that night it finally happened. And I made it the most beautiful thing I could.

CHAPTER FOURTEEN

"CAN YOU DIE FROM neon exposure?" Margot shouted over the music, shielding her eyes as we walked into the gym.

"Maybe?" I squinted at the blinding decorations. Multicolored neon lanterns hung from the ceiling, fluorescent tape zigzagged across the floor, and neon signs lit up the walls. They said: GLOW FOR IT, TONIGHT IT'S ALL LIGHT, and, my personal favorite, NEON!!!!

"Where should we take the picture?" I yelled.

Margot looked around the gym. "That one really captures the theme," she yelled back, pointing to the NEON!!!! sign by the bleachers. We made our way over, elbowing through a cluster of girls with glow-paint hearts on their cheeks. "Look happy to be here!" Margot said as we arranged ourselves in front of the sign. She stretched her arm out and snapped the picture.

She tapped a few buttons and plopped her phone into the pocket of her shimmering metallic dress. "So that's done," she said.

We stood around awkwardly for a few seconds. I caught sight of Josie across the gym, putting on a pair of oversized neon glasses and piling into the photo booth with a few other girls. On the other side of the room, I saw Ethan in a big group of musical people. They were dancing normally, not like at the cast party, and Jude wasn't there. "Should we..." I gestured to the doors. I really needed those waffles.

"Alinaaaa!" My name pierced through the music and noise. Laney was running toward me in a poufy hot-pink gown. Ada was behind her in a dark green mermaid dress. As they got closer, they did what I was afraid they'd do, which was fling their arms out and "ca-caw!" at me.

Margot's eyes widened. "Do you know them? Or do I need to remember that self-defense class I took in middle school?"

"They're in the chorus," I said. "They're harmless." Then the song changed and a fast beat pumped through the gym. Ada stopped short, grabbing Laney's wrist to pull her onto the dance floor. Laney grabbed mine, making me stumble forward. In a panic, I grabbed Margot's, and before either of us could say anything, we were whooshing through sequins and glowing white button-downs to a cramped space in the middle of the gym. I held my arms to my chest to make myself smaller, blinking at the gyrating bodies surrounding me. Aside from crowd-surfing, there was no way out. I looked at Margot, sure she would find a way to end this.

But Margot was dancing, her arms in the air. She smiled at me, her teeth radiating bizarrely in the black light. "One dance. Then waffles," she yelled, grabbing my hands and swaying them above my head. I groaned and laughed and shook her off, my hands swaying on their own as the beat grew more intense. Then everyone started jumping, and so did I, the music washing over my body, my lavender skirt swishing and spinning, luminescent in the neon lights.

We danced three songs. I'd forgotten how easy it was to move like this, with no steps or rules, and no one watching you, tallying up all the things you were doing wrong.

"Better than waffles, right?" someone shouted. Ethan danced up in a charcoal suit with a neon-purple cummerbund. Laney and Ada screamed and hugged him.

"Meh," Margot said, but she couldn't hide her smile. "Are you done Instagramming?"

"Of course not." Ethan scoffed. I had the urge to ask him if Jude was here, but I didn't.

A slow song came on just as Harrison walked up in a dapper dark blue suit. "Hey," he said, smiling nervously. I wanted to look at Ethan and gauge his reaction, but that would be too obvious. Laney started giggling uncontrollably, so she clearly wasn't concerned with being too obvious. But either Harrison didn't notice or pretended not to. He did look really nice. There was a neon-green flower in his lapel, and he wasn't wearing his beanie. Actually, he looked kind of weird without it. Like his head was naked, but I wasn't about to say that.

"Where's your hat?" Margot asked flatly, because of course she did.

"Uh..." Harrison's smile faltered.

"Are you the hat police?" Ethan said, raising an eyebrow at Margot.

Margot looked around at the group, taking in Laney's giddiness, Harrison's nerves, Ethan's irritation. "*What*, it was a simple question, why is everyone being so weird?"

"Because you're a..." Ethan held his arms out to Margot. "*Beautiful girl!*" he sang, his voice ringing out over the music.

Margot groaned dramatically, but Laney and Ada sang along. Harrison tipped his head back and sang louder than everyone, which made Ethan laugh. They all kept singing even as slow-dancing couples nearby shot us dirty looks. Ethan paused to carefully aim his phone and snap a picture of Harrison, who was singing with his eyes closed.

When it got to the part where Harrison was supposed to do a box step and spin around, he did it without looking at all like a drunk marionette. He actually looked kind of...good. Ethan's eyebrows shot up; he was impressed. Harrison gave him a shy smile.

The music changed to another fast song. My throat was dry, so I signaled that I was going to get water. As I opened the door to the lobby, my eyes took a while to adjust to the regular overhead lights. I stood there for a few seconds, holding the door and blinking, before I realized someone was standing in front of the display cases.

Jude.

"Oh," I said. His cobalt-blue jacket lay discarded on a chair and his shirtsleeves were pushed up to his elbows. He stared at me, wide-eyed.

"Um...," I said, because he was still staring. "Is everything—"

Jude shook his head. "Sorry. It just looked weird for a second."

"Weird?"

"With the black lights behind you, and that color dress, you kind of looked like a ghost." I looked down. My lavender dress did have a ghostly glow under the neon lights. I stepped forward and let the door close behind me, muffling the music into a soft blur.

"Not in a bad way." Jude rushed to explain. "Not scary. Not like a poltergeist. Like, you know, one of those, um...fancy ghosts."

He was rambling. About ghosts. Something was clearly wrong, but he didn't want me to know it. "No, I totally get it," I said, playing along. "And I know about fancy ghosts. Ever heard of the Wilis?"

"The what?"

So I started telling him about *Giselle*, not caring that now I was the one rambling about ghosts, because with each word, Jude looked more curious about what I was saying and less worried about whatever he'd been thinking about before I came out here.

"So this peasant girl, Giselle, falls in love with this guy who comes to her village, but she doesn't know he's actually a count named Albrecht who's only *pretending* to be a peasant. But Albrecht falls in love with Giselle, too. And then his family comes, and Giselle finds out who he really is, and that he's engaged to marry someone else. So she dies of a broken heart."

Jude frowned. "That's a bummer ending."

I laughed. "That's just Act One."

"Oh," Jude said, the corner of his mouth lifting. "Go on."

"In Act Two, Giselle becomes a Wili. They're ghosts of jilted girls who died before their wedding day. Myrtha is their leader, and whenever a man comes into the forest at night, they dance him to death. It's, like, badass and beautiful at the same time. Anyway, one night after Giselle dies, Albrecht comes into the forest to visit Giselle's grave."

"Uh-oh, I think I know where this is heading," Jude said. I smiled and wondered why I was going on and on about *Giselle*. Yes, it was distracting Jude from whatever was bothering him. But maybe I was also doing it for the same reason I'd listened to the Grand Pas de Deux in the car. To remember all the things I loved about ballet. To defend it against all the messy thoughts that had swirled around in my head tonight.

The ones I wasn't sure what to do with yet.

"So Giselle pleads with Myrtha not to kill him. It doesn't work, but Giselle stalls until the sun comes up and the Wilis have to go back to their graves. And Giselle is happy because she saved Albrecht, the man she still loved despite everything."

"Wow. Okay," Jude said, lost in thought. "What happens after? Is Giselle still a Wili, even though she went against Myrtha? What happens to Wilis who break the Wili code?"

I frowned a little. "I don't know. I never thought about it."

Jude nodded. Then his eyes wandered softly over my dress, my face. "You look awesome, by the way."

"Josie did my makeup," I said for some reason. "You look great, too," I added, because he did. Something about the rumpled formal wear was supremely cute. I cleared my throat and feigned interest in reading the plaques in the display case. "So, taking a break from..." I gestured behind me to the gym doors.

"Yeah." He opened his mouth to say more but then shook his head. I looked closer and saw that he had a little crease between his eyebrows and a kind of tension in his mouth that wasn't usually there. When he caught me staring, he said, "I'm fine. I was just... moping." He shook his head again, like no big deal.

I fiddled with my skirt. "Any reason?" *Your dad? Diya?*

"Nah. Just a weird night for me." He smiled, but not in his normal way. It was the first time I'd ever seen Jude Jeppson with a sad smile. It pinched my heart more than I expected it to. "Got any other sad ballets you can tell me about? I'm in the mood."

There were literally hundreds, but I'd had enough ballet for the evening. "I can't think of any. Sorry."

"That's okay," Jude said. "And hey, thanks for not telling me to just, like, shake it off and have fun. I mean, I know that's not you. But it would have been the easy thing to do."

I wondered how he knew that wasn't me. "Sure. When it happens, like when the sadness hits you, you can't really ignore it."

"Exactly." He pointed at me. "And you know, I always feel better after I let myself be sad. Like, if the sadness has a while to run around and stretch its legs, it's not so restless."

"I've never thought of sadness as having legs before."

"Oh, it definitely does. It's like a puppy, at least at first."

"Um. Sadness is like a puppy?"

"Less adorable, obviously. But yeah. It shits on everything, tears up valuable things, and whines constantly if you try to crate it for one second."

I thought about that night I realized I couldn't do pointe again. The gutting emptiness that took over and had been with me ever since. It had definitely torn up my relationship with Colleen. And shit on any optimistic thoughts my family floated by me. And I couldn't crate it for the life of me.

"I guess you're right," I said quietly. I ran my fingernail across the smooth glass of the display case. "So, was that what it was like for you? When your dad left?" I hoped I wasn't overstepping, but it felt easy to talk to him, out here in the quiet.

"Definitely." Jude looked down at his shiny coffee-colored shoes. "At first, I was still pretending everything would go back to normal. But then, at last year's Winter Formal, of all places, it hit me. I realized that, no matter what you do or say, you can't change other people. That no matter how much you love or care about them, in the end, they are who they are. And if they don't want what you want, you can't change that." Jude sighed and then looked up at the ceiling. "It was such a brutally depressing thought for me at the time. The puppy was born."

As I studied Jude's face, it softened and he turned his eyes to me. "Later, though, that same thought became kind of freeing. My dad made his choice and I could accept it or not. It helped me move on. And it helped me realize I didn't want things to go back to normal."

"You didn't?"

"My dad always wanted me to do the things *he* wanted me to do. Never liked that I was into musicals. Wanted me in lacrosse and soc-cer, like he played in school. And even when I did those things, he wasn't satisfied. Like, I'd come home from practice and make dragon pearl tea and take a bath, and he'd get all weird about it. Mumble things like 'That's not what men do.' Typical macho insecurity stuff. My mom's words. But true."

"That...sucks," I said. My dad had always supported me 100 percent. Then again, nobody thinks twice about a girl asking for ballet shoes and a tutu when they're little. But not every girl did ballet every day of the week, and asked for foot stretchers for Christmas, and canceled her tenth-birthday party because she wanted to go to class. And my dad never made me feel like I was weird for doing those things.

Also, something irrefutable in my heart told me that even if I'd quit ballet and taken up dirt bike racing or something, he would've been right there with me. He was the kind of dad who picked up tampons for Josie and me at the store without batting an eye. The opposite of macho insecurity. I couldn't imagine life without a dad like that.

"It did suck," Jude said. "But it helped me realize I was better off without him."

"So, once you realized that, the puppy disappeared?"

Jude scrunched his mouth to the side. "I don't think the puppy ever goes away. I think it just grows up. You know, you live with it for a while, and then you start training it and learning its ways, and eventually it doesn't need you as much anymore. Maybe it becomes an outdoor dog. You still have to feed it and give it exercise and pet it sometimes, when it comes back. But if you do all that, it'll let you live your life."

I let that sink in. I thought about what kind of dog my sadness was now. I crated her when I was around other people, but she escaped by accident a lot. Hence the jealousy bombs and middle fingers and the whole threatening-to-run-my-sister-over-with-a-car thing. If I was honest, though, the puppy didn't bite at me the same way it did before. I mean, I was at a school dance, and I wasn't freaking out. God, I'd recited the whole plot of *Giselle* without breaking down at the thought that I'd never dance it.

A strange warm feeling spread through my body. Maybe going to Winter Formal wasn't a way to fool my parents into thinking I was making progress. Maybe it meant that my puppy was growing up a little, leaving me alone for long enough to have fun at a neon-themed school dance.

Jude was still quiet. I sensed that he'd said all he wanted to about his dad. At least for now. So I threw out something less serious. "You haven't met Ferdinand, my friend Colleen's pit bull. He's nine and follows her everywhere, and she coddles the crap out of him. She makes him special dog treats. Like, she bakes them in the oven." It felt good to talk about Colleen like nothing had changed between us, to pretend for a moment at least.

"As she should," Jude said. His smile was less tinged with sadness this time, and I couldn't believe how happy that made me.

Maybe it was his close-to-normal smile, or turning our sadness to puppies, or the fact that we found ourselves alone together even though the whole school was ten feet away, but my mouth said something without my brain's permission.

"I'm excited to dance with you."

And then, there it was. The full, unadulterated Jude smile. Brighter than all the neon lights in the gym combined.

He didn't say anything back. He just kept smiling. As he did, his eyes roamed over my face, from my forehead to my lips, where they lingered for a second.

I suddenly worried that he hadn't understood what I meant. "Did you see the rehearsal schedule? For after break?"

"Yeah. I saw it." His eyes lifted to mine, and I was getting a little too caught up in them.

So I quickly added, "I won't dance you to death, I promise."

Jude raised his eyebrows slightly. Then he leaned forward, his mouth close to my ear. "Don't make promises you can't keep," he whispered. I couldn't say what that meant exactly, but it made my skin tingle and my heart thump.

The gym doors screeched open and Ethan, Harrison, and Celia leaned out. "Jude!" Celia yelled. "Last song!"

Ethan's eyes darted between Jude and me. I silently begged him not to say anything suggestive, anything that would make it weird. "Fred," he said sternly, blinking at Jude. Then he turned to me. "Cyd. Get your asses in here and dance."

"Aye, aye, Gene," Jude said. Then he held his hand out to me. I took it, and he led me back into the gym. We followed Ethan through the crowd to where Margot, Laney, and Ada were still dancing. A loud pop sounded overhead and silver confetti poured down on us. Margot opened her mouth and stuck out her tongue. I threw my head back and laughed. Jude looked over and started laughing, too.

Ethan must have taken a picture right at that moment, because a flash temporarily blurred everything out. Margot looked at him in exasperation and spent the rest of the song trying to grab his phone while he kept dancing out of her reach.

As I lay in bed that night, face scrubbed of Josie's makeup, I studied the picture Ethan had posted on Instagram. Margot's mouth wide open. Jude and I laughing beside her as confetti fell around us. Ethan's smiling face in the corner, which meant he'd stretched out his arm and ducked into the frame before taking the picture. That was rare. Ethan was hardly ever in the pictures he posted.

I studied my face. I looked...happy. I'd certainly felt happy, in that moment. It was something about being in that glowing room with people I didn't know at all a few months ago, but who were now my friends.

It was also something about the conversation I'd had with Jude. It was the kind of conversation that filled me up in the same way good art did, with ideas and images and moments I could keep in my head and play over and over again: Jude's smile going from sad to happy. Puppies growing up and going outside.

I stared at the picture until my eyes slipped shut.

CHAPTER FIFTEEN

I WAS STILL IN A SPARKLY MOOD the next morning, and the smell of Dad's chocolate chip pancakes didn't hurt. He always made special breakfasts when me, Josie, and Mom were all on winter break.

"Thanks," I said with my mouth full as Dad flipped another pancake onto my plate.

"You seem happy." Mom smiled cautiously over her mug of tea.

I shrugged. "First day of break."

"*And* she had a magical evening last night," Josie said, squeezing a generous glop of syrup onto her pancakes.

I froze midbite. "What?"

Josie wiped her fingers on her ratty snowman pajama pants and picked up her phone. After she tapped and scrolled, she turned the screen to me. It was the picture Ethan took. The one I'd stared at for an embarrassingly long time before falling asleep. I'd been so focused on the picture I hadn't seen the caption: *Winter Formal magic.*

I realized too late that my whole family was staring at me, probably wondering why I had a dopey smile on my face. I reached for the phone, but Josie held it away. Mom plucked it out of her hands and huddled over it with Dad, gushing about how great everyone looked. "Hey, it's Jude Jeppson!" Dad said, pointing with the spatula.

"It is!" Mom lifted up her glasses and held the picture closer to her face. "Such a handsome boy."

"Ugh, Mom." I reached over to take the picture from her, but she didn't move.

"What?" Mom's innocent expression was contradicted by the smile curving her lips. "Does he like you?"

"Are you his bae?" Dad chimed in. He loved using words he heard on TV to get a reaction from Josie and me. But Josie just said, "Good one, Dad," and they all cackled.

"No and no," I said, standing up, taking the phone, and putting it facedown on the table.

"You should invite them to Josie's show tonight," Mom said.

My stomach twisted, and even though I had half a pancake in front of me, I lost my appetite. I'd forgotten Josie's performance of *The Nutcracker* was tonight. "Um, I can't."

Mom gave me a look that said an explanation was required.

"Ethan's in Pittsburgh and Jude's in Indiana and Margot...has something tonight." I had no idea if Margot had something tonight. But I wasn't going to ask her to come. As much as she would distract me from potential jealousy bomb explosions, I didn't want her to see me on edge like that.

My phone buzzed and I grabbed it, hoping it would end the conversation. A photo of Colleen filled my screen. She was wearing a familiar white headpiece, and one of her eyes was scrunched closed. **Got a bobby pin in the eye. Wish you were here.**

She must have just finished "Waltz of the Snowflakes." KDBS used bits of white paper as snow, released from big bags above the stage. After the waltz was over, the crew swept up all the paper and put it back in the bags so it could be dropped again in the next performance. But they'd also sweep up dirt, dust, and anything else that had fallen onto the stage. So after a few performances, you'd inevitably get hit in the face with a bobby pin.

Looking at the picture, I felt the familiar pull in my heart, wishing I was there, too. But if I *were* there, I'd be changing into my Chinese Tea costume. And Colleen would be prepping for Arabian Coffee, not Dew Drop or Sugar Plum. I couldn't brush that aside anymore, or the uncomfortable feelings that came with it.

Josie finished her pancakes and put her dish in the sink with a clatter. "I'm gonna walk to Fiona's to finish our snow costumes," she said. "Her sister's driving us to the school later. You guys should get there at six forty-five." She glanced at me and then rushed upstairs.

I pushed my pancake around my plate. "Would it be terrible if I didn't go—"

"If you can go to Winter Formal, you can go see your sister dance, like she's seen you dance a hundred times," Mom said.

"My thoughts exactly," Dad added as he scrubbed some dishes.

I sighed. Case closed.

When I got into the backseat of the minivan at six thirty, I glanced at Jude's house. All the windows were dark, which made me feel a little hollow. He was going to be in Indiana visiting family all break. It was strange to think that he'd been right across the street from me for three years and I hadn't known. And that now, when he'd been gone for less than a day, I missed him.

I thought about texting him as Dad drove us to Hope Middle School, where Variations held their shows. We'd exchanged numbers after Winter Formal. I couldn't think of anything to say, at least nothing that would make sense in a text. And he hadn't texted me either, so...

I took deep breaths as we parked and I followed my parents into the auditorium. It had been ages since I was here. My winter and spring shows always overlapped with Josie's, and ran for longer, so I never had time to go. The last time I'd seen Josie dance, she was probably ten.

Mom put the peach-colored roses she'd brought under her seat, the paper crinkling and the scent wafting through the air. Mom and Dad used to bring roses to my shows, too. I rolled and unrolled the program as the lights went down and the first painfully familiar notes of *The Nutcracker* rang out.

The curtain opened to reveal six dilapidated bunk beds surrounding a table of knives. I rolled my eyes. Instead of setting the opening party scene in a nineteenth-century home, Variations set it in a dystopian boarding school/butcher shop. A techno beat, smashing glass, and a revving chain saw sounded underneath Tchaikovsky's score. The party guests leaped and gyrated and spun. There was some impressive flexibility, but nothing I saw grasped my heart the way ballet did. Not even close. Still, I clapped dutifully as each dance ended, counting down the numbers until the finale.

Josie was in a bunch of group dances, like the snow scene, where everyone wore long nail extensions on their fingers that made them look ghoulish. I could always pick her out, and not just because she was my sister. There was a musical quality to her dancing that I vaguely remembered from when we were younger, but of course it had evolved. Her movements were sharp and clean, but they always fit the emotions of the music. I checked the program and saw that she had a solo during the "Waltz of the Flowers" number—she was playing a "Rampaging Bumblebee." I rolled my eyes again.

Josie's *Nutcracker* was only one act, so before I knew it, Marie and the Nutcracker Prince were in the Land of Sweets. My mind wandered during the Spanish Hot Chocolate number, but it jolted to attention when the Chinese Tea music began. My body twitched, ready to launch into the entrechats and tiny, shuffling steps I knew so well. But what I was seeing onstage was totally different.

Three girls ran to the center, carrying in each hand a shiny green flower on a long stem. In unison, they flung their arms out, and the flowers morphed into thick, streaming ribbons. The dancers did swift turns, acrobatic jumps, and backbends, all while whipping their arms out in rhythmic movements, the ribbons making startling shapes in the air. It was mesmerizing. The ribbons seemed alive.

When the dance ended, thunderous applause echoed through the auditorium, and a strange feeling stirred in my stomach. It wasn't the jealousy bomb.

It was shame. Anger.

I was breathing so hard as the applause ended that I was afraid people would hear me. I ducked out of my seat and walked quickly up the aisle. In the lobby, I sat on the floor and flipped through the program until I came to a page labeled *A Note on the National Dances*, written by the head teacher, Yuna Lee.

> *My students and I have talked for years about the stereotypes in* The Nutcracker's *national dances. I was beyond proud when a few of them approached me, saying they wanted to make these dances more accurate, sensitive, and complex representations of dance forms around the world. I think advanced student Josie Keeler put it best when she said, "For hundreds of years,* The Nutcracker *has perpetuated narrow, racist views of different cultures. That's not how I want kids to see the world." Together, Variations students and teachers researched scores of stunning performances. With Angela Xie of the Philadelphia Chinese*

Dance Center, we learned a ribbon dance for the Chinese Tea variation . . .

I stopped reading and leaned my head against the wall.

I would always love ballet more than modern dance. Classical music more than noise music. I knew that with the same certainty I always had. But the Chinese Tea dance I'd just seen was so much better than the one I'd danced for years at my ballet school. And now, having seen what that dance could have been, all the possibilities Kira had never even considered, *I* had never considered . . .

I rubbed my face with my hands. Why hadn't I realized that the dance could be different? Why hadn't Kira? But it wasn't just me, and it wasn't just Kira. I thought about the multitude of *Nutcrackers* I'd seen onstage and on YouTube over the years. Lots of ballet companies—big and small, local and international—had similar Chinese Tea dances. Why hadn't *any* of us changed it?

The question felt much bigger than me all of a sudden, but still so personal. I mean, *I* had danced Chinese Tea all those years, *I* had perpetuated that narrow, racist view, and at the same time, thousands of other dancers all over the world were dancing it, too. Maybe it was easy for them to accept the roles they had, like I did. Maybe it was easy for dancers and teachers and choreographers and artistic directors to keep following tradition, ignoring who it hurt. Maybe, like me, they loved ballet so much, believed so deeply in its beauty, that they didn't see the ugly parts, or didn't want to.

The first strains of "Waltz of the Flowers" wafted through the auditorium doors. I was missing Josie's solo. Still, I couldn't move.

Josie had helped transform the dance into something better, and maybe if I had known what to say to Kira on cast list day last year, I could have changed the dance, too. But Variations was different from

KDBS. And besides, I was out of ballet. It was too late to change anything now.

As the cold linoleum seeped through my tights, a new kind of sadness gripped me. Different from the familiar pain of not being able to dance ballet, from missing all the things I'd once been able to do. Now I felt sadness over all the things I hadn't done, all the things I had ignored.

I sat there, absorbed in my thoughts, until I heard harps floating peacefully up and down the scale. The Grand Pas de Deux was about to begin. Something pulled me back into the darkened theater, down the aisle, and to my seat.

Onstage, a girl in a pink tutu and a boy in a scarlet coat danced ballet. Variations was doing the Grand Pas de Deux traditionally. No noise music, just Tchaikovsky. As the scales crescendoed, my body twitched again, aching to dance. Instead, I sat in the audience. Quiet tears poured down my face as I watched the dance I had once performed. The one I couldn't do anymore. The one my heart still loved, even as it broke all over again.

CHAPTER SIXTEEN

MY PARENTS WERE MIFFED at me for missing Josie's solo, but they were mostly over it by Christmas. Josie was not. She sat as far away from me as possible as we Skyped with Grandma Shiho in the afternoon before opening presents.

"What do you think Santa brought you?" Grandma asked, her wide smile deepening the wrinkles in her tanned skin.

"No fair," Josie said. "You're Santa and you already know." Grandma's gravelly laugh filled the room. We were her only grandchildren, so she spoiled us every Christmas. Over half the presents under the tree were from her.

"I think he brought us something you made," I said. Grandma was super crafty and always sent us her latest creations—puka shell necklaces or oil paintings or ceramics.

"Duh," Josie muttered, quietly enough so Grandma couldn't hear.

"I guess you'll just have to see," Grandma said. Over her shoulder, the window framed vivid green trees and bushes, a slow breeze wafting through them. I could practically feel the warmth. It was so different from the brown, leafless trees and white-gray sky outside our own window. "I have to get my gingersnaps from the oven. Love to you all."

"Miss you, Mommy," Mom said, blowing a kiss at the screen. I'd always thought it was sweet that Mom called Grandma Mommy. But this time, it almost made me tear up. Ever since Josie's *Nutcracker*, I'd felt super emotional.

After we said goodbye, Mom and Dad sorted all the presents and we dug in, starting with gifts to each other, like always. I watched Josie unwrap my present—I'd splurged on an eye shadow palette from Willa Hoang's new brand, hoping it would smooth things over.

"Thanks," Josie mumbled, not looking at me. She set it aside and flung a flat present at me.

I opened it and saw the Instagram picture Ethan had taken at Winter Formal enclosed in a silver frame with stars carved into it. I smiled. I'd looked at that picture every night before bed, so I knew every detail. But having a physical copy, in a frame and everything, made it more real somehow. "Oh, I— Thanks, Josie."

She shrugged. "Now maybe your room won't be so depressing."

I smiled at her, but she just rolled her eyes.

Next up were Mom and Dad's presents. The first was a yoga mat and outfit. The second was a Broadway songbook. "For next year's auditions!" Mom said when I opened it. The third was Princeton Review's *Best 385 Colleges*. There it was. I'd known the college talk was looming ever since my ballet plans dissolved.

"You don't have to look at it yet," Dad said. "But now you have it in case you want to flip through."

I knew Ethan had applied to a bunch of liberal arts schools in the area. And Jude to some of those, along with bigger in-state schools like Penn State and Pitt. Next year, Margot wanted to apply to schools in California and Alaska and other far-flung places. I still had no idea if I even wanted to go.

Later that night—after presents and dinner and *It's a Wonderful*

Life—I settled into my room. I put the yoga mat, Broadway song-book, and picture frame in a pile on my desk.

On my nightstand, my phone buzzed with a text from Colleen. It was a picture of Ferdinand in an elf hat. **Merry christmas, ali-oop. miss you.**

I wondered what Colleen had gotten for Christmas. Probably pit bull–themed T-shirts from her brothers and garnet jewelry from her parents. Maybe she got a new leotard for the ABT summer inten-sive audition, too. The Philadelphia one was on January eighteenth, she'd said. I wondered if I'd be talking to her by then. At times it felt possible. At others, not so much.

I stared at the text for a long time, hearing Colleen's voice as I read it again.

Mom pushed my door open with her foot, holding a mug in each hand. Hot chocolate for Josie and me. She set the mugs down on my nightstand and then wandered over to my desk, gazing at my new picture. She looked like she had when Margot came over, like her drowning daughter might have been thrown a life jacket after all.

"I'm sorry I missed Josie's solo," I said.

"Have you told her that?"

"No." Mom gave me a look. "She's been ignoring me," I said in my defense.

"Well, she probably thinks you've been ignoring her." Mom hes-itated slightly before sitting at the end of my bed. She used to sit there a lot before the injury. We'd talk about all kinds of things. Since the injury, though, I'd pretty much walled off my room.

Suddenly, a question from the back of my mind burst forward. "Do you ever miss Hawai'i so much you wish you never left?" I hadn't planned on asking her that, but lately, I'd wondered how other people felt about the things they'd lost.

Mom's eyebrows went up slightly, but then her face settled back into the thoughtful expression it always wore as she thought about a question. That was eternally Mom. Always a professor. Any question you asked got a serious answer.

"When I first got here, and I was so overwhelmed by the expectations of the new job, all I could remember were the good things I'd left behind." She tucked a piece of hair behind her ear. "My whole life was there. I felt awful for leaving it. And guilty for dragging your dad here. And a little bit like I didn't know who I was anymore."

I nodded at that last part, impressed she was able to say it out loud so easily.

"And hardly anyone here looked like me," Mom said, and smiled softly. "I knew there wouldn't be as many Japanese- or Asian-American people in central Pennsylvania as there were in Hawai'i, but my goodness. Knowing and seeing are two different things entirely. It was an adjustment."

"Was it hard?" I asked.

"Sometimes yes, and sometimes no," Mom said. "I was lucky enough to meet some amazing people here, and I love our neighborhood and my students and my colleagues. But things happened, and still happen. Like, remember at the grocery store when that guy asked me if I knew how to make 'Chinese beans,' and I said no, and then he kept complimenting me on my English?" Mom said, smirking.

"*Yes.*" Josie and I had rolled our eyes into the back of our heads at that white guy, complimenting my American-born English professor mom on her English. Things were different for Josie and me, I knew. Some people could tell right away we were biracial, and we got the "What are you?" question pretty frequently. Other times, people thought we were white. People made plenty of assumptions about us, for sure, but it was different.

When that guy saw my mom in the grocery store, he just saw her as one thing: "Asian." Not as a professor or an American citizen or even a Japanese-American, just "Asian." And to him, all Asians could make "Chinese beans" and couldn't speak English.

I thought again of the Chinese Tea dance, the view of Asian people it perpetuated.

"Did the Chinese Tea dance ever bother you?" I asked, running my fingers over the soft pilling on my comforter.

Mom nodded. "Of course. Part of me wanted you to be bothered by it, too. But another part of me didn't. You were so dedicated and so good. I didn't want anything to ruin that for you."

"Why didn't you say anything? To Kira?" It wasn't an accusatory question. I was just curious.

"I did. She thought I was being a stage mom. Apparently lots of parents complain about what role their kid has."

"This was different, though," I said, my voice coming out surprisingly loud.

Mom nodded sadly. "I know."

I dropped my head back onto my headboard. Kira had taught me so much about technique and artistry and strength. How to really hear a piece of music. How to tour jeté so it feels like you're flying. But I could admit now that she'd taught me bad things, too. How to feel small and inferior and powerless.

"When Kira let me dance Sugar Plum," I said quietly, projecting myself back onto the stage last December, feeling the silver crown on my head, "I felt like it was all okay. Like it erased everything else. I know that's not how it works, but in the moment, it felt that way." I took a long, slow breath. "But now..." I trailed off, unable to find the words.

Mom held my gaze a few moments longer. "You know, I'm glad you're thinking about this stuff. It's hard, but it's part of moving on."

Was that what I was doing? Moving on? Yeah, I was talking about ballet in ways I never had before. I'd had fun at Winter Formal. I felt all warm and glittery whenever I thought about my conversation with Jude. But part of me was still a mess. I still missed ballet desperately, even though it was far from the perfect thing I'd thought it was.

I didn't know what that meant about me.

Mom smiled warmly, and then, never forgetting my original question, went back to it. "Well, so, the longer we lived here, the more this place became ours. First mine and your dad's. And then our family's. Everything felt so different at first, but then, after all the confusion and change, I found my footing again."

I must have looked skeptical, because Mom sighed. "If I were inclined to be literary about it, I'd say it was like all the pieces of myself had shaken up and flown in different directions, flipping and spinning and rearranging themselves. Like confetti. But in the end, after the whirlwind, all the pieces were still there. Every single one. Just in different places."

The words pulled a surprising memory from my head, one I hadn't thought about in a long time. When we were fourteen, Colleen and I became obsessed with learning the tour en l'air, a step that meant "turn in the air." You started with an unassuming plié, but then you pushed straight up into the air and revolved once, twice, or even three times before coming back down and landing in plié again. It was usually a boy's step, which was why Kira never taught us. But together, Colleen and I studied online tutorials and critiqued each other's form until we could do it.

The first time I did a double tour en l'air, the only thing I felt was my own body revolving through space. And when I came down again into plié, I was shocked. I'd done it. I'd done it without Kira. I remembered staring at my reflection in the mirror afterward. I looked the same, but inside, I felt different. Like all my pieces had settled back in different places, rearranged.

After a bit, Mom stood up, pointing to the other mug on my nightstand. "Will you bring that to Josie?"

"Sure," I said, giving Mom a small smile as she left my room. A few minutes later, I dragged myself from under my covers. When I stood up, my leg felt stiff, so I rolled my ankle a few times, hearing it crackle. I picked up Josie's mug and headed down the hall to her room. Music radiated from her laptop—a hypnotic piano melody. Her door was slightly open, so I peeked inside.

Josie was choreographing, trying out different combinations and scribbling in a notebook lying open on her bed. The movements surprised me. I'd assumed they'd be like her. Tough and bold and uncompromising. There were elements of that, but there was also one part where she turned her palms to the ceiling and raised her arms, a radiant smile on her face. And then the next second, she made fists and tucked her arms in while rounding her back and scowling. The contrast was so sudden I almost gasped.

That was what she meant when she explained *Strange Harmonies* to me. Contrasts and oppositions in the world. Joy and anger. Love and hate. Beauty and ugliness.

Eventually, I backed up a few steps and cleared my throat. The music cut off, and Josie's face appeared at the crack in the door.

I held up the hot chocolate. "From Mom."

Josie took it, blinking at me like she expected something else. Like an apology for missing her solo. When I didn't say anything, she shut the door. The music started up again, filling the hallway.

When I closed the door to my room and sat back down on my bed, it was strangely silent, like I was more shut off from the rest of the world than usual. For the first time, it didn't feel like a relief.

I stood up and spread the purple yoga mat out beside my bed, put the Broadway songbook on top of my bookshelf, and carefully situated the Winter Formal picture on my nightstand, my fingers lingering on the silver frame.

I stepped back to survey my work. They were small changes, but they made my room look different. Like someone actually lived in it again.

JANUARY

CHAPTER SEVENTEEN

IN FIVE MINUTES, the first Vamp rehearsal would start.

Sitting in the auditorium, I watched Mrs. Sorenson noodle around on the piano, and Ms. Langford mark choreography onstage. Jude wasn't here yet. At first, I assumed I was nervous because I'd be learning my big dance number—the role I'd been chosen for. But the more I kept glancing at the doors, waiting for Jude to walk in, the more I had to admit it: I was nervous about him.

Over the rest of break, I'd looked at that picture from Winter Formal every night before falling asleep. It made me want to do stupid things. Like bust into Jude's house in the middle of the night so we could talk in the quiet, like we had outside the gym. Since he was in Indiana, my home invasion plans stayed safely imaginary.

But now I worried that when he saw me, he'd be able to tell how much I'd thought about him. I fidgeted with my new yoga tank top. I was wearing it with black dance shorts and tan tights. Ms. Langford had asked me not to wear pants because "your legs are the focal point of this whole number, and I need to see what I can do with them."

Maybe I was nervous about that, too.

The doors finally opened, and Jude walked in. "Hey!" he called, smiling as he made his way down the aisle.

"Hey," I repeated.

"How was your break?" He sat down next to me. "Get anything good for Christmas?"

"Oh, yeah. Princeton Review's *Best 385 Colleges*."

He gasped. "I got *1001 Things Every College Student Needs to Know!*"

"That's a lot of things you need to know."

"I should start reading it now. Otherwise, I'll only know like seven hundred things when I get to college, and then who knows what will happen."

"You'll probably die."

"I'll *definitely* die."

I smiled, relieved. This wasn't so awkward. But then Jude reached into his backpack and pulled out a package wrapped in red paper. "I have a present for you."

"Oh..." Shit. We were at the present-exchanging level?

"It's no big deal," he said, laughing a little, which made me wonder how horrified I looked. "I had a lot of downtime in Indiana, so I figured I'd make stuff for people."

I tore it open and a soft chunky-knit leg warmer slipped onto my lap. The pattern was really pretty, but it was the color that made my eyes go wide. Lavender. The exact shade of my Winter Formal dress. I ran my fingers over the soft yarn, thinking of that night—the dancing, our conversation outside the gym, the way he'd looked at me.

"I—uh—it's...thank you," I stammered.

Jude nodded, his smile fading. "I hope it's not overstepping. It's just, you said it was hard to loosen your leg up and keep it from being stiff? So I thought...maybe this could help?"

172

I'd tried to delete that whole scar interaction from my brain, but Jude had remembered. And he'd made me a really thoughtful gift. "No, it's great. It's perfect." I slipped it on. It was soft and really, really warm. I flexed and rolled my ankle a few times, savoring the heat radiating up my leg.

When I looked at Jude, he was staring at the leg warmer, a small smile spreading across his mouth.

"Alina!" Ms. Langford waved me onto the stage. Mrs. Sorenson stopped tinkering on the piano, and an odd silence fell over the auditorium. I glanced back at Jude as I stood. He gave me an awkward double thumbs-up. I did something between a wave and a salute. Good God.

Ms. Langford grabbed a bowler hat from the piano, pulled a chair out into the middle of the stage, and gestured for me to sit on it. "Now, extend your right leg out in front of you, and point your foot." When I did, Ms. Langford hung the hat off the toe of my jazz shoe.

"Now keep your leg straight and lift it up slowly, until the hat is pointing to the ceiling." I had no trouble extending my leg all the way up. Ms. Langford shook her head and told me to try it again. I did it a few more times, but she wasn't satisfied.

"The goal of this movement isn't to get your leg up high. It's to seduce someone. To lure them in. Jude!" Ms. Langford waved him over. She directed him to kneel with his face about six inches from my ankle. "All I need you to do is look at her leg." Jude's eyes flicked to mine before he did as he was told. Oh, God. Was he thinking about my scars? He couldn't see them now under the leg warmer and tights, but he knew they were there.

Ms. Langford rasped out a laugh and smacked Jude on the back. "I mean really *look* at it. You're *hypnotized*. Convey that."

Jude tried again. He *was* picturing the scars. I felt sweaty and shaky and I was ready to bolt when Ms. Langford gestured for Jude to step aside. "Allow me," she said.

Mrs. Sorenson sighed and looked pointedly at the clock. Ms. Langford ignored her, kneeling where Jude had been and proceeding to bug her eyes out and pant like a dog. It was so weird I couldn't help but laugh. Jude laughed, too, and I realized that was why she did it. To loosen us up.

Ms. Langford gestured for Jude to take his place again. "It shouldn't be that over-the-top. But I need to feel *something* from the look. Some *desire*. Think you can do that?"

"Uh...yeah. I— Sure. Yeah." Jude nodded. As he got back into his kneeling position, he took a deep breath. Then he looked. Slowly. Ankle, knee, thigh, and finally, up to my face. His eyes did look...desiring.

He was good at this. My whole body felt warm as I raised my leg up to the ceiling, knowing his eyes would follow, knowing *he* would follow, leaning in, closer, closer...

"Yes!" Ms. Langford yelled. Jude and I both jumped. Ms. Langford shot a triumphant look at Mrs. Sorenson. "See? Sometimes you gotta take the time to inject some *life* into these kids."

"Duly noted," Mrs. Sorenson said. "But there's a regional debate competition today, and we only have the auditorium for another forty-five minutes."

As they bickered, I quickly dabbed my wrist over my forehead. I hadn't thought I'd be sweating this early in the rehearsal.

Next, Ms. Langford guided us through the first part of the dance, which involved zero touching. I did a series of slinky, sexy moves around Jude, and he was supposed to resist them. "This is buildup!" she yelled over the piano as we ran through the first few eight counts for the billionth time. "There's something between you. An electrical force. *Feel* it."

I definitely felt the force, and I was *over* it. I wanted to touch. I wanted Jude's hands to lift me, or dip me, or whatever. My brain wasn't even trying to rationalize it. I tried to focus on Ms. Langford's corrections, but I was failing miserably. My movements got loose and sloppy every time I got near Jude.

"All right, enough, enough!" Ms. Langford yelled as we finished a run-through. I braced myself for a lecture. I'd let my personal life interfere with my dancing. Kira always told us to "leave it at the door" whenever we came into the studio. Meaning, whatever stresses or distractions or desires you had in your life should not work their way into your dancing. I used to be pretty good at that. Apparently I wasn't anymore.

"Za-zow!" Ms. Langford yelled. "I felt that! The beautiful dynamite!" She clapped Jude and me on the shoulders. "I wanted to push you two together by the end, even though it would cause an explosion!"

Jude laughed nervously, but I was confused. Ms. Langford said she'd felt beautiful dynamite. But I hadn't left my desires at the door—was that a good thing?

"We're almost out of time," Ms. Langford said, "but I'll teach you the first big lift before you go. It's the transition into the second part of the dance, which is all about contact. I want you to have a sense of what that'll be like."

I knew I liked Ms. Langford.

She had us go back to the end of what we learned: me standing a few feet away from Jude, preening my nails while swaying my hips back and forth. "Now, Jude, grab her hand, but Alina, you stay facing away." Jude's hand was warm and a little sweaty.

"Jude, when you pull her in, pull both in *and* up, so that you spin her around and lift her off the ground in one motion. Alina."

Ms. Langford turned to me. "You want to end up like this." She demonstrated the position, which was one arm wrapped around Jude's neck, the other extended behind her, her legs bent into V shapes.

"We'll go without music first." Ms. Langford stepped aside.

I got into position a few feet away from Jude, back turned. I dropped my arm down delicately and a moment later felt a forceful pull, and suddenly I was off my feet, whooshing around in the air until I stopped abruptly, face-to-face with Jude.

He'd pulled me in and up so hard that by the time our bodies met, he was leaning back so much I was practically on top of him. But I didn't feel unsteady. His arm, wrapped tightly around my waist, felt like it could hold me there for days. His swift heartbeat reverberated in my chest as we gazed at each other.

Well? his eyes seemed to say, a little nervous, a little hopeful. *What do you think?*

A movement in the corner of my eye distracted me—it was Mrs. Sorenson, doing a shimmy at the piano and raising her eyebrows up and down at Ms. Langford, who was fanning herself theatrically with both hands.

"The chemistry!" Ms. Langford yelled, doing a little jig.

"Fantabulous!" Mrs. Sorenson clapped.

Teacher hormones. Nothing kills the mood faster. Jude lowered me carefully to the floor. He chuckled at Mrs. Sorenson and Ms. Langford acting like giddy teenagers. I joined in, but all I could think about was his arm around my waist, and how the parts of me he touched still felt warm.

❧

"You okay?" Jude asked. As we walked out of school together, it was like he'd become a magnet. My stride kept veering closer to him until we'd bump arms and I'd startle, moving away and mumbling an apology.

"Of course, why not? I mean, why wouldn't I be?" I picked up the pace, my boots rapping against the floor. I'd stopped in the bathroom to change back into my normal clothes. I'd been both excited and annoyed to find Jude waiting for me in the hallway.

"Your guess is as good as mine," he said.

Oh, no. I could hear the smugness in his voice. When I glanced back at him, it was just as I suspected. Man, a guy does *one* good lift and suddenly thinks he's a big deal.

"Cockiness is not a good look on you," I said, shoving the door to the parking lot open and walking through without holding it.

Jude caught it with his elbow and was beside me again in a second. "Oh, I know. Arrogance kills elegance, right?"

I remembered saying that to him after callbacks. But I was too frazzled, and angry that I was frazzled, to acknowledge that we had an inside joke. "What is that supposed to mean?" I said.

"Wait, really?" Jude's smile faltered.

I slowed down finally, pulling my hat out of my coat pocket and putting it on. "Oh, right. I said that. To you."

We stopped next to Jude's car. "Yup," he said, his breath making a white cloud in front of his face. He looked a lot less confident now. It was what I had wanted, but somehow it didn't feel like a victory. I tugged my hat lower so it covered more of my ears. Jude was wearing the bomber jacket with the patches again, which was way too thin to be warm enough, along with his wonky green gloves. The whole ensemble, like everything about him right now, was both cute and annoying.

"Anyway, we now know you have the power to make middle-aged white women swoon, so use it responsibly."

Jude tilted his head to the side and looked at me curiously. "What about...," he started, taking a step toward me.

My heartbeat kicked up the tempo. Avert. Distract. That was what I should do. Because as much as I'd thought about Jude over the break, and as much as I'd nearly lost it over touching him a few minutes ago, I wasn't ready for anything real. What if I ruined it? Then he'd feel abandoned. Again. What if *he* ruined it? Then I'd feel rejected. Again. Could we handle that right now?

"What about what?" I instantly wished I could snatch the words right out of the frigid air, where they hung between us.

Jude's eyes were doing that roaming thing again. Forehead, cheeks, mouth. Then he abruptly stepped back. "Just...um, do you want to go to Fly Zone?"

It took me a moment to regroup. "The...trampoline place? Where you work?"

"Yeah, I start in an hour, but we can jump before my shift starts." The tips of his ears went red, and I didn't think it was from the cold.

"I..."

"It looks silly, but it's pretty therapeutic. Gets all your excess energy out, trust me." He rubbed his gloved hands together and bounced on the balls of his feet, not looking directly at me.

For some reason, jumping off whatever excess energy I was currently experiencing seemed like a good idea. A wise idea. The only idea. "Meet you there," I called over my shoulder as I speed-walked to my car.

CHAPTER EIGHTEEN

FLY ZONE WAS MORE CROWDED than I thought it would be on a Monday at five o'clock. Parents sat at plastic tables by the concessions stand with laptops and tired eyes, sipping coffee out of paper cups. How they were able to tune out the random shrieks of joy emanating from the trampolines only a few feet away, I didn't know.

Jude led me to the back room, where I stored my boots and bag in his employee locker, and he handed me a pair of grippy orange trampoline socks. As I followed him to the massive trampoline area, I saw a row of photographs lining the walls. I stopped short at one of a guy doing a somersault in midair, his mouth stretched into a smile I'd recognize anywhere, even upside down. "Oh my God."

Jude spun around, following my gaze to the photo. "Yeah, that's a requirement. You can't work here and not know how to do a full twisting back somersault."

"Oh, sure. I think that's a requirement in most workplaces."

Jude laughed, and the air around us suddenly felt less pressurized. Out on the trampoline floor, we made our way to the "15-and-up Section." The empty space was divided into about thirty connected six-foot-long rectangles of trampoline. The rules said one person per rectangle, so we each had our own personal jumping area and could hop from square to square. My leg, where the metal was, felt a jolt each time I hit the trampoline and was propelled upward, but I was still able to get some decent height.

It was hard not to smile as I boinged up and down, watching Jude do the same, his hair lifting and flopping.

"Show me your full twisting back somersault!" I yelled at Jude, who was happy to oblige.

After he did a few more tricks, he shouted: "You can't tell me you don't want to do some bouncy ballet right now."

I rolled my eyes but thought of an idea. A tour en l'air had to feel amazing on a trampoline. I put my arms in third position, and as I jumped, I used my open arm to spin. The height let me rotate more than I ever had on solid ground. When I landed, I couldn't stop laughing.

Without thinking, I jumped over to the rectangle in the back corner. I took a breath and then did grands jetés, springing from one rectangle to the next.

God, I'd missed this flying feeling.

Eventually, we looked at the clock and realized Jude's shift started in ten minutes. As we walked back to the employee room, the floor had never felt weirder. "Trampoline legs," Jude explained as he opened his locker and handed me my boots and bag.

"Ah," I said, out of breath. I pulled out my phone and saw a text pop up from Colleen.

Jude looked at his phone, too. "Oops, got a voice mail. One sec." I nodded and sat down on the bench to put my boots on and read the message.

Cast list posted for Giselle. Guess the Giselles.

I waited, nervous. Then she followed up with three blond-girl emojis. I deflated. Spencer. Juliet. And Camden, I found out in the next text, one of the new girls who'd transferred in this year. They would do the lead role on alternating nights.

Got Myrtha tho. ☺

Myrtha was an excellent role. Leader of the Wilis, and second only to Giselle. But it *was* second to Giselle. And Colleen deserved to be first.

Before I could stop myself, my thumbs hit the buttons and I felt a slight release of inner pressure. I was finally saying something back, and it was something true. Something I'd known was true for a long time, even before I let myself realize it.

You deserve Giselle. It isn't fair. It was never fair.

I hesitated over the Send button. Would this make things worse for Colleen? I was out of that world now, and maybe that was why I was beginning to see its ugliness. She was still in it. I couldn't force my anger onto her.

Because even if Colleen did get angry about it, Kira would just tell her the same thing she'd told us before. Ballet dancers accept the roles they're given and make them beautiful. Colleen would make Myrtha beautiful. I knew that at least.

I erased the message, wondering if Colleen could see the three blinking dots telling her I was typing, that I at least wanted to respond. I hoped that was enough for now. I knew it wasn't.

I put my phone down and looked up, seeing Jude with his phone still to his ear, a slight frown on his face. He finally lowered it and hung up. "Huh," he said.

"Everything okay?"

"Yeah, um..." He grabbed a blindingly bright orange Fly Zone T-shirt from his locker and pulled it on over his gray one. Then he hung a whistle around his neck and clipped a walkie-talkie into his pocket. "My dad called and left a message. He's back in town for a work thing for a couple of months. He said he wants to see me."

"Geez. Are you going to?"

"No," he said. I watched him delete the voice mail from his phone.

I was surprised at how sure he was. His dad sounded like a mess, but he was still his dad. "Have you seen him at all since he left?"

"Nope. I talked to him on the phone a few times, but then I stopped answering." I sensed he had more on his mind, so I put my bag on the floor, clearing space on the bench beside me. He sat down, leaning over so his elbows rested on his thighs.

"It's just, one of the ways I'm getting over the whole thing is realizing how I'm better off. Like, making peace with the ways my dad was wrong, and feeling now like I'm..." He paused, searching for words.

"Freer," I said, remembering what he'd told me at Winter Formal. "Than you were before."

"Yeah. But if I went to lunch with him, I don't know. Maybe I'd start remembering the good things about him. He's funny and charismatic as hell and tells good stories...it's probably why my mom fell for him in the first place. And once when I was little, I watched *Poltergeist* even though I wasn't allowed, and I got so scared I couldn't sleep, so he stayed up for hours, reading me *The Hobbit* until I fell asleep." Jude winced a little at the memory. "It would make the whole thing harder, if I remember the good stuff along with the bad. Do you get what I mean?"

I did. It sounded practical. Wise. "I do, except I'm the opposite way."

"How so?" Jude sat up, facing me.

"It's a long story, never mind." I wanted to keep talking about his dad. "So do you think—"

"Wait," Jude interrupted. "Tell me."

I hesitated. But his kind hazel eyes didn't move from mine, and after a few seconds, the words came up. "With ballet, I have no problem remembering the good. It's all I *want* to remember. I devoted my life to ballet, and if it's this good, beautiful thing, then it makes sense that I gave my life to it and feel broken now that I can't do it anymore." I paused for a second, gathering my thoughts.

"But if I remember the bad parts—like the fact that these two white girls in my class always got picked for the lead roles over me and Colleen, and the fact that, even outside of KDBS, lots of ballet teachers and companies choose to follow problematic traditions instead of changing them..." I bit my lip, thinking about *The Nutcracker*, about how hard it was to believe that Kira's casting decisions were fair, especially after Colleen's text about *Giselle*. "If I remember those parts, it's like I made a mistake by letting ballet be such a big part of who I am. Like I shouldn't feel so broken about losing it because it wasn't so beautiful or good. Maybe I'm better off without it. But that doesn't feel true, either."

I inhaled and held the breath for a moment before letting it out.

"Maybe because..." Jude paused. "Because you lost something you loved. Things can have a lot of flaws and you can still love them, even if you feel like you shouldn't? Maybe?"

"Maybe." Maybe ballet was like beautiful dynamite. Stunning and dangerous at the same time, so you couldn't love it simply. You had to figure out how to handle it. How to love the beautiful parts and defuse the dangerous ones. The problem was, I didn't know how I was supposed to do that. Especially when I wasn't in that world anymore.

Jude and I sat together for a while, the muffled sounds of the trampoliners just outside the door. Somehow, like in the lobby at

Winter Formal, Jude filled the strangest settings with the kind of peace that made me feel like I could talk about anything.

"I didn't realize that, about ballet," he said after a while. "I'm sorry. It sucks when something you love has such backward ideas about certain things."

"Yeah," I said, remembering Jude saying his dad wanted him to do "manly" stuff like sports instead of the musical. I guess it was hard for some people to see beyond what they thought someone should be. A ballerina. A boy.

"You said before that your dad didn't like you doing the musical. And Margot said you weren't in it last year."

Jude nodded. "Even after he left, I still heard his voice in my head. And last year part of me thought maybe he was right. Maybe I shouldn't do it. It was so weird because I *knew* I didn't believe that. And I *knew* that year would suck without the musical. And it did." He shook his head. "But that voice...I guess I'd heard it so often it got inside me."

I mulled that over, wondering how much of Kira's voice was still inside me.

Jude looked at the clock. It was a few minutes after his shift was supposed to start. We stood up slowly. "Well, if you ever want to talk, about your dad or whatever, you can text me," I said. "Or, you know, we could just talk, like we're doing now. Well, not...we don't have to be at Fly Zone. You know what I mean." As I rambled, Jude smiled softly.

"I do. I really like talking to you."

"I really like talking to you, too."

He took a breath, like he wanted to say something else. But instead, he leaned closer. His eyes bored into mine—intense, inquisitive. I felt myself leaning in, too.

Until the loud crackle of the walkie-talkie startled us both. "Jude Jeppson, report to the Dodgeball Zone. Over."

Jude fumbled with the walkie-talkie and brought it to his mouth. "On my way," he said. Then he hesitated. "Over and out," he added quietly.

I smiled, trying to hide how breathless I was, and slung my bag over my shoulder.

"See you tomorrow? At rehearsal?" Jude said as we walked to the door.

When I looked back at him, I knew that from now on, things would be different. With the dancing and the lift and the glimpses of each other's beautiful, backward things and whatever had happened just now, something had shifted between us for good. Or bad. I didn't know which it would turn out to be.

Despite that, I smiled. "See you tomorrow."

CHAPTER NINETEEN

OPENING NIGHT WAS ONLY seven weeks away, which meant rehearsals ramped up. Mrs. Sorenson blocked scenes with the whole cast, shouting and gesturing maniacally. Ms. Langford named me official dance captain, which meant I had to run through all the routines with the chorus, so I hardly had any downtime.

Jude and I were never alone, which was frustrating. I mean, we talked. We laughed. We even had another Vamp rehearsal to learn the rest of the dance, which, as Ms. Langford said, was all about contact. One move involved Jude catching my leg by his ear, then dipping me low. When Jude gripped my leg, clutching the leg warmer he'd made me, it somehow felt more intimate than if he had touched my skin. And every time I came back up, stopping six inches away from his face, he always had this look. This lips-parted, brows-wrinkled, pupils-dilated look.

Like he was a second away from closing the distance between us. And if Ms. Langford and Mrs. Sorenson hadn't been a foot away, adjusting and commenting, I would have done it for him.

By Friday night, it had been almost two weeks since Fly Zone, and I had a permanent feeling of exasperation lodged in my stomach. Tomorrow morning, I was meeting Jude, Margot, and Ethan for breakfast at Waffle Country before the first Saturday rehearsal, but that wasn't enough. So I grabbed my phone to text Jude.

Need a ride to breakfast and rehearsal tomorrow? I typed, leaning against my headboard.

That's ok, I have to stay til 2 and don't want to hold you up. The knot in my stomach tightened. Then the blinking dots appeared. **Are you coming to the rink?**

Right. A bunch of musical people were going to the Galleria ice rink after rehearsal. I thought about it for a second. **Yeah. You?**

Good. Yeah I'm going.

Cool. See you at breakfast.

Well. That was probably the most pathetic series of text messages ever. I tossed my phone onto my bed and my mind drifted somewhere unpleasant.

This was kind of a pattern, wasn't it? Jude and I would have some moment together. Something that etched itself into my brain. The scars. Winter Formal. The lift. Fly Zone. Then one of us would hit the brakes. I'd avoided him after the scar thing. He'd literally stepped away from me in the parking lot after the first Vamp rehearsal, when we'd been standing so close.

The next morning, I tried to put it out of my mind as I settled into a Waffle Country booth and inhaled the sweet smell of syrup. A minute later, Ethan and Margot walked in. Good. They'd distract me from my Jude-obsessed brain.

"Mrs. Sorenson said you and Jude are, and I quote, 'hot stuff,' " Ethan said as he sat across from me. "Care to comment?"

Never mind.

"When did she say that?" I said, opening a menu and pretending to be captivated by Waffle Country's Bangin' Breakfast Specials. "At choir practice? Weird."

"Note that she did not deny the original statement," Ethan said as Margot slid in beside him.

"Nobody's noting that," she said, dragging off her trapper hat.

"It was not at choir practice," Ethan said. "She was talking to Mrs. Tipman about musical stuff when I was passing by the teachers' lounge. You're a topic of conversation in the *teachers' lounge*, Alina. That's huge. They could talk about anything in there, but they were talking about you and Jude."

"Maybe Mrs. Sorenson and Ms. Langford are going through, like, a second puberty," Margot said. "Maybe that happens when you're middle-aged, and you get all hormonal again."

"Margot—" Ethan said, looking irritated.

"Once is bad enough. I know I'm supposed to be at the end of it, but the other day I saw a commercial for lipstick, and all I could think was 'penis.' I don't even—"

"Good lord, Margot! What's *wrong* with you?" Ethan snapped. "Alina and I were talking about the Vamp rehearsal."

"No, you were *trying* to talk about the Vamp rehearsal, but Alina clearly doesn't want to. And aren't you always going on about how you don't gossip, blah, blah, blah?" Margot closed her menu with a smug smile.

Ethan threw me a shrewd look. "It's not gossip, it's *information*." Ugh. Why did I say things people could throw back in my face later?

Ethan sighed and put a hand out in front of him, like a truce. "Look, I'll just say one thing and then I'll drop it, okay? As you know, Jude's been through a lot lately, and—"

"So has Alina," Margot jumped in.

"That's what I was going to say, Interrupter." Ethan rolled his eyes. "Jude's been through a lot lately, and so have you. It's safe to say that the fear of being hurt again is high. Maybe that's the reason all these secret talks and hot dance rehearsals haven't produced Eagle View's most *elegant* couple yet?"

"Shhhh!" I frantically looked around to see if Jude had come in.

"Oh my God!" Ethan pointed at me. "I've never seen you this dorky!" He turned to Margot. "Have you?"

She looked at me apologetically before shaking her head.

Ethan leaned back triumphantly. "Now I definitely know something's going on."

"I don't know if anything is. Really," I said quietly. Sure, what Ethan said would explain why we'd get close and then back away. *If* Jude actually liked me. But maybe he was just a good person who saw a sad person and wanted to help. Maybe his stepping back meant he just wasn't interested. "He might not—"

"He doesn't not," Ethan said, looking at me seriously.

Wait. So, he did? Coming from Jude's best friend, that meant something.

"He can't not," Margot added, nudging my leg under the table with her boot.

"And I'm not gossiping, because I'm not telling you anything you shouldn't already know. I'm stating an objective truth," Ethan said, running a hand through his curls.

"Not gossip. Very objective," Margot repeated.

"What's very objective?" Jude appeared at the booth.

"Uh...," I said eloquently.

"Puberty stories," Margot broke in. "I was telling my puberty stories, and Ethan said they were very objectively gross."

Jude gave us a skeptical look before taking off his bomber jacket and sliding into the booth. I scooted all the way to the wall so our arms wouldn't touch. The waiter came and I took the time to regroup. As we waited for our food, Laney and Ada walked in. Apparently,

Waffle Country was a super-popular breakfast spot before Saturday rehearsals. "You guys going to the rink tonight?" Laney asked.

"Fred will be there." Ethan pointed to Jude.

"Gene, too," Jude said.

"*Stop.*" Margot groaned. Jude and Ethan high-fived as Laney and Ada went to join a couple of other girls from the chorus a few booths away.

"Why do we have to go *there?*" Margot said. "I'm happy I'm not friends with Izzy anymore, but I'd still rather not return to the scene of the ice proposal."

Right. Margot and Izzy's blowout happened at the ice rink.

"Screw Izzy," Ethan said. "Create new ice rink memories with your infinitely cooler musical friends."

Jude nodded. "And if Izzy's there, we'll be like the Wilis and dance her to death." He wiggled his eyebrows at me. Ethan and Margot shared a knowing look.

"Uh-huh," I said, a bit too loudly.

Margot gave us a small, grateful smile. "All right, fine. But no bailing!" She locked eyes with me on the last part. We all swore to show up. Then, as Ethan told us about his "Make 'Em Laugh" choreography, a movement caught the corner of my eye.

It was Diya. She was sitting, alone as always, in a small booth in the back corner. She was staring at a thick packet of paper in front of her, tracing her finger over the top page. Then she shook her head suddenly, like she was coming out of a daydream. She sat up straighter and started doing a series of just-perceptible movements—tilting her head slightly to the left, then arching her back a little, then looking down over her right shoulder. She repeated the pattern a few times before finally stopping to take a bite of waffles.

Margot followed my gaze. "Never seen Robobitch here before," she said. I'd wondered if having rehearsals together would change Margot's opinion of Diya, but it hadn't. I glanced at Jude to see his reaction, but he was stirring his water around with a straw, watching the ice swirl. "God, she's so in her own world," Margot went on. "Like, everyone's here, she could sit with someone, but she's too good for us."

Diya probably didn't want to sit with people who called her Robobitch, but I kept my mouth shut.

"What's she like in 'Good Morning' rehearsals, by the way?" Margot asked, eyes darting between Ethan and Jude. "Good Morning" was the big tap number the three of them did together.

"Robobitch-tastic. Robobitch-errific," Ethan said.

I looked at Jude again, waiting for him to say something. He was the one who knew her best, right? But he kept quiet, a crease forming between his eyebrows. I rolled my neck out. Why did I care so much? Margot and Ethan and Jude were my friends. Diya was not. I hardly knew her.

I got the sudden urge to text Colleen about all this, but of course I couldn't. Plus, I hadn't heard from her since Fly Zone. Eleven days ago. The longest she'd gone without texting. I had an awful feeling I kept trying to ignore, a hollowness in my stomach telling me I'd finally lost her for good.

I couldn't lose these new friends, too. So I ignored the uneasy feeling and tried to block Diya from my mind. It got easier when our food came, and Jude's elbow brushed against mine, and he let it stay there for a few seconds before taking it away.

$\sim$

Mrs. Sorenson made it clear that Saturday-morning rehearsals meant things were getting real. "It is January eighteenth, people! Opening night will be here before we know it, and we still have a lot to do," she said, her heels clicking sharply as she paced across the stage.

Today we were blocking a scene near the beginning of the show, when Don Lockwood meets Kathy Selden for the first time. Don and Kathy exchange banter as they sit on a bench, and the chorus needed to mill around convincingly in the background, like we were regular people out for a night on the town.

Jude and Diya stood by the prop bench at one corner of the stage, and Mrs. Sorenson split the rest of us up into groups so she could place us in different locations in the background. Margot and Ethan weren't in this scene, so they were working in the choir room with Ms. Langford.

Since I was standing with Laney and Ada, Mrs. Sorenson grouped us together and told us to walk slowly from one end of the stage to the other. "You're three tourists in Hollywood. You're dazzled by everything. Got it?" Mrs. Sorenson moved on to the next group.

Laney smiled sadly while watching Mrs. Sorenson direct Harrison to pretend he was in a newsstand, selling papers. "Harrison will be so disillusioned with the world in his forties that he'll never read any newspapers. He'll just keep complaining about how there's no good art anymore."

"Have any of your Love Realism relationships turned out happy?" I asked, half listening, half watching Diya take her place on the bench.

"Of course not," Laney said. "That's why it's called Love *Realism*. I used to get a little carried away with my crushes." Ada nodded emphatically. "I'd sit around fantasizing about some guy who didn't really exist. This way, I look for the imperfections underneath all the hotness, and then I'm less likely to embarrass myself around them."

I was still pretty sure that Harrison liked Ethan, but I wasn't going to say anything. I didn't want Laney to get hurt, but it was hard to tell if she actually liked Harrison, or if it was all for the game. Still, she was right, she wasn't embarrassing herself in front of him. Ever since Winter Formal, I'd seen Laney and Harrison talking more at rehearsals and sometimes in the hallways between classes. They were definitely friendly now, and she seemed surprisingly chill about it.

Mrs. Sorenson clapped her hands to get everyone's attention. "Places for the beginning of the scene!" she yelled as we all shuffled back to our positions onstage. "Go!"

Ada, Laney, and I walked across the stage, pointing at stuff and miming conversation. But as hard as I tried to focus, I couldn't tear my eyes from Diya as Kathy—she was hilarious. Brash. Fiery. I knew she was an amazing singer, but something about this scene was beyond even that. Jude was holding his own as Don, but the stage belonged to her. I recognized her extravagant poses—the head tilt, the arched back, looking down toward her right shoulder. They were fully developed versions of the movements I'd seen her cycling through at Waffle Country. She'd been practicing this part of the scene in her head, going over it again and again. The same thing I used to do when I listened to ballet music—little ghosts of the movements as I did the dance in my mind.

We ran through the scene several more times, and my path from stage left to stage right never changed. But Diya kept trying out different things—an inflection shift here, a broader gesture there. Once she found something that really worked, she polished it, run-through after run-through. Watching her work, perfecting every little word and movement, tugged at something inside me.

My brain had cycled through so many questions over the last couple of weeks. Questions about Jude and Colleen and ballet, and I hadn't been able to answer any of them. But at least one thing was becoming clear. Why I'd felt the need to defend Diya ever since our conversation at the pre–cast party.

I understood her. She was like me.

CHAPTER TWENTY

THE MOMENT MY REVELATION about Diya clicked, my brain did an unexpected thing. It was like a roller coaster that had been moving steadily up, and then it reached the top, but instead of flying forward, it fell backward. Fast. I tried to focus on my background miming, but I couldn't keep my breathing in check, my eyes from blurring. All my darkest thoughts were flooding in.

You'll never not feel sad. No one understands you. Quit the musical. Nothing and no one will ever compare to how you felt about ballet.

No. I'd admitted there were bad things about ballet. I'd talked about it with Mom, with Jude. I'd almost texted Colleen back. I was in the musical and I'd gone to Winter Formal and had friends and a guy I liked. I was moving *on*. The picture from Winter Formal flashed to my mind—the confetti, my smile. Thinking about it usually comforted me. But suddenly it felt fake. It wasn't the real me in that starry silver frame. The real me was here, about to break down in this ugly auditorium, just like at auditions.

When Mrs. Sorenson dismissed the chorus, I rushed offstage and grabbed my bag. I felt a light brush on my elbow and spun around.

"Hey," Jude said. "Do you want to go to the rink together

tonight? I can pick you up. Or I mean, I guess it wouldn't be picking you up so much as me coming to your door, and then us walking to my car. So...do you want to walk to my car with me?" He hit me with his best smile yet. Hopeful and nervous and full of possibility.

It was what I'd been wanting for two weeks. More alone time with Jude. Proof that he wanted more alone time with me. But I couldn't get my brain to focus on that now. "I actually have some things to do before, so I'll drive myself. See you there." I tried to hurry out of the auditorium, but Margot stopped me by the doors.

"Want to come over for dinner and then go to the rink?" she asked. I gave her the same excuse I gave Jude. "I'll meet you there," I said. "Seven?" I inched toward the doors.

"Sure." Margot gave me a tight smile. "See you at seven."

When I got home, I went down a Diya Rao rabbit hole. When I was supposed to be eating lunch, I was Googling her. When I was supposed to be choosing an outfit that would look decent with skates, I was reading a profile of her in the newspaper's "High School Heroes" column, where she talked about her Broadway idol, Shoba Narayan, who was apparently the first South Asian woman in a lead role on Broadway in over a decade.

When I was supposed to be leaving for the rink, I was on the Pittsburgh Musical Theatre Song Contest website, watching Diya's first-place performance of a song called "Could I Leave You?" by Stephen Sondheim. Her performance was riveting and raw. She owned Sondheim's intricate, gut-wrenching lyrics. Before I knew it, the tears came.

This was what Diya had ditched Jude for. As I listened to her sing the final notes, all I could think was *You did the right thing.* After the song ended, all I could think was *Jude and Ethan and Margot would hate me for thinking that.*

I took a deep breath, wiped my eyes, and looked at the clock: 7:45. I was really late. I checked my phone and I had five texts.

Margot: **Where r u?????**

Margot: **If you don't get here soon I'll be so bored I'll try to do a triple axel and I WILL get hurt and it WILL be your fault.**

Ethan: **Seriously she'll do it you better come now**

Jude: **hey, everything good? if you're staying away so Margot will do a triple axel, awesome idea. but certain people really want to see you.**

Jude: **just to be clear, I'm certain people. I really want to see you.**

I stared at the screen, halfway registering the messages. Diya was still in my head, pushing out everything else. The similarities between us were so blatant I couldn't believe I hadn't noticed before. I liked Jude. She had, too. I wanted to be a professional artist. So did she. She'd sacrificed relationships for art. So had I. We were so alike, and yet all my friends hated her. Called her Robobitch. The only difference? I was never going to be a professional artist, and she still could be.

An ugly thought hit me. If I'd still been dancing, would they have hated me, too? I wanted to ignore it, to brush it aside as ridiculous, but a feeling in my gut wouldn't let me.

～

When I got to the Galleria ice rink—a big outdoor oval surrounded by lawn, pine trees, and twinkly lights—Margot was waiting for me by the concessions stand with a huge bag of popcorn.

"Where were you?" she asked, handing me the bag.

"Sorry, I lost track of time."

"Oh." Margot eyed me doubtfully. "Well, Jude was looking for you earlier. He and Ethan and Harrison went to get hot drinks because the ones here suck."

196

"Okay."

"So, what *is* going on, Jude-wise? I figured you didn't want to say anything about it at Waffle Country because literally everyone was there, but look..." She pointed to a gazebo on a hill about twenty feet from the farthest end of the rink. "No one's up there. We could talk about it."

"It's okay. I'm fine."

Margot fidgeted, pulling on the ear flaps of her hat. "You know what Ethan said, about maybe being scared of starting something with Jude because you'd been through a lot?" she said carefully. "It made me think. I know you're hurting about the ballet stuff. I never brought it up because I figured you weren't ready to talk about it. But maybe it would be good for us to talk about it."

A part of me was desperate for some relief from the mess in my head. Maybe talking to Margot would give me that. Still, that feeling in my gut held me back, telling me to be cautious. Just like Diya, Margot probably would have hated me if I'd still been dancing—how could I expect her to understand anything I was going through now?

"No, really, I'm okay." I wandered to the rink, Margot following me. We leaned on the edge, eating popcorn and watching everyone. Laney and Ada were pretending to be a figure skating pair, but Laney kept falling and laughing. Noah and Laurel were beside the rink, dancing obnoxiously to the music playing over the speakers. I still didn't see why Josie thought they'd be a good fit for her piece, especially now that I'd seen some of her choreography. But whatever.

I sighed, my mind going back to rehearsal. "Diya was really good today," I said. I couldn't help it. "She was so funny."

Margot shrugged and tossed a few pieces of popcorn into her mouth. "Too bad she's not funny in real life. She's so freaking intense."

It was the kind of answer I expected, but my stomach still sank. "Do you think she's intense because she loves musicals so much?" I asked.

Margot wrinkled her eyebrows. "What do you mean?"

"I mean...I saw Diya practicing that bench scene, the one from today, at Waffle Country. She was practicing it over and over again, like she didn't even realize other people were around. It was kind of amazing, how dedicated she was."

I waited, my heart pumping. If I could get Margot to understand Diya, maybe she could understand me, too.

"God. The ego on that girl," Margot said, rolling her eyes. "It's a high school musical. Get over it, Robobitch." I gritted my teeth, remembering when Josie told me to "get over" ballet. When something is your life, there is no getting over it. It's everything. It's everywhere.

"Maybe she sees it as something more," I said, trying to conceal how agitated I was. "Like it's part of practicing what she wants to devote her life to."

Margot shrugged, watching the skaters. "That's just it, though. She's got such blinders on. It's a drag to be around someone who's *always* thinking about the one thing they're devoting their life to. You feel insignificant and ignored and beneath them. And no one likes that. That's why no one likes her."

"But *I* was like that," I said, unable to control the volume of my voice. "Before I got injured, I had massive blinders, and I ignored people all the time."

"I mean, a little. But don't worry, you weren't that bad."

A familiar feeling of invisibility came over me. The one I got every time Kira passed me over for a role, or watched Juliet and Spencer with just a little more attention than she ever did me. The feeling that someone sees the outline of you, but not the real thing.

"No, you don't even…it isn't something I was ashamed of. It wasn't a bad thing. I was *supposed* to be dancing. I was supposed to be in New York. I wasn't supposed to be here. At Eagle View. In the musical. At this stupid rink."

"Okay…," Margot said slowly, her expression shifting between confused and offended. "You want to go?"

"I don't have anywhere to go. That's the problem," I snapped.

Margot's eyes narrowed. "What do you mean you don't have anywhere to go? You *always* have somewhere to go. You always drive separately so you can go there."

"Okay?" So I liked to drive myself places. Was that wrong?

"You always have to have a way out when you're with us."

"That's not…" I pinched the bridge of my nose. "You don't understand."

Margot laughed, but it sounded off. "Right. I could never understand the pain of the Great Alina Keeler."

"I didn't—"

"Maybe I don't understand because you never tell me anything. You won't tell me about Jude, and you know what? That's fine. That's your call. But you won't tell me why you won't come to movie nights, you won't tell me why you ditched me at the pre-cast party, and you won't tell me why you were late tonight when we had a *plan* to meet at seven and you swore you wouldn't bail. God, I've spent months tiptoeing around your feelings, making sure I wasn't doing anything to make you feel bad because I knew you were going through something. But you never did that for me. You never thought, *Oh, maybe Margot doesn't want to be alone at the ice rink, where she has bad memories.*"

Shit. I'd forgotten about the Izzy stuff. But it wasn't like she'd been *alone* alone. "Ethan and Jude were here," I shot back.

Margot looked at me incredulously. "I wanted *you* to be here."

"Why?" It sounded wrong as soon as I said it.

"*Why?* Because you're my friend. You're my *best* friend, okay? Last year sucked because of the Izzy thing. I thought junior year was going to be hell, too. But it's not. And you—you're a big reason why."

I didn't know what to say to that, because Diya's words from the pre-cast party came rushing in. *Well, of course they like you now. But you were . . . you were an amazing dancer. They didn't like you so much then.* Suddenly, it all made sense.

"Did you guys used to say stuff about me behind my back?" I asked.

Margot's eyes went wide. "What?"

"Me. Your *best* friend. Did you used to say things about me?"

"I . . ." Margot put her hands out in front of her. "It's not—"

"Hey, guys!" Laney called. She and Ada were skating toward us. Ada slid to a stop by the rink's edge while Laney plowed into it, holding on to keep steady.

"Hey," Margot said, trying to put on a calm face.

"Where's Ethan and Jude?" Ada asked. People were doing that more and more, grouping the four of us into a package. It used to feel nice. I didn't know how it felt now.

"They're coming back," Margot said quietly. "They're getting hot drinks."

"Yum," Laney said, adjusting her panda earmuffs. She smiled as she looked over Margot's shoulder. "There they are." Jude, Ethan, and Harrison were walking toward us, each holding two drink carriers.

"You guuuys!" Laney yelled as they got closer. "I keep falling and Ada's getting mad because she stole these jeans from her sister for me to wear and I'm ruining them, so Harrison, can you skate on one side of me, and Ethan, can you skate on the other?"

Ethan and Harrison exchanged a sly smile. "What do you think, Lambert?" Ethan said.

"I don't know, Anderson, you think she really wants us to?"

Ethan tilted his head. "It's hard to tell. But if there's one thing I know about sisters, it's that they're notoriously overprotective of their pants."

Harrison laughed. "Better do it, then." Ethan beamed. He and Harrison handed off their drinks to Margot and Jude and strode off to put on their skates, looking happy.

A swarm of people surrounded Margot and Jude, choosing and passing the steaming cups. I stepped back, wondering how far I could make it to the parking lot before anyone noticed.

But then Jude stepped out of the crowd. He'd finally switched to a heavier coat. It was navy blue and puffy. But he still wore the green knitted gloves. He was holding a small cup. "I got you a caramel apple latte," he said.

"Just *pick* one, you freaks!" Margot yelled at a couple of indecisive sophomores, who quickly grabbed the last two drinks. "And throw this away!" She shoved the carriers at one of them and walked resolutely up to Jude and me. "Hold on for one sec," she said to Jude as she took my elbow and started leading me up to the gazebo. "I'll bring her back, I promise."

"What's wrong?" Jude asked, following us. When I didn't meet his eyes, he stopped. I let Margot lead me up the hill.

"Okay," Margot breathed out. "Last year, like a week after my fight with Izzy, I asked you in chem if you wanted to come to this concert with me. It was like the third time I'd invited you to stuff and the third time you kind of brushed me off. I understood you were busy, but I was really lonely and not in a good place. Anyway, I was venting to Ethan at rehearsal, and I said you were so programmed and intense about ballet that you weren't just a bitch, you were a Robobitch."

My mouth hung open. Margot looked down at her shoes.

"I felt horrible about it because I knew you weren't really a Robobitch. But I guess, when I said it, someone heard me and thought I meant Diya, so the name kind of transferred to her. And then the whole thing happened with your leg, and you joined the musical, and we became real friends and I didn't say anything about it because it was a long time ago, and I honestly don't think of you like that. I was just being petty and dumb. I'm really sorry."

All I could do was shake my head, trying to process what I'd heard. When I was doing the thing I loved to do, I was just a Robobitch to them.

Anger and hurt vibrated through me. Not just because I was the original Robobitch, but because I'd tricked myself into believing I was part of this group. That they were, as Margot said, my "real friends."

"Ethan and Jude didn't call you that. I mean, Ethan may have said it once to make me feel better when I was venting that time, but it was mostly just me. I'm sorry," Margot said again.

I was hardly paying attention anymore. The anger I felt—at Margot, at myself for being so stupid, at everyone—turned into straight-up rage. "Don't be. It's just who you are."

"What do you mean?" she asked cautiously.

I wanted her to feel as betrayed and hurt as I did. "You call people names because they don't want to hang out with you. It's really fucking sad. No wonder you hardly had any friends after Izzy. She's probably the best you can do."

I spun around and marched down the hill, heading for the parking lot. Heart pumping, face flushed. As I skirted the rink, Jude jogged up beside me. "What's going on?"

"Nothing." I slowed to a stop, trying to catch my breath, looking anywhere but at him.

He ducked his head, trying to catch my eye. "Really?" I nodded quickly. "Okay," he said slowly. "Um. Do you... Do you want to skate?"

I finally let myself look at him. It didn't matter that Jude had never called me Robobitch, it still would never work between us. He wanted this life—Eagle View and the musical and his friends. He fit into it. I didn't. But I couldn't let things with Jude blow up like they did with Margot. I had to tell him maturely. Make a clean break, for once.

I nodded, moving past him to the rink. Being out in the cold for this long made my leg stiffer than usual, and the inward angle of the skates made it worse. But I kept picking up speed, hoping the rush of cold air would drown out the fight with Margot replaying in my head. It wasn't working.

Jude kept up with every change of speed, lap after lap. The circles were infuriating. Turning a corner only to end up in the same place. It was like a big, annoying metaphor for us. Getting closer, then pulling away. Even the trampoline day, which had felt so momentous at the time, was the same thing. Up and down, up and down. Like we couldn't move in one solid direction. Things would never work between us, and maybe we'd known that all along.

We turned another corner. And then everything happened at once.

At one end of the rink, Ethan and Harrison started singing "Beautiful Girl" at the top of their lungs, which made Jude and me look back at them. At the other end, Noah and Laurel started racing a couple of kids' skating aids shaped like penguins. They'd sprint for a few feet and then shove the penguins so they skidded across the ice.

I was still looking back at Ethan and Harrison when I heard Jude yell, "Whoa, whoa, whoa!"

I only saw the penguin's dopey painted smile for a split second before it knocked into my skate and I lurched forward.

Jude grabbed on to my arm to catch me, but he was off-balance too, and we were going too fast. We fell in a heap and my right ankle twisted under me as we slid to the edge of the rink.

A sharp crack echoed through the air.

CHAPTER TWENTY-ONE

TANGLED THOUGHTS SPIRALED in my head.

Broken again. Can't dance in the musical. Surgery. Can't dance in the musical. Birdie's gonna kill me. Won't see Margot and Ethan and Jude every day. Won't see them ever. Rods sticking out of my bones. More screws in my leg and I can't dance in the musical.

"Death to penguins!" Jude yelled as he sat up, raising an arm in the air to cheers from around the rink.

"Sorry!" Noah yelled back. Everyone booed. I still couldn't catch my breath.

Jude turned to me, smiling. Then he froze. "What is it? Are you hurt?" He pushed himself onto his knees and slid around in front of me. When he saw that my hands were clutching my right ankle, he inhaled sharply. "Is it—"

Is it?

I squeezed my fingers around my ankle and knew, with a strange kind of clarity, that it wasn't. It wasn't broken. It wasn't sprained or twisted. It wasn't anything. I slowly unclasped my hands and stared at them. They were shaking.

"Alina." Jude was looking at me intently.

"No…I'm okay. I…I thought I'd…I thought it happened again." Then the tears came. Ugly, embarrassing ones.

"Hey," Jude said softly as he helped me stand up. He kept a firm arm around my waist as he guided me out of the rink. Somehow I got my skates off and put my boots on. Then he walked me up to the gazebo, and I collapsed on the bench inside.

"I'm sorry, I'm sorry, I'm sorry," I blubbered.

"Why are you sorry? It was the penguin's fault. We should go on a penguin-punching expedition, you and me." He placed his hand on my back, making slow, soothing circles. I felt the warmth of them through my coat.

"That…would be…so unpopular," I managed to choke out.

"Hmm?"

"Everybody…loves penguins."

Jude smiled, and I could see his body relax. I hadn't realized how tense he'd been before.

He took his hand from my back and touched his green glove to my cheeks, drying the tears that threatened to freeze there. Then he dabbed under my nose. Just like that. Like it wasn't gross to have someone else's snot on your hand-knitted gloves.

I took several deep, steadying breaths, blinking up at the slanted wooden beams of the gazebo roof. "It was so weird," I was finally able to say. "It didn't even really hurt, but I…I *heard* my bone breaking."

Jude was silent for a moment, looking out at the rink. "Was that the first time you've fallen like that since you broke your leg?"

I nodded. There are falls where you stumble and right yourself almost immediately. And then there are *falls*, where you lose control of your body for a moment that stretches out into forever. I hadn't had that kind of fall since I broke my leg.

"Then maybe it triggered that memory?" Jude asked.

"Maybe." My brain *had* been doing weird things lately, like my tailspin after watching Diya's bench scene at rehearsal. Maybe it made sense it would do this, too. It had been a while since I'd heard the horrid sound of my bones breaking as I tried to fall asleep, but of course the fear wouldn't let go that easily.

"I'm really glad you're okay," Jude said.

"Me too." I took a breath, a little less shakily this time. "I... I thought I wouldn't be able to dance in the musical."

It was quiet for a few seconds, except for the distant sounds of skating and laughter. I glanced up at Jude. He was staring at me in a way that made my cheeks flush.

"I wouldn't have let that happen." He brushed a few strands of hair out of my face. "You promised to dance me to death. You can't let me off the hook."

I leaned in, whispering. "I promised *not* to dance you to death."

"Right," he whispered back. His breath tickled my ear. "I guess the other way sounds more exciting."

It did. All kinds of exciting feelings were swirling around in my body now that I was so close to Jude. It made my fight with Margot and my episode on the ice fade into the distance, and I liked that. I liked that a lot.

"Can I kiss you?" Jude said softly.

And just like that, everything else disappeared completely.

I pressed my lips to his. He breathed in sharply, and in an instant he was kissing me back. All around us it was freezing. But the feeling of his lips on mine made me feel warm, safe. I heard a rustling sound, and then Jude's fingers, ungloved, held my face, ran through my hair.

It was so... good. Somewhere in the back of my brain I knew the reason I'd done it was wrong. A distraction. Something to ease the pain. But I couldn't deny the way my whole body felt like it was doing something it wanted, something right.

We finally broke away from each other but stayed close, our breaths coming fast, making one big cloud between us.

"I've wondered what that would be like for a long time," Jude said, resting his forehead on mine.

"Really?"

He looked at me incredulously. "I thought it was obvious."

"There were other times it could have happened, you know."

"Yeah?"

"Winter Formal. Parking lot after rehearsal. Fly Zone." I ticked them off on my fingers.

"Yup," Jude said, his smile big and goofy and a bit dazed. "I wanted to kiss you in all those places."

"So why didn't you?" It was mostly a joke, but Jude pulled away a little.

"Because—"

Footsteps tore my eyes away from his. "Oops! Sorry!" a familiar voice said, and I locked eyes with someone I hadn't thought I'd ever see again.

"Juliet?"

"Alina? Oh my God!" I stood up and she enveloped me in a hug. I hadn't seen her for so long she almost didn't seem real. When she stepped back, she squeezed my shoulders before letting go. I stared at her face—cheeks pink from the cold, blue eyes framed by pale eyebrows.

"It's good to see you," I was finally able to say.

"You too. We've missed you. *A lot.*" She looked over my shoulder to where Jude was sitting, and then back to me with a curious smile.

"Oh. Jude. This is Juliet." I glanced in his direction. "We went to ballet school together."

"Uh, hey," Jude mumbled, stuffing his hands back into his gloves.

"Alina had the best musicality I've ever seen. And kickass extensions," Juliet said. I couldn't help but smile. That wouldn't mean much to someone outside the ballet world, but Juliet was trying to make me look good, and that was the only way she knew how.

"Colleen misses you, too, but duh, I'm sure you know that," Juliet went on. "It's awful about the ABT audition, right?"

"Wait, what—" My heart jolted. The ABT summer intensive audition. January eighteenth. *Today.* With everything else going on, I'd completely forgotten. How was that possible?

Had Colleen not done well? Was she not going to get in? Alongside my rapidly beating heart, a strange, hopeful feeling fluttered in my chest. "What happened?" I asked.

Juliet tilted her head at me, confused. "She . . . had that appendectomy a couple of weeks ago? So she couldn't go to the Philly audition today?" I froze. I could tell she was surprised I didn't know that my so-called best friend had had an organ removed from her body, but she masked it quickly. Ballet dancers are good at that. "She's totally okay. It wasn't ruptured, thank God, and she didn't need open surgery, so no super-long recovery time. But she still had to miss it. She's sending in a video, though, so it's something."

Okay. Colleen was okay. As I gulped down a few freezing breaths, my mind raced. Big schools like ABT held summer intensive auditions in cities all over the country. Philly was the closest city where Colleen could audition. Her parents had probably planned it well in advance, clearing their work schedules, arranging other transportation for her brothers. Trying to make it to another city's auditions at this point was probably impossible. Videos were okay, but it was much better to be there in person. There was so much about a dancer that couldn't be conveyed through a screen.

Still, Colleen's chance wasn't gone completely. Like mine was. She could still get in.

I realized I hadn't said anything back to Juliet. "That's terrible," I choked out.

"Juliet, come on!" a girl called from down the hill, her strawberry-blond hair streaming out from underneath a cloche hat. She was probably one of the new girls who'd transferred to KDBS this year. Maybe Camden, the other Giselle, the other Jody. Juliet said goodbye, and I watched her glide off to meet the new girl, link arms with her, and walk away.

I didn't know how long I stood there watching. What snapped me out of it was Jude, who put his hand on my shoulder. "Hey," he said gently.

I stepped away. I didn't deserve his hand on my shoulder. The kindness in his voice. It was bad enough that I'd forgotten about Colleen's audition. But there was something infinitely worse than that. For a second, when I thought Colleen hadn't done well, I'd been happy. I couldn't run away from that truth. I'd been happy when I thought my best friend had failed. And jealous when I realized she still had a chance. Something became bitterly clear then. It wasn't just my body that was broken. My brain couldn't let go of what I'd lost. And my heart—my heart clearly didn't work anymore. It was mean and jealous and awful, and it couldn't be fixed.

Margot was right the first time. I really was a Robobitch. And Jude didn't deserve that. None of them did.

"I'm *horrible*," I whispered.

"Alina. You're not," Jude said, reaching for my hand.

I stepped away again. "You don't know that. I have to go."

"Okay, but wait, let me say what I was going to say before Juliet came. Please?" I turned to him, even though I couldn't look him in the eye.

"You asked me why I didn't kiss you all those times I wanted to. It's because I was being an idiot. I wanted to give you space because when you go through something that changes everything, you don't always know what you want. I definitely didn't, when my dad left. So I told myself to step back and be your friend and if you wanted more, like I did, it had to come from you. But that was stupid. You're smart and strong and you don't need me to decide things for you. I should have kissed you when I wanted to kiss you."

He took a slow step toward me. When I didn't move, he let out a breath. "I should have kissed you at Winter Formal."

A step closer. "I should have kissed you in the parking lot."

Another step. "And I definitely should have kissed you at Fly Zone. Because when I didn't, I swear I almost cried."

I let out a shivery laugh. I couldn't help it. He was making me forget everything again. He rested his hands on the sides of my face. "I should have kissed you all those times because I know you would have told me to back off if you needed me to. And I would have listened."

I knew that was true. It was still true. He'd finally made it very clear how he felt. But it was ultimately my decision. He was still waiting for me. I hated what I was about to say. But Jude had been keeping his distance to protect me, not to protect himself. I had to protect us both. I swallowed. "I need you to back off."

We were still so close, his eyes on mine, but they glazed over. He took a dazed step back. My body sagged in the cold air that sprang up between us. "Okay," he said, setting his jaw resolutely.

It wasn't enough, though. He needed to know why it would never work.

"I didn't know my best friend had surgery because I don't talk to her anymore. She texts me and I don't text back because I'm jealous. I can't stand that she can do ballet and I can't. And just now, I was..." My breath hitched. "I was happy, when I thought she didn't do well at the audition. Because I don't want her to go to that school when I can't." I looked for the judgment in his eyes, but it never came.

"Alina..." Jude's hand reached toward me before he pulled it back. "Things get complicated when you lose something that was important to you. You do and think things you never thought you could. But it doesn't make you a horrible person."

Scars and steel don't decide if you're a dancer or not. Being happy that your best friend failed doesn't make you a horrible person. These were comforting thoughts. They just weren't true.

"I would have ditched you at Winter Formal. Like Diya did," I said. "That's who I am. I put art over people. I'm selfish. And I kissed you because I wanted to distract myself from all that."

Jude's mouth opened in surprise, and after a few seconds of silence, he looked at the ground and nodded, like he finally understood how wrong I was for him. "Okay," he said. "Okay."

A sob caught in my throat. I turned to run away, but Ethan was suddenly there. He looked from me to Jude and back to me, his eyes narrowing. "What happ—"

"I'm leaving," I said. Ethan hated Diya for hurting Jude. He'd definitely hate me, too.

As I ran to the parking lot, I cried the same ugly tears I had when I thought I'd broken my leg on the ice. Only this time, something really was broken. Lots of things. Everything.

CHAPTER TWENTY-TWO

I STAYED IN MY ROOM practically all Sunday. My phone didn't make a sound, but I hadn't expected it to. What would anyone want to say to me?

I tried skipping school on Monday, but my parents didn't buy my "I'm sick" routine. So I scooped my unbrushed hair into a ponytail, threw on a sweatshirt and jeans, and drove to Eagle View.

When I walked into homeroom, there was Margot, sitting in the same seat as always. And when I saw her—drawing a Sharpie design on her backpack—I didn't think about how she'd called me Robo-bitch. I thought about how on the first day of school this year, she was waiting for me by my locker. How she talked me into auditioning for the musical and cheered me on at callbacks and danced with me at Winter Formal. How, during the worst months of my life, she had somehow become my best friend.

Margot didn't look up, but she went very still. I walked slowly to my seat in front of hers. When I was close enough to touch it, she unzipped her backpack, tossed the Sharpie in, and took out her economics textbook. She flipped it open, never looking up. Margot had once told me that she'd rather eat goose shit than read her economics textbook, so the message was clear. Of course she didn't want to talk to me. I knew she felt lonely and friendless after the Izzy thing, and I'd stuck a knife right in that wound. I'd wanted to hurt her, and I had.

I pivoted and took a seat in the back corner. When homeroom ended, I bolted, went straight past the senior lockers without waiting for Ethan, and walked through the tunnel by myself.

"Rough night?" Paul asked after I plopped into my seat in English. "You like rough nights, don't you, Princess?"

Ethan walked in then, but just like Margot, he didn't look at me.

"You're ignoring us more than usual," Paul said, pouting. "We thought after you got some, you'd thaw a little. And she definitely got some," he whispered loudly to Jake. "Look at that sex hair."

Paul was right about one thing. I *was* ignoring them more than usual. I couldn't even be distracted by their garbage today. All I could think about was Ethan's furious expression at the rink. The same way he looked right now. Jaw clenched, shaking his head. He pulled a notebook out of his bag, knocked open the cover, and started writing. He didn't care anymore. Like at the beginning of the year, no one in here cared.

Somehow I made it to the end of the day, which meant rehearsal, and the prospect of that was even worse than school. My stomach spasmed as I stood outside the doors. A pair of sneakers squeaked to a stop as someone came around the corner into the lobby.

Jude.

"Oh. Hi," he said quietly, shifting his backpack to his other shoulder.

"Hey." I hugged my elbows and looked at the floor.

Jude glanced at the auditorium doors. "Are you going in?" There was a coldness to his voice now. No smile, no gleam in his eyes.

I opened my mouth, but then Celia and a few other seniors rounded the corner, chatting and shoving each other around. "Come on, Judey Boy!" Celia said, pulling Jude by the arm into the auditorium, and then he was gone.

I stood there for a few more seconds before walking away.

I drove home, replaying every excruciating detail from Saturday night until my head hurt. I hoped that by some miracle, my parents' Monday schedules had changed and they wouldn't be home. But when I opened the front door, Mom and Josie swiveled around on the couch.

"Don't you have rehearsal today?" Mom asked as Dad walked in from the kitchen.

"It was canceled."

"She's lying," Josie said. I glared at her, but she didn't even have the decency to look guilty. I knew she was still mad about me missing her *Nutcracker* solo, but I hadn't figured she'd rat me out.

"Thanks a lot," I muttered. I charged upstairs before my parents could say anything, slammed my door, and lay facedown on my bed.

A few minutes later, there was a knock, and before I could say anything, Dad walked in. He pulled out my desk chair, spun it around so it was facing me, and took a seat. "So," he said after a beat. "This morning you tried to get out of going to school. And right now you're missing rehearsal. I'm sensing a pattern here. What in the music world we'd call a motif."

I sighed and propped my chin in my hands. He was going for the "lighten the mood" approach. "I didn't want to go. It's not a big deal." I tried to keep my voice monotone, but it wobbled a little on the last few words.

"Sweetie...," Dad started, leaning forward with his elbows on his thighs, his hands clasped together. "I don't know what this is about, but there's something I've been wanting to say for a while. I know I haven't talked about this much. But after your injury, I was so terrified. And not just by that external fixator monstrosity, although that was..." He shuddered. "Seriously, how did no one else pass out when they looked at that thing?"

"Dad," I said.

"Sorry. Tangent. I was terrified it would be a long time before you found something you were passionate about, that made you as happy as ballet did," Dad went on. "I knew you'd find it eventually, but I didn't know *when*. And you're a passionate person, kid. I didn't know what would happen to all that passion if it didn't have anywhere to go."

Dad straightened up and drummed his hands on his thighs. "But when you tried out for the musical, I thought, *Hey, look at her. She's going for something*. And then all of a sudden you're going to a school dance, and you have *friends*..." He paused. "I didn't mean to imply that I was shocked you have friends. Of course you have friends." He laughed awkwardly.

I'd planned to keep a neutral expression through this whole talk, but my eyes rolled of their own volition. I didn't know how Dad could look so sophisticated and together as he played the piano at gigs and be so dorky in real life.

"What I'm trying to say is, I don't know what the answer is. I don't know how you recover from something like this. But I do know it won't happen in a straight, steady line. And that's all right. Just don't give up on all the progress you've made because of a setback. You've got such a great heart, kid. Remember that when things get hard."

I hadn't thought it was possible to feel any worse, but it was. My heart wasn't great, it was garbage. And I'd tricked my dad into believing I was getting better the same way I'd tricked myself.

I sat up, needing to be anywhere but here. So I left my room, grabbed my coat and bag, and got back in the car. After driving around for a while, I found myself at Waffle Country. It was what I needed right now.

~~

Strawberry Nutella waffles and my trig homework finally lulled my brain into a sluggish haze. My body seemed to realize that I'd hardly gotten any sleep the last two nights, and before I knew it, I was using my textbook as a pillow.

"What are you doing here?"

I jerked up. Diya was standing over me, her backpack dangling from one shoulder. She was the last person I wanted to see. And considering all the people I was trying to avoid, that was saying something.

"*Hello*," she said, waving her hand in front of my face annoyingly.

"I'm eating waffles, what does it look like I'm doing," I snapped. Then I glanced at the clock—4:15. Rehearsal should have been in full swing. "Why are *you* here?"

Diya hesitated for a second. Then she slid into the seat across from me and took off her pea coat. I wanted to ask her what she thought she was doing, but I didn't have the energy.

"Mrs. Sorenson and basically the whole cast told me to take the day off." She angrily opened a menu. "I'm working too hard, they said. A day off would let me come back *refreshed*. What they meant was they're all too lazy to do anything right, and they don't want to be held accountable." Diya shook her head and muttered curses under her breath.

We were both in such awful moods I was afraid Waffle Country would kick us out for bringing down its happy vibe.

"You can't swear here," I snapped at her again.

I expected Diya's signature X-ray stare, but I only saw tired eyes

217

looking back at me. I took in her long, usually shining hair, which was frizzy now and thrown up into something resembling a ponytail. She looked sad and stressed, like me.

"I mean," I said in a gentler tone, "it's Waffle Country. Have some respect."

A trace of a smile flickered on her face. Then she stared down a server and ordered bananas Foster.

"So really, why aren't you at rehearsal?" she asked when the server left.

"I'm sick," I said, taking a huge bite of waffle and dripping Nutella down my chin. Diya narrowed her eyes, pulled a napkin from the dispenser, and handed it to me.

"I heard Jude and them talking about you before I left," she said.

"Has anyone ever told you you're too blunt?" I mumbled, resisting the urge to ask what they'd said.

"Yes." Diya blinked at me, unfazed.

"Oh. Well, you are." I turned back to my homework. Diya watched me for a few more seconds before digging a binder out of her bag. Her bananas Foster came, and we both worked silently, taking a break every now and then to stuff our faces.

After a while, I couldn't concentrate with Diya there. My waffle haven was officially ruined, so I gathered my things to go.

"Want to come over to my house?" Diya asked, her eyes steadily on me.

"Why?"

She heaved a deep sigh. "My dad is going to ask me why I'm not at rehearsal, and I'd rather not have to explain. If I have a guest, he won't make me."

Huh. I definitely didn't want to go back home yet, where I'd have to face my parents again. "Okay. I'll follow you there?"

CHAPTER TWENTY-THREE

IF I'D HAD TO GUESS what Diya Rao's house looked like, I would have said modern and airy, with white couches you weren't allowed to sit on. But I would have been wrong. It was a split-level with a mix of cozy chairs and antique-looking wooden furniture. Framed photos of smiling people—old and young, some in saris, some in jeans and T-shirts—lined the walls.

As Diya took my coat in the hallway, a surprised voice called in. "Diya?"

"Yeah, Dad," she said as we turned into the kitchen. A tall man in a tie and button-down stood at the sink doing dishes. He froze, wide-eyed, when he saw me. At the table, a guy who looked like an older, male version of Diya sat with a gigantic meatball sandwich in his hands. He was staring at me, too.

"Hi?" I said awkwardly.

"Alina, that's my dad, and that's my brother, Jai. We're going to do homework," she said, turning to leave, but her dad wiped his hands on a towel and came over.

"Alina! Welcome! Great to meet you!" He pumped my hand vigorously. "Are you a senior, too? Are you in the musical?"

"Um…"

Jai grinned at my overwhelmed expression. "Diya normally repels people, so we're just a little surprised you're here," he said.

Diya narrowed her eyes. "*I'm* surprised you're eating that when Mom's on her way home." She turned to me. "Jai doesn't want his mommy to know he's not a vegetarian."

"Let's get a picture, in case this never happens again," Jai said, standing up. "I'll get the camera."

"Shush." Mr. Rao waved his hands at Jai before turning back to me. "Want anything to drink, Alina? We have soda or lemonade. Actually, you guys go ahead. I'll bring both down, with some of those cookies from Wegmans."

Wow. Wegmans cookies. He was really rolling out the red carpet. It reminded me of how my parents treated Margot when she came over for the first time after my injury.

I shrugged off the memory as Diya led me down to her room in the finished basement. "Sorry about them," she said, gesturing upstairs.

"They seem nice." I looked around Diya's room, which had huge posters hung up in evenly spaced intervals. They were for different shows, musicals I assumed, most of which I didn't recognize. *The Fantasticks*; *Anything Goes*; *My Fair Lady*; *Oklahoma!*; *Natasha, Pierre, and the Great Comet of 1812*; *Hamilton*; and a bunch more. Some looked new, and some were curling at the edges, like she'd put them up a long time ago.

I sat on Diya's desk chair and she sat on her floral bedspread. "I took the basement room so Jai wouldn't whine about me singing all the time." She pulled out her hair tie and slingshotted it across the room. It landed smoothly on top of her dresser. "He's only home from Penn State during breaks now, so I could have moved upstairs, but I like it down here."

I glanced at the posters again, and the bulletin board above her bed covered with ticket stubs and photos of her in different costumes. Her walls were a shrine to her dream, like mine used to be. "It's a good room," I said quietly.

"Thanks."

An awkward silence fell. I didn't feel like busting out my homework again, though. So I glanced behind me at her neat desk. Beside her laptop was a thick packet of paper. I recognized it—she'd had it at Waffle Country on Saturday, when she was practicing her movements for the bench scene.

I picked it up. *WHAT HAPPENED IN THE ATTIC* was printed on the front page. "What's this?" I asked.

"It's the script for a new Broadway musical," Diya said, reaching for it. When I gave her the script, she ran her fingers over it like it was a rare jewel. "It's about three sisters who've been locked in an attic their whole lives, and you don't know why, and there was a fourth sister, but nobody talks about her. You find out later the other sisters ate her. It's a comedy."

"Uh, okay?" I smiled. I didn't know if I was more surprised about the concept of this musical or the fact that I was smiling. My mood was so abysmal I wouldn't have thought it was possible.

"It's hard to explain, but it's really amazing," Diya said.

"Why do you have the script?"

"One of the casting directors saw me in a musical theater song contest I did a couple of years ago in Pittsburgh. He reached out last month and sent me the script. I did a video of me reading lines and singing, and the casting people liked it. But they said stage presence, timing, interaction with a cast, all that stuff is important for knowing who's right for the part. So they're going to see a few different girls in live productions. They're coming to see me in *Singin' in the Rain*."

"Oh my God. That's...wow. That's great, right?"

"Of course it is. Only, the role I'm up for, the youngest sister, does a ton of goofy physical comedy. The casting people know I can sing and act, but they don't know if I can be stage-funny, you know? And Kathy Selden isn't funny. I mean, she has *one* funny scene in the beginning, on the bench when she's meeting Don, but then she turns into a boring romantic object."

"But you're really good in that scene. Maybe it'll be enough to convince them?" Her pantomiming at Waffle Country made even more sense now. She needed to nail that bench scene.

Diya shook her head sadly. "I don't think so. I mean, who knows what roles the other girls have. They could be playing Ado Annie in *Oklahoma!* or the Lady of the Lake in *Spamalot*," she said, flopping onto her back. I didn't know what any of that meant, but I nodded anyway. "I tried to get Ms. Langford to replace my hula dance in 'Good Morning' with something really over-the-top. Goofy and big and showy, like Ethan and Jude's, so I'd at least have something else to work with."

"Huh." That wasn't a bad idea. There was a part in "Good Morning" where the three of them took turns doing a comical dance with a raincoat. Jude did a hilarious version of the can-can, Ethan did a hilarious version of the Charleston, and Diya did a dumb caricature of the hula.

"But Ms. Langford said I still need to look pretty doing the dance because that's who Kathy is," Diya said to the ceiling. "It wouldn't make sense for her to do something big and wild. I get it, but I wish..." She sat up and flipped through the script. "It's *such* a good role. And if one of those other girls is better than me, truly better, then fine. But I need the casting people to really *see* me. And I'm afraid they won't."

This time I knew exactly what she meant, and images of Spencer and Juliet dancing center stage appeared in my head. I looked around at Diya's posters again, and something clicked. Besides the *Hamilton* and *Comet* ones, the posters all featured white women, most of them blue-eyed, golden-haired Jodys. Maybe those women really were the best. Or maybe there were other people who were as good as them, better even, who just hadn't been seen.

I glanced at Diya, who was still flipping through the script. A spark of determination went off inside me. I wanted the casting people to see her.

"You should do something different for that part," I said. "Something big and wild and funny. You can do it on the night the casting people come to see you. Ms. Langford and Mrs. Sorenson can't really stop you, right? And you're a senior, so it's not like you'll ruin your chances to be in the musical again."

Diya's eyes widened. "I can't just change the choreography."

I remembered when I'd said that to Josie about *The Nutcracker*. I'd really believed it then, that I had to keep dancing an awful caricature year after year, just because Kira said so, just because it had always been that way. "Yes, you can. I'll help you, if you want."

Slowly, Diya smiled. "Okay. Let's do it."

So we started dancing. We flossed. We head-banged. We tried to do the worm, but that was a complete fail. We shook our butts. A lot. We learned the *Napoleon Dynamite* dance all the way through. In the middle of it all, Mr. Rao brought us soda, lemonade, and cookies. The extra sugar made our dancing even more over-the-top. After an hour, we had something we thought could work. Two counts of eight we hoped would make the Broadway casting people laugh.

"I honestly can't wait to see Ethan and Jude when I break this out on opening night," Diya said. My face fell. "Sorry. I didn't mean to bring them up."

"That's okay. I'm just...not really friends with them anymore."

"Why?"

I shrugged, trying to keep my emotions in check. I couldn't go into the whole mess right now. I'd cry for sure. So my mind traveled back again to what Diya had said at the pre–cast party. "Remember when you said that Jude, Margot, and Ethan didn't like me before I broke my leg?"

Diya nodded. "I didn't mean it the way it sounded." She crossed her arms and sat down on the bed, pursing her lips, working something out. "I saw you, you know," she finally said. "When you were the Sugar Plum Fairy in *The Nutcracker*."

"You did?" I sat down beside her.

"Yeah. You were incredible. And you were living the life I wanted. Part-time school so you could train, and then you were going to New York..." Diya shook her head, like it was too good to possibly imagine. "I was sad when I heard about your leg, and that you couldn't go anymore. And I guess, when I saw you with Jude and Ethan and Margot after all that, I just felt like it was so unfair."

"What was unfair?"

"It's unfair that the only time people in the musical ever talked to me was when I was dating Jude. It's unfair that when I won the Pittsburgh Musical Theatre Song Contest, no one congratulated me. All people did was judge me for ditching him. And it's unfair that people like you and me only have friends at that stupid school when we're not doing what we're best at, you know? Like, we can't have both. We can't have friends *and* be really dedicated to what we love to do." Diya let out a sigh, like she'd been waiting to say that for a long time.

"You're right."

"But I don't know if I *am* right. Sure, some people will always think I'm bitchy and selfish for singing at the contest instead of going to Winter Formal. And yeah, I was super pissed at Margot and Ethan for being nice to me and then doing a one-eighty after, like they couldn't *possibly* understand why musical theater was more important to me than going to a dance with a guy I'd been dating for a month."

Diya paused, her face turning thoughtful. "I know the timing was awful, but I literally got the call at six o'clock the night of Winter Formal that a spot had opened up in the contest and that I'd have to be there by nine the next morning. I had to pack and leave—there was no way I could go to the dance. It would have been great if I could have told him earlier, but I couldn't. The contest was major. It sucked that no one understood."

"I do," I said. Even after experiencing firsthand what it was like to lose my friends, to lose Jude, I still got why she'd done it. I still knew I would have done the same thing.

"Thanks," Diya said. "But anyway, what I'm saying is, you were really close with those three. Closer than I ever was with Jude or any of them. So maybe your situation is different—"

"How do you know how close we were?" I interrupted.

Diya shrugged. "I observe people. That's what actors do."

Someone else might have rolled their eyes at the way she said that. Like she was Dame Judi Dench. But it made me lean in closer, so I wouldn't miss a word. "And?" I prompted.

Diya scoffed. "I'm not going to sit here and tell you what I observed. I'm not a spy. But trust me, you guys were close. And if I've learned anything from having a super-annoying older brother, it's that when you're close, fights don't last that long."

Some tiny part of me felt comforted by that. But before I knew it, I was shaking my head. Diya hadn't seen what went down on Saturday. She didn't know the ugly thoughts I'd had and the ugly things I'd said. She hadn't seen the way Jude, Margot, and Ethan acted toward me today. Like I hardly existed.

I stood up. "Should we run through it one more time?"

By the time I got home, it was after six. My parents were stony-faced as they told me dinner was in the fridge. I told them I'd eaten at a friend's house, which piqued their curiosity, but they didn't ask about it. I guess they'd decided to give me space. For now.

Upstairs in my room, my mind went right back to everything I'd been avoiding thinking about. The ice rink. Rehearsal. I wondered if Jude and Margot and Ethan were relieved I didn't show up today. If Ms. Langford and Mrs. Sorenson were mad. We were supposed to email them if we had to miss rehearsal, and we had to have a good reason. I didn't think "I freaked out at an ice rink and realized I'm a horrible person and now my friends hate me" would count, so I didn't email.

As I changed into pajama pants, the exhaustion hit me. The lack of sleep, plus the dancing at Diya's, plus the sheer amount of sugar I'd eaten in the past few hours, made me want to crash. But I couldn't sit still. My leg kept bouncing up and down, my mind going in a million directions.

My phone buzzed on my nightstand, and I jumped.

Thanks again for helping me. I think it's going to work. I owe you. Diya.

You're welcome, I typed back, smiling involuntarily.

The dance we'd choreographed was the most ridiculous thing in the world. But helping Diya had actually been fun. And something more, too. It felt important somehow. Like we were breaking a rule that needed to be broken. At least I'd done one thing right over the last horrible few days. One thing that wasn't mean or bitter or jealous or . . .

I stood up so suddenly I got a head rush. I'd helped Diya. Even though her chance to fulfill her dream should have made my jealousy bomb explode, it hadn't.

I paced my room.

I still had this underlying feeling of awfulness about how things were with Margot, Ethan, and Jude. But another feeling was forming now, on top of that one. I'd helped an artist get one step closer to her dream without getting jealous or melting down. My brain, my heart—maybe they weren't so broken after all. Maybe they could handle more than I thought they could.

And just like that, I knew what I had to do.

I jumped back onto my bed and typed *ABT summer intensive auditions* into my laptop. When the page came up, I scrolled through the national audition schedule, passing by the Philadelphia one on January eighteenth. The last thing Colleen had texted me about was *Giselle* two weeks ago. If I had actually sent her the text I'd typed out at Fly Zone, we could have been back in touch. She would have told me about the appendectomy. I could have been there for her. I hoped it wasn't too late.

Houston, Orlando, Birmingham, San Francisco . . . my heart dropped as I scanned the list of impossibly faraway cities. I froze at the bottom. The very last audition date: *Washington, DC, Saturday, February 1, 3:30 PM.* Not this Saturday but the next. I looked up driving directions from Colleen's house to the Washington Ballet Theater, where they were holding the auditions. About two hours. It would take some doing to convince my parents to let me drive all that way, but I'd explain why I had to.

I flew downstairs. My parents were in the kitchen talking, but they went quiet when I came in. "Can I talk to you guys?" I asked.

"Okay," Dad said crisply.

"I'm sorry I left earlier. I was upset about some things I still don't want to talk about, but I'm sorry I left." Mom opened her mouth, but I held out my hand. "Wait. Please, there's something else."

I told them about the situation with Colleen. Their faces lit up when I said her name, turned worried when I got to the appendectomy, cautious when I talked about the ABT audition, and thoroughly confused when I said I wanted to drive her to DC two weeks from now.

"Sweetie," Dad said after a beat. "We could take Colleen. One of us should be able to do it that Saturday."

"I know." Tears stung my eyes, because it was true. Even if my parents were mad at me, they'd still drive the friend I hadn't talked to in months to an audition two hours away. "I know you guys would. And I love you for that. But I have to do it. I've been a really horrible friend, and I need to make it up to her, and this would be a start."

Mom sighed and looked at Dad. After what felt like forever, the two of them nodded.

"Really?" I practically squealed. Their eyes turned soft as they looked at me. Like they were proud. Then Dad headed to Mom's study. "I'm printing out directions. I don't trust the apps."

"Thank you!" I yelled as I ran upstairs to my phone.

I'm picking you up at 10am on Feb. 1st for the ABT audition in DC. For the first time in forever, I tapped Send.

Now it was my turn to watch the three dots blink, blink, and disappear. I waited. After all the waiting I'd made her do, this was nothing. If she never responded, I would understand. Even if she said *You can drive me to the audition but I won't talk to you*, I would take that.

My phone buzzed. **Ok,** she said.

Relief eased the tightness in my chest, but soon I felt anxious again, bursting with all the things I needed to say to Colleen but couldn't over text. I dug through my desk drawer until I found a notebook. I started writing. I wrote apologies and confessions. Memories and messy thoughts. I wrote until my hand cramped.

I wrote until I'd filled up six college-ruled pages. One for each month I'd disappeared.

FEBRUARY

CHAPTER TWENTY-FOUR

I PUT THE CAR IN PARK and stared at Colleen's front door. One week ago, I'd driven here to give her the letter I'd written. No one was home, so I'd put it in the mailbox. I wanted to give her time to sit with it before she had to see me. Time to figure out what she did or didn't want to say before she had to spend two hours in the car, going to the most important audition of her life with the best friend who'd abandoned her. I hadn't heard from her since she'd texted **Ok**. But she hadn't changed her mind, either, so here I was.

Colleen opened the door and walked down her front steps, carrying her dance bag in the crook of her elbow. I smiled. She looked the same as always. Hair pulled into a high bun, shoulders back, long legs floating her down the stairs like she was Cinderella entering the Prince's ballroom instead of my parents' Honda Civic.

"Hello, stranger," she said after settling into the passenger seat and brushing some Ferdinand hair from her jeans.

"Hi," I squeaked. I'd known this was going to be awkward. But there's knowing and there's experiencing, and one sucks infinitely more than the other. I took a deep breath and pushed through it. "Ready?" I asked.

She nodded, staring over the dashboard. At first, the only sounds in the car were the hum of the engine and classical music on the radio. I knew I had to speak first. And the first thing I wanted to know was if she was okay after the appendectomy, so I started there. "How are you feeling?"

"Like I'm missing an organ," Colleen said, darting her eyes to me before turning them back to the road.

"Does it...hurt?" I'd looked up appendectomy recovery, and it said you could have stomach and shoulder pain for a while.

"Not anymore," she said. "I still feel the scar tissue a little, but it's been over three weeks, so I'm fine to dance."

"Good." I breathed out. "I would have texted back," I said quietly. "I need you to know that if you'd told me about the appendectomy and missing the audition, I would have texted you back."

Colleen squinted, her eyes still on the road. "I thought you probably would have. But then I thought, what if you didn't? I knew that if I *did* text you about it, and you didn't text back, that would mean it was really over. And I guess I didn't want to face that."

"I'm sorry I disappeared," I said, gripping the wheel. "I'm so sorry. I just..." I'd thought all the things I wanted to say would be clearer in my brain since I'd written them all down in the letter, but it was still a big, confusing jumble. I pressed on anyway.

"I honestly had no idea who I was without ballet. I still don't, really. It was all such a mess in my head, and I was angry about so many things, and jealous of you, like *so* jealous, and I couldn't deal with it. I mean, I read all your texts, and I was so happy you weren't totally gone, but I couldn't...I didn't...it was too hard, so I bailed. I'm so sorry. It was unbelievably shitty of me."

I took a breath. "And I'm sorry I made it seem like ballet was more important to me than you. It's not. And if you hate me right now, that's totally fair."

Colleen was watching me closely. Then she tipped her head back on the seat and closed her eyes. "Yeah. What you did was shitty. It was kind of the shittiest."

Another quiet settled over the car. My stomach dropped. That was the end of it.

"But I don't hate you," Colleen said after a minute. "You're my best friend. I love you no matter what."

My mouth hung open. "But I...I didn't talk to you for six months."

"Like I said, the shittiest. But what happened to you, the injury..." Colleen shuddered. "I was there, remember? I saw it. I *heard* it. And I can't imagine what it would feel like to not be able to dance. To lose the thing you'd worked forever for. *That* is the actual shittiest. Of course you disappeared for a while. It sucked, and it hurt, but I get it. I do."

The sun seemed brighter all of a sudden as it streamed through the windows. Colleen still loved me. Colleen understood. I'd lost ballet, and I could never get it back. It didn't mean I could never be happy again. But it did mean that I'd lost something irreplaceable, no matter how flawed it was, and I wasn't a selfish, horrible person because I was broken up about it.

I'd done something shitty. I could come back from shitty.

"I don't know if I deserve your understanding right now," I said, trying to keep my voice steady. "But I'm really glad you're giving it to me because I've missed the hell out of you."

The corner of Colleen's mouth lifted. "Yeah, you said that in the letter. Like seventeen times."

I smiled and cringed at the same time. "Did I sound deranged?"

"Nah, you just sounded sorry. And okay, maybe a little deranged."

I laughed.

"And I missed you, too, dummy."

Then we were both laughing. And after I carefully merged onto the interstate, we started talking nonstop. We caught each other up on everything. She told me about *Giselle* rehearsals and her brother's first date and Ferdinand's obsession with the potted ficus on her new neighbor's front steps.

"It's awkward because they have a son who's our age, and he's really cute, and he's on the porch reading all the time."

"Do you guys talk?"

"Moderately. I'm usually too busy trying to make sure Ferd isn't peeing on the ficus. But he's really sweet about it."

"What's his name?" I asked.

Colleen cleared her throat. "Don't laugh."

"Oh my God."

"Swanson Vandervort." I was silent for a full five seconds before bursting into obnoxious laughter.

"It's dignified!" Colleen yelled over me. It was a while before I could stop. Leave it to Colleen to have a crush on a Swanson Vandervort.

"Colleen Vandervort has a nice ring to it," I said, blinking the tears out of my eyes.

"You know I'm never changing my name," she said. "I'm Colleen Alexander now and forever. So *anyway*, what's going on with you?"

I sighed, reluctant to bring down our happy vibe. But Colleen prodded, so I told her everything from the musical audition to the ice rink to the last awful couple of weeks—where I sat apart from

Margot in homeroom and study hall, avoided eye contact with Ethan in English, and dodged Jude altogether.

And kept skipping rehearsal. I'd missed six over the last two weeks and had gotten a chilly voice mail from Mrs. Sorenson the day before, saying she regretted to inform me that she'd have to make "other arrangements" for my part. I felt like crying every time I thought about it.

"I just wish it could all go back to how it was before," I said. Talking about it made me miss Margot, Ethan, Jude, and the musical even more.

"Can't it?" Colleen said. "I don't know about the musical, but can't you make up with Margot and Ethan? And make out with Jude again?" She raised an eyebrow.

"I . . . don't think it's that simple."

"Why?"

"Because I was so out of control that night. I got so furious at Margot, and then I started bawling with Jude when I thought I broke my leg again, and when I realized I was okay I *kissed* him, and then I told him to stay away from me and brought up his ex-girlfriend . . . I just, I blew everything up."

Colleen halfway concealed a smile. "Colleen! This is *not* a funny story!"

She put her hands up. "I know, I know. It's just, I've never seen you that 'out of control' before. I'm kind of sad I missed it."

"Trust me, you don't want that image in your brain."

Colleen snorted. "I mean, it's okay to be angry, even at your friends. It's okay to be scared, even if you weren't actually hurt. It's okay to kiss someone, even if it's not for a great reason. You were emotional that night, that's all. I don't think they'll be mad at you forever for being emotional."

"Who wants to be friends with someone *that* emotional? God, who wants to *date* someone that emotional?" I sighed, deep and heavy. "I think I just have to accept that things can't go back to the way they were."

Colleen stared at me for a second. She took a breath to say something but looked out the window instead.

"Not everything is so broken it has to stay that way, Alina," she finally said. "Some things, you can fix."

I drove in silence for a while, thinking about that. When I fell, my leg broke in a way that meant I couldn't do pointe again. It meant I could never be in the classical ballet companies I'd always dreamed of. But not everything broke like that. Colleen and I were fixing our friendship, even after six and a half months of not talking. And I'd helped Diya fix her dance in the musical, making it more likely to get her a role on Broadway.

Maybe, even though things had shattered at the rink, I could fix things with Margot, Ethan, and Jude, too. The thought filled me with hope.

It pushed me to ask a question that had been on my mind lately. "Do you think ballet can be fixed?" Even though we'd never talked about it, I knew Colleen would know what I meant.

"Yes," she said. It surprised me, how sure she sounded. "I mean, I know you can't always change a *person*. Like, Kira will probably never see as much potential in me as she does in Juliet and Spencer."

Anger bubbled up at that. "It's such bullshit that you're not Giselle. You were made for that part." She really was. She'd nail the airy, lighthearted innocence of Giselle in Act I and the willowy, ethereal grace of Giselle in Act II.

Colleen smiled wryly. "Not according to Kira." She wiggled her arms. "Too athletic, remember?"

I groaned. "Why did she always say that?"

Colleen tilted her head. "There are a lot of people in the ballet world who look at Black girls' bodies and see 'muscular athlete' instead of 'graceful, delicate fairy.'"

"Oh." I let that sink in. Ballet dancers *were* muscular athletes, but they gave the illusion of softness, delicateness. Colleen did that so beautifully it could take my breath away. Could Kira really not see that? Would other people in the ballet world not see that?

I shook my head. "I could never figure out what Kira was talking about when she'd tell you to soften your arms," I said.

"I believed her at first," Colleen said. "But then, I don't know. You get older and start seeing yourself and your strengths more clearly. And you also see what biases other people have and how they see you—or don't see you. Like, do you remember the role model project when we were thirteen? Where Kira asked everyone to choose a role model to study, and she let everyone else pick whoever they wanted, but practically forced me to choose Misty Copeland?"

"Yeah," I said slowly as it came back to me.

"I mean, I *love* Misty, don't get me wrong. She's amazing. But we're such different dancers, and anyone should be able to see that, *especially* my ballet teacher. But because Misty Copeland is the only Black principal ballerina in the history of ABT, Kira was like, 'Well, Colleen's Black, too. So she should be like Misty Copeland.'"

I squeezed the wheel, and I realized that even though Kira had limited us both, our experiences at KDBS had been really different. In some ways, Kira had grouped me in with the white girls, given me the same advantages. And if I hadn't gotten injured, our experiences outside KDBS would have been really different, too.

"I wish I'd known how to talk about this stuff earlier," I said, hating how alone Colleen must have felt at KDBS. "I'm sorry I didn't."

"I always wondered when we would talk about it," Colleen said, smiling a little. "I think we were both just so focused on becoming the best dancers we could possibly be. But then there comes a point where you can't ignore it anymore. Especially when you realize that there are a lot of other people like Kira in the ballet world."

I nodded, not knowing what to say.

"But ballet isn't just those people, you know?" Colleen said, her voice rising. "It's so many others—artistic directors and choreographers and teachers and dancers and kids who go to the ballet for the first time and fall in love with it because it isn't like anything they've ever seen. There's some ten-year-old out there now who's going to be the next great ballet choreographer, and who knows how she'll change things? And I read about how some companies are working with activists to change the racist parts of classical ballets. Plus, pre-professional schools are getting more diverse, so ballet companies could look really different soon. Ballet can evolve. And I want to be part of that."

I glanced at her. All the years we danced together, I thought Colleen and I wanted the same thing. To dance ballet at ABT. But at some point, Colleen had started wanting more—she wanted to change ballet for the better. I wished again that I'd been able to talk with her about this stuff earlier. It made me wonder how things might have been different. But it wasn't too late.

"Do you remember that day we talked to Kira after the *Nutcracker* cast list went up?" I asked.

"Oh my God, yeah. She totally guilted us for questioning her."

"Exactly! And like, ballet had trained me so well to 'follow the rules' and 'listen to your teacher' that I just accepted it. I didn't even question if what she was saying was right or wrong. It was like Kira was all-powerful."

240

"Yup," Colleen said. I took a breath and felt something shift inside me. It was like we were taking some of that power away, just by talking about it.

Something else occurred to me then. How much did accepting roles like Chinese Tea affect the way I lived my life now? I hadn't even *tried* to make things better with Margot, Ethan, and Jude for the past two weeks. I'd just assumed that things couldn't get better. Jude had said his dad's voice got into his head for a while. This was one way Kira's had gotten into mine—telling me I had to accept things the way they were, even if they weren't right.

"Anyway," Colleen went on. "Ballet has a lot of problems, but it can change. And I want to help change it."

"And I'll help you change it," I said. "However I can." I'd never felt so sure of anything in my life.

"I know you will," Colleen said. And as she did, something strange happened, and I knew I'd never be able to explain it to anyone. I saw something, like a vision, even though I didn't believe in those. It was of Colleen, looking like she did right now—eyes focused, a slight smile curving her lips—but she was wearing Giselle's famous Wili costume.

She extended her right arm, and then her left. Then she knelt into a deep curtsy, slowly lowering her head. She was doing her reverence, in front of a packed crowd at the Metropolitan Opera House.

And I was in the front row, cheering her on.

※

I watched Colleen pin a number to her leotard, throw me one last nervous smile, and disappear into the large studio with a crowd of other girls. In the quiet lobby, my leg ached from the long drive, so I rolled my ankle out. There was a piece of my heart that couldn't be all the way happy for Colleen, because it was still sad for me. But I also felt...proud. Of Colleen for being one step closer to her dream. Of me for helping her get there. Of us for wanting to change ballet. Suddenly, I thought back to dancing with Diya in her room. *That* was why it had felt so amazing. It wasn't just about helping someone achieve their dreams. It was about changing a whole art form. Opening it up to new voices and bodies. Making it better.

I realized my puppy was still growing up, despite the setback I'd had a couple of weeks ago. The thought was bittersweet, reminding me of Jude. So I did what I'd been doing lately when the sadness kicked in. I let myself feel it for a while. I sat down on the floor with my back against the wall. When classical music drifted out from the studio's doors, I tensed, waiting to get overwhelmed. But I didn't. I didn't even have to do deep breaths. Birdie had mentioned that the need to do them would fade over time. I hadn't believed her and told her that. She'd shrugged and said, "What do I know, I'm just the person who taught you how to walk again." I smiled at the memory.

After a bit, my phone started buzzing. Diya was texting me.

I told Mrs. Sorenson you had a personal issue of a sensitive nature and that's why you missed the last two weeks of rehearsal.

I asked her not to kick you out.

I have major sway with Mrs. S so you've got a chance.

Don't mess it up.

A flash of hope lit up inside me. Mrs. Sorenson's voice mail had sounded so final. But if anyone could change her mind, it was Diya. This was my last chance. On Monday, I was going to apologize to Mrs. Sorenson and Ms. Langford. On Monday, I was going back to rehearsal.

I'll be there. Thank you, I texted back.

I owed you. Now we're even.

Also you're welcome.

I smiled as the swinging doors flew open. The same girls who had fluttered into the room a couple of hours before were streaming out, breathing fast and glistening with sweat. I spotted Colleen in the crowd.

When she reached me, her eyes had a faraway look. "Ready to go?" I asked gently.

Colleen nodded and we walked to the car in silence. I knew she had to collect herself before saying anything. I'd wait until she was ready.

It was only after Colleen had climbed in, pulled the door shut, and flung her dance bag onto the backseat that she made any kind of sound at all. It was a long, shaky sigh, which she let out as she buried her face in her hands. I knew it wasn't a sign of how the audition went, only the release of the metric ton of pressure she'd felt inside the studio.

"I want it so much," she finally whispered. "And everyone was so good. *So* good." She lifted her head. "I hate this part."

I put my hand on her arm and squeezed. My grand vision of Colleen on the Metropolitan Opera House stage could only happen if the people in that room back there let her in. At the moment, we could only hope they would see how good she was in the crowd of talented girls. That they would accept her into the ABT summer intensive, and then ask her to stay at the school permanently, and then hire her into the company, and then promote her up the ranks from corps to soloist to principal. It was a long, exhausting road, and it would be full of many more moments like this one, I was sure.

But she could do it. I knew she could.

Colleen wiped her fingers across her eyes. "I know I can do it," she said, echoing the words in my head. "It's just..."

"I know." Then I was crying, too. We cried because doing

something brave didn't always make you feel brave. We cried because fixing things was hard, and change was slow. We cried for all the ways that loving something with all your heart can break it at the same time.

Eventually, we got back on the road. Somewhere between Rockville and Frederick, Colleen took my phone and found the playlist we'd made a couple of years ago. It started with Whitney Houston's "I Wanna Dance with Somebody" and ended with Mitski's "Your Best American Girl" and had Lizzo, Shakira, and Beyoncé in between. We sang along to every song, our voices loud and wild and fervent.

Because we knew, maybe since a long time ago, maybe just since this trip, that broken hearts didn't stay that way forever. That love paired with strength, whether it went into the most explosive grand jeté or the slow, steady push of your foot on the gas pedal, could change the world.

CHAPTER TWENTY-FIVE

I HELD ON TIGHT to that trip with Colleen and the fire it gave me as I drove to school on Monday, ready to fix things. Or try to, at least. Josie had missed the bus earlier, so she had to catch a ride with me.

We'd been giving each other the silent treatment again, ever since she'd snitched about rehearsal not being canceled. I was sure Josie had tattled partly because she was mad at me for missing her solo. But maybe, just like when she kept bringing up racism in ballet, she'd also done it because she cared.

"I'm sorry I missed your solo," I said.

Josie's head jerked up. "Um...transition much?"

"I won't miss it next time."

Josie blinked at me for a few seconds before staring out over the dashboard again, wide-eyed. She really hadn't been expecting an apology from me, which was fair. I couldn't remember the last time I'd apologized to her, either.

"So are they going to let you back into the musical?" she said after a minute.

"I don't know." My heart sped up. "I hope so."

"Okay, well, we're supposed to pick our dancers for the student showcase by next month, and I still need Noah and Laurel. So if they do let you back in, dance in front of them or something."

I still didn't know why she wanted them for her piece so badly. Sure, Laurel's battements were impressive, and Noah's footwork was swift. But there was something missing. Whenever I watched them dance, it was like they were too busy trying to impress everyone with their skills to really feel the music or express an emotion.

"Do you want to know what I think? About your dance?" I asked.

Josie stared at me suspiciously. It had been years since I'd taken enough of an interest in her dancing to freely offer advice. "Um, sure."

"I don't think Noah and Laurel are right for it. They don't have feeling in their dancing, and from what you were saying about *Strange Harmonies*, it needs emotional expression, not only technique."

Josie opened her mouth to argue, but then she frowned, considering.

"I saw some of what you were working on," I said. "At Christmas. It's really good, Josie. And you made it that way. I think *you* should dance in it."

Josie still didn't say anything. She switched off the radio and stared out the window. It was deadly quiet in the car as I turned into the Eagle View parking lot, found a spot, and turned off the ignition. Josie gathered up her backpack and put her fingers on the door handle.

"You might have a point," she said.

Now it was my turn to blink at her in surprise. "Really?" I said, recovering. "I mean, yeah. Just think about it."

"I will." She opened the door, giving me a small, hesitant smile before stepping out of the car and joining a group of her friends in front of school.

I took a second before getting out, my mouth stretching into a smile, too. Things weren't all the way better between Josie and me. It was hard to know what that would look like for us, honestly. But the conversation had made me feel good. And combined with the strength I was carrying from the road trip with Colleen, I walked into Eagle View with more confidence than I'd ever had before.

I got to homeroom, ready to talk to Margot. But she wasn't there. I fidgeted in my seat, looking up every time someone passed by the doorway, but she never came.

As soon as the bell rang, I rushed to the senior lockers to try to catch Ethan, but he wasn't there, either. When I walked into English, he was already in his seat, fiddling with his pen and staring out the window. I looked at my desk, and at Paul sitting behind it. He put his hands together and bowed.

I stared at Paul's smirking face and the fire inside me sparked, blazed. Why the hell had I accepted *this*? So what if I'd sat here on the first day and written my name on a stupid seating chart? Why should a piece of paper tell me where to sit?

"Hey, Ice Pri—"

I strode over to my desk, but instead of sitting down, I grabbed the sides and dragged it across the room. The desk made pretty horrendous scraping noises against the floor as I maneuvered it between Ethan's seat and the window. Then I sat down.

Everyone in class was staring at me, including Ethan. A surprised smile was spreading across his face.

Jake smacked Paul on the back. "*Denied!*" he yelled gleefully.

Paul sneered. "Dumb bitch," he said. I guess as long as I was in front of him, icing him out, he was in control of the game. But now that I'd broken the rules, he couldn't play anymore. He opened his mouth to say something else, but Ethan slapped his hands on his desk.

"Shut up, Paul," Ethan snapped. "We've all watched you try to get her attention with your bullshit. We saw you, we heard you, you failed. So stop talking."

The only indication that Paul had heard any of this was a slight twitch of his mouth. But he wasn't about to let Ethan deflect the attention away from me. "You know he's gay, right, Princess? If you're so desperate, I could've given you some." He looked suggestively at his crotch.

"From what I've heard," Ethan said, waving his hand toward Paul's nether regions, "you don't have that much to spare." He put his index finger and thumb about two inches apart.

That did it. Paul's eyes went directly to Ethan as he stood up and took a scary step toward him. But I stood up, too. As I did, I tightened my core, threw my shoulders back, and straightened my spine. With all the adrenaline pumping through my body, my ballet posture automatically kicked in. Paul kept moving toward Ethan, so I lifted my arm in front of me, blocking his way.

"Paul," I said, "if you want people to stop talking about the size of your penis, stop being such a giant dick. It's negative correlation. The more you *act* like a dick, the smaller people will assume your *actual* dick is. So be a normal human being—stop hitting on girls who don't want to be hit on, stop making racist jokes—and everyone will assume it's normal-sized. Okay?"

Silence. Then a snicker, followed by an all-out laugh. Then someone cleared their throat and my eyes shot to the door. Ms. Belson was there. "All right," she said, swiftly taking in the scene. "We'll keep these seating arrangements for now. Alina, please see me after class."

∼

Apparently there was no punishment for saying "dick" in Ms. Belson's class. It helped that I told her Paul and Jake had been harassing me since the beginning of the semester. It also helped that Ethan stayed to back me up, and that he had been keeping a record of it. Like, writing down everything Paul and Jake said to me and when in his notebook. He'd even kept the record up for the two weeks we weren't talking. Because, of course he did.

Ms. Belson apologized for not knowing, and said she'd talk to Paul and Jake, and let the principal know about their behavior. She told me to keep Ethan's record of what they'd said, because it could come in handy if I wanted to take further action.

When she dismissed us, Ethan and I made our way out the door. By now, we only had a couple of minutes to get to our next classes, but we lingered in the hallway. I smirked at the notebook he was still holding, open to the page where he had written down every one of Paul's and Jake's gross words. All along the margins were doodles of Paul and Jake getting eaten by various animals. A shark, a bear, a cute little bunny.

"Not my most sophisticated work, but very therapeutic," Ethan said. I laughed. I'd missed him so much.

"Thank you. Really," I said. "And I'm sorry for ditching rehearsals and not waiting for you by the lockers and…hurting your best friend." My face fell when I said that part.

"Alina," Ethan said, a bit exasperated. "It's not…I'm not angry at you for that. I'm sorry it happened, but you're my friend, too."

I should already have known that. But hearing it made me ridiculously happy.

"I was just mad that you decided to shut us out all of a sudden. Like we didn't matter to you."

"That's definitely not true."

"I know." We were quiet for a few seconds. "Anyway, look. You didn't even have to apologize to me, because you gave me a great shot." He pulled his phone out of his bag and held it up. I stared at the picture. It was my profile, and because Ethan had been sitting down when he took it, I looked larger than life. My arm was stretched in front of me, like I was a sorceress warding off some unseen evil.

"Whoa."

"I think I'll call it 'The Negative Correlation of Dicks Speech.'"

"You're not posting it, are you?"

Ethan rolled his eyes. "Do you think I just met you? No, I'm not posting it. But people *will* talk about it, and word travels fast around here, so be prepared."

"Got it. Will you send it to me, though?" Ethan tapped a few buttons and my phone lit up with the picture.

"You're coming to rehearsal today, right?" he asked.

"Yes," I said nervously. "I mean, if they let me back in." Ethan squeezed my shoulder, holding it for a few seconds before a teacher shooed us on to our next classes. And even though I still had knots in my stomach, I felt lighter than I had in a while.

That feeling helped me get through my second Serious Teacher Conversation of the day. Before rehearsal, I met with Mrs. Sorenson and Ms. Langford in the choir room. I convinced them I deserved to stay in the musical, listened to their lectures, and swore I wouldn't disappear again.

"You better not," Ms. Langford said as I stood up to leave. "Otherwise Cyd Charisse's ghost will haunt you." It had to be a joke, but Ms. Langford wasn't smiling. So I gave a quick nod and got out of there.

This was good. I was fixing things. I took a big breath as I walked into the auditorium. I got about two steps in when I heard a scream.

"Alinaaaaa!" Laney barreled down the aisle, a Snickers bar waving in her hand. Ada, who'd been lying on the floor with her coat as a pillow, jerked up. They enveloped me in a hug.

"We missed you!" Ada said.

"We could hardly dance without you," Laney added, doing a weird, disjointed version of the choreography to demonstrate.

"Okay, okay." I gestured for her to stop. "I'm sorry, it won't happen again."

"See that it doesn't," Laney and Ada said in unison, and then broke into laughter.

Okay, maybe in all the drama, I'd forgotten how much I liked these other musical weirdos. As they caught me up on the rehearsals I'd missed, I scanned the auditorium. No sign of Margot. Jude, Ethan, and Harrison were sitting on the edge of the stage, and a few of the other usual seniors stood facing them, tossing snacks back and forth. Ethan and Harrison were sharing a Dr Pepper, which was interesting. I'd told Colleen how I was sure Harrison had joined the musical to get closer to Ethan, and she was predictably delighted about the whole thing. I tapped out a quick text, telling her of this latest development.

She responded a few seconds later. **In some cultures, sharing a Dr Pepper means you're married. How's rehearsal?**

Ok…I hope. I'll fill you in after.

I tucked my phone away as Margot strode into the auditorium, wearing her headphones. She took them off as the senior group onstage greeted her. Ethan threw a bag of Combos at her head. She smirked, caught it, and whipped it back so fast Ethan didn't have time to react and it hit him in the face. Everyone cackled.

Maybe it had happened gradually, or during the rehearsals I'd missed, but Margot seemed completely at ease with everyone. She'd told me before that she wasn't great friends with most of the musical people, but it didn't look like that anymore.

"Gonna fill up," Laney said, grabbing her water bottle. "Don't disappear again."

"I won't," I said, distracted, as Ada grabbed her water bottle and followed Laney out. I bounced on my toes and avoided looking at Margot and the group of seniors on the stage again. I wasn't quite ready to talk to them yet, not in front of all these people. Instead, I looked around for Diya. She was sitting on the piano bench at the opposite end of the stage, studying her music.

"Hey," I said, climbing up to join her. I sat on the floor beside the bench and started stretching.

Diya gave me a knowing smile. "Welcome back."

"Thanks for talking to Mrs. Sorenson. You were right about having major sway with her. I thought I'd be groveling a lot longer."

She shrugged. "Like I said, I owed you." We fell into an easy silence, me stretching, her paging through her music.

"How's the worm coming?" I asked a minute later.

"Bad. I got a rug burn on my chin."

I snorted.

"No, seriously," she said, lifting her head and pointing to a mark on the underside of her chin. "My brother thought it was a"—she lowered her voice—"a hickey and interrogated me for an hour."

I laughed. "That seems like a weird place for a hickey."

"That's what *I* said!"

Our laughter echoed. I stopped abruptly, because the auditorium had gotten strangely quiet. I looked around and saw the senior group onstage staring at us. Margot looked away quickly, putting her headphones back on. Ethan gave me a *What are you doing?* look. Jude just seemed confused. A knot formed in my stomach. I didn't want to make things *worse* between us.

I'd turned back to Diya, trying to figure out something to say, when someone coughed behind us. I whipped around, a little on edge. It was a freshman girl in the chorus. She put her hands out instinctively. "Sorry, didn't mean to scare you."

The auditorium filled back up with the usual noises, so I calmed down a little. "You're fine," I said. The girl smiled, playing with the zipper on her pink hoodie. "I heard about what you said to Paul Manley. My sister's in that class? Anyway, I wanted to say thanks."

Geez, Ethan was right. Word traveled fast. "It was, um, my pleasure." I smiled. Because it kind of was. "What's your name?"

"Marin."

"Wait wait, what did you say to Paul?" Diya raised an eyebrow.

When I hesitated, Marin jumped in. "Oh my God, it was amazing. I mean, I assume it was. But basically..." She told Diya the whole story, starting with Paul and Jake's perpetual assholery and ending with my Negative Correlation of Dicks Speech. There was a short pause, and then Diya threw her head back and laughed, almost as hard as she had when we were dancing in her room. "That is *hilarious*," she finally got out.

"Also," Marin said, looking shyly at Diya as our laughter died down. "I think you have an amazing voice. I'm jealous of it, to be honest. A lot of people are. I think you'll be on Broadway in, like, a year, tops."

"Oh." Diya gave her a soft smile. "Thanks, Marin."

Marin nodded. As she walked away, Diya shook her head in awe. "I still can't get over the 'be a normal human and everyone will assume it's normal-sized' part." Our laughter kicked up again. I'd only really hung out with Diya once before, but it felt like we were old friends.

When I glanced at the senior group again, my happy feelings dissolved. Ethan was staring at Jude. Jude was staring at the floor, his mouth tight. Then he pushed off the stage and out the door.

CHAPTER TWENTY-SIX

REHEARSAL WAS ABOUT TO START, but Jude hadn't come back yet. He'd looked so hurt. Was it because I was friends with his ex? Did he hate her that much? Did he hate me that much?

"Alina!" Ms. Langford's voice startled me out of my thoughts. She waved me over to where she was sitting in the front row. "Good news about the ballet duet for the 'Broadway Melody' number," she said, her tone a bit clipped. She was still annoyed at me for missing so much rehearsal, and I didn't blame her.

"Great," I said, trying to show enthusiasm. God, Jude probably wouldn't want to learn another dance with me now. I was sure he'd be civil about it, like he was with Diya rehearsing the bench scene. The thought turned me cold. I'd hate being civil with Jude when we'd been so much more.

"I wanted to get someone who could do it justice, so I called around, and Kira Dobrow said she'd do it. She said you were a student of hers?"

That snapped me out of my Jude thoughts. "Wait, *what?*" I tried to remember how to breathe. "You—you're not, you're not choreographing it?"

"Ballet isn't my forte, Alina. Kira will give you something much better to work with. Your and Jude's first rehearsal with her is this Saturday."

Sweat broke out on my forehead, the back of my neck. If it was Kira, it wouldn't be ballet in quotation marks. It would be Ballet with a capital *B*. The kind I couldn't do anymore. "Um...Ms. Langford...the thing is—"

"Oh, I almost forgot, we'll need to fit you for the costume," Ms. Langford interrupted. She went on about the measurements, but I wasn't processing. Eventually, she shooed me back onto the stage. I took my place upstage right and spotted Jude. He'd finally returned. I watched Ms. Langford telling him about the duet. He nodded, a bit grimly. He didn't look for me.

Somehow, I made it through the rest of rehearsal. I felt like crap. But Mrs. Sorenson and Ms. Langford had given me another chance, along with the rest of the cast. I owed them all 100 percent. So I sang and smiled and danced full-out. It was so exhausting that all I could think about when Mrs. Sorenson dismissed us was taking a nap.

Margot zoomed out of the auditorium before I had a chance to say anything. Which was fine, because I felt so jumbled I'd probably mess it up if I tried to talk to her now. I bolted to my car, sped home, changed into my pajama pants, and sat on my yoga mat, resting my head against the side of my bed.

Fixing things with Margot and Jude wasn't as easy as it was with Ethan. And going back to the musical wasn't as easy as I'd thought it would be, either, since now I had to do ballet. Actual ballet. With Kira. I pressed my head farther into the soft mattress, tempted to crawl onto it and lift the covers over my head. To hide from reality like before. But I'd promised I wouldn't disappear from the musical again, and I'd promised myself I would try to fix things.

I took a deep breath. Kira. Ballet. That was on Saturday. That could wait for now. What I couldn't wait for any longer was talking to Jude. I needed us to be back where we were. I needed to talk things over with him in the quiet, just us, like we had before.

I ran downstairs, still in my pajama pants. Because when you get the balls to talk to the guy you've been wanting to talk to for weeks, you don't wait around. I flung the door open and almost screamed.

Jude was there. On my doorstep. Next to a woman I recognized from somewhere. Her fist was up, about to knock. "The famous Alina!" she said, smiling wide and lowering her arm. "I've been dying to meet you! I'm Isla." She shook my hand with warm, enthusiastic pumps. Oh my God. The refrigerator pictures. Jude's mom.

"Hi, um, great meeting you," I said, glancing at Jude, who was carefully avoiding my eyes.

My mom appeared behind me, guiding me away from the door. She invited them in and took Isla's bag as they exchanged mom talk about some yard sale they were planning. Jude and I hovered awkwardly. I was really glad he was here, but *why* was he here?

Isla turned back to me. "I've heard so much about you, I feel like I know you already. I can't *wait* to see you two dance together in the musical, I was—"

"We get it, Mom, it'll be the thrill of your life," Jude said.

Isla smiled slyly at me. "I have embarrassed my son." She put a hand to her heart and sighed dramatically. "My only child. The fruit of my loins. How he will ever forgive me for this grave sin, I do not know. I only hope—"

"*Mom*, okay, okay." Jude groaned. Isla raised her eyebrows at him, like *You deserved it*. Then she winked at me.

"Okay, go away now, shoo!" Isla put her hands on Jude's shoulders and spun him toward the stairs. "Ella and I have a neighborhood yard sale to organize."

As I walked to the stairs with Jude, I looked over to catch Mom's eye. I'd never had a boy in my room before, and I didn't know if it was allowed. But she was staring at the tea she was whisking like it was the most fascinating thing in the world, not even trying to hide the grin that was taking over her whole face.

When we got to my room, Jude turned to me but kept his eyes on the floor. "Sorry for that. I mentioned I was coming over here, and she was like, 'Great, I need to talk to Ella about the yard sale. I'll come with you.' I wanted to explain it wasn't a good time, but—"

"It's fine." I gestured to my pajama pants. "I was clearly in the middle of something important."

He smiled. God, I'd missed his smile. It was more strained than usual, but still.

In the silence that followed, Jude glanced around my room, taking in the bare walls, the yoga mat, the picture on my nightstand. He picked it up, studying it with an unreadable expression on his face. I sat on the edge of my bed. "You can sit down. If you want."

He carefully put the picture back in its place and sat beside me. His leg bounced up and down, his breathing was shallow.

"I . . . I've been wanting to tell you how sorry I am," I started. "For saying that thing about Diya at the rink."

"Mm-hmm," he said, distracted. Silence filled my room again until Jude let out a frustrated sigh. "Sorry, you probably don't want to talk about it, but I can't, I can't not." He fidgeted, rubbing his palms against his thighs, turning to face me, then turning away again. "God, I'm so angry I feel like I'm going to explode or implode or . . ." He trailed off, shaking his head.

I'd never seen Jude angry before. Happy and serious and sad and a little cocky and whatever emotion one feels on a trampoline—I'd seen all those. But I understood why he was angry. I'd kissed him, and then told him I would have rejected him like his ex-girlfriend did. And then I'd become friends with her.

"Paul fucking Manley," Jude spat out.

"Wh-what?"

"I can't believe he said that stuff to you. Jake, too. *Assholes*."

I opened my mouth to tell him everything was okay, but his eyes shot to mine. "I know you handled it. Awesomely. But when I heard Marin saying what happened, all I could think about was punching Paul and Jake in their stupid jerk-ass faces, which would be pointless anyway, because what would that even *do*—"

"Hey, hey." I interrupted Jude's rambling, relieved he was mad about Paul and Jake, not about the ice rink fiasco. Relieved he still cared enough about me to be mad. In his very Jude way. All the relief made me giddy. I broke into uncontrollable giggles.

Jude looked at me like I'd gone bananas. "Um..."

"Stupid jerk-ass faces?" I gasped out.

Jude kept staring at me. "I'm glad my rage is funny to you."

That made me laugh even harder. Which made Jude laugh. Which felt amazing. Us together, shaking with laughter, my stomach muscles hurting like I'd just done a hundred sit-ups.

We sobered up finally, our breathing settling back into a comfortable rhythm. I looked at him. "I really am okay."

He held my gaze steadily for the first time in weeks. "I know you are."

I wanted to hold on to that look forever. Hazel and warm. I wanted to kiss him again, but Jude looked away too soon, like the moment didn't exist for him.

"And I really am sorry about everything at the ice rink, what I said. I—"

"It's okay." Jude shook his head. "You don't have to apologize for that. I understand." His voice was quiet but firm. Like, end-of-this-particular-conversation firm. "So anyway..." He leaned back on his hands, more at ease after our laughing spell. "Looks like we've got a rehearsal Saturday?"

I sighed. "Yeah."

He squinted at me. "I watched the ballet duet on YouTube, the one from the movie. And she's not wearing pointe shoes. She's barefoot. So maybe it won't be so different than the dancing we've been doing?"

I smiled but shook my head. "My old ballet teacher Kira is choreographing it. So it'll be different. It'll be real ballet."

"Oh," Jude said, scrunching his mouth to the side. "I'm sorry."

I nodded but couldn't bring myself to say anything.

"Well," he said, "*I'm* going to be doing ballet with you, and I'll be so spectacularly bad it might distract you from everything else."

"Nah. I bet you'll be a natural. You have a ballet body."

"I *do*?" He looked down at his torso, studying it.

"I know it sounds girly, but—"

"Oh, I don't think so. I've seen guys do ballet before at my cousin's shows. I just thought you were being too nice to me."

Of course. This was Jude I was talking to. He wouldn't feel like his ego was being threatened if I associated him with ballet. He drank tea in the bath and knitted his own lumpy gloves and was just...*Jude*. And while that thought made me even sadder that I wasn't kissing him right now, it also made it easier to confess something to him.

"I'm afraid of doing ballet again," I said. "It's hard enough to move on from it, but now that I have to go back...I don't know. It's going to be so different. Most people might not be able to tell, but I will. And Kira will. I won't feel the same and I won't look the same, and I'm afraid it'll hurt. Not physically," I added. "Just, in every other way."

"I don't want you to hurt," Jude said. "Like, ever. But to be completely honest, I can't stop wondering . . ." He hesitated.

"Wondering what?"

"Wondering what you look like when you do ballet. Or no, that's not it. It's more like, wondering what ballet looks like when you do it."

I blinked at him. "Oh."

He took a deep breath. "For three years, I've seen you across the street. Listening to your music, in another universe. And I hear that you dance. And I only know a little bit about ballet, from my cousin. I mean, I know that it's pretty and involves a lot of poufy skirt things and that's about it. Seeing you, in the distance, it made sense that you'd be good at it, because you're pretty and probably look good in poufy skirt things. But then—"

Jude paused, searching for the right words. "Then, I actually meet you. And you flip me off, which is surprising. And you're smart and funny and say things like 'Arrogance kills elegance' and have passionate interpretations of Sondheim lyrics and you—you talked to me about sadness and puppies in the middle of Winter Formal. You could have just said something polite and walked away, but you didn't."

Before, all those compliments would have made me uncomfortable. Like I was getting something I didn't deserve. Now, as I thought about each one of them, I only felt happy.

Jude went on, quieter this time. "And I kept thinking . . . seeing *that* person, doing ballet, has to be something extraordinary. I know it'll hurt. I know it'll make you sad. But I also know it'll be . . . fascinating and beautiful, and I want to be a part of it. With you. Is that super insensitive? Is that awful?"

I couldn't say anything right then, so I just sat there, breathing in and out.

"It's not awful," I was finally able to say. Because I wanted to be a part of it with him, too. I wanted to dance ballet with Jude.

As soon as I admitted that to myself, I realized something else. I'd been wrong about "Finishing the Hat," but so had he. It wasn't art *or* relationships. Art *or* people. It really was both. An artist's relationships with people could change what she created, for better or worse. When I danced with Jude as the Vamp, my feelings for him let me use my body in a way I never had before, and it felt new and intense and terrific. What would ballet feel like with Jude?

What would ballet feel like when I was in love? Because I definitely was. In love. With Jude. I opened my mouth to tell him, before I lost the courage.

"And just so we're clear," Jude said, "I'm not trying to be romantic or anything. I heard you when you said you didn't want that, and I totally agree."

What? No. No, no, no. "Jude—"

"It's okay," he said. "I've been doing some thinking, and I realized I'm not ready for a relationship anyway. I'm…" He broke off with a heavy sigh. "I'm still dealing with a lot of stuff about my dad leaving. I thought I wasn't, but I am, and I don't want to put that on you. Or anyone," he added quickly.

My mouth hung open. I wanted to tell him that it didn't matter if he was still dealing with stuff. I was, too, and it didn't mean we couldn't be together. But I realized that wasn't exactly true. It would always matter to me if he was hurting. "What kind of stuff?" I asked quietly.

Jude closed his eyes for a second. "As much as I wanted to believe I was completely over my dad's opinions…I apparently still really care what he thinks about me."

"Oh." I was confused. I thought he hadn't seen his dad in a long time and hadn't planned on seeing him again anytime soon.

261

"I went to lunch with him," Jude said, his mouth tight. "After he left me that voice mail."

That surprised me. At Fly Zone, he'd seemed so sure he wouldn't. "When?" I asked.

"Last week. I figured, why keep running away from him? My plan was to look him in the eye, answer every single one of his judgmental questions honestly, and fuck what he thought."

"Sounds like a good plan."

"Except I did the opposite," Jude said, raising his voice. "When he asked me how lacrosse and soccer were going, I told him they were great. Spectacular. Made stuff up about my season stats. Didn't mention the musical at all. It was pathetic. When we were leaving, he slapped me on the back the way he used to and said he was glad I was doing so well."

Jude shook his head in disgust. "I didn't tell my mom or Ethan or anyone that I went. They all think I blew him off, and I was too embarrassed to tell them I didn't. I'm such a coward. God, and I went around giving you all that stupid advice. 'Here's the two things you should do when you're sad. Sadness is like a puppy,'" he said in a mocking voice. "I'm worse than a coward, I'm an impostor."

"You're not an impostor," I said forcefully. He was one of the most genuine people I'd ever met. True, it was hard to reconcile the Jude I knew with the one who had lied about himself to his dad. But one lunch didn't change that. "Things get complicated when you lose something that was important to you, remember?" I said, repeating what he'd said to me at the rink. I wasn't ready to hear it then, but maybe he was now. "You do and think things you never thought you could. But it doesn't make you a coward or an impostor. It just means you're in a complicated situation."

"It shouldn't be that complicated. Not after two and a half years."

I let out a frustrated breath. "I don't get it. You're, like, the least judgmental person in the world. Seriously, since I met you, you've been almost ridiculously understanding. You reassured me that I wasn't a horrible person when I felt like one. You forgave me when I was rude to you. You cut me so much slack, gave me so much room to mess up. Why aren't you giving that to yourself?"

He paused, eyebrows wrinkled. "I don't know."

"And the stuff you said," I went on. "The puppy metaphor, all of it? It really helped me. It wasn't stupid advice."

He looked at me, gauging whether I was telling the truth. I stared back, trying to communicate what he'd given me over the past few months, what he meant to me. But again, he looked away too soon. "I'm glad it helped," he said quietly. "I really am. But the bottom line is, if I'm not okay enough with who I am to be myself around *him*, then I'm not okay to be with yo—" He stopped. "To be in a relationship with anyone. But I hope...I hope we can still be friends."

I was about to tell him I wanted to be so much more than that. That I understood he was going through stuff but I loved him anyway, and we could figure it out together. But then he looked at me, and his eyes were wet, and my heart plummeted. Because it hit me, just how hard the past two years must have been for him. How he carried it all with him, even though it sometimes seemed like he didn't. How terrifying it would be to start a relationship with someone who'd already hurt him once. I wouldn't put him through that.

I forced my mouth into a smile. "Yeah. Of course. Friends."

He smiled, blinking the tears out of his eyes. "Good." He took a few seconds to compose himself. Then he gave me a light, horrifyingly platonic punch on the shoulder. "And friends help each other finish their hats."

As I tried to fall asleep that night, two thoughts kept circling around in my head.

I can't do ballet again.

I can't just be friends with Jude.

But then I stopped myself. *Why not?* I'd gotten kind of good at doing things I thought I couldn't do. I just needed to be brave. And to ask Mrs. Sorenson and Ms. Langford for one more really big favor.

CHAPTER TWENTY-SEVEN

"HI," JUDE SAID AS HE WALKED into the empty auditorium on Saturday morning, pulling off his navy puffy coat. My mouth dropped a little, because he wasn't wearing his usual rehearsal attire of gray sweats and a Fly Zone shirt. Instead, he wore a fitted white T-shirt and opaque black tights—pretty much the standard uniform for boys in ballet.

"That's...a good outfit," I said as he joined me onstage.

"Thought I'd look the part, at least."

My heart did a funny throbbing thing. Jude had worn ballet clothes. He was showing respect for ballet, for what we were about to do. It made me want to kiss him, but that was nothing new.

This past week, things had been all right between us. We'd talked and laughed, and we weren't just being civil. We really were friends again. And even though I couldn't help but want more, I was happy to have him back in general. I tried to focus on that part.

Jude squinted as he took in my fast breathing and the sheen of sweat on my forehead—proof I'd been dancing for a while. "Am I late? I stretched before I got here, so I'm ready to start."

"You're not late," I said, trying not to smile.

"Oh, good." He scanned the auditorium. "Is Kira late?"

"She's not coming." My grin broke out then, I couldn't contain it anymore.

Jude smiled, too, even though he was still confused. "So . . . who's teaching us the dance?"

"Me," I said, and then it all came spilling out. "I didn't want to learn ballet from Kira again. If I'm going to do it, I want to do it for myself. So Mrs. Sorenson and Ms. Langford talked through it and based on my experience, they actually agreed to let me choreograph."

I still felt the thrill of that conversation. The possibilities that had raced through my head as I drove home, so excited to get started I could hardly stand it.

"That's amazing!" Jude held his hand up for a high five. After our palms smacked together, our fingers interlocked for a moment before we let go.

"So should we start?" he asked, stepping back.

I nodded, all business. "The first thing we need to work on is your stance." I moved forward and put my hands on his shoulders, gently pressing down on the taut muscles. Then I grazed my fingertips along the sides of his neck, pulling upward to elongate it. I felt a series of gentle contractions as he swallowed.

I stepped back and surveyed him. "Good. The only other thing is, you need to move your pelvis forward."

He jutted it out. I snorted. "Not that much." He pushed it back too far the other way. "No . . ." It looked like he was doing the pelvic-thrusting *Rocky Horror* dance.

"Here," I said, stepping closer. "Do you mind?" I held my hands out.

He swallowed again. "Sure."

I put my left hand at the base of his spine and my right hand just under his hipbone. His breathing went a little shallow, but he didn't tense up. Ever so slightly, I pushed, bringing his pelvis into perfect alignment. "That's it," I said, quickly stepping back.

"Oh. Okay. Good." Jude nodded, keeping his body rigid in his newfound ballet stance.

"It'll feel more natural after a while, I promise," I said. And then there was nothing more to do but teach him what I'd been working on nonstop for the past week.

I directed him to stand downstage left and I took my position upstage right. I showed him how we'd run in swift circles in opposite directions, and with each revolution, we'd increase the size of the circles until we finally met in the middle of the stage. I thought the circular movements fit the whole dream-sequence vibe of the piece. Dreams didn't follow logical, step-by-step patterns. They swirled, never taking you down a straight path. Once we had the circles down, I showed him how I would pirouette into his arms, and he'd catch and hold my hips as my leg opened into a grand rond de jambe—extending my leg out and then circling it all the way to the back as I thrust both arms out to the side. That part was a lot like the balcony pas de deux from *Romeo and Juliet*, when the lovers touch each other and the whole world shifts. I'd always loved that moment. So I'd put it in.

It took a while for us to get the timing right, for Jude to catch on to my hips after I turned, but he was great at holding me steady. I smiled as I remembered our first Vamp rehearsal, when he'd pulled me into the lift for the first time. It had been exhilarating and confusing, like all the pieces of my world were rearranging themselves. When I let that memory in, my rond de jambe became oversized, effervescent.

The rest of the dance was a mixture of steps that fit the swells and dips of the music and echoes of my favorite ballets. My favorite was the part from *Giselle*. In the second act, when Giselle is a Wili, she tries to convince the other Wilis not to kill the man who wronged her because she still loves him, despite everything. She does a slow développé, raising her leg to the side, almost up to her ear, and holds it steady, like it's nothing. Like she's in complete control of her body. I'd never thought much about that part before, but it meant something to me now. Even though she lost her life, Giselle found power and peace in what happened after. But that didn't mean she lost all connection to her past. She still loved who she'd loved before, and she used her power to save him.

Lastly, we repeated the circles, but moving away from each other, the circles getting smaller with each revolution until we were at opposite ends of the stage again. I backed slowly into the wings while Jude watched, his arm outstretched, ready to get pulled into the next part of the "Broadway Melody" dream sequence.

Jude lifted the hem of his shirt to wipe sweat off his forehead after running through the whole combination for the first time. "How am I doing?" he asked.

"Amazing." He really was. He was keeping up, even though he'd never done ballet before. I rolled my ankle out. It ached a bit, but nothing I couldn't handle.

"No, *you're* amazing. *You* can lift your leg up to your ear and hold it there like it's no big deal." He guzzled down some water.

I smiled. I had to admit I'd impressed myself, too. It felt like forever since I'd done ballet, but it had come back to me in an instant. Like a song you think you've forgotten, but then it plays and you can still sing all the words.

And of course, ballet did feel different now. But not *bad* different. Maybe some of my technique wasn't the best, and maybe my ankle wobbled a little in relevé, but this dance wasn't about perfection. This dance was about dreams and desire and joy and love. I felt all that while I was dancing, maybe more than I ever had before.

"And you choreographed all this?" Jude asked, his face full of awe.

"Not all of it. Some parts are from my favorite ballets."

"Oh?" Jude tilted his head, inviting me to say more.

"Yeah. I just figured, this is the only time a lot of people in the audience will see ballet. And...maybe the last time I'll dance it."

Jude frowned a little, fiddling with the cap of his water bottle.

"I mean, I don't know. I haven't decided yet. But that's okay. Ballet will always be a big part of my life. But if this *is* the last time I dance it, I figured I might as well dance my favorite parts." The ones I'd never get to do.

Except, I was going to do them. And even if it wasn't on the Metropolitan Opera House stage, even if it was in the Eagle View auditorium—birthplace of the mysterious Happy Crack, home to tap dancers and show people and women who said "fantabulous" unironically—it was still ballet. I was still finishing my hat. Just in a different way than I'd thought I would.

If I wanted to dance ballet again after the musical was over, I'd let myself do it. And if I didn't want to, I'd let myself not. It seemed like a simple and momentous decision all at the same time.

"Should we run through it once more?" I asked. Jude nodded, taking one more gulp of water. "Just remember," I said as we walked back to our positions on opposite ends of the stage. "This is a dream, a fantasy. So don't hold back, okay?"

He locked eyes with me. "Okay." I started the music.

I took my own advice, pumping more energy and exuberance into every movement. Jude never took his eyes off mine, not once. Something just...clicked this time. We were perfectly in sync. I could feel that we were dancing something unique and wonderful and extraordinary. A dream.

As I danced, I thought back to last Saturday in the car with Colleen. I'd realized then how much Kira's voice had gotten into my head over the years. But I honestly couldn't hear it anymore. Everything I'd learned from her—about movement and music and grace—was mine now. Just mine. I could do anything I wanted with it.

I used to look at Kira with such admiration. She carried generations of ballet in her body, put there by her teachers, and their teachers before them. She was like a living ballet archive, bringing the past into the present with each class she taught. But Kira was not ballet. She was only one person. Now it was my turn, and Colleen's turn, to preserve the good things we'd learned from her and destroy the bad. Now it was our turn to dance not for her and the past, but for us and the future, whatever that future happened to look like.

When we finished rehearsal, Jude and I gathered our things, breathing hard. Silently, we walked out of the auditorium, through the lobby, and out the doors. It was like a spell had been cast over us, and if we spoke, it would be broken. When we stepped outside, Jude couldn't contain it anymore.

"That was—I mean, that was so—" He was moving his hands through the air, trying to physically grasp on to the right words. "No offense to my cousin, but that?" He pointed back to the school. "That was a different level. God, people who just judge something and decide it's not for them without giving it a chance miss out on so much. I wish they could understand that."

My eyes shot to his because I knew he was thinking about his dad. I hated that he was still hurting over it, and I worried that he still hadn't forgiven himself for lying. Still, I was glad he felt secure enough to bring it up around me, even indirectly.

"And *you*," he went on. "You're unbelievable. When you do those grands jetés it's like time stops and you just hang in the air."

I smiled, enjoying his compliments again, feeling energized by his enthusiasm, and falling even more deeply in love with him.

"I think you're becoming a balletomane," I said.

"What's that?"

"A person who really loves ballet."

"Well, yeah, that sounds right." As his eyes found mine, all his wild energy focused on me. I forgot to breathe for a second.

"My old school is doing *Giselle* in a couple of weeks," I said, recovering. "We should go."

"And finally meet the Wilis? Yes, please."

We said goodbye and I got into the car, resting my head for a second on the wheel. There. Even if it hurt a little to be with Jude now, I could still do this. I could still be his friend.

CHAPTER TWENTY-EIGHT

I WAS ABOUT TO LEAVE the parking lot when my phone buzzed. I smiled and dug it out of my bag, knowing who it was without having to look.

How did it go??

I considered my response very carefully. If I said something like *It went really well*, Colleen's romantic mind would translate it into *Jude's fallen madly in love with me*.

The dance looks great. Can't wait for you to see it!

I'm so excited!! I can't believe you choreographed. Badass move, badass move.

Jude wore ballet clothes, I couldn't resist adding, bracing myself for Colleen's response, which was five full lines of heart-eye emojis. Any news on your end? I typed. I knew she was supposed to be hearing from ABT soon.

Not from ABT. But Swanson and I talked for six whole minutes today.

Vandervort for the win!!

She responded with an eye-roll emoji.

We kept texting until my fingers got numb from sitting in my car without the heat on and Colleen had to get back to *Giselle* rehearsal.

Go dance some guys to death, I typed. **Talk to you soon.**

I finally started the car and pulled out of the parking lot, but I didn't go home. I'd gotten one best friend back. Now I needed to get the other.

❧

Margot's eyes widened when she opened her front door, but the coolness returned in a second. "Hey," she said.

"Hi." I fidgeted on the doorstep.

"My parents will be back soon, and then I have to go to TGI Fridays," she said. Margot hated her monthly Saturday lunches at TGI Fridays with her parents. She called them hostage situations.

"Maybe I can get you out of it," I said. "I'll tell them I'm having an emergency or something."

Margot flicked her eyes to me and then back to the ground. "Nah."

Oof. Blowing off a chance to get out of TGI Fridays meant she *really* didn't want to talk to me. But I had to keep trying. "Can I come in? Just for a few minutes?"

Margot sighed and stepped away from the door. We sat on a cream love seat in her living room. I'd never been to Margot's house before, even though she'd invited me several times. Fresh waves of guilt washed over me when I thought about that.

"I wanted to apologize for everything that happened at the rink," I said, getting right to it.

Margot shrugged one shoulder. "Whatever. It wasn't completely your fault. I called you Robobitch, so I guess we're even." Her tone was cold and final, and I felt a pang in my chest. I didn't want to be even. I wanted to be friends again.

Since the first day of school this year, Margot and I had clicked.

She'd opened up, which she didn't do for nearly anyone else. I knew what a privilege it was now, for Margot Kilburn-Correa to let you in. I hoped I hadn't lost it forever.

"I really miss you."

She was quiet for a moment. "Yeah, I miss you, too. But look, sometimes friendships just don't work out. And if you reach the point where you're yelling at each other at an ice rink, it probably means things are over. I should know." Her eyes flicked to the mantel, where several picture frames were arranged.

I looked at the photos. One showed Margot and her abuela at Hersheypark. Another showed Margot and Izzy at their middle school graduation, Margot dressed in the preppiest of preppy clothes, her reddish-brown hair in a long side braid.

I stared at the picture. "You still have a picture of you and Izzy," I said, confused. Margot seemed 100 percent done with that part of her life.

"I told my mom to get rid of it. But she was all, 'You shouldn't forget your past, even if you don't like it,' and I was all, 'Not everything has to be a lesson, Mom.' Anyway, she won." Margot clicked her phone on to check the time.

"That's...interesting."

"What?"

"So, after I found out I could never do pointe again...," I started, pushing through the resistance I'd always had to talking to Margot about ballet. I'd wanted to keep things light and surface between us, but that wasn't how friendship worked. You had to talk about the hard stuff. You couldn't just bail.

"When I found out, I took down all the ballet pictures in my room, and then my parents took down all the ballet pictures everywhere else in the house. They were following my lead, and I know they genuinely thought it would help me, but...I don't think it's a bad thing, to have reminders of who you were. Even if you can't or don't want to be that person anymore."

Margot was eyeing me with a mixture of curiosity and wariness, probably wondering why I was telling her all this. She dropped her eyes to her lap, not saying anything.

"But whatever," I said lightly. "I'll break in and steal the picture. I'll take some valuables, too, so no one will be suspicious."

One corner of Margot's mouth turned up and then back down again.

"Margot, I'm sorry about making you feel like you weren't worth my time," I said. "It's not true. You were my first friend outside of ballet, which was awesome. But also, since ballet was my entire life, it kind of meant I didn't really know how to function outside of it. I'm learning, though."

"I know," Margot said. Then she sighed. "Feeling like I wasn't worth your time did hurt. And it reminded me of Izzy's whole thing." She waved her hand at the picture. "Everything was on her terms, and she'd never come out of her own world to really see or care about what was going on in mine. I know it's not the same. Like, I know you were dealing with this life-changing thing, and Izzy was dealing with stuff like having to change caterers for her birthday party. *Non*-life-changing things. But still, it really, really sucked."

I nodded. "I know that. But I need you to know that even though I didn't always act like it, I did care. I do care. And oh my God, I can't believe I said that Izzy was the best you could do. It's so untrue." I took a breath. "I want you to know that you're a huge reason why I survived this year, too. You're my best friend, too."

Margot finally smiled for real. She pretended to look me over. "So what you mean is... *you're* the best I can do?"

I smiled back. "If anyone better comes along, I'll dance them to death." Margot snorted, and I felt the last bit of heaviness I'd been carrying around dissolve. All of a sudden, I wanted to tell her everything. So I did.

I told her about ballet. Kira. Colleen, and how I hadn't spoken to her in months, but then I drove her to DC. I told her about what had happened with Jude—how we kissed, and how I told him we shouldn't be together, and that he agreed.

"Whoa, whoa, whoa," Margot said, shaking her head. "Who just *agrees* like that? Who just listens to what someone says and then, like, *believes* them?"

I shrugged sadly.

"So what are you going to do? Do you still think it won't work with him?"

I bit my lip and gave one answer to both questions. "I don't know."

"Well, let's figure it out," Margot said. "Do you want to invite Colleen over? It'd be cool to meet her, and this seems like the kind of thing that should involve as many girls as possible?"

She was right. I really wanted to talk to Colleen. I wanted her to meet Margot. But she had *Giselle* rehearsal all day. "She's at rehearsal until six," I said. "And don't you have to go to TGI Fridays?"

Margot shook her head, already typing on her phone. "I get one skip a year. Looks like I'm using it now. Can Colleen come over tonight?"

I smiled and dug out my phone to text her. I spent the rest of the afternoon with Margot. We talked. We watched YouTube clips of other high schools' *Singin' in the Rain* performances, comparing them to ours. We ate a tremendous amount of Burger King chicken tenders.

At seven thirty, Colleen came over with Ferdinand because Margot said "Oh my God *yes*" when I asked if it was okay for Colleen to bring her dog. Right after I introduced Colleen and Margot, Margot dropped to her knees, said, "Hello, Ferdinand!" in a goofy voice, and started scratching his butt. So obviously Ferdinand fell in love with her. I never thought of Margot as a dog person. Then again, there was a lot about Margot that surprised me.

"How is he this cute?" Margot screeched.

"How does he love you so much already?" Colleen asked. "He usually takes at least ten minutes."

"I've got the touch." Margot wiggled her fingers.

"You want to give him a cheese peanut butter treat?" Colleen asked, digging around in her bag. "I'll warn you, though: If you give this to him, he won't leave your lap all evening. And he *will* have very bad breath."

I watched Margot giggle uncontrollably as he slurped it from her hand, her emerald Monroe piercing flashing in the light. Colleen snort-laughed in the dorky way I'd missed, raising her hand to her mouth in a gesture so graceful it almost looked choreographed. My heart swelled, and I marveled at how familiar and surprising and fascinating and beautiful people could be. Like works of art, all in themselves.

After Ferdinand set up shop on Margot's lap, we broke out some snacks and watched *Singin' in the Rain.* Our eyes bugged out when Cosmo Brown did his spectacular acrobatics in "Make 'Em Laugh." We cheered when Kathy Selden threw a pie in Lina Lamont's face. We hooted as Cyd Charisse danced with Gene Kelly. We didn't come to any conclusions about the Jude situation, but that was okay.

When the movie ended, Margot gasped. "Oh my God, how have we not talked about what you said to Paul?"

"Did Ethan tell you?" I asked, pushing the Doritos away from me because I was so full I was about to burst.

"What did you say to Paul? Who's Paul?" Colleen asked, daintily popping a chip into her mouth.

"Paul is trash," Margot said. "And no, I heard some rando talking about it in the hallway, and then Ethan confirmed." Margot turned to Colleen. "She basically told this guy that because he says racist, sexist things, people think his dick is small. I mean, it was more poetic than that, but that was the gist."

Colleen screamed. "Alina!" Then she turned mock-serious. "What has gotten into you, young lady?"

She was kidding, but I wondered the same thing. I thought about the past few weeks. I'd told Paul off. I'd helped Diya and Colleen. I'd done ballet again, and it had felt good. I'd fixed things with Margot, Ethan, and Jude. What *had* gotten into me? Whatever it was, I liked it. I shrugged, which made them both laugh.

We were cracking up for most of the time after that, and I realized how happy and relaxed I was here with them. I thought again of Diya, and how I'd felt the same way when we danced in her room. If Diya had been here, with Margot in this great mood, it could have been fine. It could have been fun. But I was so glad to have them all back—Colleen and Margot and Ethan and Jude—that I didn't want to risk it just yet.

CHAPTER TWENTY-NINE

I PAWED THROUGH MY CLOSET for the gazillionth time, cursing myself for telling Jude we should go see *Giselle* together. And cursing Margot's abuela for taking Margot and Ethan to a concert so they couldn't go with us.

I was excited to see Colleen as Myrtha, I really was, but what do you wear to your old school's production of your favorite ballet, with the boy who used to want to date you but doesn't anymore? Hanging out with Jude during rehearsals with lots of other people around was one thing. Going to a ballet with him alone on a Saturday night was totally different, and I was quickly losing my ability to function.

I finally threw on a gray shift dress, black tights, and my wool Keds before running downstairs to the kitchen. Jude would be here any minute.

I opened the fridge and grabbed the roses I'd bought this morning, tipping them to my nose. The fresh scent calmed my nerves a little, and a quiet, bittersweet feeling took their place. It wasn't a bad feeling, necessarily, but I wished I had a name for it. I'd been feeling it a lot these past couple of weeks as I hung out with Jude at rehearsals and texted with Colleen about the *Giselle* opening night.

"Aw, did you get Jude flowers for your date?" Josie said, coming up behind me.

My nerves came back in full force. "They're for *Colleen*, and it's not a date!"

Josie laughed. "You need to calm down."

"*You* need to—" I bit my tongue. I'd been trying not to snap at Josie. Sometimes, like right now, it felt like a monumental challenge. Mom came into the kitchen, carrying a stack of essays. I gave her a pleading look.

"Josie," Mom said, "why don't you go upstairs and sort through that box Auntie Ruth sent from the thrift shop? If you find anything you want, it's yours."

As Josie hurried upstairs, my shoulders relaxed. "Thank y—"

"Are you sure it isn't a date?" Mom asked, setting the essays on the table and putting water in the kettle.

"*Yes*," I said through clenched teeth.

"But are you *sure*—"

"Does this *look* like a date outfit to you?" I snapped.

Mom looked me up and down. "I have no idea. Is it supposed to?"

I groaned. "Jude and I are friends, how many times do I have to tell you people that?"

"Well, honey," Mom said, leaning against the counter. "If he were average-looking, probably only once. But he's so handsome! It's just going to take us longer to accept that you aren't together." We both froze as a shoe scraped against our walkway. Mom hurried to the window. "He's wearing a tie," she informed me.

I grabbed my coat, bolted to the door, and walked out, shutting it resolutely behind me. Jude paused midstep. He *was* wearing a tie. Goddamn it. "Hey...," he started, watching me walk briskly past him.

"Just get in the car," I said. "Trust me."

When we'd both gotten in, Jude didn't switch to the Broadway channel like I expected him to. "So how's your Saturday? What have you been up to?" he asked as I turned out of our neighborhood.

Oh, you know, just having clothing-related freak-outs and telling my family we aren't dating. "Not much. You?"

"I've just been waiting for this," he said, rubbing his hands together. "I've got a lot of theories about the Wilis, and I want to see if I'm right. Also, I'm excited to see the programs."

"Why?"

"I went to the symphony once, and in the program there was a whole section about what to do during intermission. It was like, you can have a conversation! You can go to the bathroom! You can even get a snack! I want to see if these programs give different advice."

I laughed, but it came out way too loudly, and Jude startled a little. I cleared my throat. "That's funny."

I felt Jude watching me. "Hey," he finally said. "I'm really glad we're going to this. And if you ever feel like it's too much, you know I'm here, right? You know you can talk to me about it."

I squeezed the wheel. Jude thought I was nervous about seeing my old school perform, which was partly true. But he didn't know how much he contributed to the tension coursing through my body by just sitting there and saying sweet things like that.

"I know," I said tightly. "Thanks."

We were pretty quiet for the rest of the drive, and still quiet as we walked up to the Epstein Theatre, its warmly lit windows brightening up the downtown street. It wasn't until we stepped into the crowded lobby, with its vintage hanging lightbulbs and terrazzo floor, that some of my Jude nerves faded away. I felt the energy of the people around me, dressed up and buzzing with excitement over what they were about to see.

I led Jude up the flight of stairs to the mezzanine entrance, and when we walked inside the theater, I almost gasped. No matter how familiar the red velvet curtain and the golden lighting fixtures were, they always took my breath away.

"This place is amazing," Jude said, looking up at the ceiling and down at the seats.

I smiled and pointed to the orchestra pit. "A few years ago, there was a conductor who sweat so much, he wore a towel around his neck all the time."

Jude laughed. "No way. Like a boxer?"

"Yup." I glanced up and pointed to the left balcony box. "And that's where Colleen and I would hide out and eat cheese during rehearsals." I was breathing easier now, finding my words again.

Jude pretended to be shocked. "I didn't know I was coming here with a cheese fiend."

The lights flickered, signaling the show was about to start, so we got programs, and I took Jude to our seats. They were the best ones—first row mezzanine, so we'd be high enough to see the formations of the Wilis and close enough to see the details.

The lights went down and I placed the roses under my seat as the dramatic overture swelled. The curtains parted to reveal a quaint village scene, with peasant girls miming and dancing. They all looked so lovely, each movement full of purpose and grace. A strong wave of that bittersweet feeling washed over me. I didn't notice that my hand was clenching the program until Jude reached over and rested his fingers on mine. My heart almost stopped. I loosened my grip and let the familiar weight of his hand settle into my palm, warm and reassuring and wonderful.

I knew it was just a kind gesture. Jude was full of those, so I tried to squash the stupid hope building inside me and focus on Giselle making her entrance. It was Juliet tonight, and she danced with an innocent recklessness that fit the part well. After the peasant waltz, everyone started clapping, and Jude took his hand away so he could clap, too. He looked at me with slightly raised eyebrows, silently asking if I was okay. I smiled as confidently as I could, and as the music started up again, he settled his hands back into his lap. So that was that.

As Act I played on, I kept glancing at him. Colleen and the Wilis wouldn't be on until Act II, and I was afraid he might be bored by all the peasant dancing, but his eyes were alert and following the action. After Giselle went mad and died after finding out Albrecht was engaged to someone else, the lights went up for intermission. Before I could ask what he thought, Jude started talking about what a jerk Albrecht was. "So he comes to this village and lies to Giselle about who he is and the fact that he's engaged. What did he think was going to happen?"

"He wasn't thinking that far ahead," I said, tucking in my legs so a couple could get to the aisle. "He didn't expect to fall in love with her, but he did, and then he was in over his head, and he couldn't stop it before it all came crashing down."

Jude sighed. "True. But I still completely blame him for everything that happened." He gestured to the part of the stage where Giselle had died. "Just because he fell in love doesn't mean he gets a pass. Falling in love with Giselle should have made him be like, 'All right, I need to step back and figure my shit out before this goes any further.' Right?"

As Jude and I passionately debated my favorite ballet, it felt like someone was stabbing me in the heart. Why couldn't he hate it? Why couldn't he have said "Yeah, it's cool" and then looked at his phone? Because that wasn't Jude, and that was the whole problem.

I was relieved when the lights dimmed and the curtain parted for Act II. The set was totally different—an eerily beautiful graveyard with fog rolling in from the wings.

The strings played a haunting melody, and Colleen as Myrtha bourréed across the stage. Her feet moved swiftly, but her upper body was so still that she truly looked like a spirit floating across the fog. The audience gasped, and I heard Jude whisper, "Jesus." I felt a squeeze of pride.

Colleen had the audience by the throat. She was serene and ethereal as she penchéd, promenaded in arabesque, and summoned the other Wilis. She was fierce as she led the charge against Albrecht. I found myself inching forward in my seat even though I'd seen the ballet hundreds of times. A fascinating combination of power and grace infused every turn of Colleen's head, radiated from her fingertips. I felt it in my own body, and I marveled at how this almost-two-hundred-year-old ballet could feel so alive and real and right now.

When Giselle stalled for long enough to save Albrecht, and Myrtha and the Wilis faded into the sunrise, I wanted them to come back. I wanted them to dance for a while longer.

The lights came up and the audience stood to clap. My heart felt full and exhilarated and larger than life. I hadn't realized how much I'd missed the feeling of seeing a live ballet. How much it got inside me, even if I wasn't dancing it.

When the applause died down and the audience made its way to the exits, Jude was quiet.

"So were your theories about the Wilis right?" I asked after I grabbed the roses from under my seat and we shuffled out of the aisle.

"Not at all. That was infinitely cooler. What did you think?" He watched me carefully.

I smiled. "I loved it." I gestured for him to follow me as I weaved through the mass of people in the lobby, down a long hallway, past the dressing rooms, and through the door that led backstage.

The wings smelled like wood and sweat and hair spray. I walked onto the dark stage and I ran my pinkie over the smooth velvet of the closed red curtain, like I used to before every show. Jude hovered a few feet behind me, respecting my space, even though space was the last thing I needed from him.

A movement behind his shoulder caught my eye—Colleen was gliding through the wings. She'd changed into a flowy garnet dress. I ran over and hugged her, the roses squishing between us. When we finally let go, I handed her the bouquet. "You were beautiful," I said. "Just so . . ." I couldn't find words to describe it.

Colleen smiled. "Thank you," she said. "I'm so glad you came."

Jude waited a few more seconds before coming over. "Colleen," I said. "This is Jude. Jude, Colleen."

"Hi!" they said at the same time. They were both grinning ear to ear, and they both looked a little starstruck. I knew why Jude was—he'd just seen Colleen as Queen of the Wilis. But Colleen . . . she probably thought of Jude as the leading man in the great love story she'd concocted in her head.

"I'm *so* excited to finally meet you!" Colleen said, her eyes darting from me to Jude. I tried to telepathically tell her to cool it.

"Same," Jude said. "You were awesome. I've had a lot of time to think about the Wilis, but seeing the real thing was . . ." He mimed his brain exploding.

Colleen laughed. "Thanks! So you guys are dance partners, right?" She obviously knew we were dance partners, but her eyes were zeroed in on Jude, ready to dissect his answer and use it as evidence of his love for me.

"Yup," Jude said, doing that platonic shoulder punch thing. "We have chemistry, apparently."

"Oh, really?" Colleen's eyebrows shot up. "Chemistry?" I didn't know why I hadn't predicted how un-chill she would be about this. I tried to think of a way to pivot, but a stream of people had entered the wings and a familiar voice made me freeze. Kira. She was talking to a group of parents with their young daughters in tow, some I recognized as Level A students.

As much as my feelings about Kira had changed over the last year, she looked the same—the white-blond hair pulled into a chignon, the swanlike neck and ramrod-straight posture, the air of royal benevolence as she addressed the little bunheads who looked up at her in awe, hanging on her every word.

My first impulse was to disappear without her seeing me, but I held my ground. Colleen and Jude standing by me helped, but there was something else, too. Something I was finally beginning to understand. I loved ballet with all my heart, but I didn't want to be like Albrecht and love it blindly. I didn't want to be like the Wilis and destroy it, either. I didn't even want to be like Giselle and save it without holding it responsible for the damage it had done. I wanted to love the good parts of ballet and defuse the dangerous ones. And a dangerous one was standing right in front of me.

CHAPTER THIRTY

"I'M GOING TO TALK to her," I said. "I'll just be a minute."

Jude nodded. "I'll be in the lobby when you're ready." Before he walked out of the wings, he squeezed my shoulder, signaling that he understood I had to do this without him but he was with me all the way.

"I'll come with you," Colleen said to me.

"Are you sure? I mean, I'm not her student anymore, I don't have to worry about casting next year..." I broke off. Both of us hoped that Colleen would get into the ABT summer intensive and then be asked to stay at the school next year, that she wouldn't even have to work with Kira again. But if she didn't, she'd have another year at KDBS, and it was a really important one. She'd be auditioning for companies, and she'd need attention and support.

Colleen shook her head. "Kira wouldn't not cast me in stuff because of a grudge. She's not unfair in that way. It's more like she doesn't get *how* she's unfair? And regardless, this is important to me, too. I'm ready to talk to her. I want to."

I steeled myself and we linked arms and approached Kira just as the parents and daughters were exiting the wings. My legs were shaky, just like they'd been when we walked up to her on *Nutcracker* cast list day last year. But inside, I felt different.

"Ah, excellent job tonight, Colleen," Kira said, nodding. Then she turned to me with a slight raise of her eyebrows. "Alina. It's nice to see you again." No one could make me as aware of my body as she could. But I resisted the urge to tuck my butt under my hips, inch my shoulders back, and lift my chin.

"Hi, Kira," I said, softly but steadily.

"I heard you're in your school musical." She paused. "How nice." I nodded awkwardly. I couldn't remember ever talking to Kira about anything other than ballet, and it was clearly weird for both of us.

"We missed you in *The Nutcracker,*" she went on. "Although Greta Chin made a good showing of Chinese Tea."

There it was, my opening. "I was actually wondering if I could talk to you about that."

"About Greta's performance?"

"About Chinese Tea. Um, have you ever thought about changing it?"

Kira furrowed her brows. "Changing it how?"

I took a breath and shifted my feet. "Well, right now the dance is really insensitive. Some of the movements, like the shuffling and the bowing, are actually racist stereotypes."

Kira's eyes flashed with irritation, and I thought she was going to say "How dare you" again. Instead, she lifted her chin. "My job is to preserve and pass down the world's most cherished ballets. That is what I'm doing. Besides, the dance is memorable and everyone loves it."

"Everyone *doesn't* love it," I said. Kira's mouth tightened, like it did when you weren't dancing up to her standards. I pushed myself to go further. "I think it alienates Asian people—dancers and audience members—and makes them feel like they don't belong, like they're being mocked or laughed at."

"But you did the dance for years," Kira said, sounding genuinely confused.

"I didn't always see what was wrong with it. And then when I did see, I didn't know how to say it. But I do now."

"Lots of big companies are changing Chinese Tea and Arabian Coffee," Colleen added. "It's not actually that difficult."

"Right, and it's an interesting way to think about the ballet. Like, how do you preserve the fun of Chinese Tea or the glamour of Arabian Coffee without being insensitive or hurtful?"

Kira's eyes darted between us. For the first time ever, she was speechless.

"And it's not just Chinese Tea and Arabian Coffee," Colleen said. "Sometimes I feel like *I* don't belong here."

That snapped Kira out of it. "What on earth do you mean?"

"I mean, it's easy for you to see your white students as graceful and delicate, perfect for the fairy and princess and innocent heroine roles. They're the Giselles and Odettes and Sugar Plums. But when you see me, you see 'sultry Arabian Coffee' or 'vengeful villain queen.' You *say* it's because I'm too athletic, not graceful enough for the lead roles, but the thing is, that's not true. I know it's not."

"I, well…" Kira paused, shaking her head. "You—" She broke off, composing herself. "Myrtha is an incredibly important role, and it's the one that fits you."

"But why don't I fit Giselle?"

Kira's lips parted, but she didn't make a sound. I wasn't sure if it was because she truly didn't know the answer, or she didn't want to admit it—to us or maybe even to herself. It was so clear that even after years of being her teacher, Kira never really saw Colleen.

"I think you missed a lot about how I actually dance because you had this one image in your head of what a Black dancer looks like. If you want to make sure *all* your students have the opportunities they deserve, you need to be aware of your biases."

Colleen's words hung in the air as Kira remained silent, forehead wrinkled, looking over our shoulders. All we could hear was the hum of voices from beyond the backstage doors.

"We all love ballet," Colleen finally said. "We all want to make it as beautiful as it can be. And to do that, it needs to change. It'll take a lot of work, but we can all help change it."

I nodded fiercely. "Ballet isn't this dead thing we have to preserve. It's alive, and it should evolve." I remembered Kira telling us that we should be grateful to be part of ballet's grand, unchanging tradition, in whatever roles she'd chosen for us. I was glad I didn't believe that anymore. "You should be grateful you can help it evolve."

Kira still didn't say anything. The backstage doors opened again and larger groups of people entered, laughing and chatting loudly. Someone called Kira's name. After a second, she took a breath and met our eyes. "Excuse me, ladies," she said, and walked stiffly away to join the crowd.

I exhaled and heard Colleen do the same. We turned to each other, but it was like we didn't have any words left. I had no idea what Kira would do with the conversation we just had, if she'd ignore it or do the work to help ballet change. But we'd said what we wanted to say. We were *able* to say it.

"Oh my God," I whispered.

"Oh my *God*," Colleen whispered back.

"There she is," a deep voice said from the crowd. I stepped back as Colleen's family enveloped her in hugs, piled multiple bouquets of deep red roses into her arms until she could barely hold them all.

Colleen's dad noticed me first. "Looks like all the ghosts are appearing tonight," he said, smiling. Colleen's mom hugged me. Her littlest brother, Jack, told me about his gerbils having babies, like I'd never been gone. Calvin, who was just a couple of years younger than us, waved but hung back. He'd always been protective of Colleen, and I was sure he was still mad at me. But I'd show him I was here to stay.

As Colleen's family discussed where to go to celebrate, Colleen elbowed me. "Go find Jude. And try not to burn down the building with all your"—she lowered her voice into a suggestive whisper—"*chemistry.*"

I snorted, gave her one last hug, and made my way out to the lobby, where Jude was waiting. "How'd it go?" he asked, looking at me intently.

I still couldn't find the words, so I nodded and smiled big. Jude slung an arm around my shoulders and squeezed. It made me feel like I could do anything. Fly out of this theater. Take over the world. Tell him how I really felt.

"I have the most badass dance partner, slash neighbor, slash friend in the world."

I deflated a little but tried to keep smiling. Dance partner, neighbor, friend. These weren't bad things to be.

Before we left, Jude stopped to use the bathroom, so I waited for him on a bench in the lobby. I was resting my head against the wall, trying to sort through the multitude of emotions crashing around inside me, when I saw a familiar beanie in the crowd.

I leaned forward and caught Harrison's eye. He smiled and detached himself from a group of middle-aged women, glancing around as he walked over. "Hey," he said, sitting down next to me. "What are you doing here?"

"Oh, I'm—" I realized Harrison had no idea that KDBS was my old school. After the intensity of the last few hours, it was kind of a relief. "I was here for the show. You?"

"Me too. My mom wanted to see it. I wasn't expecting so much death, but I liked it. So, um, did you come here with people?" He glanced around again. I sighed, knowing who he was looking for.

"Do you like Ethan?" I asked point-blank. Maybe it was rude, but I was completely out of filter.

Harrison paused for a second. Then he looked at his shoes. "So it's that obvious, huh."

"You should tell him," I said quickly. "I mean, I don't know how he feels about you, and I know there might be a lot of reasons why you haven't told him, and I respect that, but I just want you to consider the possibility that if you don't tell him now, it might be too late, and you won't get a chance to do it at all."

I caught my breath. Harrison was looking at me, eyes wide with confusion. "Wait, why would it be too late?"

"I don't know, it just *could* be, okay?" I said, my voice rising. "And then he might never know, which is fine as long as you're okay with that. *Are you okay with that?*"

"Whoa," Harrison said, his hands out in front of him. "I will. I mean, I've been planning on telling him."

"Hey." Jude came up to us and I startled. He looked back and forth between me and Harrison before squinting at me. "Everything all right?"

I stood up as nonchalantly as I could, telling myself to get a grip. "Yup. Bye, Harrison," I said, and for the second time that night, I walked past Jude to the car.

CHAPTER THIRTY-ONE

THE WEEK BEFORE OPENING NIGHT was called Tech Week, and it was extreme. Rehearsal every single day from four thirty to eleven o'clock. My parents were thrilled that I was so busy. To them, singing and dancing within the bounds of Eagle View sounded like good, wholesome fun. My parents had clearly never gone through a Tech Week.

"Jesus, get a room!" Margot yell-whispered as she walked into and then swiftly out of the utility closet backstage. Noah and Laurel were in there making out, but they hauled ass when they saw Margot's face. Margot sighed as she stowed her cigarette holder prop on one of the shelves. "What is *wrong* with people?"

I shrugged halfheartedly. Excitement and exhaustion and nerves were making everyone in the cast lose their inhibitions—except me. Mine were still firmly in place, keeping me from testing the waters to see if Jude had changed his mind about not being ready for a relationship.

The last few weeks, we'd been having *amazing* Vamp and ballet rehearsals together, which sometimes gave me hope. But I had to remind myself that we were playing roles. The real Jude just wanted to be friends, and I had to respect that. It sucked.

I turned to watch from the wings as Jude, Ethan, and Diya did "Good Morning." It was already ten thirty and we still hadn't finished Act 1. Mrs. Sorenson and Ms. Langford had to work through some major issues with the lights, so we had to run certain numbers a million times. We definitely weren't going to get to "Broadway Melody" tonight, which meant I wasn't going to dance with Jude tonight, which, again, sucked.

Margot and I made our way out of the wings and into the auditorium seats, where we'd left our late-night sustenance, Red Vines and root beer. I chewed on a Red Vine, my eyes glued to the front. In the middle of the fastest, most impressive tap sequence, Diya stopped and waved her hands at Ms. Langford. The pit orchestra came to a gradual, awkward stop as Ms. Langford made her way to the stage.

I couldn't tell what Diya was saying, but she kept gesticulating to Ms. Langford and shaking her head emphatically. This number was the one she hoped would get the casting people's attention, so everything needed to be flawless leading up to her surprise dance. Jude and Ethan stood off to the side, looking completely drained. Ms. Langford finally remembered they were there and dismissed them while she and Diya continued to discuss.

Ethan and Jude jumped off the stage, staggered down the aisle, and collapsed onto the floor next to where Margot and I were sitting. "That was the *worst* morning ever," Jude said, his voice muffled because he was lying facedown.

"It's Robobitch's fault, like everything is in the entire universe." Ethan rolled onto his back and flung an arm over his eyes.

"Yeah, what's she robobitching about?" Margot took a gulp of root beer, squinting at the stage, where Ms. Langford still hadn't convinced Diya to move on.

"Who knows," Ethan said. "I stopped listening to her years ago."

I knew it was late and that they had been onstage for a lot longer than I had today, which would make anyone cranky. But I couldn't stomach the Robobitch thing anymore. "Maybe you guys shouldn't call her that," I said quietly.

Compared to my Negative Correlation of Dicks Speech and my encounter with Kira, that was pretty weak. But at least it was something.

"But it fits her so well," Margot said, plucking another Red Vine out of the bag, not realizing I was serious. Jude lifted his head off the floor to look at me. The carpet had made a red mark in the middle of his forehead, which looked adorable. It made me want to laugh and forget about the whole thing, but I couldn't.

"It doesn't, though. You guys are always bad-mouthing Diya, and I know she's not the most fun person to be around during rehearsals, but that doesn't mean she's a robot or a bitch or a weird combination of both."

They were all staring at me now.

"Okay," Margot said slowly, watching me closely, searching for clues. "I saw you talking to her a few times, but I didn't know if...I mean, are you and Diya...friends now?"

"Well, yeah, but that's not the point."

"What is the point?" Margot asked.

"The point is that you guys hate her because she's too intense or ambitious or whatever. And I know that her ambition was what made her hurt Jude. But, like, you can be intense and ambitious and not be a robot bitch, you know? You can even break someone's heart and not be a robot bitch. Right?"

"Technically, sure," Ethan said. "But she didn't break someone's heart. She broke my *friend*'s heart. Therefore I hate her. That's friend code."

"Fine, hate her all you want, but..." I moved my hand in a circle, encompassing the auditorium. "People here listen to you guys. When you call her Robobitch, they all do. And I doubt they're *all* doing it because of friend code. I'm pretty sure most of them do it because she's really good and calling her Robobitch makes them feel less intimidated."

I looked at Jude then, willing my eyes away from that endearing mark on his forehead. "It's just, I don't think it's fair when a girl like Diya is called a bitch because she's passionate about what she does. I love you guys, but it's not fair."

I braced myself for their reaction, but they didn't say anything. Margot was contemplating her bottle of root beer. Ethan was watching Diya onstage, frowning. Jude was looking at me. Looking *into* me, his stare was so focused. I didn't know what he wanted to find in there. Maybe an apology for once again using his personal history with Diya to make a point?

Mrs. Sorenson finally dismissed us. I jumped up quickly. "I'll, uh, see you guys tomorrow," I mumbled, and rushed out of the aisle.

❧

During dress rehearsal the next night, I changed into the low-cut Kelly-green Vamp costume in the choir room. The choir room had turned into a second girls' dressing room, since the one directly backstage looked like a vintage costume shop had exploded—character shoes, tights, and flapper dresses all over the place.

The door barreled open and Laney ran in, wearing her canary-yellow flapper costume and brandishing a roll of duct tape. "I did Ada already, and Margot won't let me. Your turn!" She took my elbow and led me behind the filing cabinets in Mrs. Sorenson's office.

"My turn for what?" I asked as Laney cut off a strip of duct tape.

"I'm taping your boobs," she said. "You get mad cleavage that way."

"Why do I want mad cleavage?"

"You know how you have to wear a lot of makeup onstage so that your features show up from far away? This is like that, but for your boobs."

Geez. I'd never wanted my boobs to show up *more* onstage. I always saw them as a pesky distraction—throwing me off-balance, messing up my line. For our performances at KDBS, I strapped them down with a nude leotard underneath my costume.

"So...," I started, but came up blank. It was hard to make conversation with someone taping your boobs. "Uh...how's Love Realism going?"

"Harrison and I are divorced," Laney said, cutting off another piece of tape while I stood there, squishing my breasts together, looking at framed photos of Mrs. Sorenson's daughters playing with a corgi. Totally normal.

"Bummer."

Laney shrugged. "We wanted different things."

"So what happens now? Do you pick someone else and start over?"

"Of course not!" she said, offended. "I'm only fifty-six in my Love Realism timeline. I'm in Argentina right now, learning tango."

I laughed. "So no hard feelings, then."

"Nope. Harrison's pretty awesome."

"Actual Harrison or Love Realism Harrison?" I asked.

"Actual Harrison. Love Realism Harrison was kind of a moron. But I don't know, maybe something good will come out of it for Actual Harrison," she said, smiling.

"Something good?"

Laney shrugged. "Just watch for the programs," she whispered.

Before I could ask what that meant, Laney gave my boobs a nod of approval and went off to find her next victim.

I pulled my straps up and went back out to the mirror propped against the wall and... wow. Mad cleavage indeed. In my sequined green costume and seamed tights, I looked like a different person. I missed my leg warmer, but I couldn't wear it for the dress rehearsal. As I stared at myself, the choir room door opened and Ethan and Margot walked in. They looked like an old-timey photo. Margot in a champagne-colored sparkly dress with a white faux-fur wrap. Ethan in a suit, his hat cocked perfectly to one side.

Their eyes went directly to my chest. "She got you," Margot said. "I literally had to run away."

"I gave in. I kind of like it?"

"You should. Looks awesome," Margot said. Ethan nodded as they sat down on the choir chairs. I walked over to sit beside them.

"*You* guys look awesome," I said, pointing to their costumes. "Margot, your abuela is going to take so many pictures of you."

"She'd better. I'm not going dress shopping with her again, so this will have to last her a lifetime."

We smiled, and then we were quiet.

"Hey, you were right about the Robobitch thing," Margot said. We'd been running around so much, doing costume fittings, practicing dances, catching a few minutes of sleep whenever we could, that we hadn't had time to talk about it yet. "It was shitty of me to call you that when your only crime was being serious about pursuing your dream. Same with Diya. Especially since I *know* girls get called bitches for doing things that aren't bitchy at all. I mean, *I* get called a bitch for being awesome, and I hate that. I know it, and I hate it, and I still did it. I'm sorry."

298

I smiled. "Thanks. That means a lot."

"I'm sorry, too," Ethan said. "I mean, I was pissed at Diya at first. But Jude got over it, so I don't know why I didn't. I never really thought about it, I guess."

"Me neither." Margot shrugged. "Hating her was just automatic after a while." She raised her eyebrows. "Maybe we're the Robo-bitches. Anyway, we're going to apologize to Diya, too, and call out anyone who keeps calling her Robobitch. Like you did with us." She smiled.

"Exactly. Jude's also sorry," Ethan said, "but he's, you know." He pointed to the stage. Jude was probably stage-kissing Diya right now before doing his "Singin' in the Rain" solo.

I sighed in a way I hoped didn't sound wistful but definitely did.

"Okay," Ethan said, crossing his legs and facing me. "We really did come here to tell you that you were right and we were wrong. That was our goal, yes?" He turned to Margot.

"Yes." She nodded solemnly.

"We've done that, so now we're going to tell you what we're right and you're wrong about. Ready?"

"What? No. What am I wrong about?"

"You're wrong about the person you just sighed pathetically over," Margot said.

"Wrong *about* him. Not wrong *for* him, that's an important difference," Ethan added.

I fidgeted with my costume. "How am I wrong about Jude?"

"You haven't declared your undying love for him!" Ethan yelled. Before I could shush him, he said, "And you haven't declared your undying love because you think he doesn't want you to. *That's* where you're wrong."

"Look," I said. "I know he liked me before. But then he realized it wouldn't work. I mean, he told me that. He said he wasn't ready for a relationship."

Margot waved a hand at me. "But did you tell him you were? Because that could change things."

Ethan took off his hat and spun it around. "It's embarrassingly clear to everyone that Jude had, has, and forever will have a thing for you. And vice versa. All we want you to do is act on it. Preferably somewhere with good lighting, so I can get a good shot."

Margot pushed him. "Stop, this is a serious moment."

"Okay, fine. You can be boring and do it in private, if you want."

I stared hard at both of them. "Have you talked to him about this? Do you know for sure it's what he wants?"

"Well, no," Ethan said reluctantly. "He's been pretty silent on the Alina topic since the rink."

My shoulders sagged. It was all just speculation. Could I risk throwing all my heart into something only to have it broken again?

Yes. I could.

I was surprised at how certain I was about that. If things with Jude didn't work out, I was sure I'd feel shattered again. I was sure it would sting every time I saw him, maybe for a while. But I could deal with that. I had some experience with crushed hopes, after all. And even if the pieces broke apart and flew out and spun around again, I was learning how to gather them up and...not put them back together necessarily, but rearrange them into something different. Something familiar, but distinct.

I sat up straight and smiled at them.

Margot and Ethan whooped and fist-pumped. Then they pulled me onto the choir room floor for an impromptu dance party. As I swayed around in my booby costume, I thought about how at this time last year, my life fell apart. Now I was dancing with two people who cared about my life so much they wanted the pieces of it to fit together perfectly.

"Are you guys still having movie nights after the musical is over?" I asked.

"Yup," they said at the same time.

"Fantabulous. Count me in."

CHAPTER THIRTY-TWO

BACKSTAGE, I COULDN'T STOP fidgeting. Jude's rendition of "Broadway Melody" rang out, sweet and clear. I'd been hoping to catch a moment with him before rehearsing our scene to say, well, *something*. But I couldn't find time in the chaos, and now I was in the left wing, waiting for the Charleston dancers to make their entrance. When they did, and the stage was full of their brightly colored costumes, I snuck in behind them and sat on the chair set up for me in the back corner. I positioned the hat on the toe of my shoe and waited. The music shifted, the dancers exited in a whirl of color, and it was Jude and me onstage, alone.

Jude knelt next to me, I slowly raised my leg, he took the hat, and we were off. The lights, the sultry horns in the pit orchestra, Jude's adorable yellow sweater-vest costume, my mad cleavage, it all came together. I could feel the electricity in the air as I slinked around him and he stared at me like I was beautiful dynamite.

When he pulled me into the first lift I felt the tension in his body, saw the desire in his eyes. I couldn't tell if he was Don responding to the Vamp, or Jude responding to me. In the moment, I didn't care. Onstage, right now, he was mine.

"Ow-oooooow!" echoed from somewhere out in the auditorium, where Margot and Ethan were sitting. I could see Jude lose focus as he tried not to smile.

"Hot stuff, comin' through!" That did it. We broke into stupid grins.

"*Smolder!*" Ms. Langford yelled, and we quickly re-smoldered. I kicked my leg up near Jude's ear, and he caught my ankle without the lavender leg warmer for the first time. My stomach jolted as I felt the heat of his fingers through my tights. Jude dipped me, and when I came back up, I was supposed to stop about six inches away from his face. But something pulled me in closer. My lips almost brushed his.

The lights dimmed, my cue to exit. As I backed into the wings to change into my pink ballet costume, I kept my eyes on his.

He kept his on mine. The lights turned up. The chorus streamed onstage again. They started dancing the next section, but Jude was still staring at me. A second later, his head snapped back to the front and he joined everyone a few beats late.

During the ballet part, we heard no catcalls from the auditorium. There were a few gasps, like when I did the slow développé and held it. But otherwise, it was stunned silence. When the dance was over, it hurt to let go of Jude's hand and move in circles away from him, back into the wings alone. But he had a scene right after and was pretty much onstage for the rest of the run-through. At least I was giving him a ride home tonight. I'd have to talk to him then.

After we practiced the finale and the curtain call, Mrs. Sorenson gathered us onstage for one last round of notes. Margot, Ethan, Jude, and I sat in a little clump. Someone started passing out programs for the show as Mrs. Sorenson gave final pointers. In addition to the names of the cast and the order of the scenes, the program was like a mini-yearbook for the musical people. You could submit short messages for your friends, and pictures from rehearsals with funny captions.

"Alina," Mrs. Sorenson projected over the whispers and giggles, "you went in closer to Jude at the end of the Vamp dance. That was great, do that for the show."

I nodded, ignoring Margot's and Ethan's looks.

"And Jude, when you stared into the wings after she exited and missed the first part of the dance? Fantabulous. Really sold the spell she put over you. Do that for the show, too."

"Okay." Jude quickly looked down at his program. Under all that pancake makeup, I thought I spied a blush.

Then Mrs. Sorenson told us how proud she was of everyone, and how much she truly loved us all. At least, I think that was what she said—the murmurs had gotten louder as people pointed to something in the program.

"What's going *on?*" Margot hissed, paging through her program.

Laney's head poked in. "Page seven," she whispered, and then crawled away.

We all flipped through the program and found a picture of Ethan and Harrison rehearsing a scene where Cosmo Brown is leaving a party and Harrison helps him put on his coat. They had to rehearse that scene a lot without an actual coat, and in this picture, they're laughing about it. The caption read: *There's a reason I did the musical: Ethan Anderson.*

My eyes shot to Ethan. A blush crept across his face as he stared at the photo, and his mouth turned up in a slow smile. Then he looked up and the smile grew exponentially. I swiveled and saw Harrison standing in the wings. Ethan stood up, and the cast scooted away, making room for him.

"Oh my God," Jude said, scrambling around in his pockets for something. "It's a love declaration!" He pulled out his phone and ran to get a good angle. As Ethan and Harrison kissed, Jude snapped a picture, and the cast exploded into "Woooooooooos!"

Everyone gave them space but buzzed around, squealing and jumping up and down. Mrs. Sorenson and Ms. Langford had given up on the notes and were smiling at Ethan and Harrison with maternal pride.

Laney sighed contentedly.

"You knew about this?" I asked.

"Yes," she said dreamily. "All my Love Realism observations of Harrison clued me in to the fact that he had a major crush on Ethan. And then we became friends, and he told me about it. I guess he'd seen Ethan in *42nd Street* last year and was kind of infatuated, so he auditioned to see if what he felt was real. And then he tried all these subtle ways to show Ethan he was interested, but then he was like, screw it, I'll just be obvious."

"Uh, I'll say," Margot said. "Damn, Harrison's kind of a badass."

My stomach dipped nervously. As happy as I was for Ethan and Harrison, I was worried about my own love declaration. I could never do it as perfectly as that, and what if it ended badly?

Deep down, I knew it didn't matter. I had to try.

༄

"I can't get over how amazing that was," Jude said, still buzzing over Harrison's love declaration as we drove down the nearly empty roads of our town at 11:15 on a weeknight. "Musical theater is magical. You have to admit it now!"

I laughed nervously. "Did you know Harrison was going to do that? Did Ethan know?"

"Not really." Jude beamed. "I mean, Ethan started liking Harrison a while back, but he wasn't sure if Harrison felt the same way. Guess he did."

"Yeah." A tense silence fell over us. This was my opening. Now. But then "Singin' in the Rain" came on the Broadway channel. So we had to talk about how weird that was, how it was a sign that our opening night tomorrow was going to be awesome, blah, blah, blah. I kept searching for a way to pivot out of safe conversation territory, but I couldn't find one.

And then I was pulling into my driveway. It was quiet for a moment as I came to a slow stop and shifted into park. I barreled in before I could lose my nerve. "Can we talk—"

"Wait, can I say something first?" Jude turned in his seat so he was facing me.

It was hard to stop midbarrel, especially because we'd stopped so many times before. But he seemed a bit on edge, so I nodded.

"It's about the Robobitch thing. I should have asked them to stop calling Diya that. It sucks to admit, but I thought the name had some truth to it when I first heard it. I was sad and hurting and angry, and I blamed a lot of what I was feeling about my dad on her. But then I realized how unfair that was. I mean, of *course* she went to the singing contest instead of the dance. That's her passion, her future. I just never asked Ethan or Margot or anyone to stop calling her that because...it sounds terrible, but I think I got so used to it that it became kind of easy to ignore? I shouldn't have let that happen."

I fidgeted with my coat sleeves. "It's weirdly easy to ignore the bad stuff sometimes," I said.

"Yeah. Anyway, after you mentioned it, I felt horrible and started beating myself up about it. But then I thought about the question you asked me, about why I don't give myself room to mess up, why I judge myself when I don't judge other people. And I think... I think it's because of my dad. Judging myself really harshly is something I learned from him. And I don't want to do that anymore. When I mess up, I want to *do* something about it. So I apologized to Diya, and she accepted. I know it's not as easy as that, but it's a start."

My heart swelled. "It's definitely a start," I said.

Jude looked down at his hands and let out a quick breath. He glanced up at me. The sad look in his eyes, the crease in his forehead, the mouth that wasn't on mine. I couldn't stand it any longer.

"I don't want to be just friends with you!" I blurted. Jude's eyebrows shot up, but I kept going. "I want more than that, I've wanted more than that for a while, I just didn't know if—"

Jude clicked off his seat belt, flew across his seat, and kissed me.

I kissed him back as I fumbled with my seat belt. It was Jude who finally found the release button, and when I was free, he pulled me over the cup holders and onto his lap. In the passenger seat on top of Jude, my right leg was cramped, and one of the heat vents was scorching my back. And it felt like the best place in the world to be.

I didn't know how long I stayed there—I lost all sense of time— before I heard the plaintive wails of "Memory" coming through the Broadway channel. I swiveled around to turn it off, but Jude grasped my wrist. "No, wait, keep it on."

I stared into his eyes for a moment. Then I cracked up and couldn't stop. "If you can only make out to show tunes, that's a problem," I finally managed to say. He laughed but kept swatting my hand away from the button.

"Really? *Cats*? That's what you want to listen to right now?" I tried my best to be outraged but couldn't stop laughing.

Jude smiled but didn't explain himself. He only put his hands inside my coat and tickled my sides, which forced me to keep retracting my finger from the radio buttons. But as that incessant woman yowled on about her memories, *I* suddenly remembered something.

"Memory" was the only Broadway song I knew when I'd given Jude a ride home for the first time. It led to the Broadway rabbit hole, which led to "Finishing the Hat," which led to Winter Formal and sadness puppies and sexy dancing and trampolines and skating and ballet. It led to kissing. It led to right now.

"Okay. Let's keep it on," I said.

Jude's smile grew, wide and bright and beautiful. He twisted the ends of my hair in his fingers. Then he sang softly along.

And yeah, this song was cheesy. But right now, it etched itself into my heart, where I'd remember it, and this moment, forever.

CHAPTER THIRTY-THREE

WHEN I FINALLY WALKED in the front door, it was midnight and Josie was in the kitchen getting a glass of water. Her eyes widened at the sight of me. My stage lipstick was smeared all over my face. I knew because it was smeared all over Jude's face, too.

"What the hell?" Josie stared at me in horror.

"Hey!" I said brightly.

"Why is your face like that? Why are you smiling? Are you all right?" she asked, utterly weirded out.

"I'm great, actually. Really great. What are you doing up?"

Josie still eyed me suspiciously but seemed convinced I hadn't been possessed by aliens, at least. "I couldn't sleep. I'm stressed about showcase auditions. I haven't found a duet partner yet."

"Really?" That surprised me. "But it's such a great piece. I'm sure tons of people want to do it."

"They do. But nobody's been right for it. Their dancing doesn't fit with mine the way I want it to. It's too similar. There needs to be some clashing, some dissonance. That's what'll make it exciting."

I searched my brain, trying to think of possible solutions, things she could try during auditions.

Josie traced the rim of her water glass. "Would—would you want to do it?"

I blinked at her. Me and Josie dancing together, for the first time in a decade. It would be weird. But maybe also . . . fun? Modern dance still wasn't my favorite, but it would be interesting to try something new. "As long as you don't make me wear a sailor suit, then sure."

"Deal—wait, you'll really do it?"

"I'll really do it," I said, smiling.

Josie smiled back. "Okay," she said. "Cool."

After I climbed the stairs to my room and wiped the lipstick off my face, I searched my bag for my phone. There was no way I was falling asleep anytime soon, and I had to text Colleen and Margot about what had happened with Jude. I didn't care how late it was.

When I finally found it underneath my jazz shoe, I saw I already had a text from Colleen.

I got in.

I read the words again. Oh my God. ABT. She got in.

I gasped, excitement swirling like confetti in my stomach, goose bumps standing out on my arms. She'd sent the text a few hours ago. I'd been so busy with rehearsal, and then with Jude, I hadn't checked my phone in forever.

I texted back my congratulations with a million exclamation points and firework emojis. I felt those fireworks crackling through me, bursting out in explosions of color. Colleen was going to be amazing, and I was so proud of myself for helping her get there. For being part of this incredible beginning.

Thank youuuuuuuuu!! she said back. **I'm excited but also nervous but also excited. Aaack!! I need to start hoarding pointe shoes.**

Summer intensives meant dancing on pointe for hours every day in hot, humid weather, which made the shoes wear out more quickly. And pointe shoes weren't cheap, so it was the one drawback of summer intensive season.

And then I remembered, I still had a few unused pairs. Ones I'd gotten in preparation for the ABT intensive last year and then packed away.

I have three pairs. We're still the same size right? I texted back. **Let's go shopping for the rest this weekend? After I pick you up from class?**

Yes please!

I'd told Colleen that whenever getting access to one of her parents' cars was complicated, I'd take her to class. So on Saturday, because of Jack's soccer game and Calvin's math modeling competition, Colleen and I would be driving to KDBS together for the first time in forever. I couldn't wait to geek out with her in person about ABT. And Jude.

I went to my closet and got the pointe shoes out. They were beside the old Capezio box where I'd put all my ballet pictures.

I took a breath and opened the lid. I thumbed through photo after photo of me and Colleen. I put a pile of them on my bed.

Then I snuck downstairs to Mom's office, where we kept the color printer. I logged on to her computer, brought up Ethan's Instagram, and scrolled through. There was Jude at auditions, flushed and smiling after he sang "Maria." There was Margot dancing at the pre—cast party, looking like a badass mermaid queen. Harrison singing "Beautiful Girl" at Winter Formal.

The whole year so far was there, but beautified. Or maybe it had really looked like that and I was only now noticing. I printed out a bunch of pictures and snuck back upstairs.

I found some adhesive putty in my desk drawer and got to work, putting all the old pictures back on my walls, interspersed with new ones. Colleen and me in *A Midsummer Night's Dream* next to Jude at auditions. Colleen and me in *Coppélia* below Margot at the party.

When I finished with my walls, I grabbed one more photo. It was of me getting my first pair of pointe shoes. I had braces and was smiling so much my mouth took up half my face.

I was eleven. I'd had no idea what was going to happen in the future. I still didn't.

I snuck downstairs again, careful not to wake anyone. I propped the photo against a frame in the middle of the mantel. Then I crept back to my room, turned the lights off, and finally went to sleep.

MARCH

CHAPTER THIRTY-FOUR

"I'M HEADING OUT!" I called as I hurried down the stairs, my hair finger-waved and pinned into a fake bob. I grabbed my bag and triple-checked to make sure I had my makeup, costumes, and character shoes. As I dug around, I heard Mom, Dad, and Josie coming in from the kitchen. "Okay, leaving for real now," I said. "You have the tickets, right?" When I slung my bag over my shoulder and turned around, they were all staring at me. Mom's eyes were misty. "You look beautiful. We can't wait to see you dance."

"We're so proud of you, sweetie," Dad said.

My chest warmed and tightened. Then Josie cleared her throat. "Let's not forget, I'm the one who did the hair." She came over and primped it. "This is professional-level work."

Dad slung his arms around both of us. "We're proud of *both* our talented girls."

"Aaah, Dad, don't mess it up," Josie whined, flinging a hand out to protect my hair. "I need a picture."

"Good idea," Mom said. "Alina, why don't you stand by the—"

"No, just of her hair," Josie said. "I'm building a portfolio so I can get a part-time job at a salon in a rich neighborhood and make buttloads in tips."

"Good, I'll probably need a loan soon," I said, keeping my head still as Josie snapped pictures.

"Why?"

I shrugged. "Because I'll probably apply to colleges in New York, and it's expensive there."

The room went quiet except for the click of Josie's phone camera. I looked up and saw Mom and Dad sharing a look of pure joy. I guess they hadn't known where I stood on the whole college thing. I still didn't know what schools I'd apply to, or what I'd major in, but I had time to figure that out.

Josie stepped back, satisfied with the pictures. "All right, let me take a real one," she said, directing me to the mantel. When she held the phone up, my mouth stretched into an embarrassingly gigantic smile.

And I kept smiling, all the way to Eagle View and the auditorium and backstage. This whole day, I'd felt such happiness glowing from every part of my body. The anticipation of opening night, the memory of the kiss, the fun of talking about it with my best friends, and the heart-pounding eagerness to see him again.

Jude.

I weaved my way through the packed hallway backstage, full of cast members chattering with nervous energy. My phone buzzed.

It's cool if I wear a T-shirt with your name spelled out in glitter, right?

I knew Colleen was joking, but I also wouldn't put it past her to actually do it. If you do, I'll bring a bullhorn to your ABT debut.

Totally worth it. Break a leg tonight (but, you know, not really).

I'll try my best.

I put my phone away and saw Margot at the stage door, decked out in her sparkling gown. "You look amazing!" I said, smacking her in the bicep.

"*You* look like you made out with Jude." Margot smacked me back.

We hit each other a couple more times and then made our way to the wings. Behind the curtain, the stage was dim. Crew members were zooming around, getting everything ready. Ethan and Jude were center stage, backs to the closed curtain, as Mrs. Sorenson gave them a pep talk and fixed their bow ties. Margot went to get her cigarette holder prop from the closet, and I stepped onto the stage.

As soon as I did, Jude's eyes went right to mine. His expression, serious a moment ago, completely changed. His eyebrows went up and his mouth opened slightly, like he was surprised to see me. I felt a jolt of surprise, too. Surprise that I hadn't made the whole thing up, that he was right here in front of me.

After all the kissing last night, Jude and I sat in the car and talked about everything. Ballet, Winter Formal, the ice rink, Jude's dad. Jude said his father could make him feel like he was the most important person in the world one day, and like a total disappointment the next. He said it scared him that he still found himself wanting his dad's approval, and it made him not trust his own instincts. But he didn't want to deny himself the things he wanted because he was afraid he'd mess them up somehow.

I told him I'd been scared, too. That I'd wanted to protect us both from getting hurt, and that was why I said the stuff about ditching him like Diya did. He made it clear that he would want me to do something I was passionate about, even if it meant missing something like Winter Formal. He made me promise I wouldn't compromise for his sake on something I really wanted. In my heart, I already knew that I wouldn't, but it was good to hear all the same.

I watched Ms. Langford hurry to talk to Mrs. Sorenson, and as soon as they were both distracted, Jude ran over to me. "I want to show you something." He took my hand and led me to the middle of the stage, right behind the curtain. Beyond it, I could hear the familiar sound of an audience rustling, finding seats, chatting.

Jude opened the curtain a tiny bit, gesturing for me to peep out. "Look at the back wall," he whispered. I looked out at the wooden acoustic panels in the back of the auditorium. There, in the crack between two panels, was a shoddy smiley face—two misshapen eyes and a crooked mouth—made out of faded red construction paper.

I squinted. "What is—oh my God. *That's* the Happy Crack?"

"That's the Happy Crack. Someone a long time ago made it to remind everyone to smile during the show, and we find it in Mrs. Sorenson's office every year and put it up."

"Who made it?" I asked. The paper looked faded, even from the stage.

"No one knows. It's probably, like, twenty years old."

I started giggling.

"What?" Jude smiled at me as we stepped away from the curtain, back into the dimness of the stage.

"I'm sorry, but the Happy Crack is a total letdown. You guys built it up so much."

"You'll see," he said. "You'll understand the Happy Crack one day."

He circled an arm around my waist, and I put my arms over his shoulders. "So also," he said, pulling gently on one of the waves Josie had meticulously crafted. "I called my dad today."

"Really?"

"I said if he wanted to see me again, he could see me in this. I have no idea if he'll come. But we'll see."

I ran my hand through his hair. "I think that's great."

"I think *you're* great," Jude said, giving me his cockiest Don Lockwood grin.

"Save it for the show," I said, leaning in nevertheless.

Our lips were almost touching when a hand made a swift slicing motion near our faces.

"No smudging your makeup!" Ms. Langford said. "Wait till after," she added with a wink before walking away. Before, that would have killed the mood dead. But now, nothing could make me stop wanting to kiss Jude.

❧

Diya's sparkling voice resonated through the auditorium as the orchestra played the first jaunty notes of "Good Morning." It was the end of Act 1 already. I couldn't believe how quickly it had gone by. The audience was responding to everything just right, and that feedback was energizing us. We were performing better than we ever had.

I crept into the wings to watch. I looked at Diya for any signs of nervousness, but I shouldn't have worried. Instead of wrapping the coat around her waist and doing the hula, she flung the coat dramatically to the side and started head-banging, pelvic thrusting, all the things we'd practiced. Our inspiration was the *Rocky Horror* dance at the pre–cast party. We wanted to capture that sense of wild abandon, of letting go completely.

At first Jude and Ethan stared at Diya, completely dumbstruck. Then they snapped their heads around to look at each other, like *Do you know what's going on?* It was so synchronized it almost seemed choreographed, too. The audience ate it up. And then, the grand finale: Diya did the worm. Or, failed to do the worm, which was the plan. It was funnier that way. The audience started cheering before the song even ended. I wanted to know where the casting people were sitting, how they were reacting, but that was impossible. Still, whatever they thought, Diya killed it.

When she exited into the wings, we hugged. I wanted to whisper that she'd done awesome, but I felt emotional all of a sudden. Performing did funny things to you. I kept quiet—I knew Diya would understand what I meant to say.

And then, before I knew it, it was time for "Broadway Melody." Sitting onstage behind the Charleston dancers, I could feel the audience beyond the fluorescent costumes. I knew that in a few seconds, there would be nothing between us anymore. I'd be dancing by myself for a real audience, for the first time since the injury.

The dancers dispersed, and I was alone in the spotlight, leg extended, hat on the tip of my toe. I looked out into the audience. And I saw the stupid Happy Crack.

I kept looking at it, during the Vamp dance and the ballet part afterward. In its pitiful mouth and mismatched eyes, I saw all the kind but woefully inadequate "maybe it's for the bests" I'd heard over the past year. I still didn't believe in that sentiment. Those words—*best, beautiful*—used to mean only one thing to me. Now I realized they weren't always straightforward. Beautiful things had bad parts, and bad things had beautiful ones, and I knew now that I could work with that. I could hold on to the beauty and the good. I could try to fix the bad. I wasn't certain anymore about what I wanted to devote my life to. But that was okay. *I* was okay. I was here. I was dancing.

At the curtain call, I watched the chorus run onstage to take their bows as everyone belted out a reprise of "Singin' in the Rain." Mrs. Sorenson had told me I could choose which costume to wear for my bow—the green Vamp dress or the pink ballet one. Tonight, I chose the pink.

Jude snuck up behind me in the wings, adorably handsome in his old-fashioned suit and hat. He took the hat off and held it out to me. "Hey," he whispered. "You finished it."

I kissed him, threw the hat on my head, and walked out onstage. The house lights were on, so I could see the audience clearly. Everyone was standing. There were Mom and Dad, second row center, clapping wildly. Jude's mom was beaming beside them. Josie was in the upper level, yelling with her friends. Margot's abuela Isabel cupped her hands around her mouth and shouted "Brava!" Birdie held a tiny baby, gripping her hand and waving it at me. Colleen and her two brothers jumped up and down, screaming my name. In front of them were a couple of elementary school kids, looking up at me in awe. I wondered if Jude and I had shown them ballet for the first time.

I was supposed to bow. But I felt too much to do only that.

So I extended my right arm, and then my left. Then I knelt into a deep curtsy, slowly lowering my head.

Acknowledgments

The biggest thanks in the world to everyone who helped turn *The Other Side of Perfect* into a book and to everyone who read it.

Allie Levick, who has exceeded all expectations I ever had for a literary agent: Thank you for loving this story from the beginning, for helping me tell it, and for your endless encouragement and expertise. Alex Hightower, editor extraordinaire: Thank you for your incredible revision notes that always made me dig deeper, for your kind, thoughtful guidance, and for being an unwavering champion for this book. So grateful to be part of this dream team!

Thank you to the amazing people at Poppy and Little, Brown Books for Young Readers for giving Alina such a good home: Farrin Jacobs, Jen Graham, cover designer Jenny Kimura, cover artist Anne Pomel, and the rest of the incredible team. I can't thank you enough!

To foreign rights agents Cecilia de la Campa and Alessandra Birch: Thank you for all the wonderful work you've done to give Alina's story a wider reach. To fantastic film agents Mary Pender and Olivia Fanaro: I've loved all of our conversations about this book. Thank you for your insight and dedication!

A huge thank-you also goes to my authenticity and sensitivity readers: Phil Chan, author of *Final Bow for Yellowface*, thank you for that incredible book and for your generosity in reading, critiquing, and discussing *The Other Side of Perfect* with me. For anyone who wants to learn more about racism, anti-racism, and the current anti-racist work being done in ballet, read the book and visit the website: yellowface.org. Thank you also to Sonora Reyes and Ravi Teixeira—your help was invaluable.

I'm also so grateful for the wonderful friends who read Alina's story at various stages and gave me both excellent feedback and much-needed encouragement: Hillary Bliss (30FT superstar), Asmaa Ghonim, Kate Peters, and Casey Wilson (who has read so many versions of this book, I can't thank her enough).

Finally, thank you to my family—Andrew Wilson, Mark, Jean, Adam, Natania, Hiro, and Ronin Turk—not just for reading and supporting me and my work throughout the years, but for being the best people in the world.

Barb Colombo

Mariko Turk graduated from the University of Pittsburgh and got her PhD from the University of Florida, where she studied children's literature. Growing up, she danced, performed in her high school musicals, and broke her leg—all of which she clearly can't stop thinking about. She loves drinking tea, reading and watching stories of all kinds, and spending time with her family. She currently lives in Boulder, Colorado, with her husband and daughter. *The Other Side of Perfect* is her first novel.